Adrienne Wilder

MW01153983

In The Absence
of
Light

Adrienne Wilder

This book is dedicated to:

Anyone and everyone who has ever been misunderstood, cast out, or ostracized for simply being who you are.
Forgive the ignorant. They know not what lies within the layers of our reality.

***

When you choose to download or upload and distribute copies of the books I write, you chisel away at my ability to write full-time.
I live a very minimal life, just so I can afford to do this. Writing is my dream, please don't take that from me.
And while it is a labor of love, it's also work.

***

Chapter One

Toolies was located on one of the few paved roads running through Durstrand. Breakfast—hot, deep fried, and homemade—could be ordered all day long. At night when the church-going people were at home reading their Bibles, Toolies broke out the spirits.

I'd driven by the place a dozen times going to and from the hardware store, but I'd never stopped because my idea of a bar doesn't boast the world's fluffiest biscuits.

But it was late and I was too tired to drive the thirty miles to Maysville where they had some semblance of civilization. Unlike Durstrand, in Maysville the cell phones had a reliable signal, the water came to you in a pipe rather than a hole in the ground, and the TV received an actual signal without satellite service. It was only three channels, but three was better than none.

The place was packed, which meant maybe a dozen people, including the busboy and the bartender. There were several trucks parked across the road, so half the patrons were probably from out of town.

As long as the beer was cold and fresh, I didn't care.

A few customers looked up from their drinks and meals just long enough to give me a once-over. I guess I passed inspection because they didn't kick me out. It was nice to know I hadn't forgotten all the idiosyncrasies of a small town despite twenty years in Chicago.

The mournful wail of country music followed me to the bar. A woman at the end talked to the bartender over the edge of her shot glass. He excused himself and walked over. "Welcome to Durstrand. What can I get you?"

"Whatever's on the tap and not watered down."

He filled a glass. "You're the fella from up north who bought the old Anderson place, right?"

"Yeah. How'd you know?"

"Patty told me." He set the beer on the counter.

"Who?"

"She's the agent that sold you the house, and my second cousin."

First, second, third, it was just like back home in that dirt bowl I'd grown up in.

"'Bout time someone bought that house." He wiped up a dribble of beer from the counter. "It was starting to look rough."

"I think it passed rough a few years ago." I sipped the beer. Smooth, medium body, very little carbonation. It was the kind of beer found in a luxury restaurant, not a bar. Most definitely not a bar in some Podunk town in the middle of nowhere.

"You like it."

I nodded. "Really good."

"You sound surprised." He laughed. "Don't feel bad, most people are."

I took another drink. It went down better than the first. "I think I've found my new

4

favorite bar."

"Good to hear. So what brings you to Durstrand?"

I shrugged. "Needed a change of scenery, I guess." It was a part truth. I did need a change but only because, with the death of so many old-school businessmen, the rules had changed in a way I couldn't. A man's word was no longer gospel and people only kept their promises to keep from getting shot.

Don't get me wrong. I wasn't shy about using a gun if I had to, but it wasn't my first choice or even my second. After all, dead men can't pay the money they owe.

"What do you do for a living?"

"I'm retired, but I used to own a private shipping company."

"So you're the guy responsible for all those 'Made in China' tags on the stuff we buy now days."

I laughed. "No, no. Not by a long shot. My specialty was cars." Antique, modern, concept—very few that had less than five zeros behind a fat whole number.

"Did you make a good living?"

I bit back the smile. According to the statements from my offshore accounts, I'd made several lifetimes of a good living. "Reasonable."

"Then why did you by that shit hole farmhouse?" I choked on a swallow of beer and the bartender grinned.

I wiped my mouth. "I like to work with my hands. I figured a fixer-upper would give me something to do."

"You must be really bored."

I had two, maybe three years to burn before I could risk moving any funds and finding a nice beach house on some remote island way out of US jurisdiction. Until then, I had to mind my Ps and Qs, thanks to a certain son-of-a-bitch FBI agent.

"Yo, you serving drinks or what?" One of the men on the other end of the bar held up his glass.

"I better get that." The bartender held his hand out. "By the way, I'm Jessie Church."

"Grant Kessler." We shook, and he left to take care of the half-drunk patron.

I nursed my beer while scrutinizing the quaint atmosphere. What a joke. Roosters mixed with beer signs, nature scenes on china plates mounted to the wall. A vintage poster of Betty Davis's good side next to a severed deer head.

In other words, the place had all the appearance of a redneck, alcoholic grandma.

A busboy wearing worn-out jeans and flip-flops went to one of the back tables. It was hard to tell how old he was, seventeen, eighteen. Not too tall, but almost too thin. His baggy shirt hung to one side flashing a scattering of freckles on his shoulder.

He cleared the dishes with exaggerated care. Every so often, his left arm would jerk and he'd raise his hand to his temple and flick his fingers like he was tossing out thoughts.

The man sitting two seats down spit out "Faggot" loud enough there was no way half the bar didn't hear him, let alone the kid.

He continued clearing the table. A fork. A spoon. Napkins.

My neighbor elbowed his buddy. "Bet Morgan there will suck your dick for twenty bucks."

"You're kidding me. He'd probably pay twenty bucks for me to let him." They laughed.

My neighbor leaned back on the stool. "You hear that, Morgan? Jim says he'll let you suck his dick for twenty dollars."

The busboy—Morgan—lifted a dirty glass and held it up to the light hanging over the table. His wayward hand opened and closed several times near his shoulder before returning close to his temple to toss more thoughts.

He repeated the behavior while turning the glass back and forth.

"Hey, Morgan." Jessie whistled loud enough to make my ears ring. Morgan didn't respond until he did it again.

Morgan turned.

"The dishes, Morgan. They're not going to jump into the sink on their own."

Morgan put the glass in the tub and finished clearing the table. He moved to another booth occupied by a guy in a rumpled business suit.

The man caught Morgan by the wrist and leaned close. Morgan kept his head low and his shoulders hunched. The guy spoke, and Morgan shook his head.

My neighbor yelled for Jessie. "Empty glass here. You might want to fill it."

"Hold your horses, Mike." Jessie went back to the conversation he was engaged in with a guy in overalls.

"Slow service and queer help. What kind of place you running here?"

"Hey," I said. "Do you mind?"

Mike snorted. "Should I?"

In Chicago, very few men would have talked to me like that. They knew who I was and who my associates were. But I was in Durstrand now, and nothing more than another corn-fed white boy among a town full of the same. No one owed me favors here. Hell, they didn't even owe me respect.

"That's what I thought." Mike sneered at me and banged his mug on the counter. Jessie stormed over and replaced it with a fresh glass. "'Bout time." Mike drank half in a few swallows.

As Morgan passed me on his way to the back, Mike grabbed him by his shirt. I caught my neighbor by his wrist. "Back off."

"Who the fuck do you think you are?"

"Just someone who thinks you're making a mistake you'll regret."

"Really?"

"Yeah. Really." I tightened my grip, and for a moment, Mike's eyes widened. "Now let go."

"I think he has a thing for you, Morgan," Mike said.

Morgan dropped his head and waves of blond hair hid his face.

"I'm not going to ask you again." I lowered my voice in the way I knew could grab a man's attention and shake his survival instincts into action.

Mike held my gaze, and I wondered if I was going to have to make good on my threat. I didn't want to cause trouble with the local PD, but I'd learned long ago never say what you aren't willing to act on.

The bravado in Mike's expression crumpled to embarrassment, then anger. I let him shake out of my hold.

"Asshole." He turned back around and glared at me from the corner of his eye.

To Morgan, I said, "You okay?"

6

He held the bin against his hip with one hand and the other hovered close to his temple. Dark brown eyes met my gaze before disappearing under his bangs.

Morgan tapped his fingers against his palm before flicking his hand and snapping his fingers.

"Do you need me to get Jessie?" Before Jessie could walk over, the kid fled into the back.

"He'll be fine." Jessie propped his elbow on the counter.

Mike and his buddy laughed at the TV and ate peanuts.

I glanced back at the way Morgan went. "What's wrong with him?"

The question was meant for Jessie, but Mike answered. "Boy's *dain bramaged*."

Jessie took the glass of beer out of Mike's hand. "Get the fuck out of here before I throw you out."

"Just calling it like I see it."

"Out, Mike. Or I'll phone Louise and tell her I saw you making eyes at one of my waitresses."

The smirk on Mike's face shriveled up and he jerked himself off the stool. A few choice words followed him to the door. He pulled instead of pushing. Twice. His buddy helped him figure out how to get it open, and they left.

"You know he's actually a halfway decent guy when he's not drunk." Jessie leaned over the bar. "I'm just glad Morgan didn't hear Mike say that."

"I think the whole bar heard Mike call him a faggot." The word left a bitter taste on my tongue. I washed it down with a mouthful of beer.

"Morgan doesn't care about people calling him queer, faggot, or any of the other colorful labels they come up with. I just don't want him hearing Mike call him retarded."

"I think the PC term is mentally disabled."

Jessie shrugged. "Whatever they call it, Morgan isn't. He's autistic, and it pisses him off when people insinuate that he's retar—I mean, mentally disabled."

"That doesn't even make sense."

"Sure it does. Morgan is gay, he's not disabled."

"He's gay?"

"Yup."

"Who decided that?"

"He did."

Was he kidding? Someone like Morgan wouldn't even know what sex was let alone sexuality. I bit back my argument and attempted to hide my disbelief behind another swig of beer, but my glass was empty.

"Still doesn't give anyone the right to call him names."

"No, it doesn't. But trust me. If it bothers him, he'll deal with it."

"How can you say he'll deal with it? He's helpless."

"I'm going to pretend I didn't just hear those words come out of your mouth." Why not? Morgan had obviously been scared to death. Why else would he run to the back?

The guy in the business suit stopped at the bar and laid a twenty on the counter in front of Jessie, and said, "Food was decent and the beer good. Thanks again."

Jessie slid the money into his pocket. "See you in three months?"

"There abouts." Business suit headed in the direction of the bathroom.

7

"Now, what was I saying?"

"That Morgan will deal with the name-calling."

"Yeah. That. He will, so don't worry." Jessie held up my glass. "You want another?"

"No thanks." I slid off the stool. "I've got to get up early." I did have to get up early, but I didn't want another drink because I didn't trust myself not to shoot off at the mouth.

Because how could any half-decent human being think someone like Morgan could defend themselves. I don't know why I expected anything less. Small town, small minds. I had firsthand experience.

I mean, all the good church-going people back home didn't see a damn thing wrong with a father putting his son out on the street for kissing a boy. It wasn't like Chicago didn't have bigots; everyone there hated someone for some reason, so it evened out.

I laid a five on the counter and hit the john. For a men's room in a bar, it was clean. The scent of plywood and fresh paint overrode any trace of beer piss. There were gaps between the tiles around the urinal close to the door and supplies to install a new one on the floor.

Nice to know I wasn't the only one with unfinished projects. I'd just zipped up when a low murmur came from the direction of the stalls. A whimper followed.

Wouldn't be the first time I'd walked into a bathroom with two guys exchanging a quick hand job. Either way, it was none of my business.

I washed up and plucked a paper towel from the dispenser. The stall reflected in the mirror, along with two sets of feet toe to toe. One wore shiny dress shoes, the other flip-flops.

Another whimper, small, frightened…

I kicked the door and the lock gave way enough for me to yank it open.

The guy in the business suit whirled around. "What the hell?"

Morgan's shirt was partway up, and his jeans were undone. Tears gleamed on his flushed cheeks.

"You sick son of a bitch." I grabbed the Suit by his tie and hurled him out of the stall. He hit the garbage can and rolled off to the side.

"What the hell is wrong with you, man?" He held up a hand.

"Me?" I snatched him by his jacket and yanked him to his feet.

"Stop." Morgan slapped his hand on the stall wall while holding his jeans up with the other. "Stop. Stop. Stop." His hand jerked up, and his fingers danced next to his temple. Then a high-pitched keening sound inched out of his throat. He swung out as if to hit the stall again, but his arm jerked up and his hand returned to his temple, tossing thoughts in between snapping his fingers. His expression twisted up and that strange wounded animal sound hissed from behind clenched teeth.

While my attention was on Morgan, the businessman slithered out the door leaving his jacket behind in my grip. I dropped it.

"It's okay." I started to walk over but didn't want him to think I was trying to box him in. Or worse, do the same thing the other guy had done.

Morgan took a few steps forward, back. Finally he made his way out of the stall. He pulled his hair with his dancing hand.

"It's okay, Morgan. Everything will be okay."

He turned away, turned back. The flush in his face was almost beet red. Did I leave him and go get Jessie? Or did I just call the cops? I felt around for my cell phone.

8

Morgan raised his chin, and I was held in place by the raw anger burning in his dark eyes. He was the first person who'd ever stopped me with a look.

Morgan flicked his hand at me. "Thanks for the cock block, asshole." Then he turned and left.

****

The hardware store had become my second home over the past few weeks. Sometimes I was there twice a day. To be honest, it surprised me Berry hadn't got tired of looking at my mug, despite how much money I spent.

While I did spend it, I was careful not to flash too much and always played the part of pinching pennies. I kept just the minimum in my savings account up north since I didn't want so much as an overdraft fee to catch the attention of the FBI. Not that overspending at a hardware store would normally do that, but since their failed sting on my operation, they'd developed a personal interest in my life.

"Hey there, Grant. What can I do for you?" Berry came from around the counter.

"Need more nails and my sander copped out on me this morning."

"Told you that cheap model wasn't fit for the job." He grinned and stuck his thumbs in the straps of his overalls.

"Yeah, you did."

"Should have listened to me."

"Yeah, I should have done that too."

He jerked his head in the direction of the aisles. "You need me to show you where they are?"

"Nope. I've pretty much got the place memorized."

"You know, if I gave you a job here, you'd get ten percent off."

I laughed. "If I worked here, I'd never get the house fixed. Maybe when I'm done, we'll chat." We wouldn't. Don't get me wrong. I liked Berry, but working for the man would make it too easy to be his friend and I didn't need friends in Durstrand. I just needed a rest stop before I went on with my life.

Hardware, power drills, and skill saws covered the shelves. The sanders were on the end next to the Sawzalls.

The bells on the door clanged, and Berry called out a greeting.

I picked up one of the sanders. The shelf was just short enough for Morgan's crop of blond hair to flash over the top as he walked past.

He hummed while he paced up and down the aisle.

I stood on my toes.

Morgan stopped in front of the cutting tools located directly on the other side. Like before, he held his dancing fingers close to his temple.

"I need the red-handled glass cutter." His gaze stayed on the floor.

Berry walked over. "I'm sold out, but the Martin brand is really good."

Morgan's shoulder jerked, and he clenched his fist. "Has to be the red-handled one." He dug through the shelves.

"You may have to wait then. I've got an order coming in tomorrow. They should be on

9

the truck."

"Need it today, Berry."

"And I'm out."

"You're supposed to keep extra for me. We agreed." Morgan rocked on his toes.

"And you buy them faster than I can put them on the shelf."

"They go dull."

"That's why I keep telling you to use the Martin. They last twice as long." He took one out of the package.

Morgan shook his head. "Need the red one."

"What if I gave this one to you on the house, just to try it?"

"I only buy the red ones."

"You wouldn't be buying it. It would be a gift."

Morgan fell still and took the tool from Joe's hand. He held it up to the light, turned it around, and flipped it over. When he lowered it, he traced the flat side with elegant fingers belonging to his strong hands. Tawny muscles made subtle lines on his arms, and there was a hole in the side of his shirt. When he moved to the right, it flashed his navel.

Between the bad lighting and his build, I'd misjudged his age at the bar. He was not a boy but a hell of a gorgeous man.

I jerked my gaze away.

What the fuck was wrong with me? There I was in the goddamned hardware store lusting after some poor disabled guy. The sick feeling in my stomach was compounded by the fact that my dick didn't seem to care Morgan wasn't normal.

I grabbed one of the sanders Berry recommended and headed to the back where he kept the nails. There were only two boxes of one-and-a-half inch galvanized so I grabbed both. I turned around and slammed into Morgan. He stumbled back, and I caught him by his arm to keep him from falling into a rack of hammers.

"Jesus, I'm sorry. I didn't see you."

"You should pay attention then. I'm hard to miss." He flicked a look up at me, and his mouth curled in a way that made my cheeks burn. Then he went back to staring at the floor.

I let him go and tried to figure out something to do with my free hand. Morgan brushed by.

A ripped seam at the corner of his back pocket flashed a patch of bare skin.

Goddamn. He was commando.

Morgan bent over at the rolls of wiring. The thin denim tightened over his ass, and a few more threads threatened to give way. He turned a little, and if I hadn't known better, I would have thought he purposely flashed me.

When he stood again, his jeans rode low enough to show off the dimples on his lower back. He caught me watching, tilted his head, and smiled.

I fled to the register.

I needed to make a trip into the city to find a piece of ass before I got myself in trouble.

"Is that all?"

I put my stuff on the counter. "Yeah, that should do it." Had Berry noticed me watching Morgan? I prayed he didn't. I'd wind up burned at the stake sure enough.

And I'd deserve it.

Berry turned the sander over. "Damn sticker must have fallen off. You remember how much this was?"

"No." I hadn't even looked at the price because I'd been too busy watching Morgan.

"Hang on while I look this up." Berry dug a book out from under the register.

Morgan appeared at the end of the aisle and sauntered toward me. He stopped a few feet away, and I did my damnedest to keep my eyes from wandering over parts of him they did not need to wander over.

He reached around me and dug through a bucket of chocolates on the counter. My ass wound up pressed to the cradle of his hips and the line of his cock followed the crease of my crack. I gritted my teeth and held the edge of the counter until my knuckle joints showed under the skin.

Morgan plucked a piece of candy from the container, unwrapped it, and his wayward gaze met mine. Almost in slow-motion, Morgan slipped his tongue from between his parted lips. He teased the surface of the candy, leaving a shiny wet line on the edge before slipping it into his mouth. Then proceeded to suck the chocolate from each fingertip with enough force to hollow out his cheeks.

"Here it is." Berry tapped the page and rang up the sander.

Morgan rubbed against me one last time before stepping back. I fumbled for my wallet while fighting off fantasies of those lips on my cock.

Berry's bushy white eyebrows bunched up. "You okay?"

"Huh?"

"Your hands are shaking."

"Uh, no, I'm good. Probably too much coffee."

He squinted up at me. "You sure? You look kinda feverish. There's a bug been going 'round. You'd better watch yourself; you don't wanna get sick."

Oh, I was already sick as they came. Just not in the way Berry worried about.

"Yeah, I'll do that." I grabbed my things. "I'll see you tomorrow probably."

He smiled, and his gaze slid from Morgan to me. I didn't wait around to find out whether or not he suspected anything.

By the time I got behind the wheel, I had the father of all hard-ons pressing against the back of my fly. Jesus Christ, when the hell had I turned into the kind of man who lusted after someone with the mind of a child?

Although it hadn't been a child rubbing off on me.

I had to have imagined it. Morgan could barely lift his eyes. But when he had, it was like he knew how good he looked and what a body like his could do to a person.

"Get a grip, Grant." I glared at myself in the rearview. "You're turning into a class-A pervert."

I started the truck and backed out. The road was clear so I made a right. Red flashed in my periphery. There was barely a thump when the bumper of the truck caught the rear wheel of the bike, but it was enough to shove it over and toss the rider on the ground.

"Fucking hell." I threw the truck in park and got out. Broken spokes on the wheel tangled in the bumper. The rider was on his knees examining his bloody elbow.

"I'm sorry. I didn't see—"

Morgan glanced up at me. "You really should pay attention to where you're going." He stood and ran a hand over one of the busted spokes. "Damn it."

11

"I'm sorry."

"You said that already." He tried to tug the bike free, but the truck wouldn't let go. Morgan gave up and wiped his scraped palm on his shirt, leaving a bloody smear.

"Wait here." I tossed a thumb over my shoulder. "I'll go inside and call an ambulance."

"What for?"

"You're hurt."

"It's a scrape and a few bruises. I don't need an ambulance." Morgan rocked and flicked his wrist and fingers next to his head. "If you want to do something, help me get it loose." I tried to figure out where to grip the thing without getting too close to him. "Sometime today would be nice."

We untangled the spokes, and he examined the crease in the wheel. "Here." He pushed the bike in my direction. "You carry that and I'll get the rest." Morgan picked up a flip-flop and put it back on. Then he put his bag of supplies in the bed of the truck.

"What are you doing?"

"You wrecked my bike. I don't have any way home. So you're going to give me a ride." He pulled the bike out of my hands and hoisted it over the edge of the truck bed.

Morgan shook a rock out of his other flip-flop, then climbed into the cab. He tapped the dash, flipped the visor down then up, opened the glove compartment.

That boy in my truck could only land me in jail.

Morgan leaned out the window. "I've got somewhere I need to be so if you don't mind I'd like to get going." He counted his fingers against his palm then dropped his hand into his lap.

When he wasn't doing those strange movements, I could almost convince myself there was nothing wrong with him except he couldn't look me in the eye more than a second or two.

I got in the truck.

"What about seat belts?" He looked around.

"Doesn't have any."

"It's illegal to drive without a seat belt."

"The truck is older than I am, it didn't come with any. The law doesn't apply."

Morgan kept searching. Maybe he didn't believe me. Finally he stopped and propped an elbow on the window. "You should see about getting some installed."

I squeezed the steering wheel. "Do you want a ride or not?"

"Why else would I be in your truck?"

Oh the reasons I could come up with. And unlike the lack of seat belts, none of those could be legal.

"Where do you live?"

"Porter's Creek Road."

"Where is that?" Close. It had to be close. Anything longer than three miles was playing with fire.

"You know where the reservoir is?"

Damn it. So much for close. "Yeah."

"Porter's Creek is about five miles from there on Water Way."

"You bike ten miles into town?"

"If I had a car, I wouldn't be on a bike."

No wonder his ass looked so good. I cursed myself and started the truck.

Fall painted the dense forest edging the road in shades of gold and red. Every so often, a fat leaf would flutter down and get caught on the windshield. Soon the limbs would be bare. It had been a long time since I'd seen so many trees, and having grown up in Alabama, I'd never experienced this kind of color.

Bits of sunlight broke through the canopy, scattering into nameless shapes on the road. The fragments of light slid across the hood of the truck and trickled into the cab.

Morgan held his hand out over the dash and wiggled his fingers through the luminous patches.

His mouth tilted into a soft smile, and for some reason, the combination left me with the strangest feeling of ignorance.

I thrummed my fingers on the steering wheel and kept an eye out for Water Way. After a few more miles of eerie silence, where Morgan chased the light through the air, the sign appeared on the right.

"Five miles?" I glance at him. He held his hands closer to the windshield. The light shifted direction, pulling it back to the edge of the dash. "Morgan?"

He tilted his head and continued to dance his fingers. The expression on his face didn't have a name, but it was peaceful.

I squeezed the steering wheel. What was I supposed to do to get his attention? Jessie had whistled so I decided it was worth a try.

Morgan blinked a few times. "Yes?"

"Five miles?" It was a fight to keep my eyes on the road with him looking at me. Somehow I knew it was a rare moment that wouldn't last.

"Five miles, eighteen mail boxes, not counting the airmail box."

"Airmail box?"

"You'll know it when you see it." He put his hands in his lap. "So what do you do?"

After the lengthy silence, my brain seemed to have trouble deciphering his words. "I'm retired. Sorta."

"Retired? You don't look old enough to retire." He tapped his fingers in an odd rhythm on the dash. It took me a moment to realize he was matching the beat of the wheels as they hit the streaks of tar filling the cracks in the asphalt.

"I got lucky."

"So you must be rich?"

He had no idea, and neither did that two-faced son of a bitch FBI agent. Living in a farmhouse in the middle of nowhere was a small price to pay to keep it that way. "Not really."

Morgan stopped tapping the dash. "Airmail." He pointed up. Ahead of us a mailbox had been fastened to a post no less than twenty feet tall.

Airmail. I snorted.

"Do you think they use a ladder or just shimmy up the pole?" Morgan tilted his head, following the airmail box as we passed it. I started to laugh but stopped because I wasn't sure if he was serious. I mean there was no telling what he understood.

Morgan graced me with a momentary view of his dark gaze. His smile cocked to the side. "I was joking."

"I knew that."

"No, you didn't." He knocked on the windshield. "Three more then turn on the road with the dead tree on the side. Watch for the squirrels because they'll run out in front of you."

"I know the truck is old, but I'm pretty sure it will hold together if we hit a squirrel."

"It's not the truck I'm worried about."

I slowed down as we approached the remnants of a massive oak on the shoulder of the road. Splinters of wood jabbed at the sky. A couple of squirrels sparred with each other at the split in the base. They disappeared in a flash of brown fur as we passed.

I took a left onto Porter's Creek. Before I could ask where to next, Morgan said, "White house with the picket fence with lots of bottles. He pointed."

Bottles?

I had my answer as soon as I turned up the drive. An assortment of bottles lined the narrow cross beams of the picket fence surrounding the front yard of the farmhouse. Top and bottom, the colored glass was twice as bright against the white wash. They'd been organized by hue ascending from light to dark. Size and shape didn't seem to matter.

There were no cars in the driveway. It wasn't uncommon for people in a town like Durstrand to be too poor for a car, but no one came to the door. I pulled to a stop next to a pile of firewood waiting to be split. An ax stuck in the center of one of the stumps.

"Your parents home?"

"Parents?"

There was a fresh cord of wood on the porch next to the porch swing. It was gray like the shutters. All the paint on the house was so perfect it couldn't be more than a couple months old.

Morgan hopped out of the truck. "Why don't you come in and I'll fix you a glass of tea."

I got out to help him with the bike.

"I've got coffee if you prefer that?"

"I appreciate the offer, but I can't." I started to get the bike.

"Leave it." He picked up his bag of supplies. "I'll take it to Jenny's when you give me a ride back into town."

"Wait..."

But he'd already cleared the porch and walked inside.

What the hell did I do now?

His voice floated out the screen door. "Tea or coffee?"

"I can't stay."

"What?" The hazy image of his silhouette was swallowed by the shadows.

Against my better judgment, I followed him inside. The living room furniture was rustic and neatly arrange around a large wood stove. There was no wall between the living and dining room. The kitchen was in the back. All the appliances were well kept but products from generation that preceded my parents.

"I'm in here." Morgan's voice came from behind the half-closed door on the side of a small nook to my left. The sight of his bare ass stopped me in my tracks. "Tea's in the fridge, coffee's in the cabinet over the stove." He turned around, and I stumbled back. The tight confines didn't offer much of a retreat, and I wound up knocking my hip into the dining room table.

Morgan came out of the room dressed in a clean pair of jeans with holes in the knees. He held a T-shirt in his hand.

"Can't find the coffee?"

He rolled a shoulder and stared at the floor. "Or did you want something else?" His dark

14

eyes glittered from behind a curtain of blond curls. Morgan closed the space between us, and my lungs squeezed tight. "Problem, Grant?" He fondled the sleeve of my shirt and trailed his fingers across my chest, stopping over one of my nipples.

He tipped his chin up. This close the full weight of his gaze hit me with the force of a punch to the ribs. He flicked his tongue over his plump bottom lip leaving the pink flesh glistening.

More than anything, I wanted to press my mouth to his and drown in his taste.

"What are you thinking?" Morgan drew a line with his thumb from my chin to the front of my jeans. He palmed the growing bulge and squeezed. "Whatever it is must be pretty interesting." His exhale warmed my ear. "So is it, fucking me or sucking my cock?"

I couldn't have told him if I wanted to because the rush of jumbled thoughts made no sense.

Morgan's bangs brushed my cheek. "Hmmm?" He popped the button on my jeans. "How about I make this easy and start for you?" His free hand fluttered next to his temple.

The disjointed behavior kicked me in the balls, and I pushed his hands away from my crotch. "Is there someone I can call to let them know you're here?"

He raised an eyebrow, but his stare remained focused near my shoulder. "Call?"

"Yeah, whoever it is that takes care of you."

Morgan stepped back. "Care of me?"

I felt around for my phone but couldn't find it. Damn thing was always falling out of my pocket in the truck. "You mentioned someone named Jenny."

"My aunt."

"What's her number?"

"Why?"

"So I can let her know you're all right."

Morgan jerked away and raised his fist. I fully expected him to hit me, but it hovered near his temple. The tendons stood out on his wrists and his knuckles were white. A tic jumped along Morgan's jaw accompanied by that high keening sound I'd heard before. He stepped back.

"Look, I'm sorry people have taken advantage of you."

His nostrils flared.

"I don't mind helping you, but you don't have to do… that. I'm sure your family… aunt… whoever wouldn't want you to…"

"What? Have sex?"

"I don't expect you to understand."

He took another step back. "Because it's hard to understand."

"Yeah, exactly."

He spun on his heel and went into the kitchen. The rattle of condiments in a refrigerator was followed by cabinet doors slapping against wooden frames.

I followed him. "I'm sorry if I offended you."

He set the pitcher he held on the counter hard enough to make tea slosh over the top. The tension in his shoulders fell away and he dropped his head.

"It's okay." His voice was so soft I almost missed what he said. "It's just hard, you know." Morgan wiped his face with the back of his hand. His inhale was more of a sniffle than a breath.

"I'd be a liar if I said I did." But it could only be hard. If I'd trusted myself, I would have

15

put an arm around him and held him while he cried.

"Are you sure you don't mind giving me a ride into town?"

"I'm sure."

"And you won't expect me to… you know."

"Of course not."

"I appreciate that. The nurse who takes care of me doesn't like it when I ask for a ride."

"Why not?"

He shrugged.

"There has to be a reason." And whatever it was, it wouldn't be good enough.

"She says…" A shudder ran down his back, and his sob was almost a choking sound. "She says she does enough. You know, with the cleaning, and the cooking, and other things. She says driving me around…" He flexed his grip on the counter. "It isn't in the job description. So I ride the bike and it's *so* hard."

"Isn't there anyone who can give you a ride?"

"No." He sobbed again.

"Please don't cry."

"I just wish I wasn't so useless."

"You're not."

"I am too. I can't do anything."

"You wash dishes for Jessie."

"So?"

"That's doing something."

"But anyone can wash dishes. I wish I were smart like everyone else. Maybe I could even drive. I'd love to drive, but I'm too stupid."

Goddamn it. I walked over and pulled him into a hug. "It's okay." He shook his head. "Yeah, it is. I bet there are a lot of things you can do other people can't."

"There isn't."

"I don't believe that."

Another sniffle. "Sometimes I can count toothpicks."

"Toothpicks?"

"You know in that movie, that guy, he's special like me. He counted the toothpicks."

"Okay, that's pretty impressive."

"Nah, everyone like me can do it."

"Well, it's impressive to me."

"Really?" The broken tone of his voice was replaced by an almost childlike excitement.

"Yeah, really." My smile was wasted on the top of his head.

He pulled away and wiped his nose on his arm. The waves of Morgan's hair kept me from seeing his tears. I didn't want to see them. I hated myself enough as it was.

"Can I show you?"

"Sure."

He opened one of the drawers. "I won a whole dollar once from Jessie. He didn't think I could." Morgan laid a screwdriver on the counter, then a pair of pliers. "I know I have some." He opened a different drawer. "Here they are." The box filled both of his hands. "Sometimes I forget where I put things. You know, being like I am."

16

"I forget things too so don't worry about it."

"Take this." He held out the box. "See, it hasn't been opened. So you get to open it."

I turned it around and broke the tape seal with my thumbnail. "Okay, now what?"

"Take out some toothpicks. Any number and don't let me see them. Then dump the rest on the floor."

"The whole box?"

"Yeah, all of them. Then I'll count them really fast."

"There's like a thousand in here."

"One thousand and five hundred." He pointed to the box. "But I can count them, promise. Now take some out." He covered his eyes. "I won't peek, but make sure you don't let me see."

"I won't. Promise."

I kept the flap raised and counted out a dozen or so. Even if he got the number wrong, he'd never know it. Nope. I couldn't stand the idea of breaking his fragile ego.

I slipped the toothpicks into my pocket and dumped the rest on the floor.

"Okay, you can uncover your eyes."

"You sure?"

"Yeah."

"You dumped all of them out?"

I shook the box. "Every single one."

Morgan tapped his fingers against his palm and then snapped them close to his ear. I still couldn't see his eyes, but he slowly turned his head as if following the flood of toothpicks covering the kitchen floor.

"Morgan?"

He stared. "Hang on."

The clock on the wall ticked off the seconds of silence. I ran a hand over the top of my head. "You finished yet?"

"Almost." He flicked his thoughts, then managed to corral his wayward hand into one of his pockets. His shoulder jerked a few times like it wasn't happy with the arrangement.

I cleared my throat.

"Okay, got it," he said.

"All right, how many?"

Morgan raised his head, and there was nothing soft, subtle, or innocent in his eyes and not a single tear on his cheeks. "Fuck if I know, but you better start cleaning up the mess you made. I've got somewhere to be." He shoved past me. "Dust pan is in the closet. I'll be waiting in the truck."

The screen door slapped shut, and I was left standing in the kitchen holding toothpicks.

****

It didn't take me as much time to clean up the toothpicks as it did to shore up the courage to walk out and get in the truck.

"Took you long enough." Morgan flicked thoughts. "We going or what?"

"You don't have a nurse, do you?"

17

"Guess what, Mr. Rocket Scientist, I can even wipe my own ass, or did you think I wore diapers?"

"No, of course not." My cheeks burned.

"Only because you saw my bare ass while I was getting dressed."

"I'm sorry, okay." God I wanted a rock to crawl under. "I'm sorry for…"

"What? Making assumptions? Or throwing toothpicks all over my floor?" His shoulder jerked. "Or maybe you're sorry for having some stereotypical idea about how I should act and what I can and can't do."

I sank in my seat. What could I say? "You're right. I deserved that."

"No, what you deserve is a punch to the face." Morgan jerked his head to the side and fluttered his fingers. "Will you quit staring at me?"

I cranked up the truck.

"It's called a tic," he said.

"Huh?" I glanced before I could catch myself.

"This." He tapped his fingers on his palm like he was counting down. "It's involuntary. And the rare times it isn't, it keeps me from knocking people around."

"I really am sorry."

"That's okay. You're obviously mentally handicapped on the subject so I'm just correcting the problem."

"I didn't think you were—" His glare choked me.

"Don't patronize me. I hate that almost as much as I hate being treated like there's something wrong with me. Bad enough you cock blocked me the other day. You gotta talk to me like I'm three."

"I thought he was making you do something you didn't want to do."

"And why would you think that? Let me guess, because people like me aren't supposed to have sex?"

I wasn't about to admit it, but that's exactly what I thought. Morgan narrowed a look at me. So much for hiding it.

"You were crying." It was my last defense in an argument I couldn't win. At this point, I could only hope he'd spare flaying me alive and just hack my head off.

"You thought I was crying."

"I saw tears."

"So your eyes have never watered when you're about to shoot a load? Mr. Salesman was rubbing my dick in the best way. You know how long it's been since I got laid? This town isn't exactly a banquet for single gay men."

"I didn't know."

"No. You just assumed that it was impossible for me to have a perfectly normal and healthy sex life. Not my problem if you have no idea what that's like, seeing you've never had sex."

The truck veered too far to the right and the wheel beat over the gravel shoulder. I pulled it back onto the road. "I've had plenty of sex."

"All right, good sex."

"I've had good sex too."

"Really? Turn here." Morgan pointed.

I did. "Yes."

"You realize masturbation doesn't count as sex, let alone good sex."

I swerved again almost taking out a mailbox. "I'm not talking about masturbating."

"Toys then."

"Not masturbating, not toys."

"Now, come on, Grant. Everyone masturbates. See, I knew you weren't having sex."

"That's not... of course I... Jesus."

"Jesus? Seriously? Okay, now you're just getting weird."

I ground my jaw. "Stop twisting everything up and turning it into something you know damn well it's not."

"Why, can't stand the competition?"

I glared. "Look, I said I was sorry."

"Oh you're sorry, all right. Just not in the way you want to believe." Morgan propped his elbow on the window. "Cavander Road is up on the left. A mile down you'll see a garage. Pull in there." Fragments of sunlight trickled into the windshield. Morgan leaned forward with his palm up as if he could collect the bits of sun into a pool in his hand. The tension and anger in his expression was replaced by a serene smile.

I concentrated on the drive. It didn't take long to get to the road. We topped the hill, and between a cow pasture and a dilapidated convenience store, a red metal-sided building with three bay doors faced the street. There were a dozen or more cars scattered across the front lot. Some old, some new, some in serious need of being scrapped. Men stood under the racks of cars occupying the garage.

I pulled in and parked the truck in the only available spot that looked like it wouldn't block anyone.

Morgan returned from wherever he'd gone and got out. "You mind helping me with the bike?" Before I could answer, he'd slammed the door.

I met him at the bumper and took the bike as he lifted it over the edge. He landed beside me. "Thanks."

A woman walked out of one of the bays. She wiped her greasy hands on her overalls while giving me the once-over. Her attention went to Morgan. "What did you do to your bike, boy?"

He jabbed a thumb at me between hand flutters. "Aunt Jenny, this is Grant, he ran over me in his truck. You got any moon pies? I missed lunch."

"Just bought a new box. They're in the office, under the register."

Morgan carried his bike away, leaving me standing there in front of a woman who put most linebackers to shame. She narrowed her eyes.

Morgan poked his head out the door. "Go easy on him, Aunt Jenny, he's a city boy."

"City, huh?"

"Yes, ma'am."

"Where?"

"Chicago."

She snorted. "You don't talk funny."

"I was born in Alabama. Moved up Illinois when I was fifteen."

"Alabama." And she said it like it explained everything. It must have, because she let me live. "This way."

The office was a small room off the left side of the garage. A door in the back led into the bays. Men drifted around the work area, chatting about life while they exchanged tools and helped each other dig through the guts of various cars.

Morgan sat on the counter, dangling his legs over the edge. He'd already eaten half a moon pie.

"So what does a Chicago transplant do for a living?" Jenny said.

Morgan waved the moon pie at me. "He's retired."

"You look awfully young to be retired."

"I—"

"He got lucky."

"Morgan, let your boyfriend talk."

The blood rushed to my cheeks so fast the room tipped. "He's not... We're not..." I tried not to choke on the words. "Morgan and I aren't dating."

"What's wrong, Morgan, you don't like him?"

"I'm not the problem."

Jenny raised her eyebrows at me. "You straight or stupid?"

"Well, he ain't straight, that's for sure." Morgan devoured the last bite and hopped off the counter. "Is Robert here?"

"Yeah, honey, he's in the back working on the Chevelle."

Morgan picked up the bike and carried it with him into the garage.

Jenny shook her head at me. "You fell for the toothpick thing, didn't you?"

If my face burned any hotter, I was going to catch fire. "Yeah."

"Don't worry." She patted me on the shoulder. "Everyone does."

"That doesn't make me feel better."

Morgan stopped by a trashcan and disposed of the moon pie wrapper. One of the grease monkeys whistled at him. "Heard you scared some poor shoe salesman out of Toolies. Ran off like his ass was on fire."

"Who says it wasn't?"

"Your dick isn't all that, Fruit Loop."

Morgan held up his middle finger. "See that, Ronny? Still bigger than yours."

Several of the men laughed, and Ronny tightened his grip on the wrench he held. "Faggot."

"Faggot? Really? What are you, twelve?" Morgan laughed. "Oh, that's right. I'm talking to the carpet muncher who failed the third grade. Like what? Four times?" He held up his fingers and counted them off. "In case you're wondering, four is this many."

Ronny threw down his wrench and took a few steps in Morgan's direction. Jenny stayed quiet.

I, on the other hand, had every intention of getting in the way.

"Don't." She held my arm.

"You can't expect me to just stand here."

"Yeah, I can. And you will."

Ronny cast a quick look at the other men. They'd stopped what they were doing to watch. Morgan stood stock-still.

20

Ronny took a few more steps.

Morgan tipped his head. I couldn't see his expression with his bangs in the way, and I was pretty sure Ronny couldn't either. But after a few moments, Ronny turned on his heel and stormed off.

The men went back to work like nothing had ever happened.

"See." She let me go.

"Yeah, and what if the guy hadn't walked off?"

Jenny shrugged. "Boys will be boys."

"How can you say that?"

"Because Morgan is perfectly capable of taking care of himself."

"And so that makes it all right to stand around while people abuse him?"

She shook her head at me. "How would you like it if every time you had a confrontation your aunt ran to the rescue?"

I rubbed the back of my neck.

"Yeah, that's what I thought."

"I just hate…"

Morgan exchanged a few laughs with one of the other men, then disappeared into the back. I had to force myself not to follow.

"He's fine, Grant."

I blew out a breath.

"I'm not going to pretend Morgan hasn't had his share of bumps and bruises. But he's a grown man. Believe it or not, I do understand how you feel," she said. "It took me a long time to quit running after him to check him over every time he fell down, and sometimes I still stepped in when I probably shouldn't have. And then there were times my sister Lori and I couldn't protect him even when we tried. Like high school."

I knew my own stint hadn't been easy. I didn't hide the fact I was gay, but I didn't advertise it either. I suspected quite a few knew, especially when I misread another guy. But I think most of them were too afraid to say anything.

Someone small and pretty like Morgan wouldn't have stood a chance.

"What happened?"

"What didn't happen?" She rolled her eyes.

"That bad?"

"Let's put it this way. Three months into the ninth grade, I had to pull him out."

"Someone cause problems?"

"Several someones. They had this fall dance. Have for years. Even back in the stone age when I was in high school."

I would have laughed if her expression hadn't held so much pain.

"Everybody was going with someone, and Morgan wanted to go with someone too. He asked a boy he'd had his eye on, and the kid panicked, went home, and told his older brother who was a senior."

Dread blanketed my shoulders, and I slumped against the doorframe. Jenny nodded at me like she knew exactly what I felt. She probably did.

"I told Morgan not to go to that dance, but he was hell-bent to prove he was not ashamed of who he was or who he liked. He got that from Lori, my sister. Anyhow—" Jenny crossed her arms. "—Brad Beckmen, that was the name of the boy's brother, he got a few of his classmates together, and when Morgan showed up at the dance, they jumped him right there in the middle of the gym, held him down, smeared makeup all over him, and forced him to wear a dress. All the while, the entire school stood there and watched." She shook her head. "It was bad. Real bad."

"Damn."

"You're telling me. And then the damn fools went and let him up. Only five to one. They didn't stand a chance."

I couldn't be hearing her right. "Are you saying Morgan beat them up?"

"Beat them up? More like messed them up. Broken arm, a knee, gave one of them a concussion when he kicked him in the head. Knocked out all his front teeth. Dr. Pope did his best, but last I saw Karl, he still looked like he was part mule. Not sure what happened to Neal and Todd. They left town about a week later. And Wilson? He still walks with a limp.

"Their families were all hot to trot to press charges until they realized it was an eighty-five pound boy who kicked the ever living shit out of their football stars. As if that wasn't bad enough, that many players out cost us the championship."

I tried to imagine Morgan laying out five guys probably twice his size, but I couldn't do it.

"You wanna beer?" Jenny slapped me on the shoulder. "I keep some in the fridge."

"Uh, no thanks."

"So what about you, Grant?" She got a beer from inside the door. "How does a thirty-something year old man retire and wind up in the armpit of the south?" She pulled the tab, and it popped with a hiss.

"Not a whole lot to tell."

"Yah, those with the juicy stories always say that." She slurped a sip. "Fess up, or I'll tell Morgan you said he'd look good in pink."

I was pretty sure she was joking but just in case… "I ran a small international shipping business. Made enough money to live happily ever after and got out."

"Uh-huh." She eyeballed me from over the edge of her beer can. "And for shits and giggles you decided to move from Chicago to down here?"

"I was tired of the city." It was true. "I picked the farthest spot on a map without winding up in the ocean." Also true.

She took another swig. "You married?"

"No."

"Got kids?"

"No."

"You ran a shipping business?"

"Yeah."

Jenny wiped her mouth. "My granddaddy used to tell folks he drove cross-state delivering Bibles. Everyone believed him too, till he got caught with almost two hundred gallons of moonshine in his truck. So what did you ship? Drugs? Guns? Or was it desperate people?"

"None of those. Ever."

"Then what?"

"Art, jewelry, antiques, occasionally rare books. But my specialty was cars."

"Nothing else?"

"I'm sure there have been a few odds and ends over the years but never guns, drugs, or people."

"Most folks don't have those kind of ethics. Especially when they're looking at money."

"It's why I got out. Business was going in a direction I wasn't willing to travel."

"You in trouble with the law?"

"No."

"Ever been in trouble?"

"I don't have a record."

"That doesn't answer my question." She rocked back on her heels.

"I've made enemies on both sides for my unwillingness to cooperate."

She smiled a little. "So I don't have to be concerned about Morgan when he's in your company. 'Cause I sure would hate to have to shoot that pretty little ass of yours with a load of rock salt because you got him hurt."

I held up my hands. "I swear. You have nothing to worry about. There's nothing like that going on between us. I was just helping him out, that's all."

Jenny finished her beer and dropped the empty into the garbage next to the wall.

"So you're straight?"

"No."

"Well, you don't look stupid, even if you did fall for the whole toothpick thing. But like I said, everyone does, seeing how he's so good with those big brown eyes and that sad little voice that can pull your heartstrings. Manipulating little shit, do you know how many times he fleeced me for money by pretending he needed a present for someone's birthday party when he was actually buying dirty magazines from Billy Thomson up the road?" She tossed a disgusted glance in the direction Morgan had gone. "He knows how to play a person."

"I think I've realized that."

There was movement in the shadows, and Morgan stepped out. He tilted his head in my direction but didn't lift his chin. His hand escaped his pocket and fluttered next to his ear. A spasm yanked his shoulder, and he turned away.

"Boy, he sure does like you." Jenny stuck her hands in her pockets.

Morgan's laugh mixed with the clank of tools.

Jenny leaned closer. "And from what I can tell, you seem to like him."

"I do like him. Just not like that."

"Really?"

Was there anything this woman couldn't see? "It would be wrong."

She gave me a look. "Wrong? How do you figure?"

Morgan rocked on his feet while he spoke to a redhead who joined him in the back. Instead of the floor, Morgan stared at the ceiling.

I would have been a liar if I'd said I wasn't attracted to him. Anyone who wasn't blind would be. But at the same time, I couldn't understand why Jenny didn't agree with how I felt.

Morgan's strange movements and refusal to make eye contact made it obvious he wasn't like other people. How could pursuing a relationship with him be anything but wrong?

Jenny clicked her tongue. "Morgan is apt to knock your teeth out if he sees you looking at him like that."

"Like what?"

"Like that." She pointed. "You've got that 'he's not right' all over your face."

"Well, he isn't." I could not believe the words actually came out of my mouth. Jenny's expression said she couldn't either but for a completely different reason.

"That's where you're wrong. Morgan's just like any other guy his age. He just sees the world a little bit differently. Maybe he even sees things we'll never have the pleasure of experiencing."

"He's autistic."

Her eyes widened. "And your point?"

"That means…" I didn't even want to say it.

"What? He's defective?" She laughed. "If you knew the hurdles he's overcome in his life, you'd think he was Superman." Jenny jerked her chin in Morgan's direction. "That boy's beaten the odds, no matter how big, every time they were thrown at him. When he was two, they said he'd never walk. Four, talk. Six, he'd never read and write. Twelve, he wouldn't survive on his own and never hold a job.

"As you can see, he walks and talks just fine and he was accepted to Duke University before he even graduated. And I'm sure you've seen his house. Restored it from the ground up. Did everything by hand. Wouldn't let anyone help. Took him two years to make it livable and another to make it nice. All of that by the time he was twenty-two. So tell me, Grant. What had you accomplished by the age of twenty-two?"

I dropped my eyes.

"Yeah, that's what I thought."

"Are you done making me feel like the world's biggest jerk?"

Jenny threw back her head and laughed. A few of the workmen glanced our way, but the interruption was barely a speed bump in their conversation. She punched me in the arm. "I like you, Grant. You're okay."

"Is that why you'd use rock salt instead of buck shot?"

She grinned, but it didn't reach her eyes. "Just do me a favor. If you're not interested in him, tell him now. Don't lead him on, then reject him. He's been rejected enough by the people in this town. A lot of them he thought were his friends."

"I think that happens to a lot of men and women when they come out. Especially in a small town like this."

Her smile turned serious. "You don't give the folks in this town enough credit. Very few ever rejected him because he's gay. People can deal with that because they don't have to see it if they choose not to. But that?" She nodded at Morgan. The redhead had the bike upside down at the edge of the bay door. He spun the wheel and the reflector sprinkled the floor with rainbow fragments.

Morgan wiggled his fingers through the scattered light.

The redhead spoke to him, but Morgan didn't appear to notice.

"I've always wondered where he goes when he does that," Jenny said.

"You've never asked?"

"Nope."

"How come?"

"Hasn't anyone ever told you to never ask a question unless you're a hundred percent sure you want the answer? Especially if you want Morgan to answer. He'll tell you and you may not like what he has to say."

The redhead flipped the bike back over. He clapped Morgan on the shoulder, and he walked in our direction.

"Don't believe anything Jenny says." Morgan waved at her with his wayward hand. "I did not break Wilson's knee, Beckman's arm, or knock out Karl's teeth."

Jenny folded her arms across her barrel chest. "You didn't, huh?"

"No. Wilson had a trick knee from a dirt bike accident, Beckman's arm was fractured, not broken, and Karl lost his teeth because he slipped on a puddle of punch Annie spilled on the floor, and smacked his face against a bench." Morgan leaned over to me. "She loves telling that story. Get a few beers in her, and she'll have me kicking the ass of the entire football team and scoring the finishing touchdown."

"From what I heard—" Jenny huffed. "—if you hadn't scored your senior year, we would have at least made it to the playoffs."

Morgan lifted a shoulder. "Not my fault the quarterback couldn't walk in the morning." He tugged on my arm. "C'mon, I need a ride home so I can get a shower and dressed. I work tonight."

We walked to the truck and got in. I was a couple miles down the road when Morgan said, "You bought the old Anderson place, right?"

"How did you... never mind. Yeah. I did. Why?"

"I get off at eleven and didn't want you to have to drive far from my place after it was dark. Deer get suicidal this time of year. Even though it's just a few miles, make sure you drive safe."

"Wait. I can't pick you up."

"You expect me to walk ten miles, at night, in flip-flops." He wiggled his toes.

"Wear tennis shoes." I didn't really mean it. Even in tennis shoes, it was too far.

"I can't tie the laces. Besides, you let me walk home and someone might tote me off. And I'm too good looking to wind up toted off. Then you'd miss me."

I pulled into his driveway and stopped by the picket fence decorated with glass bottles. The large flowerbeds around the perimeter were empty but had enough greenery left to suggest the flowers would be impressive come spring.

"C'mon." Morgan opened his door. "I'll make you some lunch."

"What time do you go in?"

"Four."

"How about I run home for a bit, then come back at three thirty?"

"Why waste the gas? You can just hang around here." He got out.

"Morgan, I know what you're trying to do."

"Really?"

"Yeah."

"And what am I trying to do, Grant?"

"I think you know."

"How could I? According to you, I'm not even capable of taking care of myself." He marched up the stairs. "Hope you like chicken salad."

For the second time that day, I was going to make this mistake. And it was a mistake. Mostly because my dick couldn't be convinced otherwise. Tomorrow, I'd make a reservation at a hotel in the city, spend a few nights there, get laid, and purge this out of my system.

For my sake and Morgan's.

I found him in the kitchen. He had two plates on the counter with sandwiches and was pouring a second glass of tea. "Might as well grab it, I don't wait tables for a reason."

I picked up the plate and he shoved a glass of tea in my hand. Morgan joined me at the dining room table.

"So." He drank some of his tea and turned his plate around before taking a bite. "What do you like to do while being retired?" His arm jerked, and he tossed thoughts in my direction.

I reached for my sandwich. Morgan got there before I could and turned the plate halfway around.

"Was upside down," he said.

"The sandwich?"

"No. The plate."

"How can you tell?"

He wiped a glob of mayo off with his thumb and sucked it clean. "The cottage motif."

I picked up half the sandwich. There was a house etched in blue on the center of the plate. "So, what do you do?"

"Right now I'm working on the house I bought." The chicken salad had just enough mayo to soften it, and celery to give it crunch. It was all enhanced by an undertone of something mildly spicy but not salty. I had no idea what it could be.

"Hope you didn't pay much for the house. It's a dump."

"Berry tells me the same thing every time I go into his store."

"Then I bet he sells you something to fix it."

"Yup."

"I guess since you bought it, that means you're staying a while."

"That's the plan." For now. I ate my sandwich.

"I'm glad to see someone taking care of it. Had a lot of renters move in and out. None of them appreciated the place." Morgan jerked his head to the side, smearing a line of mayo on his cheek. He wiped it away without a pause.

"Did you know Mr. Anderson?"

"I think everyone knew Joe. He was like a grandfather to anyone under the age of sixty." He broke off a piece of bread but didn't eat it.

"What was he to you?"

"Like I said…" He squished the chunk of bread between his fingers. "He was the closest thing I ever had to a grandfather, and I guess a father."

"You knew him pretty well then?"

"Yeah. He helped Lori when she got sick." There was something else in that statement, and it made his words heavy.

"Since you call Lori by her name, I take it she wasn't your real mother."

"If by that you mean, did she give birth to me, then no."

"Where are your parents?"

Morgan polished off half his sandwich. "No clue."

"So, how are you related to Jenny and Lori?"

"I'm not. Good thing too."

"Why's that?"

"You want some cookies? I made some killer pecan chocolate chips." He was gone before I could answer. There was the rattle and thump of the fridge door, and he returned with a Tupperware container. "They're made from almond butter instead of flour so I keep them cold." He took off the lid and set the container on the table.

A mound of lumpy cookies filled the bottom of the Tupperware box.

I took one.

"You need at least two." He put a couple more on my plate.

"That's three."

"I know." He took three for himself.

On the first bite, rich chocolate and mellow pecans hit my tongue in a taste explosion carried on the back of slightly sweet almond butter. A moan escaped from my chest.

Morgan met my gaze and grinned at me.

God, he was gorgeous. "They're good. You're right."

"Of course I'm right." He ate one.

"Humble too."

"No need to be humble when it's the truth."

I could only smile.

"Hey." He snapped his fingers. "You know if I go in early, Jessie might let me off early too. That way you won't have to be out so late."

"About that." I finished off the last bite of chicken salad. "You sure there's not someone else who can give you a ride?"

Morgan kept his gaze down and somewhere at the edge of the table. He wiggled his fingers close to his ear. His knuckles whitened when he made a fist. Then with his other hand, he forced the wayward one to his lap.

His shoulder jerked a few times then stilled. Morgan drank some tea, put the glass on the right side of his plate, moved it to the left, and then back. "Sure. I can ask Marty. He washes dishes on nights I bus tables. Might have to wait a bit. But hey, I'll give him some gas money and make it worth his while to pick me up and drop me back off."

Some of the tension left my body. "Thanks."

"No problem."

It was the lilt in his voice that made me ask, "You sure?"

"Yeah, yeah, why?"

"I just... I just wanted to make sure you'd be okay."

Morgan lifted his head enough for me to see his smile. "I'll be fine, no worries."

"Okay, good." I stood and reached for the dishes.

"Leave 'em. I'll clean up."

"I don't mind."

"You're a guest. Guests don't do the dishes. Aunt Jenny would tan my ass if she found out. C'mon, I'll walk you to the door." At the edge of the porch, he offered me his hand. "It was good meeting you, Grant."

"You too." For some reason, exchanging handshakes felt odd. "See you around then." I went to the truck. Before I could crank it up, Morgan had already gone back inside.

Chapter Two

I finished the porch.

Twenty years out of the country hadn't impeded my ability to cut a straight line or hammer a nail. What began as grayed, warped planks was now a smooth surface begging for a rocking chair or bench swing. I couldn't help but stand back and admire what I'd done.

Gravel crunched and a sedan came around the trees and up the driveway. It stopped behind my truck. In a small town like Durstrand, people only showed up at your house to visit or if they were lost.

If only I was so lucky.

Dressed in a nice suit, I almost didn't recognize Agent Shaldon. He'd never worn anything beyond ratty jeans and a comfortable button-up around me. Even then, it wasn't for very long.

I was willing to bet he'd even gotten rid of the jockstrap in favor of FBI standard issued tighty-whities.

"Long time no see, Grant." He walked up. "How are you?"

"I was good…" I looked at my watch. "Until about thirty seconds ago."

"Great to know you haven't lost your sense of humor."

"Who says I'm trying to be funny?" I hung the hammer off the edge of the porch. "Why are you here?"

"Because you didn't do a very good job of hiding. Any pimple-faced teenager could have found you with your social security number and Google maps."

"Who says I was trying to hide?" I knew how to hide. Trust me, I was the best when it came to making items big or small disappear right in front of the FBI's best surveillance team.

Sometimes it was all about distraction, other times fancy accounting. I was good at both, and if by some chance, I took on more than I could handle, enough people owed me favors to cover my loose ends.

"So you haven't skipped town?"

"Skipped town? They still use that lingo in the FBI?" I clicked my tongue. "How disappointing."

"That doesn't answer my question. Why did you run?"

"Run?" I smiled and tilted my head. "Running insinuates I've done something illegal. Which I haven't."

"You seriously believe your own bullshit, don't you?"

"It's not bullshit. Everything I ever did is on paper. Even the IRS doesn't have a beef with me. Hell, Jeff, I fucked you every night in my bed for over three years and you couldn't find dirt under my fingernails."

His smile turned brittle.

"Now, hurry up and tell me what you want. You're messing up the neighborhood."

"Nothing particular. I was just in the area and thought I would say hello."

I laughed. "Jesus Christ, you people seriously need to update your FBI handbook of excuses. That's almost as bad as, 'I have some incredible art to show you back at my place.'"

"Worked for you."

"Yeah, it did. Now I know why you were so quick to take the bait."

He took a toothpick out of his inside pocket and stuck it between his teeth.

"Gonna have to do more than chew on a splinter, Agent Shaldon, if you have any hopes of blending with the natives. Might want to start with that suit. Nothing screams city boy like a three piece and Italian leather footwear."

"Maybe I'm looking to introduce some variety."

I picked up a box of nails and put them in the toolbox. "Go home, Mr. FBI agent, you don't belong here."

"You used to like having me around."

I slammed the toolbox lid shut. "Yeah, well that was before I realized you were a shit-eating liar."

He took off his sunglasses. "I never lied to you."

"No. Of course not, Jeff. You just forgot to tell me you were undercover with the FBI. And the fact you copied shipping documents and reported my every move to your superiors was a figment of my imagination."

"They thought you were involved in human trafficking."

"Anybody with two functioning brain cells could take one look at my operation and know I wasn't set up for that kind of thing. And you, of all people, knew I'd eat a bullet before I got involved with anything like that." I lifted my shirt high enough to show the scar under my right pectoral. "In case you forgot." Even after a year, the flesh was still tender and turned pink in the shower.

He looked away. "I lied about who I was, but I didn't lie about the rest."

"Truth built on a lie is still a lie."

He opened and closed the earpieces on his sunglasses. I learned a long time ago it meant he had something important to say but wasn't sure where to start.

And it could only be important if he came all the way from Chicago.

"You want something to drink?" I picked up the toolbox and carried it up the steps.

His gaze flicked from the door to me.

"Yeah, that means you'll have to come inside. Unless you want to stand out here and work on your tan. Although it's not exactly the best time of year to lay out in the sun, but at least the mosquitos won't eat you alive."

"You sure you don't mind?"

"If I did, I wouldn't have asked." I went inside. The porch steps squeaked, and the screen door whispered.

"Do you want me to shut the door?"

"Nah, trying to air out the place."

Jeff stopped at the end of the runner where it met the dark cherry hardwood.

"It's okay to walk on. The finish is dry; it won't mess up your shoes."

"It's not my shoes I'm worried about." He took a tentative step. "You did this yourself? Never mind. Of course you did."

"You don't know that, I might have hired me a couple lowlife FBI agents down on their luck and looking to make a few extra bucks."

He shook his head. "If you'd hired lowlife FBI agents, they would have used the wrong color finish and tried to fix it by tearing the whole thing back up."

"More like burn it down and get trapped inside in the process."

He laughed, and I hated how hearing it made me miss him.

Him. The Jeff I knew. The guy from upstate New York who got kicked out when he told his dad that his new wife tried to make a move on him. The man with a gummy bear addiction that would land most people in a mental ward, couldn't hold his liquor, was allergic to cats, and sang like a canary when I fucked him from behind.

And maybe he was still was that Jeff, but when he couldn't give his people the dirt they wanted, he used me to try to get to the people who would make them happy.

That was my eye-opener. The moment that forced me to realize my style of business had gone out decades ago and I didn't have the stomach to do what it took to not wind up a victim statistic on the list of FBI gun violence report.

"This will be a really nice place when you get finished with it." He ran a hand over the wall. "Real wood."

"Yup."

"Must have cost a fortune."

"It wasn't cheap, no. But I wanted the place as close to original as possible."

"So you must be doing pretty well then."

I rolled my eyes. "You can't help yourself, can you?"

"It's just a question."

"Nothing with you is *just* a question." Too bad it took me three years to figure that out. Never claimed I was the brightest crayon in the box. "C'mon. I'll fix you a glass of tea."

I took out the pitcher and two glasses. The sunlight hit the edge and made elongated triangles on the counter. I ran a finger through the spot of light.

"Something wrong?"

"Nah. You want lemon?"

"No thanks."

I poured two glasses and brought them to the table. Jeff stood with his hand on the back of a chair.

"You can sit down if you want."

"Sorry." He took a seat. "I was just admiring the place." He nodded at the stove. "Does that use wood?"

"Yeah."

"And you plan on cooking on it?"

"Hell no. Not only would it take an hour to heat up a bowl of soup, I'd die of heat exhaustion in the summer. I'm using a countertop hot plate until I find a used stove I can afford."

He cut me a look. "You can't afford a stove?"

"I'm sure you've seen my savings accounts by now, so you know the answer to your question."

Jeff took a swig of tea and almost choked. I grabbed a napkin and handed it to him.

"You act like you've never had iced tea before."

"Yeah, tea, not syrup."

31

I raised the glass. "Sun brewed, thank you very much."

He wiped his mouth.

"C'mon, it's not that bad."

"I didn't say it's bad, it's just really sweet. Caught me off guard." He looked in his glass.

"Just water, sugar, some dead greenery, and a day's worth of sun, promise."

He managed to keep the next mouthful down but still scrunched his nose up. "And you drink this?"

"Every day, by the buckets."

"I guess it's an acquired taste." He set the glass down on the napkin.

"I sure hope they don't try to put you undercover anywhere past Virginia, you wouldn't last a day before you wound up as feed for someone's hogs."

"They don't really do that."

I arched an eyebrow.

"Okay, so there've been a few rare instances."

"Rare instances? Or just rarely caught."

He tried to laugh, but it fell short. "Quit fucking with me."

"If I was fucking with you, I'd have you bent over the counter." His cheeks reddened, and I didn't even attempt to hold back my smile. "As for the rest? Pigs do eat anything and everything. Kind of hard to prove there's been a crime when there's nothing left."

"There's always something left." He said it like a challenge. "DNA, hair, blood, skin."

"Good luck trying to dig all that out of three feet of pig shit."

The flush in Jeff's cheeks faded as quickly as it had appeared.

I rattled the ice in my glass. "What the hell attracted you to the FBI? You've never had the kind of stomach a person needs to deal with the kind of shit they see."

"It wasn't my first choice."

"Really?"

"You'd know that if you'd stuck around long enough to ask."

"I don't make a habit of rubbing elbows with pit vipers."

"They knew you were innocent. They had the proof in years' worth of intel. You didn't have anything to worry about." He fumbled with his napkin.

"You never were a very good liar."

"I fooled you." He clenched his eyes shut for a moment.

"Yeah, you did. But only because I broke the rules and let myself get led around by my dick."

Jeff started to take a sip but put the glass back down. "How did this happen?"

I shrugged. "Which part? You backstabbing me, me getting shot, or trying to fix the mess you and your buddies made that almost got a lot of people killed? Take your pick. And if you don't like 'em, there's more, those are just the first three off the top of my head."

"I meant what I said about how I felt."

I leaned back in my seat. Jeff Shaldon, or Jeff Myers as I knew him. Dark hair, blue eyes, pretty, but built on testosterone and sculpted by a high-dollar gym membership. There wasn't a damn thing out of place. Even the scars he'd earned made him all the more desirable. He was the first guy I'd ever considered bottoming for, but for some reason, I could never go through with it. My subconscious must have known something I didn't.

It was rare to see him with his shields down. Rarer to see him vulnerable. Sitting across from me at the kitchen table, he was a gaping wound.

That wasn't like him either. He was either truly sorry or… A much better liar than I ever gave him credit for.

"So where do they have the mic? On your chest or your crotch."

Crow's feet appeared at the corner of each of his eyes.

"Maybe I should get on my knees, you know, to make sure they get everything loud and clear." I looked under the table. "Can you hear me now?"

"I took it off."

I propped my elbow on the table.

Jeff ran his hand over the top of his head. "I told them you'd make me in five minutes and putting a wire on me wouldn't help."

I checked my watch. "I must be slipping, that took at least fifteen."

"You were distracted." He shrugged.

"And you give yourself too much credit." I emptied my glass. When I stood, I took Jeff's untouched drink with me to the sink. "What were they hoping for? That I'd confess my love in between rattling off my imaginary black book and bank account numbers?"

"Probably. But they learned a long time ago you were too smart for that."

"See, now you're giving me too much credit."

"Like you said, there isn't a grain of proof you've ever done anything illegal."

"Maybe because I haven't." I held his gaze when I said it. The confidence in his eyes dimmed a little. I gestured toward the front door. "You know the way out."

"I haven't even told you why I'm here."

"Maybe I don't give a shit."

"I think you will."

"Wouldn't be the first time you've been wrong. The door is that way." I pointed just in case he'd forgotten.

Jeff stood and pushed in his chair. "Two minutes."

"Two minutes too long."

"I'm only asking for two minutes of your time. Just hear me out."

"Why?"

"Because you owe me."

How quick a man could forget someone taking a bullet for him. I dug my fingers into the counter to keep my fist from flying out and connecting with his face. Last thing I needed was to assault an FBI agent. No matter how bad he deserved it.

"Start talking."

"Carson Lorado has been in touch with a lot of your clients."

"It's a free country."

"He's up to something."

"Probably looking for business."

"We don't think so."

"Then what else could it be?"

"No clue. But what we do know, is that he made trips to Egypt, Russia, and Cuba."

"That's an odd combination."

"Exactly. His movements don't make a bit of sense. We were hoping you might have a way to find out what he's up to."

I crossed my arms. "You're the guys with the millions in surveillance equipment."

"That's not what I mean and you know it."

No, he wanted my contacts. The nonexistent little black book, at least outside my head. "Discretion, Jeff. It's the number one rule. Right up there next to trust. Which I realize is a difficult concept for you to grasp."

"Damn it, Grant." He knocked his chair into the table. "This is serious. Carson is up to something and whatever it is it's huge. So big that Ruford and Zada closed up shop and got out of town."

Old-timers, but they'd evolved with the current market, moving from money laundering to drugs and guns.

They were men who shot first but made sure to aim for the knees. Then they'd pick your bullet holes while they asked questions. You lie, you died slow and painful. You told the truth and they'd make it a clean shot to the head.

They were not men who scared easily, and they were not men who gave up their business without bloodshed and a body count.

"Now do you understand?" Jeff said.

"Your two minutes are up. Should I walk you out?"

Jeff smoothed out his tie. I never imagined he'd look so good in a suit. And he did look good. "It's okay, I know the way."

"Jeff."

He stopped in the doorway.

"Do me a favor. Next time you want to talk to me, call me on the phone. No need to waste the taxpayer's dollars so we can yell at each other in person."

He smiled, but it wasn't happy. "Tax payers didn't pay for my plane ticket. I did."

With that, he left.

****

I blame my trip to Toolies on Jeff showing up at my door. Or maybe I just really needed a beer. Either way, I went, and Jessie had a glass from the tap on the counter before I made it across the room.

I'd waited until late in the evening, hoping since it was a Thursday, the place would be dead. It wasn't crawling, but there were more liquored-up people than I'd expected.

A group of young guys took up a line of tables. Their shouts and laughter drowned out whatever broken heart song leaked from the jukebox.

I sat at the bar.

"Bachelor Party." Jessie propped an elbow on the counter. "Preacher's daughter is getting hitched."

"Congrats."

"For the third time."

I choked on a mouthful of beer.

"Go easy on that. You drown on your beer and you'll make me look bad."

I wiped up the droplets with a napkin. "Can't have that."

"Nope. Sure can't. So, where you been? I thought you and me hit it off and you'd be a regular."

"Been working on my house."

"Fall in on you yet?"

The grin on my face made my cheeks hurt. "It hasn't fallen in, but I have gone through the floor a few times."

"Just as bad."

"Ruined two pairs of jeans."

"Wear them anyways."

"They look like Swiss cheese."

"Don't know if you've noticed or not, but ragged out is back in style."

I couldn't help but think of Morgan. People moved around the bar, and others watched TV.

"He'll be out in a bit," Jessie said.

"Who?"

He raised an eyebrow at me, and I picked at a spot on the counter.

"I think it's a good thing, myself," he said.

This was not a conversation I wanted to have right then. "Business good?"

"Steady. Especially this time a year with all the truck drivers coming through. When it gets close to Christmas, it'll get rough, then go dead until after New Year's. I'd take a vacation in February, but the regulars would probably break in and raid the tap while I was gone."

"Gotta love dedicated customers."

"Want me to get you a burger?"

"No thanks. Wait. I thought the kitchen closed at nine."

"Usually does. But with a bunch of drunk guys, I figured to keep them fed and they can buy more beer. A win-win situation."

Someone at the other end yelled for a drink. Jessie knocked on the counter. "If you change your mind, holler and I'll get you a plate."

"You got it."

He grabbed liquor bottles from the shelf and went to refill shot glasses.

Another tune came on the jukebox, sounding like the one before. Someone laughed high and loud, and the bachelor crowd let out a cheer. There wasn't a game on so there was no telling what they were happy about.

Considering it was twelve twenty-something year olds doing all the yelling, it could have been anything.

They passed vulgar hand gestures back and forth. I bet none of them had ever built a house by the time they were twenty-two. It wouldn't have surprised me if a few of them had never even held a job. I was also willing to bet every single one of those guys would fall for a certain toothpick prank.

"Hey, you."

I turned on reflex. So did several other people sitting at the counter. But the trucker and his girlfriend weren't talking to any of us.

Morgan cleared at the neighboring booth.

The trucker snapped his beefy fingers like he was calling a dog to heel. "Boy, I'm talking to you."

I wondered how Morgan could ignore the loudmouth, until I noticed the two white strands leading from his ears to the iPod hooked to his belt.

Morgan picked up his tub of dishes and walked past the trucker to the table behind him. His face reddened, and he turned as far around as the space between the bench and the table would allow. "You. Hey, you." He moved to the end of the bench. "You listening to me?"

I gritted my teeth. According to everyone who knew Morgan, he was capable of taking care of himself, but it didn't stop my pulse from hitting the top of my skull.

One dish after another, Morgan set them in the tub. Then he lifted a dirty glass up to the light and turned it back and forth.

The trucker got out of the booth and shoved Morgan hard enough to make him stumble back. The glass tumbled out of his fingers and the tub of dishes slid off the edge of the table. Silverware, broken plates, and food were tossed all over the truck driver's boots.

"You mother fucker, you did that on purpose." The man shook his foot in an attempt to dislodge the clumps of slaw clinging to the leather. "I oughta make you lick'em clean. You hear me? Boy?" He made a grab for Morgan.

Head down, shoulders slumped, and as far as I could tell, he wasn't even looking at the man, yet he swung his arm in a downward arc with the kind of precision you rarely saw outside of choreographed fights scenes in movies, and knocked the man's hand away.

Just as quickly, Morgan went back to standing like a ghost. The only change was his wayward hand going to his temple to toss thoughts. His usually controlled hand opened and closed over and over at his side.

The truck driver laughed. "What the hell is this?" He imitated Morgan's tic.

I got up.

"Don't." I didn't even notice Jessie beside me until he put his hand on my shoulder. "He'll handle it."

"Well, he's not handling it."

The truck driver brayed like a mule.

For the first time in a long time, I itched to have a gun in my hand. "Either do something, Jessie, or I will."

Jessie curled his bottom lip and let loose with one of those ear-splitting whistles. The truck driver looked up. "Quit antagonizing my help."

"Your help? You call this help? No wonder I can't get another beer. You got retards working for you."

No one deserved to be talked to that way. Definitely not Morgan. I started to walk over, and Morgan raised a hand at me.

The truck driver jerked his head at Morgan, and to me, he said, "This your girlfriend."

By now, all eyes were on Morgan and the trucker, but no one said anything. No one stood up to help.

"Fuck this." I shook free of Jessie's hold.

Morgan lifted his chin, and his bangs slid back. In my line of business, I've worked with all kinds of people and I've met more than my share of stone-cold killers. Not because I wanted to but because it was business.

36

Only on rare occasions was I ever in their sights since most of them were there to pick up a package or accompany a large money exchange and nothing more. But once you've been in the presence of walking, talking violence, you're forced to realize some monsters are real.

In that moment, that flavor of savagery rolled up at me from the depths of Morgan's dark brown eyes. It was only a flicker, but it was enough to stop me in my tracks.

He knelt down and began cleaning up the broken plates.

The truck driver scuffed his boots across the mess, slopping food and bits of porcelain across Morgan's apron. He moved on to picking up the silverware.

Patrons went back to staring into their glasses or watching TV. When Morgan had the last large shard tossed into the bin, he picked it up.

I'm not sure if the truck driver was looking to pick on someone the size of one of his legs or trying to show off. I don't think it was to impress his girlfriend; she was slumped over her mixed drink and hamburger.

Either way, the trucker grabbed Morgan's arm.

"All hell," Jessie hissed.

Before I could get a foot off the ground, before I could shout out a threat to the son of a bitch truck driver, Morgan snatched up a shard of broken plate from the bin. The crash of broken dishes brought the room to another standstill, leaving the sad song of some lost love to serenade the trucker as he stared at the length of plate jutting out of his palm.

Jessie waved at one of the waitresses. "Call an ambulance."

A high-pitched keen broke through the pause. Morgan balled up both fists close to his head. He turned like he wanted to run only to rock back. A tight grimace marred his face, and he shut his eyes so tight it made creases at the corners.

I ran over.

Jessie nodded at the trucker, still staring at his hand. "Make him sit before he faints."

I didn't give a rat's ass if he fainted. As far as I was concerned, someone needed to push his ass into a ditch. I did as Jessie asked.

"He stabbed me. The little retard stabbed me." The trucker showed me his hand. A trickle of blood cut a path down his arm and soaked the cuff of his flannel shirt.

"Yeah, well, you deserved it." I never claimed to have good bedside manners. I lifted his arm. "Hold it up."

"I'm gonna sue the little shit. I'm gonna sue this whole fucking place."

"And shut your piehole before I stuff the napkin dispenser down your throat."

"Look at me, Morgan." Jessie made an attempt to cup Morgan's face. "C'mon, son, look at me."

Morgan jerked away.

"It wasn't your fault." Jessie pulled him back. "You hear me, this was not your fault."

Now there was more blood and drama here than on TV, the patrons inched closer.

Jessie waved them back. "Please, go sit down."

And just like you'd expect drunk people to act, none of them listened.

"Take him to the office. It's behind the kitchen." Jessie pushed Morgan toward me.

I tried to guide Morgan with a hand on his back, and he twirled to the side. His chest pumped with every breath, and saliva made white flecks on his lips.

"You'll have to make him," Jessie said.

The truck driver yelled at his girlfriend to call his lawyer.

"He won't hurt you, Grant." Jessie nodded at the kitchen. "Go."

I touched Morgan's shoulders, and he yanked away.

"Fine, you stay with him." Jessie nodded at the truck driver.

"Wait." I waved him back. "I'll do it." But I had no idea why I wanted to. I got a firm hold on Morgan's arms and pushed him. He pulled, but when I didn't let go, he gave up and I steered him into the kitchen.

An older black man met me just beyond the racks of pots and pans. "This way."

I followed.

He turned on the light in the office. "See if you can get him to calm down, I'll call Jenny."

We both jumped when Morgan barked out, "No." He opened and closed his one fist while the other tossed thoughts in rapid succession. "Don't, Tony... don't call her." His shoulder seized up for a second. "It's late." It did it again. "I'll be okay." He nodded and didn't seem able to stop. "I'll be okay."

Tony looked at me.

"Don't, Tony. Don't..." Another cry ticked out from behind Morgan's clenched teeth. He worked his jaw as if to free it from some unseen vice. "Don't... call. Please."

"You know she won't mind."

"No. I know. Don't."

Tony nodded. "Okay, but if you change your mind..." He shut the door, sealing Morgan and me inside the office.

I grabbed the chair sitting next to the wall. "Here, sit."

Morgan jerked his arms and braced his chin to his chest.

"Please sit before you fall." It occurred to me that maybe he couldn't. I lowered him into the chair.

His arms continued to jump and the cords in his neck stood out. I took him by the wrists and forced his hands into his lap. I held them there and massaged his pulse with my thumbs. The grimace on his face eased, and the pause between each breath grew longer. With every exhale, the strength in his jerking limbs waned.

"You okay?"

He nodded. His wayward hand opened and closed, and his fingers tapped off against the heel of his palm.

"You sure?"

He shook his head.

"You want me to tell Tony to call Jenny?"

His face reddened with the effort to force out the word. "No."

I continued to rub my thumbs over his wrists, and he sank against the back of the chair. Eventually the tension left his body, but for some reason, I still didn't let go.

"Is he going to be okay?" Morgan raised his head but dropped it before I could catch his gaze.

"Who? The truck driver?"

He nodded.

"I hope not."

He made a sad sound. "I can't lose this job."

"Why would you? He assaulted you."

"Because Jessie can't afford to get sued." He made two fists, but it lacked the abruptness of a tic. "I can't believe I did that."

"Me either."

Morgan winced.

"No, I mean, that was pretty impressive. And here I thought you said Jenny made up that story about you beating up the football team?"

"Not funny." Yet he laughed, and I smiled.

"You won't lose your job." Again he almost looked at me. And damn it, I wanted him to look at me. I cupped his face and tipped his chin up. A tear escaped down his cheek. I wiped it away with my thumb. "Did you learn to fight like that the same place you learned to count toothpicks?"

He tried to drop his gaze, but I shook him a little because I wasn't done staring at him yet.

"Self-defense class."

"Why did you take a self-defense class?" There was a pale white scar over one of his eyes and another one across the slight dip at the bridge of his nose.

I hadn't seen them until now, since he kept his head down most of the time and the scars were faint. But I'd seen enough beatings in my time to know the kind of marks they left behind. Morgan either healed really well or had a damn good plastic surgeon.

I traced the one leading from his eyebrow to his cheek. "Who hurt you?"

"A mistake." He pushed my hand away. I didn't try to stop him again when he dropped his chin and averted his eyes.

"Does that mistake have a name?"

"Why do you care?"

I didn't have a clue, but there was no denying the urge to hunt the asshole down and make them bleed.

"Well? Does he?"

"He's in jail so it doesn't matter."

"What happened?"

Morgan's wayward hand returned to his temple, and his fingers fluttered. "I'm really tired so I'm gonna go home and get some rest. Can you ask Jessie to let Sheriff Parks know I'll come to the station after I sleep for a few hours?" Just like that, he'd shut me out.

"Sure."

Morgan stood, easing his weight from one foot to the next.

"Did you hurt your ankle?"

"No, just stepped on something sharp a few days ago."

White socks covered his feet and the strap connected to the sole of his flip flop made a crease between his first and second toe.

"Getting a bit chilly to wear those."

I think he looked down, but it was hard to tell.

"I'm gonna go. Marty is supposed to meet me at the corner store." Morgan bundled up his torn earbud wires and stuffed them in his pocket. On his way out, he took off his apron and hung it on the hook next to the door.

He hesitated for a moment with his hand on the knob, but before I could ask him if there was anything else, he was gone.

****

Except for a few gawkers too drunk to drive home, the bar was empty. Cops tend to have that effect on places like Toolies. Even if there's nothing illegal going on, people will get nervous and jump ship.

I met Jessie in the parking lot. He leaned against the hood of a patrol car with one foot on the bumper while he talked to a blond-haired cop who was almost as wide as he was tall.

"Grant, this is Deputy Patrick Harold."

We shook.

"You saw what happened?" Deputy Harold took out his notebook.

"Sure. The truck driver assaulted Morgan. Twice. The second time he defended himself."

Patrick chuckled. "I'm on your side. This is just standard."

I kicked at a piece of gravel. "My apologies."

"No problem."

"So what now?" Jessie said.

Patrick put his notebook in his front pocket. "I charge your esteemed patron with assault. Convince him that it's a wise choice not to sue, otherwise he could wind up in jail."

"What do you mean *could* wind up in jail?" I said.

"If I book him, he's more apt to retaliate by getting lawyers involved."

"And I already told you I don't care," Jessie said. "Let him try."

"You sure?"

"Yeah. I have a really good lawyer and Morgan's been through enough." The way Jessie said it made me think of the scars.

Patrick and Jessie shook hands. "Call me if you need anything."

"Morgan wanted me to tell you he was tired and to let the sheriff know he'd come to the station tomorrow to talk," I said.

"We won't need to talk to him." The deputy got in his cruiser. "There's more than enough witnesses so he doesn't need to worry himself. Tell him to rest."

Jessie moved off the hood, and the deputy drove off.

A cab pulled into the parking lot, and two of the bar flies helped each other into the back.

"How's he doing?" Jessie said.

"He says he's okay, but honestly I think he's shook up more than he's letting on."

"He is. Morgan hates it when people see him like that."

"What do you mean?"

"His reaction. You saw it. He shuts down. It's hard to watch, and he knows it."

"Do you think we should call someone?"

"Tony said he offered and Morgan said no."

"Yeah but—"

"Then don't. Morgan has worked hard to be independent."

"This has nothing to do with independence."

"It doesn't, huh?"

"No. Not if he's hurt."

"Yeah? And when's the last time someone played nursemaid to you after a brawl?"

Never. At least not of my own freewill.

Jessie nodded as if he'd read my mind. "Me either."

A few more people wandered out of the bar. The neon sign overhead transformed them into red and black silhouettes.

Another cab drove up and took a few more home.

Jessie toed the gravel. "If you're so worried about him, why don't tell him you're too tired to drive home and you need to crash on his sofa?"

"After I drive him home?"

"Haven't you been picking him up every evening?"

"No. He told me he'd hitch a ride with Marty."

"Marty Bower hasn't worked here since June." Jessie spit out a curse. "No wonder he's been dragging his ass." He started across the parking lot in the direction of the bar. "He couldn't have gotten far, I'll lock up and go find him."

"I'll do it." After all, this was somehow my fault.

"You don't—"

"I know I don't. I want to." I took out my keys. "You take care of the bar."

Jessie nodded. "He'll take Dent Hill Road as a cut through." He pointed east. "It's about two miles down, Water's Way on the right. It's nothing but a pig trail so you'll have to look hard or you'll miss it."

"Thanks."

I did miss Dent Hill Road, twice. I was about to give up and go get Jessie when on the third pass the headlights caught the reflective paint on the only corner of the street sign not swallowed by Kudzu.

I was surprised to see how far Morgan had gotten considering he limped with every step. As I approached, he held up his thumb and stepped into waist-high grass clogging the shoulder of the road. Just the kind of thick weeds snakes loved to hide in.

I stopped. He opened the door and froze.

"Why didn't you tell me you needed a ride?"

Morgan shut the door.

I leaned over and rolled down the window. "Get in and I'll take you home." He walked, and I let the truck idle up next to him. "C'mon, Morgan. Get in."

The missing tic returned.

"Morgan, get in the stupid truck."

He limped faster.

I put the truck in park and got out. "Morgan." He still didn't stop so I blocked his path. "Get in the truck and let me take you home."

He pulled his hand to his side but couldn't keep it down.

"Please," I said.

Crickets chirped, and dead grass crinkled under Morgan's constantly shifting feet. He made a half-turn like he might try and run but instead went over to the truck and got in.

I slid in behind the steering wheel. "You should have told me you needed a ride."

41

He leaned against the door.

"Why didn't you say something?"

Puffs of dirt mushroomed up ahead in the headlights and gravel pinged off the undercarriage in sharp bursts.

We reached the main road. It was longer, but it would be quicker than crawling at a snail's pace down a pig trail. Morgan draped his hand out the window and wiggled his fingers in the wind.

"You told me Marty was going to give you a ride. Jessie said he hasn't worked for him since June." The knowledge Morgan had been walking twice a day for over a week sat in my gut like sour milk.

He laid his head on his arm.

"If I'd known you'd have to walk, I would have given you a ride." But Morgan didn't tell me, because I'd made it clear how much I didn't want to. I scrubbed a hand over my chin, then squeezed the steering wheel.

The hum of the tires and the rumble of the engine filled the silence. Deer watched us from the side of the road with their ears cocked, and I slowed down once to keep from running over a raccoon.

I counted the mailboxes and turned onto Porter's Creek. The headlights slid across the picket fence. Colored glass flashed to life before fading back into the dark. I stopped in the shadows just beyond the soft glow of the porch light.

The rumble of the engine was replaced by chirping tree frogs.

"I'm sorry." I leaned back in my seat. "I'm sorry I made you feel like you needed to lie. No, no, that's not quite right. I gave you no choice but to lie." I dried my palms on my jeans. "I'm sorry, Morgan."

I couldn't see his expression so I flicked on the light. "Will you at least yell at—"

Morgan's eyes were closed, and a sigh left his parted lips after each slow inhale.

I shook my head. "You're an asshole, Grant." If only Morgan hadn't been asleep so he could agree with me. I went around to his side. It took some maneuvering, but I was able to open the door and not have him fall out.

He muttered and made a halfhearted flick of his hand before slumping against me. I slipped an arm under his knees and another around his ribs. By the time I got to the porch, I had to stop and catch my breath. Either I was getting weak or tenacity weighed twice as much as muscle.

The door was unlocked. Did he even have a key? It wouldn't have surprised me if he didn't. Locking a door had been a foreign concept to me until I moved to Chicago.

One of his flip-flops fell off in the doorway of his room. After I laid him down, I went back for it. The foam was mashed paper thin under the imprint of his heel and toes. The rest of the sole had been chewed up by the gravel.

For all the protection it offered, he might as well have been barefoot. I dropped his shoe by the bed and took off the other one. There was a dark stain on the underside of his sock. I turned on the bedside lamp and checked him over. He didn't have any cuts or injuries.

The truck driver had been bleeding, but that wouldn't explain how blood got on the bottom of his foot. The flip-flops had landed cockeyed, and there was a mirror image of the bloodstain on the sole of the left one.

I peeled the sock off Morgan's foot. Thick bandages wrapped around his foot sporting brownish red star bursts and his first three toes were black and blue. I took out my pocketknife and used it to cut away the gauze.

The cotton strips pulled away with a sticky sound and the shadowy stain grew. When the last piece fell away, I was glad I'd missed dinner. On shredded flesh, Morgan had carried himself to and from Toolies for over a week.

I cradled his foot in my lap. There was no sign of infection, and the only smell was copper and a little sweat. I checked his other foot, and of course, it was in the same condition.

If he had bandages, there was a good chance he had other first aid supplies. I found a box under the sink with a montage of aspirin bottles, Band-Aids, heartburn pills, and tubes of antibiotic cream.

Scrounging up something to clean him with was more difficult. I had to settle on a roasting pan for the warm water and dish soap.

When I returned, he was still on his back with one arm across his stomach and the other tucked under his chin.

I laid a towel under his feet and wet the washcloth. Morgan whimpered and tried to pull away when I pressed the wet cloth to the bottom of his foot. I held it there until the dried blood let go, then gently cleaned the cuts.

The thick calluses on the bottoms of his feet were the only reason they weren't raw hamburger.

When his feet were clean, I patted them dry.

Morgan slid his hand in my direction, and I held it. "I'm sorry…" he said.

"This isn't your fault."

He mumbled something else, and I pushed his bangs back. Sleep had no effect on his crumpled expression.

"Dillon…" He tightened his grip. "Dillon…"

"Shh—" I started to pull away, but he wouldn't let go.

"I'm sorry." Tears pricked the corners of his eyes. "Please don't be angry. I tried. I tried." The plea was barely a whisper, but it still screamed with desperation.

I put Morgan's hand on his chest. "No one's angry, Morgan. Everything's all right."

"I'm sorry I messed up. I didn't mean to."

I shushed him again.

"I'm so sorry."

What could he have possibly done to make him beg so hard for forgiveness? I ran my knuckles down his cheek.

"I'm sorry for being a freak."

My chest squeezed tight, and I could barely swallow around the lump in my throat. "You're not a freak."

"I'll do better. I promise… I promise." Morgan fell still, and some of the pain left his expression. I'd thought he'd escaped whatever nightmare held him until he said, "Please, just don't hit me anymore."

****

The scent of salty bacon and buttered toast teased my senses, and my stomach growled.

I rolled over to get up and almost fell onto the floor. I lay there, knees dangling over the edge, one hand planted on the ground, holding me up with no idea how my bed had gotten so small. Then last night came back to me.

My knees protested about being twisted into a position where I would fit on Morgan's narrow couch. Then of course, my shoulders had to voice their opinion on my sleeping arrangements. A sentiment echoed by a sharp twinge in my neck.

Soft metallic scrapes came from the kitchen. I stood, and the dull ache in my knees shot into a hot line to my back. I wound up right back on the couch.

I massaged the offending muscle into submission before I tried again. Then I made a pit stop in the bathroom on the off chance my bladder might decide it had aged fifty years in a single night like the rest of my body.

By the time I was done washing my hands, most of my joints had forgiven me for the inadequate sleeping arrangements.

In the kitchen, Morgan stood in front of the stove wearing jeans and a long-sleeved shirt. His sun-streaked hair laid in defined curls, suggesting it had air dried some time ago.

Bits of gauze stuck up around the edge of the fresh pair of socks on his feet. A large rip in the leg of his jeans revealed the sharp lines of his ankle as it led into the firm muscle of his calves. The tear widened enough at the top when he moved, flashing the back of his knee.

I stuck my hands in my pockets to keep from doing something stupid like walking over there and finding out how far I could reach up the leg of his jeans.

"Do you like bacon?" Morgan said.

"Uh... Sure."

The hand he held the spatula with slung droplets of grease on the stove. Morgan wiped it up with a dishrag without missing a beat between turning the bacon and stirring the eggs.

"Go ahead and sit down. It's almost done."

"I feel like I should help."

Another spasm bent his wrist. The spatula escaped, bounced off the counter, and landed on the floor. Again, without hesitation, he had the utensil under the tap washing it off. He returned to the stove.

"Can I?" I said.

"What?"

"Help."

He turned his head enough for me to get a glimpse of his chin. A tiny patch of razor burn glowed at the edge of his jaw. "You can get the juice out of the fridge. I made coffee too. The pot is in the microwave. Sorry I don't have a coffeemaker, but the teapot seems to work just as good."

There was apple and orange juice in the fridge. I didn't know which one he wanted so I carried both of them to the table.

Morgan already had the dishes in place.

"Glasses?" I stopped right behind him.

"You might want to back up."

I did and just in time to avoid a flick of grease. The glob became a dark spot among the many others on the sleeve of his shirt.

"Over the cookie jar."

"Huh?"

"You asked where the glasses were." He pointed, but his hand was quick to retreat to its place next to his temple. He opened and closed his fingers, but the movement was slower than before. After a few flicks, he picked up the pan of eggs and moved it off the burner.

I got the glasses and put them beside the plates.

"Sorry my sofa isn't very comfortable." Morgan walked into the dining room carrying a bowl of eggs. He left it on the table and went back to the kitchen. When he reappeared, he had the bacon and toast.

"Go ahead." He sat and fixed himself a plate.

I lowered myself into a chair.

"It's nothing fancy, but it will eat." He handed me the eggs, and I set it next to my empty glass. "My toaster has it out for me." He scraped a blackened edge of bread with his finger. "It's either undercooked or burnt. I'd fire it, but it's thirty years old and will probably work for another thirty years compared to a new one that'd die after six months."

He passed me the plate of bacon. I laid it next to the eggs.

Morgan corralled pieces of runaway eggs and herded them away from his bacon. Then he proceeded to break the strips into pieces that I bet you could have measured with a ruler and every one of them would have been right at two inches or dead-on.

He made three rows and stacked them at the edge of his plate. "Do you want me to get the coffee?"

"I'm good."

"I don't normally drink it, but I've got milk and sugar. At least I think I have milk, it could be bad. I can't remember when I bought it last. If it is, I can open a can of goat's milk. Probably taste better that way." He stood.

"Please sit down."

"It'll only take a minute for me to get—"

"Why didn't you tell me the truth?"

He fluttered his hand. "I'll be right back." I tried to stop him, but he slipped by. I followed him into the kitchen.

Morgan leaned on the sink, clutching the edge with one hand while the other maintained its standard spot next to his temple.

Even with a shirt covering his back, the tension pulling at his shoulders was visible.

"Maybe you should just go," he said.

"If that's what you want. But will you answer my question first?"

"You made it perfectly clear you didn't want to give me a ride. What did you want me to do? Beg?"

"No, but you should have told me you didn't have a ride. Hell, you should have told anyone. For God's sake, you walked your feet raw. You need to call a doctor and make sure you don't wind up with an infection. I'll even give you a ride to see him so you—"

"Stop it, Grant." He thumped his fist against the edge of the sink. "Just stop. I do not need your pity. I do not want your pity. I'm not handicapped. I'm not a child. I'm a grown man able to make my own decisions."

"Well, you made the wrong one."

"And you never have?" He rocked forward. I wasn't sure if it was one of his strange movements or he was trying to take some weight off his feet.

45

"I'm sorry about…" I ran a hand over my head. "About being an…"

"I think the word you're looking for is asshole."

I opened my mouth, then shut it. All I could do was nod. "You're right. I'm sorry for being an asshole."

"Apology accepted. But I still think you should leave."

"If I do, are you going to keep walking your feet raw?"

"Jenny said my bike should be ready today. Her parts man Will has a delivery to make, so he can drop it off on his way over there."

"What if I don't want to go?"

Morgan gripped the edge of the sink, lowered his head, and a hard whine ticked out of his throat. "It doesn't…" His knuckles whitened, and his arms trembled. "It doesn't matter what—" His right shoulder jerked. "You want." Again. "This is my house and I'm—" The whine returned and then stopped. "I'm telling you to leave."

Any attempt at arguing would have sounded like pity. I guess it would have been pity. So not only was I an asshole, but a lying asshole. Did you get double points for that?

I paused at the kitchen doorway. "Deputy Harold said not to worry about going to the station, and Jessie said he wants you to take the day off."

Morgan nodded. "If you see him around town, tell him I'll be in by five."

I bit off another rising argument. "Do you need a ride?"

"My bike will be here by then."

"In case, it's not. Do you need a ride?"

"Honestly, Grant. I'd rather walk."

Chapter Three

I didn't go to Toolies for several weeks, and I avoided the hardware store; moving from project to project, leaving them unfinished as I ran out of supplies.

The last nail sank into the floor joist I'd spliced by attaching a fresh board to the one blackened by a leaking pipe. It was probably overkill, but I needed something to do.

I climbed out of the opening where the kitchen sink and cabinets used to be. With the linoleum gone, I'd been able to get a good look at the aged hardwood floor. Except for a few pieces where the fridge sat, it was salvageable. But I'd have to finish it in a shade close to black to hide the water stains.

In the long run, it was a good thing it didn't need a drastic overhaul, otherwise I would have faced getting the new pieces of wood to match the color of the old. Even with everything being finished at once, there would be a difference since the new wood wouldn't be aged. I was willing to bet a local carpenter might know a few tricks to keep the patch from showing.

I wiped the sweat off my face with a dishtowel. With the days getting shorter, I'd been spared the effects of the Southern heat, but the winter would be short and I'd need to get an AC unit installed if I planned on surviving the summer.

As a kid, we'd only had an attic fan to draw in a breeze from the open windows. But after living with the spoils of the modern age, I couldn't fathom ever doing it again.

I realize I had plans to live out the rest of my life on a beachfront, but there's a big difference between baking nicely in the sun with an ocean breeze to kiss your skin and melting inside the liquid air of a farmhouse.

I toed an empty box of PVC connectors. There was nothing left for me to do, so it was time to bite the bullet and get my ass into town. While Durstrand was small, it was unlikely I'd run into Morgan. Although I think the idea of not running into him bothered me more.

Stopping at Toolies would solve the problem. And that had to be one of the worst ideas I'd had in a very long time. Needless to say, by the time I shored up enough courage to go to the hardware store, the sun had fled in favor of the night.

Berry appeared from between the aisles with a broom and dustpan. "Long time no see, stranger. Where you been? And you'd better not tell me at that new chain store in Maysville."

"Nope."

He narrowed a look at me.

I held my hands up in defense. "I swear, Berry, I am your loyal customer. I've just been busy is all. Now I've run out of everything so I came by to reload." I took the list out of my pocket. Berry left the dustpan and broom behind the counter. I handed him the list.

He put his glasses on and held out the piece of paper at arm's length, then brought it back to the tip of his nose. "Wow, you did run out of everything." He rubbed his chin. "You in a hurry?"

"No, sir."

He waved at the door. "Bring your truck around back, and we'll load her up."

I got my wallet out of my back pocket.

"I've already shut down the register. Just pay me next time you come in."

"You sure?"

"Positive. After all, I know where you live."

We loaded the small things: hardware, pipe, nails, glue, and various other items.

During several trips back and forth to my truck, no one else came in the store. The back porch was on my to-do list this week so we moved to the lumberyard. If I cut around the pallet of cinder blocks, I could still catch a glimpse of the inside of the building through the porthole window in the back.

"You expecting someone?"

"What? No, why?"

"You keep eyeing the storefront like you're expecting someone to come in."

I didn't even try to convince him I wasn't.

"If you got questions, Grant, ask. If I got answers, I'll tell 'em."

I dusted my hands off. "What can you tell me about Morgan?"

A smile pulled at Berry's lips. "What do you want to know?"

It was a perfectly logical reply. "I'm not sure, to tell you the truth. Anything, I guess."

"He's single."

I arched an eyebrow at him.

"And he really likes you."

"I don't know about that."

"He does." Berry puffed out his chest like I'd insulted him.

"How do you figure?"

"He looks you in the eye. He only looks people in the eye if he really likes them and trusts them."

"I think you're making a big deal out of nothing. Morgan only looks at me for a second or two."

"That's a second or two more than most people."

I chuckled.

"I'm serious." He jabbed a thumb at his chest. "I've known him since he was in diapers and can count on one hand the number of times Morgan has looked me dead in the eye and still have all five fingers left over."

"Aw, c'mon."

His face turned serious.

"You really mean it?"

"Yeah. I do. He likes you, Grant. A whole lot."

"Why? He barely knows me."

"I guess he sees something in you no one else can. Like he seems to see things other places no one else can."

If Morgan could really see who I was, it made no sense why he liked me. There were things I didn't like about me.

The plywood was stacked in the corner.

"Just wanted to make sure you were aware of that," Berry said.

"I'll keep it in mind."

He pointed a finger at me. "Now don't you dare downplay your interest. I saw you watching him a couple months ago when he was here."

I grabbed up the first sheet of plywood I could get my hands on.

"Hang on and I'll help you."

Together we loaded up the last item on my list.

Berry handed me the end of the tie-down. "So you decide what questions you want to ask yet?"

"I've only heard him talk about Jenny and Lori. He said she raised him." I ran the strap through the eyebolt on the side of the bed. "When I asked him about his parents, he didn't answer me. Do you know where they are?"

"Dead, I suppose. Or run off. I don't think anyone really knows what happened to them except maybe Lori."

"How's that possible?"

"No one ever saw them, so I'm pretty sure they weren't local. Lori just showed up one day with Morgan in her arms. I think he was two, maybe three." Berry rubbed his chin. "He wasn't older than four. Couldn't have been."

"She just showed up with a toddler?"

"Yup."

"And no one asked questions?"

"Sure, they did. She just didn't give no answers."

I propped an elbow on the edge of the truck bed. "Where do you think she got him from?"

"Don't know. Really don't care." He locked the strap in place on his side.

"Has anyone ever tried to find out?"

"Are you kidding? Small town like this? Gossip is less of a recreation and more a civic duty. He'd been legally adopted. The names of the parents wasn't available. She didn't snatch him if that's what you're thinking."

I guess it sorta was. "Does he have anyone to look in on him?"

Berry snorted. "Morgan don't need no looking after. Trust me. That boy has his life together better than seventy-five percent of this town."

"It's just…" I was doing it again. Yet I couldn't stop myself.

"It's hard." Berry took off his ball cap and reshaped the bill. "A lot of people who don't know him think the same way you do, and a lot of people who do know him have a hard time accepting him. Even when they saw what Lori started with. It's amazing, you know. How he's gone from a little boy who didn't hear or see you, even when you talked right at him, to a self-sufficient, educated adult."

"Jenny said people thought he would never walk, talk, or even read and write."

"And Morgan proved everyone wrong. He's always proving people wrong." Berry watched the front of the store for a moment. "Sad to say, I was one of those people. I think the only one who ever had faith in him was Lori, but she was as stubborn as a team of mules."

"Did anyone help her?"

"A little here and there. But Lori wouldn't let anyone handle Morgan. She quit her job keeping house for some rich family she'd worked for since she was twelve and spent every waking moment with him. But she didn't coddle him. Oh, no. She had expectations, and she patiently waited for him to meet each one."

"How did she afford to stay home with him?"

Berry scrunched up his face. "Not sure to tell you the truth. She got money from somewhere. She weren't rich or nothing, but she didn't want for anything and neither did Morgan."

"What about the scars on his face?"

"Morgan was in a relationship years ago." Berry slapped his ball cap across his knee. "He moved off with the guy. Dillon, I think was his name. Morgan was barely seventeen. No one heard from him until the hospital called."

"Was Dillon the reason why Morgan was in the hospital?"

Berry frowned. "Yeah."

"What happened?"

"Dillon was abusing him. One day, it went from bad to worse."

"Why didn't he leave?"

"I don't know."

"How did he get away?"

Berry fumbled with the end of the tie-down before tucking it between a couple slats of wood. "He didn't. Neighbors complained about the stereo playing loud all night. When the super showed up, no one answered, he let himself in and found Morgan.

"All I know is it was bad and Lori wouldn't elaborate. Honestly, though, I don't even think Lori knew for sure how serious it was until she saw the aftermath.

"Lori. She didn't cry when her momma died, or her daddy. She didn't cry the day Tom Daniel's horse kicked her in the arm and broke it in three places. Wasn't a doctor in town back then. Was three days before she could get someone to take her to the hospital. Even the day she saw the mess Dillon had made of her boy she did not cry. She just picked up the pieces and went to work to make it right.

"She wasn't just strong, Grant. She was made of iron. Her willpower could move mountains, and by God, it did." Berry took a few measured breaths. "Nope. She never cried. Not until she brought him home and the doctors told her she needed to put Morgan in an institution because he would never come back. I was there. I saw. It was only one tear, but it might as well have been a river."

"What do you mean he wouldn't come back?"

"He turned into that little boy again. The one who didn't see you or hear you. He just wiggled his fingers through the sunlight. They said it was the trauma. He shut down because of the terrible things that man did to him and went away where he would be safe."

"But he got better."

"Yeah." Berry nodded. "He did." He inhaled a shaky breath. "Because Lori refused to accept any other outcome. She shut herself up in that old homeplace on Maple and sometimes months would go by before I saw her. When she did come to town, Morgan was always with her and she was never ashamed of how he acted. She just went about her shopping, incorporating Morgan into the routine just like she did when he was young. And every time she showed up in town, he'd gotten a little better, until one day he was riding his bike and working at Toolies.

"She loved that boy, Grant. She loved him so much she lived when she should have died."

"Was she sick?"

"Cancer. The doctor wanted her to go into the hospital and do that chemo treatment, but

Lori refused. She said Morgan needed her too badly. So she kept going. And going. About a week after Morgan started his job at Toolies, she let go." Berry wiped his eyes with the back of his hand. "Everyone thought Morgan would—you know—go away, but he didn't. He sold the old homeplace to pay her hospital bills and moved to the one he lives in now. Rebuilt it and himself."

"And Dillon's in jail?"

"Yup. He deserved worse, but seven years was the best they could do."

Berry was right. Dillon did deserve worse. But even death was too easy a punishment. There were far more suitable ways to extract penance for what he'd done to Morgan.

I've seen the results left behind by debt owed to private lenders. Even the toughest men crumbled under the kind of torture the monsters could deliver. I'd never imagined myself capable of that kind of cruelty.

I guess I was more of a beast than I'd ever given myself credit for. Because if I'd been given the chance to get my hands on Dillon, I would have started with pulling out his toenails and ended at his teeth. I would have broken every joint, severed every finger.

And when I was bored with his screams, I would have shoved an ice pick in his gut, pulled up a chair, and watched him slowly bleed out.

Berry cleared his throat and forced a smile. A patch of skin on one cheek was still shiny. "So what about you?"

I still had questions about Morgan, but Berry had already relived enough. "Not much to tell. Born and raised in Alabama, got kicked out when I was sixteen, went to Chicago, never looked back."

"What'd you do in Chicago?"

"I moved people's valuables when they sold or bought them, or when they just plain old wanted to relocate to the beach home or winter cottage, here in the US and abroad."

"Musta been good business. Jessie's cousin said you paid cash for the Anderson house."

I laughed. "Nice to know small town news still moves fast."

"Even faster now, thanks to cell phones. Otherwise it would take at least two days for the gossip to get around. Now, I practically get text alerts on the hour every hour." Berry grinned. "So why'd you quit your obviously successful shipping company?"

There was a tone to the question that made me wonder how much Jenny had told him. "Got tired of it."

"Never knew a man who got tired of money."

"It wasn't the money. It was the people. I got into the business when a handshake was more binding than a three inch legal document." When men did business and didn't dig graves. "The tides changed and I couldn't—wouldn't—change with it."

Berry nodded like he understood. "Well hopefully you find happiness here in Durstrand."

The only place I had intentions of looking for happiness was that long stretch of virgin beach where the water was so blue you could see the treasures hidden just below the surf. And yet the usual anticipation I felt when I rolled my fantasy future through my head didn't happen.

It was only when I went back to thinking about Morgan my heart took on a subtle flutter.

I got in the truck. "Thanks for all your help." And answers. I didn't say it out loud, but I think he saw it in my eyes because his smile trembled.

"Any time."

I started the truck and gave it some gas to warm it up. Berry walked over, and I rolled down the window.

"I meant what I said about being happy here. I think if you allow it, you'll even find someone to love."

****

The parking lot at Toolies was almost full. It was still early, even for a small town, so the dinner crowd hadn't quite moved out and the drinking fans hadn't moved in.

I pulled around the back where there was more parking. Morgan's bike was propped up against the rear door. I exhaled a sigh of relief that I hadn't realized I was holding.

The bar was full so I took up a booth that hadn't been cleaned yet and pushed the dirty dishes to one side. Then I plucked a few napkins from the dispenser and used them to clean up crumbs and spilled coffee.

A waitress walked up. "There are some clean booths over here."

"This is fine."

Her smile faltered. "Are you sure? We're pretty backed up. It may be a few minutes before one of the busboys can clean it."

I took ten dollars from my wallet and handed it to her. "Whenever is fine. Just make sure it's Morgan."

"You must be Grant." With that, she walked away.

A family of five left and a familiar bar groupie wandered in with his girlfriend. They parked it at the counter.

A few booths up, two men with high-dollar haircuts and very nice suits stood to leave. Durstrand sat between Maysville and Alto. Both were a metropolis of corporate offices and high-end living. In just the few months I'd been here, traveling businessmen had become a frequent sight. And since Toolies was the only place offering fresh cooked food on the main stretch of highway, it was no surprise a lot of people stopped.

The two suits didn't speak to anyone and left money on the table. The hairs on the back of my neck stood up when they walked by. I turned, but they were already out the door and lost between the neon glow from the sign and the night.

Just two businessmen. That's all.

The young people near the jukebox parted ways, clearing the view across the room. Morgan stood in the doorway to the kitchen, talking with my waitress. He didn't appear to respond to what she said so I was surprised when he headed my way.

He cleaned the dishes with the efficiency achieved with practice but with careful precision found in people who took pride in their job. He stacked each plate, lined each glass along the edge, and filled them with silverware. When the plates were clear and the used napkins piled on the plates, he wiped down the table.

Morgan put the bin in the booth across from me and slid in next to it.

He removed his earbuds but didn't lift his head. His wayward hand creeped up, and he tried to hold it down. After a moment of fighting, he gave up and flicked thoughts in my direction.

"Your feet doing better?"

His shoulder twitched.

"Did you let a doctor look at them?"

Morgan tipped his face up at the light and wiggled his fingers close to the bulb, making shadows on the table. He chased them with his free hand.

I rested my arms on the table. "I'm not even sure why I'm here."

He dropped his chin to his chest, and the curtain of blond waves slid into place.

"I feel like I should apologize, but I'm not sure how."

The small jumps and stutters assaulting his muscles calmed, and his hands sank into his lap.

"I'm not going to lie to you. I wasn't sure how to react. You know, to the tics. It threw me off. But I like you. A lot. And I think that messes with my head more than the... I'm sorry, you know. I'm sorry that I lack the ability to understand." I scrubbed my face.

Morgan sat motionless.

"Will you say something? Anything? Even if it's fuck off, I never want to see you again." And if my heart broke, it wouldn't have surprised me.

Morgan cocked his head to the side, turning it just enough to part his bangs. His gaze was distant. Or maybe he was staring into the parts of the world I'd never be able to see. Places most people would never be able to see.

Because they just weren't gifted enough.

"Please, Morgan, I—"

"I get off work in half an hour." He picked up his bin and went into the back.

The waitress reappeared with her ticket book in hand. "Decide what you want?"

Had I?

I guess in thirty minutes I was going to find out.

****

I'm willing to bet, if I'd had a stopwatch, it would have ticked off the thirtieth minute just as Morgan opened the back door to Toolies.

He pushed his bike over to the truck. I got out and helped him put it on top of the wood and tie it down.

The poor lighting in the back parking lot eliminated any chance I had at catching a glimpse of his face, and left the rest of him shadowed in slaps of gray. Now that I knew how precious a gift it was for Morgan to meet my gaze, I was desperate to have him look at me.

I was even more desperate to touch him.

He said nothing, so I said nothing, and that nothing continued after I turned out on the main road and on Water's Way.

When I slowed to look for his street, he said, "Keep driving."

There were no street lamps this far out of town, only the occasional house with a front porch light. Sometimes they were close enough to the road to break the darkness, but mostly they just fed the shadows.

Several more miles down, there was only the headlights leading the way to nowhere and the dash lights to assure me we hadn't fallen into an ink well.

The road narrowed, and the pavement ended.

What began as a county maintained road turned into a washed-out gravel strip, half hidden by waist-high dried grass. The untamed trees along the shoulder hung low enough for the branches to claw the roof of the truck. Those disappeared, and a pasture edged with barbed wire flanked us on both sides.

The gravel road ended at a cattle gate. It was open, and Morgan didn't tell me to stop.

Creaks and groans rose and fell as we rolled over the lumpy earth. Grass brushed against the undercarriage. The perpetual sigh followed us another mile.

"Stop here," Morgan said.

I did.

"Turn the truck off."

I did.

"The lights."

I hesitated.

"Please."

I thought I knew what darkness was until the night swallowed us whole, leaving absolutely nothing. I hoped to see a few stars, but cloud cover had erased them.

The steering wheel in my hands assured me we hadn't ceased to exist. "Is there a reason why we're out here?"

Fabric whispered against fabric and the old vinyl seat squeaked. Morgan quit moving, and once again I was left to question whether or not I'd ever been real.

"When I was nine," Morgan said, "I wanted to be a ballet dancer. Lori emptied out the extra bedroom and put a mirror on the wall. She even installed a railing that went all the way across the room.

"We had a small TV and a VCR, and she built a shelf in the corner to sit everything on. Every week she'd check out instructional tapes, and any movies with dancers from the library, and I'd watch them over and over.

"I followed the dancers on the video. I did everything they did. Just like they did. I practiced and I practiced.

"Lori saved up some money so I could take real lessons at a small private school in Alto. They made you do auditions to get in, and it was a thirty-mile drive one-way. Sometimes they'd run late, and you'd have to go home and come back. It took three trips before it was my turn."

Morgan laughed a little. "I wasn't even nervous because I'd watched those videos every day. I'd practiced every day. I knew the moves perfectly.

"I was the best." Silence reigned until Morgan sighed. "But they denied my application before they even let me show them what I could do."

"Why?"

"Because they couldn't see me."

I hated to admit my ignorance, but I didn't have a choice. "I don't understand."

"The light is a funny thing, Grant. We think it shows us what we need to see, but in reality, it blinds us. That's why I brought you here. I wanted you to see me."

He was right. The light did blind people. I knew firsthand just how misleading it could be. Switch a few parts, tuck a masterpiece in a load of half-assed art, and people wouldn't give it a second glance.

In Morgan's case, the light had let me see the tics, the muscle spasms, and his strange movements, and I'd been distracted by them. The dark took it all away and left me sitting next to a person, not a behavior, a human being, not perceived defects. Someone insightful, quick-witted, determined, generous, kind, and armed with a wicked sense of humor.

Someone definitely smarter than me.

Someone I did not deserve.

I'd been so close to being like those dance instructors who threw away a once in a lifetime chance. But instead of leaving me to the mercy of the light, Morgan had led me into the darkness, where it had no more power over me.

How did you replay that kind of gift? How did you repent for being unable to see it?

I didn't know, but I wanted to try.

"What's your favorite color?" I said.

"Blue? You?"

"Yellow or green. It's a toss-up."

"What kind of music do you listen to?" Morgan said.

"I'm not particular. Depends on my mood really."

"Me either. But I like to listen to classical when I work on my sculptures."

"You sculpt?"

"Sorta."

"How do you sorta sculpt?"

He laughed. "It's hard to explain. I'll have to show you sometime."

"I'd like that... I tried to draw when I was in high school, but it didn't work out."

"How come?"

"Well, for starters, I couldn't draw." I grinned even though he couldn't see it. But I had a feeling he would know anyhow.

"I would definitely say that'd be a requirement."

"I might have gotten better if I'd kept at it, but playing football was easier, and I got to stare at a lot of nice ass."

"If art isn't your thing, what is?"

"What do you mean?"

"What kind of hobbies do you have?"

I hadn't really thought about it. "Right now it's fixing the house. I'm pretty sure that'll keep me occupied for a while."

"And after?"

"I don't know. I could get a dog."

Morgan laughed again. It was my new favorite sound. "A dog isn't a hobby."

"Okay a boat."

"Neither is a boat, unless you plan on building it."

"Not unless I want it to sink."

"Then you're zero to two, Grant. Better think fast."

I tugged on my bottom lip. "Well, I could take up fishing."

"Hmmm, yeah. That could work."

"Do you fish?"

"Sometimes. Not as much as I used to. I'm too busy with work and my sculptures."

"You're definitely going to have to show them to me."

"I will. I promise."

"Did you learn to sculpt in college?"

"Never went." Was that disappointment in his voice?

"Jenny said you got a full scholarship."

"I did."

"Then how come you didn't go?"

Morgan snorted.

"What?" I said.

"Nothing."

"I must have said something funny."

"The fact you even asked."

"Why you didn't go to college?"

"Yeah."

"Well, why didn't you?"

He shifted in his seat. "I don't do well with change, so I stick close to home."

"Lots of people get homesick when they go away to college, Morgan. It's perfectly normal."

He sighed. "Will you say that again?"

"Say what?"

"Normal. How it's perfectly normal."

****

Pale pink and yellow bled into the night from the east. As light returned to the world, so did the trees, the grass, the roads.

So did I. And so did Morgan.

But I'd been changed by the dark. I promised myself I'd never forget there were things beyond the light, and if I wasn't careful, they'd be lost.

Forever.

And now everything I'd missed about Morgan was revealed. His longish nose and rounded chin. The dusting of a fine gold five o'clock shadow.

Morgan was average height with square shoulders. Yet still looked stronger than seemed possible. But I think that was because his strength had nothing to do with the tawny muscles running down his elegant arms and legs.

I parked in front of his house, and he got out.

"Do you want to go get some lunch after a while?" I said.

"I might not be up."

"Well, how about supper?"

"As long as it's not Toolies." Morgan graced me with a rare glimpse of his eyes.

"Promise." I made an X over my heart. "No Toolies."

"You realize the only other place to eat on Sunday is in Maysville."

"Is that where you want to go?" I'd take him. Even if the truck broke down and I had to carry him on my back.

Morgan leaned against the doorframe. "It's probably not a good idea on the weekend. It gets really busy and loud."

"Okay."

56

"I know that doesn't leave much." He shook his head. "Actually it leaves nothing except the convenience store hotdogs."

I tapped my fingers against the steering wheel. "Do you have a grill?"

"Sure."

"Then how about this. I bring the beer and the steaks and you supply the grill and charcoal."

"Will wood do?"

"Absolutely."

"Okay, what time?"

"Five, five thirty."

"Sure. I'll see you then."

I didn't drive away until he was inside and out of sight. When I got home, I unloaded the truck, took a shower, and ate breakfast. But the strange hum in my body wouldn't still.

I went ahead and laid down even though I wasn't tired, and after staring at the ceiling a while, I resorted to counting down the minutes as they ticked off the clock on the bedside table.

Time slowed just to be spiteful.

I was about to give up and go do something productive when my cell phone rang. I retrieved it from the bedside table where I'd left it, my wallet, and a handful of crumpled dollar bills.

"Hello?"

"It's me." Jeff.

"Why are you calling me?"

"You told me to use a phone the next time I needed to talk with you, rather than buy a plane ticket."

"I told you that I'm not going to help you." I sat up. "I won't betray the confidence of my clients."

"Well, you may not have a choice."

"Is that a threat, Agent Shaldon?" In my line of work, threats got people killed. Because where I came from, threats were nothing more than the echo of future actions.

"No threat, Grant. At least not the kind you're thinking of."

"What other kind is there?"

"A heads-up." There was a rattle of movement and a moment of background noise that sounded an awful lot like... an elephant? "Where are you?"

"The zoo."

"Why are you calling me from the zoo?"

"Because I wanted to make sure what I have to tell you couldn't be heard by any of our surveillance teams or any other interested party."

"Are you saying I need to worry about the FBI spying on me?"

"Only if you've done something illegal. Which you have clearly stated many times, you haven't. And as you've so eloquently pointed out, you have the paperwork to prove it."

"Who's the other interested party?"

"Carson Lorado."

"Why the hell would Carson care about what I do? I'm nothing to him."

"He's a paranoid son-of-a-bitch who kills like people take vitamins, as preventative medicine."

"Touché." Jeff was right. Carson was exactly the kind of man who turned business into bloodshed. His way of thinking had spread through my neighborhood like a plague, turning prospective clients and partners into dangerous investments. Apparently even the criminal world had gotten so lazy it was easier to shoot people than deal with them. "How do you know he's got an interest in me?"

A child squealed somewhere beyond the rise and fall of happy music. It faded until the silence was almost absolute.

I was about to ask Jeff if he was still there when he said, "Someone hacked my computer."

"And you think Carson did it?"

"Whoever it was only went for one thing."

"What?"

"My travel plans."

"To here?"

"Exactly."

"Have you considered one of your playmates might be trying to dig up dirt on you? After all, I was fucking you."

His exhale hit the speaker hard. "My playmates knew I went down there. They wanted me to wear a wire, remember?"

"And you took it off."

Another exhale.

"You motherfucker."

"I had to."

"You care to tell me why?"

"If I hadn't worn it, Hines would have sent someone else. And someone else might have gone after you in a way to make you fuck up. You know as well as I do how this game can be played. Hines wants you in here bad, Grant. He knows you have information, and he wants it."

"And you still think the break-in was Carson?"

"One of Carson's associates was hit by a bus almost a week ago."

"Sounds like Karma."

"More like someone upstairs is looking out for you."

"How so?"

"Don Wallis, Carson's first choice hit man. He had a slip of paper in his wallet. The numbers didn't make sense when I first saw them, but I felt like I'd seen them before. Then it hit me. They were the date, time, and flight number on my itinerary. He even had the coordinates to your house plugged into his GPS. He'd stopped for gas right off I-65 South. A bus hit him when he pulled out."

"He was headed here." It wasn't a question but an obvious fact.

"Yeah."

"Do your friends know?"

"They do."

"I don't suppose they sent a welcoming committee." Jeff's silence was all I needed. "Told you nice suits and Italian leather didn't mix well in this town."

58

"Lots of business people go through Durstrand."

"Yeah, but they don't walk around like they have listening devices crammed up their ass." I think he almost laughed, but I couldn't be sure. And I wasn't going to ask to find out.

"They're not there to help you."

"You don't say."

"But they don't want to miss out on the chance you might spill valuable information."

"You mean they want to listen in while I get various body parts cut off, burned, or electrocuted."

"With Don Wallis dead, Carson will send his second, Ulrich."

"Great. I've always wanted to know what it felt like to be dressed out like a deer. Wait, I thought he was in prison."

"He must have gotten out early."

"How the hell does a killer get out early?"

"Well, technically he didn't go to jail for killing anyone, he went to jail on illegal weapons charges; second, it's not all that uncommon for a DA to make a deal for a chance to catch bigger fish."

Bigger fish like Carson Lorado. Even I knew Ulrich wasn't that stupid. "Was it worth it?"

"They lost track of him a few days after he got out."

"What a surprise." I rolled my eyes. "I hope the DA at least got something useful before Ulrich disappeared."

"False leads, old addresses, empty bank accounts." Jeff moved again. Voices rose and fell. Quiet returned. "Look, I need a reason for the SAC to see you as something more than collateral damage."

"Is Hines still the Special Agent in charge?"

"For now."

"Lovely." Just what I needed, the man with a personal beef to pick with me.

"He wants information more than he wants to get back at you."

"You sure about that?"

"I'm not saying he'll forgive you. I mean it's kind of hard to forgive a man that almost cost you your job."

"I don't have any idea what you're talking about." Thank God Jeff could not see me smile.

"You sank almost a million dollars' worth of computer equipment into the lake."

"Not my fault the barge sank."

"With some help."

"I was fifty miles away arranging transportation for an antique car collection. I had witnesses. Eight, if I remember correctly. One of whom was a judge."

"Ex-judge turned criminal."

"Retired judge because the authorities couldn't make the case stick."

"Minor details."

"Weren't those the exact words that maintenance man said when questioned about the hull damage? You'd think Agent Hines would be grateful I chose to upgrade the life boats and life jackets since he couldn't swim."

Jeff did laugh that time. "Just between you and me, it was brilliant."

"Sorry, can't take credit for something I didn't do."

The seriousness returned to Jeff's voice. "You need to watch your back. And if Carson really is sending Ulrich, you need all the help you can get."

Again, he was right. And I hated it. "What would it take to move me from the glue truck?"

"Simple, Hines wants your shipping routes, client list, times, dates, items you moved, and where."

"My preverbal black book, aye?"

"Yeah." There was a ruffle of fabric as if Jeff might have shrugged.

"What does he plan on doing with it?"

"I'm assuming he'll use it to pin down bigger fish."

"Like Lorado?"

"Possibly."

"Revealing my trade secrets won't help him arrest anyone."

Jeff made a frustrated sound. "Damn it, Grant, I'm trying to help you."

"Really? Since when?"

"Since the day I fell in love with you."

That stopped me cold. I sat there on the edge of my bed, goosebumps crawling over my skin, heat pushing up sweat droplets over my upper lip. "You better hope no one is listening in on this phone call."

"I'll call you from the unemployment line if they are."

"More likely prison."

"What happened between us wasn't illegal, it just happened."

If only I'd seen it coming, so I could have put up a wall. But Jeff was right, what we had was nothing more than an evolution of companionship. An inevitable end.

"I'm sorry, but my black book isn't up for sale."

"Has it occurred to you maybe Hines isn't the only one interested?"

It hadn't until he said something, but sending Ulrich to torture the information out of me would be overkill. Even for Lorado. Besides, Lorado had his own techniques. If Lorado was gunning for me, he had a completely different agenda. Not that it made the situation any less dangerous.

"Are you still there?" Jeff said.

"Yeah."

"Will you cooperate so I can help you?"

"No."

"Damn it, Grant," Jeff growled into the phone. A sound he never made except when he pulled my hair while he fucked my mouth. "Do you hate me so much you're willing to get yourself killed?"

"That's where you're wrong, Jeff."

"So you don't hate me enough to lock me in a shipping container and push me into the ocean?"

"No. I hate you enough not to waste a good shipping container. But I don't play that way, as you well know. It's why I got out."

"Lucky me."

"You have no idea." No idea how close I'd come to tracking his ass down and making the rumor of Mr. Jeffery Meyer's demise front page news.

****

The phone call with Jeff was enough to suck the life right out of me. But before I fell asleep, I unpacked my 9mm from the bag in my closet and put it under my pillow.

I wasn't too concerned with Ulrich sneaking up on me. That wasn't his style. He liked to watch your expression when you saw him coming.

According to rumor, it was his version of wank fodder.

I didn't know of anyone who'd ever survived a meeting with him. But Jeff confirmed traces of semen found at one of Ulrich's supposed shops. They just never found evidence to prove he'd actually killed anyone there.

But he did. I heard the screams on the tape he played for the man's son who owed his boss money. The son asked me if I thought it was legit. My answer made him throw up.

I was up by three, had the steaks picked up from the local butcher by four, the beer by four thirty, and pulled into Morgan's drive way by five on the nose.

I think he would have been impressed. I know I was.

A trail of white smoke curled up from the other side of Morgan's house. Sweet hickory mixed with the spicy scent of crisp fall air. I grabbed the cooler and headed around the back. Paving stones with bits of colored glass made a path beside the picket fence lined with an array of glass bottles, all sizes and shapes, and a rainbow of colors.

As I rounded the house, delicate stems of copper weighted with circles of colored glass spun on invisible strings hanging from tree limbs. Each turn caught the streaks of sunset and scattered droplets of blue, green, and orange over the grass.

Morgan stood in front of a stone hearth. Coals glowed red under the iron grate.

"That's one hell of a grill. You must really like to cook out."

He wiped his hands on his jeans "It's only a grill when I have company."

"How often is that?"

"Not often enough."

A bucket of broken bottles sat on the stone edge containing the fire. More were lined up on a small section of wall.

"Do you use the glass to make the wind chimes?"

Morgan took the cooler and put it on the picnic table. "They're kinetic sculptures." He fluttered his hand next to his temple and snapped his fingers. "Do you mind if I get a beer?"

"Go ahead." He pulled out two and offered me one.

I took it. "Are those the sculptures you wanted to show me?"

"No. They're inside in the sunroom." He indicated the large screened-in porch. It had to be almost as big as the house. Definitely not standard for a bungalow.

"Did you build that?"

"Yeah. I had to rebuild a lot of the outside wall when I bought the house. So I decided to do it then."

I popped the top on the beer and took a drink. "Berry said you bought this place after your mother died."

"Lori—I didn't like to call her mom."

"How come?"

"Because my mother gave birth to me and didn't want me. Lori wanted me and she loved me. Mom isn't a good enough word to describe her." Morgan took out the steaks. "These are nice. Must be from Mack's."

"How can you tell?"

"You don't get steaks like this at the grocery. So unless you butchered it yourself, there's only one other place they could have come from. How do you want yours cooked?"

"Medium rare."

"I'll try. It's hard to get the temperature right for grilling." He used a poker to coax down another grate folded to the back wall of the hearth. The steaks hit the metal with a hiss.

"What do you normally use it for?"

"To melt glass."

"Is that how you get the edges so smooth?"

"Yeah." He added some spices to the steaks. "I made potatoes, but I used the oven. Last time I tried to bake them on here, I burned them. The time before that, I forgot about them and they disintegrated."

"Well at least you've improved."

"More like I quit trying to rush cooking my potatoes." He turned the steaks with another iron tool, forked at the end.

"Did you make those too?"

"What?"

"The poker?"

"Uh, no. I bought those from Bill Timmons. He does ironwork. Makes fancy gates for a lot of the upscale subdivisions they've been building in Maysville. I needed something to turn the glass. I use fireplace pokers most of the time, but turning the glass requires special shaped ends. Especially for the small pieces."

"From artist to cook. I'm impressed."

Morgan tilted his head and flashed a grin. "Would you mind getting the plates? I forgot to bring them out."

"Sure. Where are they?"

"On the counter. The potatoes are in the bowl with the silverware. Just go through the back door. The kitchen is right there."

Everything was where Morgan said it would be. On my way through the sunroom, a row of strange shapes on the far end caught my eye.

Reddish metal clashed with fragments of colored glass as it twisted around or balanced on spikes of steel mounted to heavy wooden bases.

"If you want medium rare," Morgan said. "You'd better hurry."

I brought him the plates. The spices he used blended with the smell of grilling meat. He flipped the steaks and droplets of grease fell from the first grate to the second. The melted fat bubbled and turned black.

"Go have a seat." Morgan waved the spatula at the table.

"I'm feeling kind of useless."

"Then set the table."

Of course, why didn't I think of that?

I put out the silverware and had picked up the first glass when bits of colored light broke over the ground. The misshapen blobs swam across the stones making circular patterns slither up the back wall of the house to wink out. The source was another one of Morgan's kinetic sculptures.

"Grant?"

"Uh, yeah."

"I need a plate."

More colored light moved across my boots on my way to him.

Morgan nudged me. "Pay attention."

I held out the plate, and he rescued the steaks from the fire. It was a physical battle not to follow the moving splashes of color with my eyes. I made it back to the table without spilling anything.

Morgan sat in front of me and speared a steak with his fork. I unwrapped the potatoes. More glowing fragments moved over the table. I held out a hand to see what it looked like sliding over my skin. The movement of the setting sun was minute, but it made a drastic change in how the shapes were cast and where they appeared. It was only a few minutes before they migrated their dance over the back of the house, turning the white wash into a rainbow of colored sunlight.

"If you don't eat your steak, it's going to get cold." Morgan smiled at me around a bite of meat. Half his potato was gone.

I concentrated on cutting up my steak.

"It's beautiful." Although beautiful seemed too simple a word to describe the montage turning circles in his yard.

Morgan shrugged.

"You don't think so?"

"It's not that."

"Then what?"

"It's not quite right."

I chewed a bite of meat. Whatever he'd put on the steak gave it a robust, warm flavor. "What do you mean?"

"I can't get the patterns right. It's too smooth."

The dance of light shifted positions. I was tempted to watch them climb higher on the house, but I was afraid I'd get lost again. "Compared to what?"

"Sunlight."

"But it is sunlight."

"It's not the same."

"You're going to have to explain what you mean." After all, light was light.

His shoulder twitched, and he tossed thoughts in rapid succession. "I'm not sure I can."

"Try."

"The light. It moves in waves, and they break over objects." He wiggled his fingers, cutting a shadow through the patch of light seeping through the last of the fall leaves. "What comes from my kinetic sculptures doesn't flow right." His serious expression smoothed out, and his eyes focused on the world I couldn't see. I tried, though. I tried to catch a glimpse at whatever it was holding his attention.

Another patch of color passed over the table, turning my potato green, then blue before

63

flickering out.

"You're trying to make what you see, aren't you?"

He blinked several times, and his gaze came back from wherever it had gone. Morgan resumed eating.

"Is that what you're doing?"

He nodded.

"But it's not right?"

"No. I can't figure out the right angle. I think I'm close, though." As hypnotic as the moving colors were, I wasn't sure if I should be impressed or scared.

"Is that what it's like?"

He drank some of his beer. "What?"

"When you…" How did I say it?

"Zone out?"

I nodded. "I guess it's as good a word as any."

"No. I told you, it's not right yet. There's more, but I'm not sure how to incorporate it into the prisms."

I dug around in my potato. Morgan passed me a small tub of butter from the bucket of ice on the table. "Thanks." I added a small chunk and stirred it in. "I thought prisms have edges. The shapes you make are smooth."

"They have edges, just not on the outside. I tried the standard prism shapes, triangles, squares, anything with actual sides. Like you said, an edge. But it only split the light. I needed it to move." He rolled his hand in a waving motion.

The movement caused his shirt to slide down his upper arm. The stark line of his collarbone went to the hard edge of his shoulder. Against the white T-shirt, Morgan's tanned skin was a shade closer to brown sugar. "That's not really the right word, but it's the only one that comes close. Light isn't easy to translate."

"Translate? You make it sound like you're talking about a language."

He tilted his head. "It is. Just not what you hear." He snapped his fingers. "And it doesn't make actual words. But there is a rhythm and a visual tone."

"How can you see sound?"

"Sound moves in waves, and the light moves in waves, but the light doesn't move faster or slower, which is how sound changes pitch. The waves are constant."

"But the tone changes?"

"Again, not like you think. Not in the same way sound changes. It breaks, splits, and alters shape depending on how it hits something. The patterns are words just not made with letters, but it still speaks. And by that, I don't mean it talks. Like I said, it's hard to explain."

Apparently it was also impossible for me to understand.

The muscles in Morgan's forearm flexed. He rolled his arm, revealing the lighter underside. The veins in his wrist made pale blue lines, making it possible to see fine white scars crisscrossing over his skin.

I caught his hand. There were no ridges to suggest the cuts had been deep. I rubbed my thumb over the ones on the heel of his palm. Those were smooth as well.

"What happened?"

"I work with glass and wire, what do you think?"

"You should wear gloves."

"They get in the way." Morgan relaxed his hand, exposing his palm. There were new red scratches in the center. "It's not as bad as it used to be."

"How bad did it used to be?" I lifted my eyes to find him watching me.

"When I first started, my fingers resembled mummies."

"How do you keep from getting that cut up now?"

"Like they say, practice makes perfect." He pulled free, and at the same time, his gaze slid to the edge of the table. He ate and I ate. When we finished, he gathered the plates and I picked up the empty bottles. With any other person, these extended moments of silence would have been awkward. But with Morgan, they were more like a part of him. A detail like eye color or freckles.

Was there another secret in the quiet I couldn't see or, in this case, hear?

He put the dishes in the sink, and I dropped the bottles in the trash. When I turned, Morgan was right there. Close enough that his body heat radiated through my clothes and the musky scent of sun-warmed skin filled me with each breath.

"I want you, Grant."

An electric chill ran up my leg, becoming a heavy weight in my groin.

There was nothing I could desire more in that moment than to take this beautiful man to bed, strip him down, taste his flesh, and bury my cock in his ass. But I couldn't shake the nagging fear doing so would be wrong. I didn't know if I was afraid I'd somehow ruin him or afraid of losing myself and knowing I would never be able to understand enough to give him what he deserved.

Morgan slid his hands up my chest to my face and pulled me down. His velvet lips met mine, and he invaded my mouth. The spices from the food we'd eaten left a mild burn with each stroke of his tongue.

I moaned, and Morgan drank it down. He kissed me harder, and I wrapped my arms around him. There was no more space between us, and his erection pushed against my hip from behind his jeans.

Was he going commando again? The memory of those dimples above the swell of his ass made me want to find out.

I slid my hands up his side and over his ribs and the dips between them. Morgan wrapped a leg around my thigh and pulled himself up my body. I was forced to tilt my head up in an attempt to keep eye contact. The second attack on my mouth was brutal, and my lips ached under the weight of the kiss.

"Morgan…" I wasn't sure he heard me so I gripped his hair and turned my face away. "Morgan, you need to stop."

He bit my neck and drew a wet line to my ear. Morgan latched onto my earlobe and sucked hard enough to make it sting. God, that mouth on my cock would be heaven.

"Morgan." He pulled back only because I made him. His flushed cheeks made his brown eyes darker. "Stop."

He searched my face for a moment before his gaze was lost with a turn of his head and his bangs slid into place. Morgan unwound himself from my body, and my hands burned with the memory of his flesh.

"I'm sorry," I said.

He walked into the living room. I followed.

"You're beautiful, you're…" I scrubbed my face. It did nothing to ease the fire in my skin or my frustration. "It's just that the idea of being with you makes me feel guilty."

He turned just enough that I knew he looked at me.

"I don't know why." I said. "Maybe because you deserve better or more or hell… I don't know."

"Try."

"You're young." It was the best I could do. Mostly because it was all I could come up with. Like his struggle to vocalize what he saw in the light, I struggled to voice what I felt.

"So you think you're too old for me?"

"I'm not sure."

"I see."

"God, Morgan. I feel like I would be taking advantage of you."

"Why?"

"What if I can't give you what you want?" Because even if I was capable, I couldn't allow it to happen. I was leaving as soon as it was safe for me to move my money around.

"And what do I want?"

"I don't know."

"Exactly. You don't. I'm twenty-four years old. An adult. Not a kid. I'm a man perfectly capable of making choices."

"I just don't want to use you."

"I'm perfectly capable of taking the risk."

"What if I hurt you?" Or myself.

"Are you planning on hurting me?"

"Of course not, it's just…"

"You're older?"

"Yes."

"You know more than I do?"

"No."

"So are you really trying to protect me from you or yourself from me?"

Why didn't it surprise me he read through me? He could already see the world beyond the layers of my understanding. "I don't know."

Morgan shrugged and walked away.

I followed. "Please understand."

He stopped next to his bed. How the hell had I gotten in here? I stepped back until I was in the doorway.

Morgan shrugged again. "I do."

I'd expected him to say a lot of things, but that was not one of them. "You're not mad?"

"Nope."

"Are you sure?"

"Positive."

"This isn't about you being autistic."

"I know." He stripped his shirt off, uncovering his flowing shoulders and length of his back. He faced me. His smooth chest was interrupted by dark brown nipples, and his flat stomach by the faint happy trail widening below his navel. The dusting of caramel-colored hair disappeared

66

beyond the hem of his shorts.

My mouth went dry and my heart stuttered. "What are you doing?" The words came out on a squeak.

"Changing my clothes. I have a sculpture to finish. You're welcome to stay and watch"— he unbuttoned his jeans—"me work." Morgan went to his dresser and pulled out a long-sleeved shirt. "I'm really sorry, you know."

"For what?"

"For coming onto you. I mean, it's gotta be embarrassing. But it makes sense why you pushed me away before."

"What are you talking about?"

"Well, you know, being too old to, you know..." He waved a hand. "Get it up."

"That's not why I wanted you to stop."

"No, it's okay. You don't have to make excuses. Like I said, I get it." Morgan tossed his shirt on the bed and added a pair of sock. "You're right. I should explore because if it all goes downhill at sixty—"

"Sixty?"

"Don't get me wrong. You look really good for your age."

"You know damn well I'm not sixty."

"Oh, excuse me. Fifty-nine."

"I'm thirty-six."

"You sure? You look so much older."

"Yes, I'm sure."

"Well then, you should probably see a doctor." Morgan picked up his flip-flops and sat on the bed. He laid them next to the shirt and socks. "I think I read somewhere your prostate can cause erectile dysfunction." He flicked his hand near his head. His shoulder jumped and one of his flip-flops fell off.

I walked over and picked it up. "I don't have problems getting it up. You should know. You were rubbing off on me."

"Hmm—" He took the shoe. "I didn't notice."

"You didn't notice?"

"Oh... so it's that."

"It's what?"

"Nothing."

"It's what, Morgan?"

"Well, with as built as you are, I thought you'd be, you know, bigger."

"Excuse me?"

"Don't get upset. You might strain your heart."

"There's nothing wrong with my heart."

"At your age, it's better not to take a chance." He smirked.

I knew he was baiting me. I knew, and yet I couldn't stop myself from getting pissed. Angry and horny do not mix. I knew that from experience.

"Don't get upset; I'm just looking out for you." Morgan stood and unzipped his shorts. They fell to his ankles. He pushed past me and went to the dresser again. This time he took out a pair of jeans. Holes speckled the thighs.

"Are you going to stay?"

After this conversation? "I don't know."

He tossed me a few thoughts. "If you decide to leave, I'll help you to your truck. I'd hate for you fall and break a hip." Morgan sauntered back over to the bed, flopped down on the edge, and spread his knees. The gap in his boxers flashed an uncut cock and neatly trimmed hairs.

I willed myself to walk out of there, but my legs were in cahoots with my dick.

"Are you okay?" Morgan said. "You looked flushed."

"I'm fine."

"Might want to get your blood pressure checked when you pick up your prescription for those little blue pills."

I clenched my teeth. "My blood pressure is fine."

"Do you think bad blood pressure might be why you can't get it up?" Morgan reached out and squeezed my crotch. A shock raced up my legs. He goosed me again. "Have you considered packing? I mean at least that way it being small wouldn't be so noticeable. Just a sock. Or maybe two socks, you know so you'll be about average."

"There's nothing wrong with my dick either."

Morgan grinned at me. "Prove it."

"No."

"Here." He rolled to the side and grabbed an address book from inside the nightstand. "I'll give you Aunt Jenny's number. She'll know who to refer you to. She volunteers at the nursing home a few days a week."

He stood, and I glared. Morgan tapped the book against my chest. "I know, maybe you should go to Chestnut Hill yourself. I'm sure there are lots of older people like you who would totally understand your issues."

"I am not old and my dick is way above average."

Morgan met my gaze and held it. Pure mischief gleamed in his eyes. Someone like him should never be capable of that kind of look. "Don't worry, Mr. Kessler." He pressed his chest against mine. "Your secret is safe with me." He rubbed his palm over my crotch.

"Don't even pretend you can't feel that." I forced him to run his hand down the length of my hardening cock pressed against my thigh.

"Yeah, I feel it." His coy expression turned into a look of concentration. "Sorta."

I tightened my grip over his. "Sorta?"

"Can't be too sure. Your jeans are in the way."

"If you can't feel my dick, my jeans aren't the problem."

"Sorry, Grant, but that could be a wrinkle in your briefs for all I know." Morgan popped open the button on my jeans. "Here, I'll even give you the benefit of doubt and check." He pulled down the zipper.

I pushed his hands away. "Morgan, you're playing with fire."

"I thought it was your dick." Morgan shoved his hand down the front of my pants. His cool fingers soothed my burning flesh. "I'm not sure, but I think I found it." He stroked.

I broke. God help me, I just broke.

I grabbed him by the face and smashed our lips together. Morgan speared my mouth, fighting for control of the kiss. His hip bumped the end table and the clock hit the floor. He turned, taking me with him in a single fluid arch, giving me a hint of the skillful dancer he could have been.

The movement dislodged my jeans from my hips, and they fell to the floor. Morgan sank his fist in my hair, pulled my head back, and attacked my throat. His teeth coaxed tingling lines and sent them racing to my balls.

I groaned.

"I'm going to blow you, Grant. I'm going to give you the best damned head you've ever had." He forced me to step backward, and the back of my knees hit the edge of the bed. Morgan rode me all the way down. I bounced on the mattress, and Morgan went off balance. I took the opportunity to roll over him. He slithered away, and I made chase.

"Why are you running? I thought you wanted this?"

He averted his gaze as a tic jerked his head to the side. For a moment, there was only the soft expression of a naive young man. It caught me off guard, and I sat back.

Morgan raised his eyes. A wicked grin spread across his face. He locked his legs around my waist and grabbed the iron headboard. I was flipped to the side with enough force I almost went over the edge. Morgan caught my arm and pinned me with his body on my chest.

He found my nipples with his agile fingers and pinched them. "Am I being too rough on you, old man?"

"Call me old one more time and I'll show you the meaning of rough."

Morgan hissed as he rocked against me. The head of his cock slid over my stomach. I reached for him, but he yanked my shirt over my head and twisted the material until it bound my hands. Then he arched over me.

"Still think you're up for this?" He nipped my chin, my lips, and licked a line up my jaw. There was a metallic click somewhere above me. "Wouldn't want you to overexert yourself. Being old an all, you should probably take it easy."

"I warned you." I made a grab for him and a cold line bit into my wrists. I shook my arms enough to slide the shirt out of the way.

Handcuffs bound me to the iron trellis of the headboard.

Morgan grinned.

"What the hell do you think you're doing?" I rattled the cuffs, and they clanked against the metal.

"Told you. Gonna give you the best head you've ever had." He climbed off and stripped me of my boxers. My cock jutted high, dark red at the head, and aching to be touched.

I may be average in everything else when it came to appearances, but I wasn't ignorant to the fact I had a dick to be proud of.

Morgan licked his lips. Just the sight of his pink tongue flicking out made me gasp.

He kicked off his boxers. His beautiful cock curved toward his stomach and precum glistened in the folds of skin cradling the head. Morgan straddled my ribs, putting the smooth globes of his ass inches from my chin. I forgot about the cuffs and tried to reach for him. The metal scraped the wrought iron.

He leaned forward, giving me a perfect view of his hole and balls dangling between his legs. An inferno covered the head of my cock.

"Fucking hell, Morgan."

He hummed on the upstroke and sucked the tip. My balls pulled tight, and a rising tension extended up my torso, threatening to toss me right off the bed before he even got started.

Holy shit, he was right. I forgot about the cuffs and lost myself in the feel of a silky tongue swirling over the glans and tight lips stroking the upper part of my cock. Morgan didn't keep me at the back of his throat, instead he concentrated on the last few inches, massaging and working the flesh until the only thing that mattered was the rush of pleasure he coaxed into the head of my dick.

The wave of euphoria twisted around me. "Oh, God."

Morgan caressed my thighs, my calves, rocking forward until his head was pulled between his shoulders. His touch danced around my ankles. Electric lines retraced the path his hands had taken.

Morgan did some strange rolling movement with his tongue, applying pressure to the slit. The slow build of need spiraled out of control.

I barked out a cry, and right at the edge of release, Morgan stopped.

Every breath I exhaled was accompanied by an explosion of black spots in front of my eyes. When my vision cleared, Morgan's face was so close our noses almost touched.

I swallowed several times in an attempt to alleviate some of the scratchiness in my throat.

Morgan danced his fingers over my face.

"All right, let me up."

He closed his eyes.

"Morgan, I want to touch you." Because if I didn't, I'd lose my mind. He sat back, and I moved my feet to gain purchase. The clink of more metal echoed from the end of the bed.

At some point, he'd managed to cuff my ankles to the footboard.

"Morgan?"

He took out a bottle of lubricant and condom from the drawer.

"Morgan, this isn't funny anymore."

He unwrapped the condom and sheathed my cock. Then poured a generous amount of lubricant into his palm.

The oily liquid ran down his fingers. He rubbed them together until they were shiny.

Morgan rose up on his knees and put his hand behind his back. The squelch of lubricant let me know exactly what he did.

One, two, or three? How deep did he go? What did he look like stretched tight around his fingers?

Not knowing twisted my insides more than all the times I'd ever watched those details with past lovers because being denied the show let my imagination take over.

Morgan gasped with each roll of his hips. The movement tightened his muscles, and they cut shadowy lines down his torso and thighs. A low lean groan echoing in his chest turned into an open-mouthed cry. The sound shot through me.

I fought against the restraints hard enough to make the bed tremble. I needed to touch him more than I needed to breathe.

A slice of sunlight broke through a gap in the curtain and flowed over Morgan's body, painting his tan golden, turning his blond hair a fiery orange.

My heart missed several beats, then surged in one hard thump in my chest.

Morgan removed his fingers from his ass and knee-walked over me until he was positioned over my hips. He gripped my cock with his slick fingers. Static points flared under his fingertips, and a tremor ran through my body.

70

Then the smooth dip of his ass cheeks brushed the head of my cock as he pressed it to his opening. The tight ring of muscle was forced over the sensitive tip. It gave just enough for the head of my cock to enter and then tightened again just below the glans.

Again he took me another inch, and again his body clenched. Morgan relaxed his legs, and the weight of his body pulled him down until he sat cradled against my pelvis.

Tiny droplets of sweat beaded over his skin as the flush underneath darkened. Morgan stayed there with his chin on his chest.

"Morgan?" Had he hurt himself? The occasional shudder of his thighs muscles and his leaking cock suggested just the opposite. "Morgan, talk to me."

He slid his hands up my chest, tapping his fingers and tracing unseen lines. A sigh left his lips as he stretched forward.

Morgan caressed my face, traced the cords in my neck, and drew lines down my shoulders. Then he made bizarre patterns on my chest each point of contact growing hotter until every nerve in my body burned.

I thrashed under him, trying to get closer, trying to get away because each brush of his flesh to mine was a threat to my sanity.

"Goddamn it, Morgan." I made an attempt to thrust, but I couldn't get enough slack in the ankle restraints for purchase.

Morgan dragged his hands up his body drawing those strange patterns until he cradled his own head. He tightened his thighs, and his ass cheeks clenched like a vise. Then he shifted his weight, riding forward and back.

The muscles in his abs flexed in a wave of tension that passed all the way through his body and down my cock. Again he rode back and forward, but this time rolled his hips. The movement only took an inch out and back in, but it was more intense than a full stroke.

He swiveled his hips one way, his torso another, rocking, rocking, rocking until he undulated like something liquid.

A desperate cry escaped his parted lips. With his eyes clenched shut, his brows down, I couldn't decide if the expression he wore was pleasure or pain.

Then he looked at me. Not the fleeting kind of glimpse but a hungry, feral gaze belonging on a wild animal.

I'd been wrong to think Morgan was the naive one.

He arched back, twisting his body, lifting himself up and dropping back down. With every stroke, he rode higher.

The movement was slow, but it was enough friction to push me back to the edge, just not enough to shove me off the cliff.

"Please, Morgan." I ached with a kind of pleasure I'd never known. "Please, please, please." My eyes watered. Morgan put his hands closer to my knees. He leaned back until most of his weight was held by his arms and his feet were flat beside my hips.

The new angle tugged my insides. While Morgan fucked himself with my cock, he fondled his balls on his way to his dick. There he teased the folds of foreskin, pulling it over the head to massage the tip.

There was no escaping the cuffs, but I fought them in hopes of finding some way to increase the friction.

"Morgan, Morgan, oh God." Fighting the tears cascading down my temples and soaking my hair was as useless as fighting Morgan.

He repositioned his knees until they flanked my sides again and reached back. The elegance in his movements proved again what the ballet school had missed.

The cuffs couldn't have been standard because they fell away with a flick of his fingers and fell from my ankles. Morgan sat up just in time to counterbalance my body as I planted my feet against the mattress and lifted him off the bed. Hands on my chest, he stayed mounted only because of the strength in his thighs.

The urgency to come took over. Sweat joined the tears but did nothing to cool the fire spreading under my skin, and the bit of freedom he'd given me wasn't going to be enough to find release. After what Morgan had done, I wasn't sure I'd ever come again. Or at least survive it. Frustration boiled out of me in a half yell, half groan.

And suddenly my hands were free. I grabbed Morgan and flipped him over, pulling out in the process. Driven by the need for release, I pushed his legs up and his limber body folded. In one hard thrust, I shoved my cock back in his ass.

Then I fucked him. I fucked him harder than anyone I'd ever been with. Like some mindless animal, I took him over and over, knocking him against the headboard. The pain in my nuts broke free and the electric crackle seared through my body. Muscles in my legs seized up, but I couldn't stop. Everything whited out, and for a moment, there was nothing but the explosion of pleasure. I roared as I came, and the euphoria washed through me in waves. With every pulse of my cock, my strength drained until I could barely hold myself up.

I breathed, but there wasn't enough air.

A drop of sweat fell from the end of my nose to Morgan's lips, and he smiled.

****

I couldn't remember the last time I slept so deep after sex. I could, however, remember the last time I came so hard that I thought a heart attack was imminent.

Never.

Maybe, I was getting old.

No. No I was not even going down that road. I was not old. I had at least another twenty years of hard sex, and if things went south? Like Morgan had said, they made little blue pills.

But something told me even if I fucked every day for the rest of my life, no other man would make me come like that.

Dear God, what the hell?

Maybe Morgan was right. I'd never had good sex.

Thing is, I knew I had. It was Morgan. Whatever it was I experienced with him was something close to religious. The thought made me laugh.

Morgan stirred. Tucked against my body, he was a line of warmth that went from shoulder and ended somewhere around my ankle.

The reddish-orange sun breaking through the gaps in the curtains had been replaced by a cool line of purple.

I'd not only slept. I'd slept all the way till morning.

Morgan exhaled a sigh and made a small sound. Almost a whimper but softer. A wrinkle cut across his forehead, and his full lips turned down.

Was he dreaming about Dillon?

I turned enough to cradle him close to my chest and rubbed his back in long, languid strokes.

"Shhh—" I kissed his forehead. He sighed again, and the tension faded. "That's it. You're safe."

I might not have been there to save him then, but I was here now, and I was going to do my damnedest to never let him have nightmares again.

Again?

Again was forever, and I wasn't going to be here forever. Just a couple of years, three at the most. My destiny was unspoiled beaches and clear blue water. A place as close to heaven as I could get without actually dying.

But who's to say I wasn't going in the other direction? I could almost guarantee I was. It might have worried me if I believed in those sorts of things, but I could only believe in what I could hold, see, and feel. So far, I'd never had a reason to have faith in anything.

Until the day I experienced one of those fairy tale miracles, I never would.

I caressed Morgan's cheek.

And miracles were no more real than fairy-tale true love.

Morgan pressed closer. His touch wandered up my chest. Along the way, he tapped his fingers in measured beats that left me wondering if the world he looked into sometimes had music along with the secrets hidden in the light.

His hand went to the side of his head but did nothing more than brush against his temple before tucking back under his chin.

I moved a lock of hair hanging in Morgan's face, and he opened his eyes. The distant gaze I'd come to know was different, and I had the strangest feeling he wasn't looking through my reality and into the world only he could see. He was looking through me.

Then he blinked and his gaze returned. "Hey."

"Hey, yourself."

He glanced over his shoulder at the window. "It's morning?"

"I think so."

He pushed himself up.

"What's wrong?"

"The sunrise. I can't miss it."

He grabbed his boxers off the floor and put them on, hopping from one foot to the next, on his way to the door. Morgan headed to the back of the house. I grabbed my jeans and followed.

My attempt to dress and run was far less graceful, and I wound up stumbling into the wall. After that, I took the ten seconds to pull them up before I wound up falling and busting my ass.

I caught up to Morgan on the back porch. The morning sky was bleached white around the line of trees at the edge of the pasture beyond the east side of his house.

Morgan knelt in front of the odd mass of wire and glass I'd seen yesterday. Close up, it was even stranger, but every bend and coil of copper had been arranged with care around droplets of colored glass.

Morgan's expression tightened with concentration.

"What's going on?"

He put his finger to his lips and continued to stare. I stared too.

The thin fog rising to the sky glowed and pale yellow rays poured into the screened-in window as the edge of the sun broke the horizon. With each second, the light shifted until it spread in puddles on the wall behind me.

Geometric shapes appeared within the droplets of light. They split, sprinkling dots of color over my shoulder and the wall. I knelt beside Morgan so I wouldn't be in the way. More color appeared as the sun climbed. What began as points turned into shapes. Their movements were minute, but time seemed to have slipped away, leaving only us and the fragments of light.

My knees protested, and the tingling sensation crawling over my feet turned into a numbing blanket. I needed to move, but I was held in place by the shift of glowing line. The sections touched, squares separated, triangles shattered. As the sun rose higher, the light intensified until the kaleidoscope of color covered a large section of wall.

Morgan used a pair of pliers and adjusted the branches of wire holding the glass in place. The changes weren't noticeable, but it altered the collage, tearing spaces between the seams of color, turning the arc of light until the near flawless edges spiked with ridges.

Finally Morgan turned around. He tilted his head one way, then the next. His face scrunched up and he shook his head.

"What's wrong?"

"It's still not right."

"What do you mean?" It was incredible.

"The shape isn't right." The shadow of his hand followed the lines of color where they jutted beyond the blue and yellow squares. "These don't move like they're supposed to."

"It's supposed to move?"

"It is moving but not in the right direction. It should be cresting higher, otherwise it's just gibberish."

Even though I didn't stand a chance seeing what he did, I squinted at the starburst built of colored shapes in hopes I might catch a glimpse at what Morgan saw. But my sight wouldn't go beyond the beautiful kaleidoscope.

Morgan blew out a breath hard enough to pop his cheeks. He picked up the sculpture and the color painting the wall broke apart and disappeared.

"I was hoping it would at least be close." Morgan set it down on a workbench and began disassembling the wire, releasing the pieces of glass.

"Wait." I tried to stand, but my stiff knees refused to bend. When I finally got to my feet, the blood rushed into legs and every step turned into pins and needles. "Don't take it apart."

By the time I got to the bench, Morgan already had most of the glass removed.

"Why did you take it apart?"

"It wasn't right." His shoulder jerked, pulling his hand against the metal. The strand of copper wire he'd unwound raked the back of his hand and a crimson line darkened.

Morgan continued to work, and the tiny droplets turned into dripping lines.

"Hang on, I'll get you a paper towel." When I returned, his thumb was bleeding too. "Here." I held his hand and patted the cuts until the blood slowed. "I hope you've had a tetanus shot in the last five years."

"Maybe. I don't remember." He held his head down, and his wandering hand twitched beside his temple. Another jerk almost pulled his wrist out of my grip. "Sorry."

74

"For what?"

"You know."

I smiled at him. "And what do I know?"

His bangs parted just enough for me to see his gaze locked on the floor. I cupped his chin and brought his face up. The veil of golden locks slid away, and he looked at me.

I never thought just eye contact could make me feel so important.

Morgan smiled too. "I need to go to the hardware store."

"Can I go with you?"

His smile turned into a grin. "Sure. But you'll have to drive."

"I can do that."

"We should probably eat breakfast."

"Good idea."

"And shower before that."

"Yeah, we are kinda ripe."

"Brush our teeth."

"Mmmm." I ran my thumb over his bottom lip. Morgan caught the tip between his teeth. "You probably shouldn't do that."

"Why?"

"Because I'd really like to get a shower before you suck my cock."

"I'm just biting your thumb."

"Keep doing that and you won't be."

"You did wear a condom."

I wrinkled my nose. "I prefer to be clean."

"Okay, just give me a minute." Morgan returned to working on the sculpture.

"You're still going to take it apart?"

"It won't ever be right if I don't. I already have too many that don't work." He nodded at the cabinet on the other side of the porch.

"Do you mind?"

"Go ahead."

I walked over and opened the doors. Wide shelves were packed with coils of wire and colored glass. Some formed domes, others walls. A few had moving parts that spun when you pushed them.

"Why do you keep them in here?" They may not be right, but if they were able to put on half the show his current one did, it was a waste.

"Where else would I put them?"

"I don't know. Anywhere. Just as long as they can be seen. People need to see these." I picked up one with an organic shape. When I turned to the side, the layers of wire and color blended together in a way that reminded me of those 3-D images I used to find in boxes of Cracker Jacks that transformed into a new picture depending on how you held it.

But they'd been nowhere as impressive as the tiger taking shape.

"Damn, Morgan, these…"

He sat motionless at the bench with his head down.

"Morgan?" I carried the tiger with me and set it down on the table. "You okay?" I knelt. "Morgan?"

His breath shuddered out. "Don't ever say that."

"Say what?"

"People should look at them."

I leaned back a little. "Well, they should. Heck, they should be put on display. Have you ever considered having a showing?"

Morgan shot past me so fast I fell back on my ass. He fled into the backyard.

"Morgan." I took off after him.

He stopped just in front of the trees where the disks of light spun in slow circles. Morgan's wayward hand tangled in his hair and tic after tic assaulted his shoulders.

I caught up to him. "Hey." I tried to turn him around, and he spun away. "Morgan, what's wrong?"

The hand buried in his hair tightened until his knuckles turned white.

"Stop, you're hurting yourself." I grabbed his wrist. When he yanked again, I was ready. "Morgan, please, stop. Whatever it is, it will be okay." At least I hoped it would be. "Talk to me, Morgan. I can't help you if you don't talk to me."

His jaw worked hard enough to bunch his cheeks.

I crushed him to my chest. "Please tell me what's wrong." He struggled, and I held him tighter. "Morgan, please, please, just tell me."

The tics slowed, and his hand opened up. I untangled his fingers. Golden strands clung to his skin. I smoothed his curls back into place.

His breath huffed against my chest.

I kissed the top of his head. "It's okay." I don't know why, but I rocked him and he began moving with me. His muscles relaxed until we were molded together. "I've got you."

He slid his arms around me. "Just don't ever say that again."

"What? Let people see your sculptures?"

He nodded and squeezed me.

"Why? They're beautiful." And hiding them away just seemed wrong.

"They're mine to look at."

"You showed me."

He nodded.

But he also looked me in the eye, and according to Berry, it wasn't something Morgan did. "You haven't ever shown them to anyone, have you?"

"No."

"Not even Jenny?"

"No."

"Anyone?"

"Lori."

"Just Lori."

He exhaled a sigh.

"How come?"

"Because they're mine and I don't want to share them."

"But—"

He dug his grip into my back. "No. No, Grant. No." A wounded keen trickled into his exhale.

76

"All right." I petted him. "Okay, I won't ask. I swear, I won't ever ask again." Even though I didn't understand, I would respect it. Morgan relaxed again, becoming pliable in my arms. Holding him filled me with an indescribable comfort. As if the mere act reached inside of me and cradled my soul.

It was terrifying in a lot of ways, but like the patterns of light he captured in those drops of color, it was wondrous.

Without a doubt, there was no place, nothing as exotic or rare, as that moment right there with him.

Never again could I claim miracles didn't happen.

Chapter Four

Durstrand had one grocery store; The Frugal Mart. It was old, worn out, the F was missing off the sign tacked to the shingled roof, and I don't think there was a single buggy with all four working wheels. They either locked up, wobbled, or screeched to a halt at random moments, giving you the power shopper's equivalent of whiplash.

When I first went there, I told myself the cracked tile, faded walls, and sagging aisles gave the place character. The second, it was atmosphere. The third, nostalgia.

After that, I had to concede that the place was just falling apart.

But it seemed to be where everyone shopped—shuffling down the cramped rows, hovering over the meat cooler, or wasting the cold air in the freezer section by standing with the door open—rather than traveling to the neighboring city where the supermarkets and mini-malls pockmarked the scenery like a bad case of acne that would never go away.

I made the out of town trip once, walked a mile, and endured product placement rather than putting an item where it made sense. There were plastic smiles of overworked, underpaid employees who not only didn't want to help you, they didn't want to be there. Crowds, lots of crowds, because everything was always on sale. And after I'd wandered aimlessly for a couple of hours, running from one side of the store to the next caught in some perverse scavenger hunt, I stood in the line. Then there was the one open line in a row of fifty closed ones trying to check out a store full of tired suburbanites, their screaming kids, and clueless teenagers.

Yup. I made the trip once.

The next week I returned to the decrepit grocery store where the bread was made by little old ladies looking to support their retirement checks and most of the canned goods were in glass jars.

Where the freezer stocked beef, pork, chicken, lamb, goat. Turkey, wild. Deer, when in season. Duck, always with a sticker on the package reminding you to check for buck shot. And last but not least, rabbit. Which by the way, tastes nothing like chicken.

There were no organic sections because almost everything came from someone's farm.

Even the hot sauces were cooked up in someone's kitchen. Who needs a commercial touting potency when your product had a name like Five Alarm Fire and Fire In the Hole. And caution labels warning spilling the hot sauce on your wood floor would eat off the finish.

In those chain stores, there might be a hundred different cereals, gourmet frozen dinners, and every kind of cookie imaginable, but you'd never find honey organized by the kind of pollen the bees collected or moonshine jelly.

Nope. Never.

The Frugal Mart did have one thing in common with those big department stores. There was only one lane open. But then, there was only one lane.

I parked next to a guy unloading boxes of eggs and jars of milk. Both the boys helping him waved at us.

"I really appreciate this," Morgan said.

78

"I asked."

"You still didn't have to."

"No. But I wanted to."

A tic jerked his shoulder up and he flicked thoughts. "You realize people are going to talk when they see us together."

"Is that a bad thing?"

"Depends."

"On what?"

"How creative they get with the rumors."

I laughed and so did he.

An elderly couple got into the car in front of us. The wife smiled at her husband who glanced our way. They unloaded their groceries, and while the man pushed the cart back to the store, the woman took out a cell phone.

"Wow, that was fast," I said.

Morgan sighed. "I was really hoping it wouldn't be one of the church ladies."

"How come?"

"Because by the end of the week, they'll have me pregnant with your third illegitimate baby."

"You're kidding."

"Could be worse."

"Worse? How can it be worse than you getting pregnant?"

Morgan tipped his head. "I'm not sure. But that's Betty Lawson, so I'm sure she'll think of a way."

She cupped her hand over her cell phone and turned in her seat.

"Does she really think we can hear her?" I said.

"Don't know."

She smiled and cast a quick glance our way.

"What do you think she's saying?" I waved at her, and her eyes widened.

"Probably shouldn't do that."

"Why not?"

"She'll tell everyone you were making eyes with her."

"That wouldn't be good."

"If Marsha Wells hears about it, which she will, she'll start sending over her daughters with pans of casserole."

"I'm gay."

"Then you better really hope Candice Jones doesn't get the news while it's fresh."

"What will she do?"

"She'll show up at your door and try to convince you you're just going through a phase and with the right woman you won't be gay."

"Let me guess, that right woman is her."

"You got it."

The husband returned, and his wife tried to pass him the cell phone. He declined, and while his wife returned to her call, he gave us an apologetic smile. The kind of expression begging for understanding and at the same time conveying just how helpless he was to stop it.

When you lived in a small town and someone gave you a look like that, it was gonna be bad.

"We should probably nip this in the bud," I said.

"How do you plan on doing that?"

I caught the old man's gaze again after he cranked up the car, and nodded at his wife. His brows crunched up. I pointed. He looked at her then me.

"What are you doing?" Morgan said.

"Just wait." I pointed at his wife again and nodded.

He hesitantly tapped her on the shoulder. She shooed him off. He glanced at me, and I encouraged him with a wave of my hand.

He shook her by her shoulder until she yanked the phone away from her ear. Halfway through whatever she said to him, he jabbed a thumb at us.

She turned, and I slipped my hand around to the back of Morgan's head.

"What are you—"

Our mouths met, and his words turned into a moan. I didn't just kiss Morgan. I forced his lips apart, penetrated his mouth, and fucked him with my tongue.

He gripped my shirt, holding me where I was. Morgan countered me by nipping my bottom lip and then seizing control. It was my turn to moan.

When we parted, both of us panted and I was hard as a rock. I ran my thumb over Morgan's cheek and traced the line of his jaw. His freshly shaven skin was velvet under my fingers.

I brushed another kiss close to his eye, and he laid his head to the side, exposing his neck. The soft place under his ear was too much to resist, and I sucked the skin, leaving behind a glowing red dot.

"What's she doing?" Morgan said.

"Who?" Then I remembered what started this. I looked. Betty's mouth hung open next to the cell phone dangling in her hand. Her husband grinned and gave us a thumbs-up as he backed out.

Morgan's exhale brushed the shell of my ear. "When we get back, I want to pick up where we left off."

I chuckled. "I think I can make that happen."

Morgan started to open his door. One of the young men helping unload the truck stared at us.

"I don't think I've ever seen anyone turn that red," I said.

"I thought the same thing when you came." Morgan lifted his head just enough for me to see his smile.

"No, I don't."

He shrugged.

"I do not turn red."

Morgan got out, and the boy followed him with his eyes.

My door opened, and Morgan poked his head in. "You coming?"

I shifted in my seat.

"You better do something about that," Morgan said. "Or you'll have every eligible bachelorette following you home."

"Well if they all brought casserole dishes, at least I wouldn't have to cook."

Morgan punched me in the arm. "C'mon. Walk it off."

The reflection of a dark gray Bronco flashed in the side mirror. Nothing about the car was out of place, but a cold streak ran down my spine. The two men in the front seat wore white T-shirts under their flannel button-ups. Just two good old boys. That's all. My instincts growled a warning.

"What's wrong?" Morgan had his face tilted in the direction of the store. His wayward hand fluttered next to his head.

I rubbed my knee and made sure to favor it when I stepped out. "Just an old football injury acting up. Must be going to rain."

"Really?"

"Yeah, it tends to do that."

"Oh." Morgan held up a finger above his head.

"What are you doing?"

"Shh—" He closed his eyes.

A lady with a buggy full of kids walked past. She eyed Morgan then me.

Morgan turned a circle and switched hands. He bent his wrist so his finger was horizontal. Two teenagers walk between the cars. The one with the emo hair elbowed his friend. They both laughed.

"Uh, Morgan?"

"Shh—"

I scrubbed a hand over my head.

Finally Morgan dropped his arm and headed for the store. I followed.

"What was that all about?"

The automatic doors opened with a shudder, and Morgan pulled out a buggy from the line of them in the foyer. "Do you want your own, or are we putting the stuff in the same cart?"

"One, I guess."

"You sure? I need to get a lot."

"Yeah, I don't need much."

He swung the buggy around. The second set of automatic doors screeched when they opened.

"They really should oil those," Morgan said.

"Are you ever going to tell me what you were doing?"

"Bread is on aisle one, I need whole grain and peach. If they don't have peach, strawberry. Have you ever tried the banana? It's really good." He cut a hard left, almost running over my foot.

"Hold up."

Morgan stopped in front of the rack of bread. "Barometric pressure is too high. Been high for a week. Means no rain. At least not anytime soon. My guess would be three days of sunshine, rain starting on Monday. Then it's going to get cold, so make sure to bring in any potted plants you have on your porch." He put two loaves of whole grain bread in the buggy.

"Are you telling me you can tell what the barometric pressure is just by sticking your finger in the air?"

"Peach..." Morgan walked down the aisle. "They're always moving the peach bread. And if Harold isn't moving it around, that Hatchet lady hides it behind the apple." He stopped again. "Sure."

I rubbed my temple. "Sure? Sure what?"

Morgan shook his head. "Pay attention, Grant. Not paying attention is why you ran over my bike."

"That was—"

"Barometric pressure is nothing more than how much the air weighs. Heavier the lower, lighter higher. Causes your joints to swell." Morgan reached behind the row of apple bread and came up with a loaf of peach. "See?" He held it up. "Hatchet strikes again. You want some, there's another loaf back there?"

"Uh, no, I'm good."

Morgan took it out and carried it with him to the end where there were various bags of rolls. He rearranged the bags and set the peach bread in the gap he made. "Do you think between the wheat and rye is better or the raisin and cinnamon?"

"What?"

"Let's go with the wheat and rye. She's shorter than me so looking up should throw her off her game."

"Are you hiding the bread?"

"If I don't hide the bread, then she'll think she's won." Morgan pushed the cart over to the produce. "Anyhow. Barometers." Morgan stopped beside the bananas. He picked up one bunch, then the other. "Did you know that when the barometric pressure has a rapid increase that your capillaries are more likely to clog up? Number one cause of brain aneurisms in men over thirty." He tipped his chin up, but his gaze stayed somewhere around my arm. "You haven't been having any headaches lately, have you?"

"No, why?"

"Just checking." He put both bunches of bananas back and grabbed a bag of oranges. "But most of the time it just squeezes you a little."

"The pressure?"

"What else would squeeze you?"

"I—"

"And it tingles. If you concentrate hard enough, you can actually feel your pores closing up. So that's why, when I put my finger in the air, I can tell what the barometric pressure is." Morgan took my arm and pushed it up. "Here you try."

"Morgan..."

"Go on."

I kept my arm up.

"Raise your finger?"

"I really don't—"

"Finger, Grant. Up!"

I put up my finger. Two men walked past me. The one didn't even notice, the other guy stopped and stared. I started to drop my arm, and Morgan pushed it back up.

"Give it a minute."

"Morgan..."

"C'mon, Grant, I'm trying to teach you something here."

I relented and kept my arm up and waited. And waited some more.

82

"Feel anything?"

"No."

"Maybe you should raise it higher."

"I don't think…"

Morgan shoved my arm up as high as it would go. "There."

A young couple heading our way stopped. The guy turned the buggy around and steered his female companion in another direction. She peeked back at us when they rounded the corner.

My face turned hot.

A kid walked up. He couldn't have been more than five. He stuck his hand in the air and stayed there until his mother dragged him away.

"This isn't working."

"Are you sure?" Morgan leaned to the side.

"Yes. I'm very sure."

"Maybe you should stand on your toes?"

"I don't think that's going to help."

Morgan rubbed his chin. "Hmmm. It worked fine when I did it." He stood beside me and raised his finger. "Yup. Definitely feel it. It's way up there. Practically in the stratosphere."

"Well it's not—"

"Wait…" He closed his eyes. "Wait…"

"My arm is really getting tired."

"I know, just hang on." Another long minute dragged. People actually began to bunch together over by the lettuce to watch us.

"Well that explains everything." Morgan dropped his hand back down.

"What?"

"Seems like I got my o-meters mixed up."

"Huh?"

"Happens sometimes. Barometer, bullshitometer, I'm sure you can understand how easily it can happen."

Morgan left with the buggy.

I put my arm down. The crowd broke up, and a lady wearing a hairnet stopped beside me and squeezed my bicep a couple of times. Then she walked away without saying a thing.

If I'd been given a choice of standing around with my goddamned finger in the air or facing Morgan, I would have chosen the former. No matter how many little old ladies felt me up.

Morgan had already cleared the produce section and moved into the meats. I stood next to the buggy while he examined packages of pork chops.

He made a choice, then moved down to the chicken.

"Mor—"

"Do you like dumplings?" He held up a Styrofoam tray of chicken strips.

"Yeah, sure."

"Even if you didn't, you'd like mine. Everyone does." He put them in the buggy.

I trailed after him like a kicked puppy. "I didn't mean—"

"Ham?"

"What about it?"

"Do you like it?"

"Yes."

Morgan checked the prices. His wandering hand tossed thoughts and his shoulder jerked hard enough to yank his head to the side.

"I'm so—"

"I think I need eggs." He dug his grocery list out of his pocket. "It's not on the list, but I'm pretty sure…"

"I'm sorry, all right?"

Two mothers with their gaggle of children turned and looked at us. They kept staring so I tried to look busy by grabbing a package out of the cooler and tossing it in the buggy.

"Are you sure you want to buy that?" Morgan cocked his head. With his hair in the way, I couldn't tell if he was watching me or looking in the buggy.

"I have no idea."

He handed it back to me. Pig tails. Lovely.

"You look like more of a donkey tail person to me."

"What's that sup—"

Morgan walked over to the dairy section while holding his finger in the air.

I was never going to live this down. If I lived through it at all. I caught up to him at the milk cooler. "Okay, you're right. I'm an ass."

He shut the freezer. "I'm sorry, I couldn't quite hear you."

"I said, I'm sorry."

"Oh I heard that part just fine, but those last few words kinda faded out." He held up two containers of milk. "Lactose intolerant?"

I took the bottles of milk from Morgan's hands and put them in the buggy. As soon as his wayward one was free, it fluttered at his temple. He dropped his head and stepped away. The freezer door shut, expelling a puff of frigid air.

I cupped his face. His shoulder jerked, and I petted his cheek with my thumb. Morgan made a fist at his temple. The tendons stood out on his wrist and his entire arm trembled. I didn't know if it was because he fought the tics or was angry.

"Please," I said. "Please look at me."

"Why?"

"Do I need a reason?"

"Yes."

"Because you have beautiful eyes."

He bit his lip.

"Because I love it when you do."

Morgan tensed his shoulders.

"And because it's a gift I don't deserve, but for some reason, you've chosen to share it with me."

He slowly blinked and shifted his gaze. The brown of his eyes had turned close to black under the shadows of sadness and self-doubt.

"I… Am… Sorry." My voice trembled under the weight of the words. "I did not mean to hurt you."

"Then why did you lie about your knee?"

I had a hundred very legitimate excuses. All of which would have been for his benefit.

84

Lies that you told to protect people were the most believable because they were the kind of lies you bled for, so even the worst liar could weave tales of protective netting.

I didn't like lying, but when it came to keeping the people around me safe, I had a silver tongue.

Even if Morgan never found out I'd lied to him, knowing I had would taint everything from that moment forward. And he would find out. He'd look through me like a window and read it off my soul.

Telling him the truth could also push him away, but I owed him the choice.

"Let's finish the shopping. Then when we get back, I'll explain everything."

Morgan brushed his fingertips over the back of my hand and stepped away. "Would you like to stay and have pizza for dinner?" He fluttered his fingers next to his temple.

"I'd love to."

"C'mon." He tugged me up beside him. "I need to keep my eye on you."

"Why?"

"Dolores has been following us around since aisle three."

I looked. There she was, the lady in the hairnet. Purse over her arm, yellow and blue print muumuu, and house slippers. She waved.

"I don't know why."

"How can you say that?" Morgan stopped at the cheese shelf. "You've got good looks, nice legs, arms, and a gorgeous ass. And you do a killer Statue of Liberty impression." He picked up a chunk of mozzarella and put it in the buggy.

"You're never going to let me live that down, are you?"

Morgan laughed.

****

With a stomach full of homemade pizza and a fresh bottle of beer, Morgan and I sat on the top step of his front porch.

I wasn't quite sure how we got out there. If it was my idea or his idea or it just happened. But there we were, hip to hip, beer in hand. With the porch light turned off, and only the kitchen light on in the back of the house, we were left to drown under a new moon and an ocean of stars.

There hadn't been many things I missed when I left my home in that no-name town in the armpit of Alabama. And the few things I did miss were quickly forgotten.

Except for the stars.

For a very long time, I yearned to see those billions of glowing points. To count shooting stars or witness the rare meteor shower. But after years of looking up and seeing the moon, and the few patches of starlight burning just bright enough to survive the afterglow of the city, I succumbed to the belief something so perfect could have never existed.

I was so convinced, even after I arrived in Durstrand, I hadn't bothered to look up. And once I did, I had no idea how I would ever be able to look away.

Occasionally a barking dog would interrupt the fading tree frogs, but otherwise it was quiet in the way only the country could be.

We sat for a very long time, saying nothing, sipping on beer, and breathing the night air.

I learned then, there are patient men in this world and then there was Morgan.

"I'm not sure where to start." I drank some of my beer. It wasn't anywhere as good as Toolies, but it was good enough to calm my nerves. "And a lot of what I need to tell you, I've never told anyone."

"Why not?"

"Because it was in my best interest, and the best interest of others, not to."

The darkness was not infinite like it had been in the truck the other night in the pasture, so gray smudges highlighted Morgan's hair and left commas on his beer bottle.

"You could always start at the beginning."

I propped my elbows on my knees. "I guess that would make the most sense."

"Lots more sense than standing around with your finger in the air."

"You have a point." A breeze shuffled past us, bringing the promise of winter with it. "When I was fifteen, I told my dad I was gay. It was Wednesday. Pot roast night. My mom always made the best damn pot roast.

"I'd been trying to come up with a way to tell him all day long and right there between 'pass the green beans' and 'do you want some butter on your bread,' it popped out." I huffed a laugh. "My dad didn't miss a beat. He stood, picked up my plate and glass, and carried them into the kitchen. Then he walked to the closet and took out my jacket and handed it to me. But he didn't send me out completely empty-handed. He gave me twenty bucks and told me to never come back."

"What did you do?"

"Not much I could do. I started walking. Clay wasn't as small as Durstrand, but it was small enough. I slept in a cow barn the first night. Earned me the worst case of chiggers I've ever had. And the twenty bucks was gone in three days. After I spent the last buck twenty-five on a Waffle House grilled cheese sandwich, I sat outside next to the dumpster and cried. A woman from our local church recognized me and asked me what was wrong. I told her what my dad did and why, and she told me she'd pray for me and walked away."

Morgan put his hand on my thigh.

"Three nights later, it turned cold and all I had was a jacket. I had no idea a person could be that tired, cold, and hungry and still walk around. I was on some dinky highway I can't even remember the name of, when this guy pulled up and offered me a ride.

"I was scared to death he was going to expect me to have sex with him, but as long as he gave me something to eat, I decided I didn't care."

"Did he?"

"No. He just took me back to his hotel, let me eat myself sick on a bag of Oreos, take a shower, and crash on the other double bed. The next morning, he told me his name was Cody West and he was going to Chicago and wanted to know if I'd like to go with him. I had nothing to lose so why not.

"I think I was in love with him two weeks after he picked me up, but we didn't have sex for almost eight months after we met. By the time it happened, I was masturbating every night to fantasies of fucking him in the back of his Impala."

"Wow."

"Car was the ugliest green color. I have no idea why anyone would have fantasies about anything in a car like that, except maybe to throw up." I shook my head. "Cody was thirty-nine going on eighteen. A liar, a con artist, and always looking for a get-rich-quick scheme. Cody would have sold his own grandmother, if he had a one, in a thousand to one chance at that big score. By the time I figured him out, I was in love. Or thought I was."

When I closed my eyes, I could still see his apartment. At the time, it had been the Ritz, but looking back, I knew it was only a few steps higher than a rat-infested alleyway. But we weren't going to be there very long. Tomorrow, next week, in a month or so, that friend, contact, or associate was going to come through and Cody was going to take me to Europe or Australia.

"I got a job doing deliveries. Sometimes along with tips, I'd bring home brownies from one of the upscale restaurants I ran packages for. Cody loved those stupid things. Made him horny as hell too."

A car engine echoed through the darkness and a faint beam of light grew brighter. It passed the driveway and disappeared in a wink of red taillights.

"Then one day, when I came home from work, the apartment was empty." Dirty dishes in the sink, trash full, and empty Chinese food containers on the coffee table. The usual.

"Did something happen to him?"

"Nah. All his shit was gone, and he left me a note. Said something about how he had some business in Atlanta, but he'd be back in a week."

"He didn't come back?"

"No. And Surviving in Chicago is a lot harder than surviving in the middle of nowhere. It's a lot colder too. But I had the job with the delivery place, and Eugene, the guy who owned it, let me sleep in the back room. After a few years, he started to teach me the business. A few years later, I figured out what his business was really all about."

"Aunt Jenny said you did something illegal."

Illegal. I called what I did a lot of things but never that. Truthfully, illegal was the only right word and I knew it. But until the moment the word left Morgan's lips, it had no weight. Now it crushed me.

"I helped people ship stolen goods. Desperate people fleecing rich folks and then selling what they stole to other rich folks. I'm telling you, the rich buy some pretty weird shit." After years of seeing people burn millions, the one thing I swore I would never do: I would never buy something just to look at. Whatever I owned would have a purpose. "Mostly it was antiques and cars. Really expensive cars."

There was the hollow clink of a beer bottle touching the porch on the other side of Morgan. Mine was close to empty. I drained it and put it beside me on the porch.

"I'm not going to try to pretend that what I did wasn't wrong. I might not have taken things that belonged to me, but I helped people take things that didn't belong to them. I've shipped thousands of items across the country and the ocean."

"Did you hurt anyone?" Morgan shifted his weight, and his elbow brushed mine. "Grant?"

"Yes. But not like you think. I did what I did for money. Putting people in a condition where they couldn't pay me was not conducive to my goal. I learned if a person owed me money, they would find it when they needed me again. And the people who used my services always needed me again. Clients got the first job on credit. Ship now, pay after. If they stiffed me, they pre-paid plus half just to make it worth my while." I rubbed the scar on my chest. "But sometimes things happened."

"Like what?"

I'd hoped he wouldn't ask, but at the same time, I was glad he did. For the first time in my life, I could purge my soul of the sins I'd committed. They weren't the deep dark sins of a lot of men, but it doesn't take a very big splinter to make you worry the skin.

"Sometimes people tried to steal from you or the people you worked for. Sometimes other businessmen took it personal when you were a better job than them. And there were clients who lied about what they wanted to ship and were not very happy with me when I turned down the contract. Those were the most dangerous because by then you'd seen the product, and if you knew what they were moving, it could make you a liability."

"Did it happen a lot?"

"Eugene taught me to respect my fellow businessmen, to be gracious to clients, but to never let people run over me. You never mixed friendship with business. A person was either an associate, which meant you never took their money or moved in on their people, or they were a client, which meant they paid you for a service, you did not give them a service to be paid.

"But there was always someone who would eventually test you and I never pulled a gun without the intention of using it.

"That's why I quit. The rules I'd learned to do business by were fading out. If you weren't leaving a body count, people didn't take you seriously. And if your competition couldn't intimidate you, they went after your clients.

"I was a businessman, providing a service. It was bad enough when I had to worry about my own ass, but when the people I worked for were threatened, I took it personal."

Another vehicle turned onto the road in front of Morgan's house. This time the engine lacked the smooth hum of a car or truck. The heavy chug of thick tire tread chased the single headlight to the other end of the street. Then the wind shifted and the putrid earthy smell of chicken shit overrode the spicy fall leaves.

Not long after, the tractor was out of earshot and the smell went with it.

"Did you go to jail?"

"First rule in shipping is to make sure you always had your paperwork in order. Second rule, make sure your client does too. And I am damn good at paperwork and balancing a checkbook, and paying all my taxes."

"Then why did you come to Durstrand?"

"About four to five years ago, I met a guy. He wanted a job. I gave him a job. I liked him, he liked me, so it was no surprise when we wound up in bed together. Then things went from occasional, to casual, then serious."

"Did something bad happen to him?" Morgan's exhale warmed my arm. I extended my fingers and found the edge of his elbow.

"At first I thought he was married, or had kids and was running from child support. Then I wondered if he was trying to steal from me, but he never skimmed any money, even when I gave him the chance. He turned out to be FBI.

"He was good at playing the part. I let my guard down, and it almost got people killed." No matter how pissed I was at Jeff and his damn blue eyes, the truth was I was solely to blame. "There's another rule when you do this kind of work. I don't know if Eugene ever told me or if it was just something I picked up from being in his circle, but you didn't piss off the authorities. You treated them with respect. You never gave them a reason to have a grudge. But if they crossed you. If they fucked with your people, not the merchandise, shit can be replaced, but the people who were your bread and butter and relied on you for your confidence, you dealt with them.

"Clean, quick, and with no trace it was ever done, you dealt with them. People would know, but there would never be anything left to prove what you'd done or how. And that can be scarier than a body."

I curled my fingers into a fist. Somehow it felt wrong to touch Morgan now. I was soiled. "I should have. If he'd just gone back to where he belonged, it would have blown over and no one would have known. But his superiors convinced him to set up a shipment or two under the guise of him going into business on his own.

"Fucking idiot. He called a couple of people he knew I had contact with and pushed them into a job by being willing to do it cheap. Stupidity is only outdone by greed when it comes to the number one cause of death.

"One of my competitors got wind Jeff was underselling me, which meant he was underselling them even more, they took it personal, the client got involved, so did their kids. Bullets got thrown around, innocent people died. I got in the middle of it all, trying to fix what he fucked up."

"Is that how you got shot?" Morgan turned. His chest pressed against my arm, and his touch slid over my shirt. He rubbed the scar under my pec. The hypersensitive nerves tingled with electricity while the surrounding skin went numb.

I caught his hand. Not to push him away but to keep him there. I wanted him to touch me other places, but I hadn't earned that right back. There was a good chance I never would.

"Like I said, number one cause of death." Morgan sat back. I cleared my throat. "Jeff got between one of the shooters and the client's little girl. He knew he would die, but he did it anyhow, and if he was dead, I couldn't get the pound of flesh he owed me."

I'd like to think the deal wouldn't have gone bad if Jeff hadn't agreed to pick up the goods at the client's house. It would have. Jeff might not have been in the middle of it and neither would I, but Marx was already there with a gun to the man's head.

I would have never agreed to meet a client in their home, and my customers knew that, so they would have never asked.

"Who shot you?"

"A very angry guy with a really ugly mug."

Morgan laughed, and in spite of the tangled knot growing ever larger in my gut, I laughed too. Then we fell quiet and there was only the night, the frogs, and that one lone dog off in the distance.

"After he disappeared from the community, rumors spread about his demise. I never told anyone who he was. It was safer for people to think he'd paid for disloyalty with a bullet to the head."

"Who were the men in the Bronco?"

"If I had to guess, FBI."

"Are they following you?"

"Apparently."

"But you made it sound like they couldn't arrest you."

"Which is exactly why they're only following me."

"What do they want?"

"Information. Names. Dates. Locations. The measurements of my dick."

"Nine and three quarters."

"Excuse me?"

"Nine and three quarters."

"My dick is not ten inches long."

"No, I said nine and three quarters."

"Even I'm not that self-inflated."

"Have you ever measured it?"

For fear of setting off Morgan's bullshit o-meter, I had to fess up. "Just under eight and a half."

"When?"

"What does that have to do with anything?"

"Well, if you did it before the age of twenty, you probably gained an inch."

"My dick is not... okay, even if it was, when did you measure it?"

"I had it in my ass. I think I would know."

"Is this where you tell me everyone has a built in ruler and all I need to do is bend over so you can show me how to use mine?"

Morgan snorted. "No, but we can test that theory if you want."

If I said anything but hell yeah, it would have been a five-alarm bullshit fire. "My dick is not that big." And as soon as I got the chance, I was whipping out the tape measure to prove it.

"Okay, you got me, it has nothing to do with it being in my ass and everything to do with the length of your hand, minus the width of your face, plus the length of your nose."

In high school art class, we'd been taught how to know the proportions of the human body. Fingertip to fingertip, height. Ears from the corner of the eye to the nose. Corners of the mouth to the center of each eye and so on.

It sounded plausible.

I put my thumb on the heel of my hand and measured to my fingertips. Then I *guestimated* the width of my face, then my nose which was right at the same size as my thumb.

"Done measuring?"

I'd made sure to move quietly, but I think if I'd been on the other side of a wall he would have heard me. "Yeah."

"Well?"

I measured again.

"Statistically if you have to measure more than once, it means you need to cut your first answer in half."

"In half?"

"Defensiveness suggests you're trying to make up what you lost, which means you need to take off at least another quarter."

"If that's the case, I just went from ten inches to one and a half."

"You probably measured your head wrong."

"I would have had to measure it wrong three times over. Hell, by your calculations, my head would have to be so big that I couldn't fit through the front..." I had the insane urge to put my goddamned hand in the air and point to the sky. "You're doing it again, aren't you?"

"Only a little."

"How come I fall for your shit? You're not even a good liar and you get me every fucking time."

"You underestimate me."

Morgan was right. "I'd apologize, but I think I've run out of my quota for the year."

He chuckled. "It's okay. Everyone does. I'm used to it."

And that was wrong because of why it happened. "I don't want to be everyone else."

Morgan's arm jerked, and his elbow grazed my bicep. He snapped his fingers, and in the dark, his fingers were a fluttering blur next to his head.

"Mor—"

"How come you picked Durstrand?" He jerked again. "I'm assuming you made a lot of money and you can probably go anywhere you want, but you came here. No one with money wants to live here unless there's a reason." A small sound was pulled from him with another tic. "And how long were you going to stay? Since you don't have a reason to stay, it can't be too long. But it has to be more than a year since you bought the Anderson house. As long as it's going to take you to fix it up, two years would be pointless. So is it three or four years?"

I struggled to swallow. "I don't know for sure."

His breath shuddered. "My guess would be three years. So why would you come somewhere you don't want to be and commit yourself to staying for three years when you could live anywhere you wanted? And where is it you want to live, Grant? Where do you dream of being for the rest of your life? What do you dream of waking up to every morning? Mountains, valleys, desert?"

"The ocean." The confession left a pain in my heart.

"But not just any beach. Someone who ships expensive stolen cars, pisses off the FBI, and gets shot would want a special beach. Somewhere far away and out of jurisdiction of the people who could cause him a problem. I'd say Tahiti, but that just seems cliché. So where were you thinking?"

"Maldives or Seychelles."

Morgan sighed. "I think I've seen pictures of Seychelles. Very pretty." He shifted, and it left a gap where we'd been touching. It was only an inch at the most, but it might as well have been miles. "You should be really happy there."

I used to be sure I would. But that was before I had any real idea about what happiness was. Granted, it was only a taste. Just a few precious drops. But what I'd been given in my time with Morgan amounted to more than I'd ever drank from the first thirty-odd years of my life.

Morgan stood, and the wooden slats squeaked. "Grant?"

"Yeah."

"Would you mind staying the night?"

I sat up. "You sure?"

"You don't plan on staying around. You're just doing something to fill the space in between now and Seychelles. I get that. But I figured, you know, when you're not working on the old Anderson place and playing tag with your FBI groupies, you might want to do something recreational like fucking me. But if you'd rather watch TV or do crossword puzzles, I understand."

"I don't have a TV, and I hate crossword puzzles."

"I never cared for them either. Both, I mean. TV and crosswords. Have you ever really looked at the questions they come up with on those things? Wonder how much they pay someone to do that job? And is it by the hour, or the word?" The screen door squeaked. "I've gotta brush my teeth, and then I guess I'll meet you in my room. Don't take too long, or I'll start without you." The wood frame knocked against the jamb and then immediately squeaked again. "Oh, and there's an extra toothbrush that I bought for a dime at the dollar store in the medicine cabinet. You can't miss it. It has Kermit the frog on the handle. Not very manly, but at least your breath won't taste like garlic. Not that I mind garlic but sometimes the other spices I use in my pizza sauce will irritate my dick so make sure you brush all the way to the back of your throat.

"And I mean it when I say I'll start without you, so don't dawdle."

The door shut again, and a light clicked on in the dining room, muting the stars. A few minutes later, it clicked off, the next break in the darkness came when he turned on his bedroom light.

I went inside and disposed of my beer bottle before hitting the john and stuck the smiling face of a legendary Muppet in my mouth so I wouldn't leave a rash on Morgan's cock.

When I got to his room, Morgan was propped up against the headboard, knees bent, feet flat on the bed and his cock in his hand.

There was a bottle of lube and fresh box of condoms on the bedside table. He hadn't just opened the box, he'd taken one of the rubbers out of the package.

"I get this feeling that you're in a hurry."

"Been thinking of your mouth since the cookie aisle."

"Cookies make you horny?"

"No, your mouth makes me horny. We just happened to be in the cookie aisle when I started fantasizing." Morgan moaned.

I took off my shirt. "You sure you need me? You seem like you're doing fine on your own."

"I told I would start without you."

"I didn't take that long."

"Long enough." He rolled the foreskin over the tip in short slow strokes. Fluid coating the wrinkles of skin glistened in the lamplight.

I shed my jeans and boxers. Morgan raked a look over me and licked his lips.

"Fucking hell, Morgan, I could come just watching you."

His mouth curled. "Is that a challenge?"

Was it?

Morgan gripped the iron bed frame with his free hand and arched his back. The perfect curve of his body popped his hips, spread his legs wider, and pushed his knees to the mattress. His head fell back, and the column of his neck almost brought the top of his head to his toes.

"You ever bend the other way and suck your own dick?" I stroked my cock.

"How do you think I got so good at it?" Morgan spread himself out on his back and pulled his knees to his chest flashing me with the tight circle of his puckered hole.

I ached to bury myself.

Morgan spread his thighs and effortlessly folded himself in half.

I climbed on the end of the bed. Morgan watched me through the space between his legs. The head of his cock rested on his chin. He smiled at me when I moved up.

"You better get comfortable." He picked up his head and took his cock into his mouth.

"Holy fuck, Morgan." I smoothed my hands over his ass. Morgan hummed on the upstroke. His lips were so tight that he barely left any saliva behind. Then he flexed his hips, giving enough bend for him push his dick all the way to the back of his throat. His gaze met mine, and my tongue stuck to the roof of my mouth.

I don't think I'd ever been so jealous about a blowjob in my life.

Heat spread over my cheeks and ran down my chest.

At the tip again, he tongued his slit. I lowered myself down and licked a line up his taint to his balls. A shudder ran through Morgan's thighs so I did it again.

His heavy sac pulled tight, and I took one of his balls into my mouth. Morgan's eyes widened. I moved to the other, and he sucked his cock to the back of his throat.

I leaned back enough to grab the lubricant.

"I'm going to use my fingers on you." I made a show of pouring the oil over my fingertips. It made glistening trails all the way to my palm. I dribbled more over Morgan's hole. It constricted, and his balls pulled tight again. "Gonna start with one, then maybe two. If you sing pretty for me, I might even give you my cock." I licked the base of his dick and met his mouth at the head. Morgan slipped his tongue across mine and fed me the subtle salt of precum.

I spiraled my finger over his entrance until I was at the center, then pushed. Morgan's breath went faster with every inch. I pulled back slow, and he whimpered into my mouth.

I broke the kiss and lapped at the head of his dick. "Blow yourself, Morgan, I want to watch you suck your cock."

He didn't hesitate. Morgan bobbed his head, and I thrust my finger. The pink in his cheeks darkened and tears pricked the corner of his eyes. I raked my teeth over his nut sac and fondled them with my tongue.

"Gonna give you two now." I wasn't even sure if he heard me. His hole contracted hard enough to pull at my fingers. I sank them in one push. Morgan released his cock and cried out.

His hips fell enough that I was able to catch the head of his cock in my mouth. I sucked him all the way to the back of my throat and filled his ass with the full length of my fingers again. Morgan dropped his legs over my shoulders, pinning my head between the muscles of his thighs and proceeded to thrust.

"God, Grant. More. Need more…" A wanton cry preceded every pump of his hips. I pushed deeper and faster. "Yeah, yeah, like that…" Morgan pulled the tip of his cock to my lips so only the first few inches filled my mouth and thrust in rapid fire. "Suck, suck hard." I did, and he threw back his head and yelled. "More…"

There was no way I could finger-fuck him faster. I added a third.

Morgan yanked the headboard hard enough to rattle the bed. "Close…" He inhaled so deep his chest swelled until his ribs made lines under his skin. "Relax your throat… now, Grant, now."

I leaned forward so he'd feel me pull my tongue back. Morgan dug his heels into the space between my shoulder blades and forced my head down by locking his thighs. His cock hit the back of my throat.

I struggled to breathe out of my nose and not lose rhythm.

His thrusts slowed for a moment. I wasn't sure if the change of pace was for my benefit or his. Then his eyes darkened with heated need. I held his gaze and hummed.

Morgan withdrew to the tip again, then shoved his cock past the back of my tongue with the same kind of rapid thrusts he'd done with the tip.

I knew then what was really meant by the phrase, fucking like rabbits.

"Gonna…" Morgan keened. "Gonna come…" He slung his head. Golden locks heavy with sweat slapped his cheeks. "Gonna come, Grant, almost, almost…" His legs tightened hard enough to make my ears ring. "Oh God…" His thrusts faltered, and a wash of hot cum pumped from his cock, filling my mouth. "Yes…yes…"

A wave of tremors ran down Morgan's body, leaving him collapsed on the mattress. His grip on my head loosened until his legs went limp and slid over my shoulders. I continued sliding my mouth over his throbbing cock, tonguing the folds of foreskin until there was nothing left.

When I was satisfied, I sat back. "I don't think I've ever seen anything like that." I kissed the inside of his leg. "Jesus, Morgan, you could put some of the top porn stars to shame." He whimpered when I pulled out my fingers. I felt around for the bottle of lube and dropped it twice trying to pop open the lid. The second time was because I kept pushing down the cap from the wrong side.

It clicked, then squirted too much in my hands. Droplets made oily circles on the bedspread bunched up around my knees. My hand shook, an echo of the aching need in my balls.

The first stroke I gave my cock shot an icy bolt across my nerves, and I had to grit my teeth to keep from yelling. Lubricant oozed from between my fingers. Morgan pushed himself up on his elbows. His bangs were in his eyes, but I knew he was watching. The weight of his gaze as firm and real as strength of my grip on my cock.

Morgan fondled his balls. His softening cock jumped. He moved to tug at the foreskin around the head of his dick. He used the velvet skin to the stroke himself while making small circles just inside the folds with his index finger.

It didn't seem like much, but his flagging dick hardened.

I sped up my strokes, and the squelch of lubricant against flesh turned into a steady click. Morgan undulated against the mattress. It was a simple movement but one that rippled his body and made his tawny muscles flex under his skin.

"Grant…" Morgan twisted to the side. The new angle allowed him to keep watching me while allowing him to use his other hand. Morgan sucked on his fingers.

I regretted not being patient and waiting for that mouth, but it was too late now. The spiraling pleasure took me to the edge.

Morgan pulled his fingers out of his mouth and tweaked each of his nipples. With each pinch, he gasped, a sound so small and yet it rocketed through me.

"Wanna see you come, Grant."

He wasn't going to have a choice. I pumped my hips. Morgan returned his attention to his cock. The flush was back in his cheeks.

I should have fucked him. If I'd know he was so fast to recover, I would have. But a lot of guys didn't want a dick in their ass right after they'd come.

If only I had, though. If only I'd sank myself to the hilt in his hole. The memory of his ass squeezing my cock as I came drew a moan out of my throat.

"What are you thinking about, Grant?" Morgan twisted the other way. "What's going through your mind when you watch me?"

"What do you think?"

He smiled. "Me." He moved his free hand to his balls. "You're thinking of my mouth." He wet his lips with his tongue. "You're thinking about my mouth on your cock, sucking you. Taking you to the back of my throat." Morgan widened his knees. "Or is it something else?"

"You... tell... me." The need to come swelled into a pain. All I needed to do was let go, yet I couldn't make myself do it. I wanted to watch Morgan more.

His smile turned into a lopsided grin. "I know that look."

I huffed a breath. "Really?"

"Mmmmhmmmm." Morgan pulled a knee up and rolled over. "You're thinking about my ass. About me riding you."

I was now.

"Did you like that?" Morgan moved his hand between his legs until his fingers were at his entrance. I knew how limber he was, and yet watching him angle his shoulder into the mattress so he could watch me while he held his ass in the air was nothing short of a magic trick. He rubbed his opening.

I had to open my mouth so I could breathe.

Morgan pressed against his hole. The ring of muscle clenched so tight it almost disappeared. Then it relaxed and Morgan sank two fingers deep in one push.

"Oh hell, Morgan." I tipped forward and had to put my hand on his ass cheek to hold myself up. "Fuck, fuck, fuck..." Sweat burned my eyes.

"What are you waiting for? I can always stop, go ahead, Grant. Come..."

"Don't you dare."

"You've got to be tired of watching me do this." He pumped his fingers faster. "Gotta be getting boring by now."

"Never."

He started to laugh, but it transformed into a long, lean moan. "Feels good, Grant, so good." Morgan rocked his hips.

"What? What feels good?"

"You. Your cock. Thick. Deep. You've got big fingers, but a bigger dick. I like that. I like that a lot."

My muscles jumped, and my rhythm faltered. The electric current building inside me stuttered. I glanced at the condoms. Could I get one and be inside him before I shot all over the place?

No chance.

I tightened my grip and fucked the tunnel of my fist. It was nothing like Morgan's ass. I could squeeze tight enough, but my skin was too rough to be mistaken as anything but the palm of a hand.

Tomorrow, I told myself. Tomorrow I was going to fuck him against the wall. Day after that, over the sofa. The next one, across the kitchen table. I was going to fuck Morgan until he wouldn't be able to ride that stupid bike, let alone walk to work. But it would be okay, because I'd give him a ride. Hell, I would even put a pillow in the truck for him to sit on.

It might have been funny if I hadn't meant it. And I did. Goddamn me, I meant every word. I wanted those coming days and the days after them.

Two to three years. That was a lot of time for blowjobs, hand jobs, and fucking. I counted the possible months, the weeks, the days, the hours, but the numbers got too big and my mind blurred.

Morgan cried out with every plunge of his fingers and thrust of his hips. He still hadn't closed his eyes. Desire and raw need still shadowed the brown, but there was something else I didn't have a name for. But I'd seen it before when Morgan watched the light and the world disappeared for him.

In that moment, the light took a backseat to me.

Two to three years might have been a lot of time for sex, but it would never be enough time to have him look at me that way. He might still never look at me the same way again. It could have been a fluke or even my imagination.

And it could take a lifetime to find out.

Lines of cold crackled down my spine, and my body tensed. My cock thickened in my hand, and a tingling wave engulfed me, crashing harder and harder with every pulse of my cock. Cum sprayed the back of Morgan's balls.

A shudder ran down his thighs, and he shoved his fingers deep one last time. Morgan jerked and came, each surge rocking him.

When he stopped, he fell over on his side. Somehow he'd managed to catch most of his cum in the palm of his hand.

"Tissues." He waved at the bedside table. I opened the drawer and pulled out the box. Morgan wiped his hands and the back of his nuts. Bits of deteriorating tissue stuck to his skin.

"Wait here." I retrieved a wet washcloth from the bathroom. "Here." I sat beside him and wiped his hand clean. "Raise your leg." Morgan propped his heel on my shoulder.

"Feels good." He gave me a lazy smile.

I finished wiping him off and tugged the comforter down. Morgan was boneless as I pulled the blankets out from under him. He made a sleepy sound and pressed himself to my chest. I'd never been one to enjoy a bed partner clinging to me while they slept, but Morgan fit against me. Almost as if our bodies were interlocking puzzle pieces.

I lay there a very long time, holding him and petting his hair. Every so often, his breath would pull deep and he'd sigh against my neck.

I counted his heartbeats.

I traced the shell of his ear.

I carefully arranged locks of his curly hair, not caring it was hopeless to make sense of the mess.

Morgan had been right about so many things.

Except one.

I did have a reason to stay here in Durstrand. And that reason was asleep in my arms.

****

"I don't mind giving you a ride to Toolies."

Morgan put his plate in the sink. "And I don't mind riding my bike."

"It's going to get cold tonight."

"It gets cold every winter. That's why it's winter."

I pushed my empty plate away, leaving a smear of honey on the table.

"Do you want any more French toast?"

"If I eat any more, I'll be sick." I picked up my coffee cup and went for a refill. Morgan had used a ceramic pot to heat water in the microwave and tea bags to hold the grounds. It was crude, but damn it was good.

To think of all the times I'd gone without brewed coffee because I didn't have a coffeemaker when all I needed was a box of empty tea bags and a cup of hot water.

I leaned against the counter. "Are you sure you don't want me to give you a ride?"

He tossed thoughts in no particular direction. "Yeah. I've got to work late tonight."

"I don't have anywhere to be."

"Grant." His hand opened and closed.

"Okay. But if you change your mind, will you call me?"

Morgan ran his fingers along the sink where the sun dappled the porcelain.

"Will you?"

He turned. "Yeah. If I change my mind, I'll call."

It was all I could ask for. Morgan had slept with me, that didn't mean I owned him. I don't know why I felt like I did. I'd never felt possessive about anyone before, not even Jeff.

I was worried being overprotective of Morgan had nothing to do with caring about him and everything to do with pity. He didn't need my pity, he deserved my admiration. "Do you want to do something tomorrow?"

"Are you asking me out on a date?" Morgan propped his hip against the counter.

I smiled around the edge of my cup. "I guess I am."

"I don't know, I should probably ask Aunt Jenny if it's okay, since you're so much older than me."

"Shut up."

He laughed and so did I.

"Do you like movies?" Morgan tilted his head.

"Durstrand has a theatre?"

"A drive-in."

"You're kidding. I haven't seen one of those since I was a kid."

"I don't know if you've noticed or not, this town isn't exactly up to date. I can't remember when anyone even built a new house here."

He had a point. "I'd love to go to the movies with you. What's playing?"

"Probably something that's been out of the city theatre for thirty years." His shoulder jerked. "But we can get popcorn, hotdogs, and drinks. Believe it or not, the hotdogs are really good."

"Can't beat a good hotdog. Count me in."

"You wanna pick me up about seven?"

Actually I didn't want to leave. I wanted to push him back into his bedroom and do wondrous things to that very flexible body of his.

The curtain of hair concealing his eyes parted just enough for me to know he watched me. Morgan licked his bottom lip, then pinched it between his teeth.

Fucking hell.

"I should probably get dressed." He pushed away from the counter. "Don't forget, tomorrow, seven sharp."

"I'll be here, but I don't want you to hesitate to call me if you change your mind."

****

97

I was about a mile from home when a dark sedan pulled up behind me. It could have been any one of thousands of sedans cluttering the streets in the city. Which is exactly why it didn't belong.

I turned onto a back road. The driver hesitated before following. Pot holes dropped the front end of the sedan and steep ruts tossed it back into the air. The driver slowed down, but the gullies made it impossible to avoid bottoming out.

When I was pretty sure there was no chance of reversing down the road, I stopped. The sedan pulled a few feet from my bumper. I got out, they didn't. Sunlight glinted off the windshield, concealing the driver.

I had a feeling about who it was. Call it instinct. Call it luck. In reality, it was probably my dick remembering what it was like to be buried in the man's ass.

The automatic window hummed as it sank into the door.

Jeff was dressed casual.

Well, about as casual as a man could get in a two hundred dollar shirt.

"Where's your tie?"

He took off his sunglasses. "Left it at home. Thought I'd blend in better without it."

"The jeans are a nice touch."

"I thought they were."

"But you need to pick a cheaper brand, TRR are way out of the pay grade of the folks around here."

"Anything less wouldn't have gone with the shirt." He smoothed out an imaginary wrinkle on the front.

"I thought you went home."

"I did."

"Then why the hell did you come back?"

"I had some vacation time saved up. Thought this would be a nice place to kick back, read a book, you know, vacation things."

"Most people go to the beach, Vegas, or Colorado to ski."

"Too cliché."

"So is riding around in a dark sedan. You might as well tattoo FBI on your forehead."

"I'm not trying to hide."

"Nah, I guess not. You've got a fake set of good ol' boys to do that."

Jeff clenched his jaw.

"Don't worry, they did a much better job of blending in this time. No one else noticed." I leaned down. "I'll ask you again. Why are you still here?"

"I need you to cooperate."

"You mean you need me to divulge private information between my clients and myself."

"Criminals, Grant. The correct term is criminals."

"Until you have evidence proving otherwise, they are clients. And the last time you dragged me into court, a judge agreed with me."

"It doesn't change the facts."

"According to the facts, every job I've ever done has been legal, and by the books. You don't even have a typo to hound me on."

Jeff met my gaze. "I'm trying to help you."

"Really?"

"They're going to arrest you."

"On what charge?"

"Hines found out about your *off the record* storage unit."

I was very careful not to even blink. "It's off the record because it has nothing to do with my business." Which was true.

"Yeah, well, they're going to search it."

"They need a special piece of paper first."

"And they'll get it."

"On what grounds?" There was no way they had any. I knew for a fact they couldn't have any. "On what grounds, Jeff?"

"Does it matter?"

"If I need to give my lawyer a heads-up, yes." It had to be a bluff. But if it was, Jeff had one hell of a poker face.

He put his sunglasses back on. "Think about it."

"Nothing to think about." I stepped back.

"I'll call you in a few days. Until then, you'd better not so much as double park."

I went back to my truck and got in. Jeff was still trying to get the car turned around without taking out the oil pan when I pulled away. I stomped the gas and gravel shot out from under the spinning tires. It pinged off the body of the sedan and left snowflake shaped chips spiderwebbed across the windshield.

I headed into town to find a disposable cell phone.

****

Common sense told me there was no way they'd get a warrant.

Legally.

But the FBI had more ways around the letter of the law than I did. There wasn't much in the warehouse beyond personal affects—very valuable personal affects, but there was a box with numbers, names, and places. It had nothing to do with my shipping business, but if it got out, a lot of people would be in danger.

My three rules: no weapons, no drugs, no people.

About five years ago, I'd broken the last one. The first time was an accident and the reason I sank the barge. A shipping container belonging to someone else got switched with mine. It didn't happen very often, but of all the people to accidentally wind up with his cargo on my boat, it was Lorado. In the long run, I guess it was a good thing. At the time, I was ready to prepay my funeral expenses.

Because when I realized there were people in the tin can, I had to get them out. Then the only way to make sure Lorado didn't know what happened, and how it happened, and where they went, was to sink the barge. The FBI surveillance equipment was a surprise bonus.

Yeah, the first time an accident, I can't say the same for the next dozen or so repeats.

I could have told Jeff what was in the file and hoped he'd keep the information confidential, but that was about as likely as the FBI apologizing for ever hounding me.

Being hounded by the FBI wasn't what worried me. They were nothing more than ill-tempered, oversexed ankle biters. Lorado and his buyers were not.

If the FBI uncovered that information, it would get out. I could handle one hit man but not an army. And I wouldn't be the only casualty. They'd kill the people I'd stolen from them, and their families. That's a lot of blood to have on your hands.

Even when you're dead.

I left the drug store with a cheap pay-as-you-go phone and drove around until I found a decent signal. Then I dialed a number I'd hoped I'd never have to use again.

Rubio Venice was more than a friend. The bond we had was the kind forged when you thought you had thirty seconds to live. A connection when you knew one fuck-up would bring down a hail of bullets. A kind of soul mate, I guess, because he was willing to snap your neck before letting you fall into the hands of the men you're trying to elude.

The phone rang a few times before it picked up. "Hello?"

"It's me."

"I would tell you it's good to hear your voice, but we both know it would be bullshit." Because a phone call meant things were very bad.

"The file maybe compromised."

"By who?"

"My fan club."

"They have a warrant?"

"Not yet but they claim they will."

"They're baiting you."

"Yeah, probably."

"Then why are you worried?"

"There are too many people involved for me not to be."

There was a shuffling sound, a click, then the high-pitched cry of seagulls.

"You on vacation?"

"Winter home."

"How's the weather?"

"Beautiful."

I could practically hear him smile.

"You should come visit me sometime." Rubio said. "Meet the grandkids."

"You have grandkids now?"

"Four of them."

"You only have two daughters."

"And now two sets of twins." His sigh conveyed so many things. But gratitude was the loudest. "What do you need me to do?"

"I'm not even sure I should ask. Like you said, they're baiting me."

"True, but you still called."

Because that night, half frozen, up to our necks in saltwater, about to go our separate ways, he'd put his hand on my cheek. The happiness in his eyes couldn't be concealed by the shadows.

Instead of thank you, he'd said, "Call me when."

There was no explanation needed. I knew what he meant. When you need me, when you know something, when either of us needs to watch our back.

I hoped to never make the phone call, but there I was.

"Yeah." I exhaled the frustration building in my chest. "I should have never kept the documents, I'm sorry."

"I'm not. We could have needed. We still might need them."

"Not sure which risk is greater now."

"I am. You did the right thing, Grant."

"Only now it could blow up in our faces."

"And we could have died a dozen times over that year, and yet, here we are."

We were. And so were a half dozen families, including Rubio's.

"The documents need to disappear, but they'll be watching me and any of my contacts." Except for a man I knew as Rubio Venice. He was dead. Only Rubio knew who and where he was now.

"Is there anything else of value in the storage building?"

There was. Monetarily at least. "Nothing I can't replace."

He laughed. A thick rich sound with only a hint of his place of origin. Some country in the darkest corner of the world, where people survived on nothing, and sold their daughters and sons in order to survive. When they didn't sell them, they were taken. Then the family didn't even get compensation for their loss.

Rubio had lost four daughters to human traffickers and a son. We were able to save two of the girls. The boy lived too, but I'm not sure if we really saved him or not.

"Do not worry. I'll take care of it," Rubio said.

"Are you sure?"

He laughed again, only this time it was softer and even sad. "I think that is my line, my friend."

"Maybe, but you're the one who's putting their life on the line."

"It isn't worth much anyhow."

"Now who's stealing whose lines?"

The sound of waves in the background filled the silence.

"Rest easy, Grant. Be well. And again, call me when."

He hung up.

I stomped the cell phone into the gravel on the shoulder of the road. When it was in enough pieces to make it impossible to use, I kicked them into the creek running through the drainpipe under the blacktop. It was still swollen from the recent rain, so the remnants would be miles away from there by morning.

Getting out of the business was supposed to have made my life easier, not complicate it. But that was the FBI for you.

The scar on my chest ached, and I rubbed it. How come none of the other reminders from my past ever did?

If I had to guess, it was because I'd gambled with more than my life with Jeff.

And I'd lost.

****

I pulled into Morgan's driveway at five till. He leaned against the post on his front porch.

Dressed in ragged-out jeans and a T-shirt, he resembled one of those barely legal models for those high-end clothing stores.

Which of course made me feel like a fucking pervert all over again.

A few days ago, it would have sent me running for the hills, but I'd had my hands on his body, felt his mouth on my cock, been buried inside him, and I'd watched what this beautiful man could do to himself.

The memories alone were enough to make me hard.

He came around to the passenger side and got in. I hoped he wouldn't notice the complication currently occupying my jeans.

"You're late."

"No, I'm not."

"Three minutes after."

I looked at my watch. "Says I'm right on time."

"Then your watch is wrong."

"I just set it."

"Still wrong."

"According to who?"

Morgan held up his wrist. "Mine says three minutes late."

"Then your watch is wrong." After all, this could work both ways right?

"My watch is atomic, yours is digital, mine sets itself according to USNO."

"What?"

"The United States National Observatory Master Clock."

Of course he'd have a watch synchronized with Department of Defense. How silly of me to think otherwise.

I tapped my fingers on the steering wheel.

"We can go now." Morgan opened and closed his hand next to his temple.

"You sure we have time? After all, I'm late."

"Don't worry, told you seven, but we didn't need to leave till seven thirty."

"Then why did you tell me seven?" I held up a hand. "Never mind. I don't want to know."

The truck stuttered as I reached the end of the driveway. "Right or left?"

Morgan pointed left. "That way."

I turned, and the road took us farther into the backwoods of Durstrand. "I would have thought a drive-in would have been closer to town."

"We could have taken Apple Lane and cut behind the rec center, but then you have to go all the way around Newman's farm to get to it. This way will be a straight shot, and we won't have to dodge the cows."

I wasn't about to ask him what he meant. When we got to our destination, I didn't need to.

A narrow dirt road led to the manicured patch of land surrounded by barbed wire and cows.

Lots of cows.

Lots and lots of mooing cows.

There were more cars than I expected seeing; the place was in the middle of... well... a cow pasture.

"What the heck possessed someone to build a theatre out here?" I found a spot as far from the bovine choir as possible.

"Newman's got money. Likes movies. Decided to build a theatre."

"You'd think he would have built it closer to town so it was easier for people to get to." I cut the truck off.

"He built it for the cows, not for people." Morgan opened his door.

"You're telling me some farmer put up a movie screen for a bunch of cows."

"Why else would he put it in the middle of a cow pasture?" Morgan got out. "C'mon, while the hotdogs are fresh."

I followed him to the concession stand, which of course was nothing more than a miniature barn. The guy loading the kernels into the popcorn machine was old enough to be my grandfather.

"Morgan." He came around the corner and gave Morgan a quick hug. "Been too long since I've seen you."

"Seventeen days."

"See, too long." There was a jewel-encrusted cow on his ten-gallon hat. "Who's your friend?"

Morgan's shoulder twitched, and he tossed thoughts. "This is Grant. Grant, this is…"

"Mr. Newman."

"Why yes, I am." He held out his hand, and we shook. "You must be the fella that bought the old Anderson place. I was sure it would fall in before someone rescued it."

"It almost did."

He laughed and slapped me on the shoulder hard enough to rock me on my heels.

"So what will it be?" Mr. Newman tottered back around the counter.

"Two hotdogs, a drink, and a couple of those." Morgan pointed to the brownies among an assortment of baked goods inside the glass counter. "What do you want?"

I had no idea. "The same, I guess."

"Be right up." He went to the rear of the shack. The scent of cooking meat and hickory permeated the air.

"Fresh hotdogs and homemade brownies, I'm impressed."

"Wait till you taste them." Morgan reached over the counter and grabbed two drink cups. "Here."

The soda fountain faced the outside. I was putting a lid on my drink when Newman reappeared with a tray of hotdogs decked out in every assortment of topping one could imagine. He even gave us forks.

"Do you want ice cream on the brownies?"

"Yes, sir," Morgan said.

Newman opened a floor freezer next to the popcorn machine.

I reached for my wallet. Morgan put a hand on my wrist and shook his head.

Newman returned with our ice cream covered brownies. Morgan added them to the tray.

"Enjoy the show. And don't be a stranger, Morgan." A teenage couple stepped up behind us. Morgan ushered me toward the truck.

"We need to pay."

"He doesn't charge."

"What?"

"You should have your ears cleaned out. You always ask me to repeat myself. Wax build-up can make it difficult to hear." The preview screen came on, giving me enough light to see the coy smile Morgan threw in my direction. "Of course at your age, maybe you're just going deaf."

"I'm not going deaf."

Morgan beat me to the truck and put the tray on the dash.

Ah, the advantages of a thirty year old truck.

"You realize if we eat all this, we're going to be sick."

"Nah." Morgan dug into one of his hotdogs with a plastic fork, and I did the same. I have no idea what was on it that made it spicy, sweet, and rich, but damn, it was good. Thank God they came in bowls.

"I've never had a hotdog like this before." I polished off the last bite. The movie screen turned blue. When the opening credits began, I rolled down the window and took the speaker off the pole. The hook barely fit over the door. I adjusted the volume, but it didn't put a dent in the static.

"They're good. Everyone says that Betty, his wife, was the one who came up with the recipe. She had a café across the road from the hardware store, but Mr. Newman closed it after she died."

"Must have been a while ago." The hardware store had a lot of age on it.

"Almost fifty years."

"She was young."

Morgan switched out his empty hotdog bowl for the brownie and ice cream. "In her twenties, I think."

I did the same. It took a lot of will not to moan when that brownie hit my tongue. "What happened to her?"

"Not sure. Unlike you, that was way before my time."

I glared at Morgan over the edge of my fork. His bangs moved to the side enough for me to catch a hint of a smile.

"But, from what I've heard, she died in childbirth."

Which had to be one of the top tragedies for a young couple. It didn't seem like dying in childbirth would be possible this day and age, but medical knowledge had changed a lot in fifty years. In Durstrand, it was unlikely they had the meager advances available at the time.

"That's why he has the cows." Morgan caught a glob of ice cream on his thumb and licked it off. "She was raising a baby calf, and after she died, Mr. Newman kept it. It had baby cows, and then there were more cows…"

As if they knew they were being talked about, the cows mooed.

"Every year, Mr. Newman has this great big cookout and the whole town shows up."

I choked on a bite of brownie.

"Free hamburgers, steaks, it's really good, best hot dogs ever." Morgan nodded at the empty tray. "You need to make sure you go next time."

"Wait," I cleared my throat. "He eats the cows?"

"What else would he do with them?" Morgan put his empty brownie plate with the rest of

104

the trash.

"I thought he had the cows because of his wife."

"He does."

"Then how can he eat them?"

"What do you think they were going to do with the first cow?"

"I don't know, I just thought, well… I don't know what I thought, but it sure wasn't grinding them up and making burgers. That just seems wrong."

"Why?"

"They remind him of his wife."

"And she ran a restaurant. C'mon, Grant, this is real life, not a Hallmark movie. Man's gotta eat."

On the big screen, a horse trotted around a track. Music played. Well, sort of. Thanks to the crappy speaker, it was more like a scratchy record.

Playing a scratchy record.

"Is this Seabiscuit?"

"Probably. He usually shows animal movies or musicals. Says it makes the cows happy and they taste better."

Great. Happy cows make better burgers. Sounded like a bad slogan for a fast food chain. Although if the hotdogs were any hint as to how good the cookout would be, I definitely needed to go.

I propped my elbow on the window and watched the screen. "I think this is Flicka, not Seabiscuit."

Morgan shrugged. Between the darkness of the cab and the tilt of his head, I couldn't tell if he was looking at the screen or out the passenger window.

I picked at the clear coat on the steering wheel. I really needed to get a cover for the thing. There was a hole in the seat next to my thigh I'd never noticed. At least there wasn't a spring sticking out. Yet.

"You're bored," Morgan said.

Since lying was out of the question. "A little."

Morgan's shoulders fell. I was just about to apologize when he said, "Me too."

The horse ran around on the screen. Characters talked. The dialog came over the speaker in chunks broken apart by white noise.

We stared out the windshield.

"So," I said. "You want to do something else?"

"Yeah."

"Got anything in mind?" Was there even anything open this time of night besides Toolies?

"Wanna make out?"

On the screen, a boy chased a horse.

Make out? I tried to remember the last time I'd done that and couldn't. Which made me feel old. And damn it, I was not old.

"Sure," I said.

Morgan was across the seat straddling my thighs before I could blink. He sank his hands in my hair and attacked my mouth. His hot wet tongue slid between my lips. Instantly hard, instantly desperate, I cupped his ass and rocked against him.

"Fucking hell." I barely got a breath in to say the words before he was on my mouth again.

Morgan yanked on my shirt, freeing it from the waist of my pants. The heat of his touch slid inside my jeans.

"I want you." He opened the button and then pulled down the zipper. "I want you, Grant. Right now."

Yeah, yeah, I wanted him too. The fact we were inside a truck seemed insignificant.

I lifted my hips so Morgan could get my jeans down my thighs. My knee hit the steering wheel. I fumbled to find the lever to adjust it. With Morgan in front of me, it felt impossible. Then it was there, a button on the bottom side. I flipped it, and the steering wheel went up. It gave Morgan enough room to lean back.

His skillful hands released my cock.

I barked out a cry, and he drank it from my lips. With just a few pumps of his hand, the ache in my balls condensed.

Morgan dragged his teeth along my jaw to my ear. He bit down on the lobe. It wasn't a gentle bite either, but an act of hungry desperation.

The urge to come was almost too much. I fought with his jeans, got them open. Commando, he was commando. Why the fuck was that so hot? I gripped his cock and precum painted my wrist as he thrust into the tunnel of my fist.

"Need more," he whimpered. God that sound, that fucking sound. Helpless, hot, wanting, and yet in control.

I stroked faster.

"No, no, not that." He pressed his body to mine, making it impossible for me to move my hand.

"Morgan…" Closer and my cock slid along the cleft of his ass.

"I want you to fuck me, Grant."

"Ah, damn it. Damn it…" He had to go and say those words. Like that. As if I wasn't already on the brink.

"No room."

"Plenty of room."

"No condoms." I sucked at his throat. The soap he'd used flavored his skin.

"Front… right… pocket."

"Lubricant."

"Front pocket."

I dug through Morgan's pockets and found the condoms in the right one. "You planned this?" Like I really cared if he did.

"Always prepared, Grant. Boy Scout code." He tweaked my nipples hard enough to make me drop the strip of condoms.

"Fuck." I stuck my hand down the gap between the seat and the door. My fingertips brushed the edge of the foil package.

Apparently I was moving too slow. Morgan got the small bottle of lubricant out of his pocket. While I was trying to snag the strip of condoms, there was a snick and burp.

I pinched one of the foil squares between my middle fingers and retrieved them. Morgan was already up on his knees with his hand behind his back. The wet sound of his fingers sliding in and out of his ass was way more interesting than the static ridden dialog from the movie we were supposed to be watching.

"There's not enough room."

The changing colors on the big screen highlighted him in red, blues, white, then yellows and greens. Like his beautiful glass sculptures, the bits of broken light danced. I could have jerked myself off to the sight of him.

"Gotta get your pants off." I tugged, but with his legs spread wide, there was no way.

I tried to lift him up, and his ass hit the horn. It gave one sharp blare before he scooted forward and over my dick.

"This isn't going to work."

"Shut up, Grant." Morgan leaned back, raised his legs, and bent his knees. His shins wound up pressed against my chest. This was never going to work. Then he planted one hand on the door and his elbow on the wheel. My cock slid along his oil-slicked cleft. The puckered skin of his hole rubbed the head. "You gotta help me here, Grant."

I wasn't even going to ask how he could possibly be comfortable rolled up like a spit ball. After all, this was a man who could suck his own cock.

I scooted lower in my seat, braced my feet against the floorboard, and got a hand under him. The infinitesimal space made it almost impossible to maneuver.

"Now, Grant."

I found his entrance with my fingers and used them to line up my cock.

Morgan made a high-pitched keening sound. "Grant, for god's sake."

"I'm trying, trust me." My attempts to angle were either too high or too low. Then I was right there—fucking hell he was tight. The heat of his body enveloped me. I lifted my hips, readjusting the angle, and sank to the hilt into his ass.

"Holy shit." A tremor ran down my legs.

"Don't you dare come, yet."

Intense, why the hell was it so much more intense?

Morgan used his arms to lift his body, gaining a few inches then coming back down on me. That one stroke was all I needed. Who gave a fuck why it felt so good?

I locked a hand on Morgan's shoulder, the other on his hip. Between the seat at my back and my feet on the floorboard, I was able to get enough leverage to pop my hips.

We found a rhythm, however awkward, and I pounded him as hard as I could. Morgan bounced on my lap with his head back and mouth open, singing that beautiful music he could make. I tightened my hold on his hips, yanking him down to meet me. Our bodies slapped together in a violent clash of flesh.

"Fuck, fuck, fuck…" My arms trembled with the effort to lift up higher. Morgan readjusted his arm on the steering wheel, taking on some of the weight. The horn blared again, but the hell if I cared. I was too far gone. Cock moving in and out of his body, never wanting to stop and so desperate to finish my heart clawed at my ribs.

"Want you to come," I said.

"Not yet." Morgan barked in pleasure again and again. His swollen cock curved toward his stomach. The head glistened in the poor light. The scent of musk and sex soaked the truck cab. Even with the windows down, fog clouded the edge of the windshield, closing in until only the center was clear.

"Harder." The cords on Morgan's neck stood out. "Harder, Grant, harder."

"The truck was your bright idea." A cramp pulled at my left calf; I extended my leg to ease it and came dangerously close to sliding out of him. I bent my knee back.

"Yesss—" Morgan grabbed me by my hair and pulled me forward. With one arm propping him off the steering wheel and the other on me, our bodies were crushed together so tight I could barely take a full breath.

His bangs slid away. The lack of light erased irrelevant details, leaving behind the raw, unrelenting desire. No man had ever looked at me that way. Not even in the throes of sex. Like the light, he watched something inside me, something no one else could see, and I didn't know whether to be frightened or honored.

"Want you to come. Want you to fill me. Can you do that?"

I either would or die trying, that much I knew for sure.

I fucked him.

Sweat made my clothes stick to my skin. My jaw ached from clenching my teeth, the joints in my knees screamed, muscles knotted, and my pulse beat so hard black spots danced in front of my eyes.

But I didn't stop. Couldn't stop. The mask of bliss sweeping over Morgan's face was worth anything.

I seriously began to wonder if I was going to live up to my vow. Then the sudden rush of electric euphoria swept over me. I threw back my head with a shout. Morgan's body tightened around my pulsing cock. Wave after wave, beat after beat, Morgan flexed his ass.

I collapsed and was able to unfold enough to breathe.

Morgan pulled my hair. "Not yet, you don't." He moved to his knees. His stiff cock curved toward his stomach. "You're gonna suck me?"

"Yeah." Hell if I knew how.

Morgan raised up on his feet and perched his ass on the steering wheel. His back pressed to the roof, his arms on either side of my shoulders on the back of the seat, he created an arch with his body, giving me perfect access to his glorious cock. I slid forward on jellied legs and almost dumped myself into the floorboard. He caught me before the horn did much more than yelp.

The thick rich flavor of precum filled my mouth as I took him to the back of my throat. Morgan moaned. Like the musical cries he made, it was a sound unique to him. He pumped his hips, driving his dick into my mouth.

The angle made it difficult for me to get to his balls so I plunged two fingers in his hole.

He jumped, and his head smacked the roof. "More." He twisted a handful of my hair. I gave him three, and he cried out. Morgan fucked my mouth while I did the same to his ass. The heat of cum slid down my fingers with the slick remnants of lubricant.

His gasps, his pleas, it added to the obscene squelch of my fingers moving in and out of his body.

I pulled to the tip, sucked hard, and he yanked my hair again. I took him deep, swallowing around him. It must have been exactly what he wanted because his breathing hitched.

"Almost, almost."

For a moment, his cock went so deep I couldn't breathe, then he backed out. I tightened my lips around his length and his thrust shortened, giving me half, but increasing the speed.

108

"Almost, Grant. God, your mouth, I love your mouth. I love your dick, too. And your fingers. Harder, harder, please..."

I twisted my arm at an uncomfortable angle, but it gave me enough room to shove my fingers all the way to my knuckles. I found his prostate.

"Oh, God, yesss—yessss...." Morgan bucked his hips. The back of his thighs hit the horn, and it chirped with every rapid thrust, then his wanton cries drowned everything out. Liquid heat shot over my tongue, salty, bitter, rich, and earthy, his cum filled my mouth, trickled down my throat. I swallowed as much as I could and kept sucking. Morgan rode out his orgasm long after he had nothing left to give. He rocked, he breathed, he pulled my hair.

I removed my fingers from his ass and looked for something to wipe them on. Then it dawned on me why I needed to clean them in the first place.

"Damn it."

"What?"

The condoms sat on the seat next to me. "Jesus, Morgan I'm sorry, I..." I knew better. I fucking knew better. "I'm clean. I swear. I haven't been with anyone since I got out of the hospital and they..."

"It's okay." He tilted my head back and took my mouth. I slipped him the flavor of his cum, and he moaned.

It was then I heard the strange popping sound. No, no, not popping.

Clapping?

I didn't even want to look, but I did.

Cars in front of us, beside us, behind us had become perches for their passengers. No one in the parking lot watched the movie any more.

Someone whistled. Another person shouted. Then I'll be damned if they didn't start shouting for an encore.

Morgan gave me a crooked smile.

"No," I said.

"But our fans are calling our name."

I didn't even take the time to pull up my jeans. I just dumped Morgan in the passenger seat and cranked up the truck. Just as I started to back out, I remembered the stupid speaker hooked on the door.

It landed on the ground with a thump. At least I managed to not run over it.

And damn Morgan, he was still laughing at me when I took a left back onto the main road.

****

I stayed over because after an encore, and an encore to the encore, there was no way I was going to walk, let alone drive.

But as exhausted as I was, I couldn't fall asleep.

I lay there in the darkness with Morgan's head on my shoulder, his exhales warming my cheek.

When I'd been in the business, I rarely slept if I was outside of my apartment. Even if I'd been going for days organizing a shipment. I put a couch in my office for those short lulls when I could catch an hour nap.

But no matter how hard I tried, how achy, how much my eyes burned, I couldn't get them to close. My body remained on high alert until the package was safe and my client was happy.

Then I could sleep for days.

It was like that there in Morgan's bed. As if for some reason, I had to wait until it was safe for me to rest.

Outside the wind blew hard enough to rock the dozens of kinetic sculptures hanging in the trees. The soft chink joined the fading fall tree frogs. I glanced at the clock, it was three a.m. I didn't have anywhere to be tomorrow so the lack of sleep was no big loss.

My internal clock ticked and the spring wound tighter.

I wasn't afraid or worried, just… waiting.

Morgan whimpered, and the building tension popped.

The moonlight poured into his bedroom window, illuminating things as bright as a streetlamp. Shadows made heavy outlines over Morgan's features.

His eyebrows crunched up, and he frowned in his sleep.

Tears pooled in the corners of his eyes.

"Morgan?"

Another sound but it was less a whimper and more like a sob. His wandering hand made a halfhearted jump to his temple. "I'm sorry."

"Shhh—"

"Please don't be angry." He opened his eyes, but I knew right away it wasn't me he saw. The hurt, pain, the weakness, was not the Morgan I knew. "I didn't mean to embarrass you."

It was wrong, but I didn't try to wake him up. I wanted to know what memory plagued his sleep. Asking him in the morning would have been the better choice. But in the light, he would be the Morgan I knew. The independent wall of wit and charm. This vulnerable Morgan would have been covered back up.

He slowly ducked his head and his wandering hand pressed against his temple. A tear slid down his cheek and smeared on my chest. "Please, please, please." He tensed. Bogged down by sleep, it was like watching a movie in slow-motion.

It took me a moment to realize Morgan was protecting his face. "Please don't hit me."

God, I was such a bastard. "Shhh—" I combed my fingers through his hair. Sweat weighed down the soft curls. "It's okay, you're all right."

"I tried. I tried. I'm sorry. Please, please, please stop, Dillon. I love you. I love you, and I didn't mean to."

"Morgan." I shook him. "Morgan, wake up." I reached over and turned on the bedside lamp. Morgan's gaze was still distant. Was he asleep, awake?

Neither.

Wherever Morgan had gone was beyond the place where nightmares lay. I wanted to believe he was watching the layer of the world I couldn't see, but this time it was different. His features held no sense of wonder, no calm, they were just… empty.

The first time I killed a man, I'd been unable to look away as the life left his eyes. The moment he took his last breath, he changed. It was as if the entire world shifted around him and he was suddenly separated from it. He'd gone from a living person, to an inanimate object.

There were nights I'd wake up with the memory so fresh I smelled the blood. My heart would pound. Sweat would soak the sheets. Fear held me hostage until I convinced myself it was in the past. A deed done. I'd have to live with it because I'd done it to survive.

I thought nothing could disturb me more.

What I saw in Morgan's expression made looking into the eyes of a dead man insignificant. Because Morgan was still alive and yet he'd slipped into a place where only inanimate objects belonged.

I shook him again. His wayward hand made a lazy movement. Then he wiggled his fingers at the tip of his nose.

I sat up and took him with me. He flopped against my chest. Neither fighting nor going willingly. Just there and not there.

"Morgan." I patted his cheek. "Morgan, wake up." I shook him again, and again, and again.

Where was my phone? In the truck? Had to be. I didn't remember it being in my pocket when I put my keys in there.

I started to go get it when Morgan dropped his hand into his lap and the living-dead expression vanished.

He blinked a couple of times. "I want to go home. Please let me go home."

"Okay. Okay, I'll take you home." We were at his house, but I would have agreed to anything to lead him out from the nightmare…

"You won't be mad?"

"No, no, I won't be mad. Everything will be all right. I'll take you home, Morgan."

"You promise?"

"Yeah, I promise."

Morgan nodded. "Thank you."

Then he pressed himself against my ribs and fell back to sleep.

I didn't. I held him. Sitting there in the middle of the bed while he slumped against me, I petted him, shushed him, and prayed the nightmares would stay away.

It wasn't until the sky outside the window lightened I dare to lay him back down. Even then I kept him tucked under my arm. I don't know if it really did any good, but the dreams didn't come back and I was finally able to sleep.

****

The smell of coffee dragged me out of bed and forced me to put my jeans on. In the kitchen, Morgan stared out the window over the sink.

The smooth length of his back pulled my gaze to the swell of his ass. Two dimples peeked over the edge of his boxers, divided by the very tip of his crack. His hair was wet, and the scent of soap clinging to him left me longing for another night at the movies.

Then I was forced to relive my stupidity. Now I just had to figure out a way to bring up the topic. "Morning."

He continued to stare.

"You mind if I get a cup?"

"I was going to cook breakfast, but I'm out of bacon, and I don't have any buttermilk to make biscuits. My biscuits aren't all that great anyways, but I'd like some with gravy. I thought

111

maybe you could take us to Fran's. Their lunch is terrible, but the breakfast is good. I wonder why that is? Good breakfast, bad lunch?" Morgan sipped his coffee. "I have to be at work by two. You'll have to bring me back here, otherwise I'll be late. Takes at least thirty minutes for me to get there on my bike."

Since he didn't say no, I got a cup from the cupboard. "I want to apologize for last night. I don't know how I forgot…" No, no that was a lie. I knew exactly how I forgot. "I got carried away. I didn't think. But I promise you, I'm—"

"Sugar's over the microwave with the powdered creamer. There's milk, but it's just milk. Some people like it better than the creamer. I like the creamer most of the time."

I moved a small stack of mail out of my way so I had room to fix my coffee. "If you want, I can go to the health clinic in town and get tested again. What about you?" I hated to ask, but I had to.

"Never gone bareback. I get tested twice a year. Haven't had more than a blowjob in the john at Toolies in two. So? Biscuits and gravy?"

I propped my hip against the counter. "You sure make for interesting morning conversation."

"I'll go get dressed." Morgan put his empty cup in the sink. "I made sure to leave you some hot water, but it won't stay hot for long. Unless the water heater has caught up. It's a good heater so it might have. I bought it for fifty bucks. Berry had it on sale. Has a gouge in the side, but it's only aesthetic. I'll be ready in fifteen minutes." He started out of the kitchen but paused in the doorway. "No."

"No, what?"

"I don't want to talk about it."

Talk? Last night. He meant last night. "I hadn't really thought about asking."

Morgan nodded. "You would have. So I'm just telling you now."

"Okay. I promise not to ask."

"Good. You should hurry. She makes the biscuits fresh, and they go quick."

Morgan was already in the truck by the time I was showered and dressed.

I opened the driver's side door.

"You're late."

"Had to shave."

"Still late."

"Had to wash too. And get dressed. Unless of course you expected me to go naked."

He cocked his mouth to the side. "Is that a question or an option?"

I rolled my eyes.

"You should get a watch."

"I have a watch." I showed him.

"A better watch."

"This one cost five hundred bucks. I can't afford a better one." I started the truck, and it belched a cloud of white smoke.

"You're burning oil. Need to get Jenny to take a look at it."

"I already looked at it. It's nothing serious."

Gravel crunched under the tires. Every so often, we'd hit a rut and bounce on the seats.

"Shocks are bad."

"What's with you this morning?"

Morgan flicked thoughts. Then he did something I'd only seen him do when he had the run-in with the truck driver. He rocked. Over and over, Morgan flicked thoughts and rocked in his seat.

I stopped the truck. "What's going on?"

"You really should take better care of your truck. You're lucky to have it. If I had a truck, I'd fix an oil leak, no matter how small."

I drummed my fingers on the steering wheel. "Then maybe you should get Jenny to find you one. I'm sure she could get good deal."

"Can't drive."

"It's not that hard."

"Can't tie my shoes either. Or tell left from right. Neither one of those is hard."

He had me there. "And I can't make the beautiful works of art like you."

Morgan fell still. "I could teach you."

"I'm not sure it would work, but I could try, I guess."

He nodded.

"Would you like for me to give you some driving lessons?"

"Can't drive."

"Yeah, you said that."

"You sure?"

"I wouldn't ask if I wasn't."

"Hasn't gone well before."

"Well, maybe this time it will."

He nodded. He kept nodding. Then he went back to rocking in his seat.

"Morgan?"

"We should get going, or they'll be out of biscuits."

"What's wrong?"

"If they run out of biscuits, we'll have to settle for waffles."

I put the truck in park.

"We'll be late."

"Then you'd better start talking. About something besides biscuits and the fact my truck leaks oil."

His shoulder jerked.

"I told you I'd go get tested."

A high-pitched cry ticked out of the back of his throat. It snapped off with another hard twitch that jerked his entire torso.

I watched helplessly as Morgan fought with the onslaught of tics. I wanted to comfort him, but I was afraid it would only make things worse. The rumble of the truck engine kept us company for a good five minutes. His body calmed until he was only rocking and flicking thoughts.

A tractor drove by on the road in front of us, carrying a round bale of hay.

Morgan pulled a folded sheet of paper from his pocket. Wrinkles covered the surface. He held it out to me.

I took it and opened it up. The letterhead was from the Alamo Prison Facility. It was a notice of a parole hearing.

113

"They sent me a letter." Morgan's voice was flat. He no longer rocked, but his hand remained close to his temple. "They're gonna let him out."

"That's not what this means."

"They're going to let him out." He thumped his fist against the door. "After everything they promised."

"It's a hearing. It doesn't mean they're going to grant him parole."

"He'll come back here." Morgan's shoulder jerked. "He'll come back here, Grant."

"You can contest it, you know." I glanced at the piece of paper. "You've got six almost seven months. You could take time off from Toolies. I'll even drive you there." Atlanta was a good four hours away, but I'd do it.

"I can't."

"They have to let you dispute it."

"I can't."

"Why not?"

"Because I can't. I can't, Grant. I just can't." The flush in his cheeks hardened his features. "He knows I can't. Everyone knows I can't."

"Do you have a lawyer?"

Morgan flicked thoughts.

"Do you have a lawyer?"

"No."

"Then we'll get you one."

"They cost money I don't have."

They were expensive. The good ones were really expensive. My retainer with Harriet Price was a hard hundred grand. And I hadn't even needed her beyond a phone consultation yet.

"I'll make some calls." I'd have to use my standard account. There wasn't much there, thirty grand maybe. If Harriet wanted more, then I'd be shit out of luck. Touching the offshore accounts would be like ringing a dinner bell. Jeff and all his frat boys would be on my doorstep by morning.

"No."

"Look, you need a lawyer. I have a lawyer."

"No."

I slammed my hand against the steering wheel. "Yes."

Morgan fell still again.

"I'm sorry." I scrubbed my jaw. "I didn't mean to yell, it's just…" I took a breath. "We all need help sometimes, Morgan. Everyone. I want to help you. Please, let me."

"I can't leave Durstrand. I just can't."

I'd be a liar if I claimed to understand why. So I said, "If Ms. Price insists on a face to face, we'll figure something out."

Morgan dropped his chin to his chest.

"Can I keep this in case she needs me to fax it?"

He nodded.

"Try not to worry. It'll work out." And if it didn't, killing Dillon wouldn't be a problem. It went against everything I believed in and left me worried that maybe I wasn't as different from Lorado as I claimed.

I could only hope it wouldn't come to that.

I put the truck in gear and the transmission clinked.

"Probably should get that checked."

I put the truck back in park, and slid over next to Morgan. He startled when I cupped his face and tilted his chin up. I kissed him, long, slow. Right there in the driveway, I made love to his mouth. I worshiped his exhales. I savored his taste.

And in all my years, I'd never kissed anyone like I did him. I never wanted to. But Morgan wasn't just anyone.

When we broke apart, the tension was gone from his body and he all but melted in my arms.

"Why?" The question was barely a whisper.

"Why what?"

"Why would you do that?"

I thought a moment. When I came up with nothing, I knew better than to try and lie. "I'm not sure."

He lifted his gaze. The amount of trust in his eyes made it hard for me to breathe. Resignation was the last thing I'd expected.

Not just because I was in awe but because I knew how dangerous it was for him to hand over that kind of power. The fact he could do it so easily after a terrible experience made me realize Morgan was far stronger than I'd ever given him credit for.

Morgan brushed his lips against mine. "We should go."

"Or they'll run out of biscuits."

"And we'll have to eat waffles."

"Can't have that."

"Would be a waste of gas."

I scooted back over to my side and we turned onto the street.

****

Fran's was one of those mom-and-pop places so "mom-and-pop" they'd started out as a house and at some point evolved into a place of business.

It wasn't located on a back road, but it definitely wasn't in town. Although, *in town* for Durstrand, wasn't much more than a drug store, grocery store, and a gas station edged by a thirty mile stretch of highway leading into Maysville.

I parked under a large oak tree. There was a swing dangling from one of the branches some ten feet off the ground. Over the years, bark had swallowed the rusted chains wrapped around the limbs and weather had rotted the wooden seat.

Morgan and I didn't speak for the entire drive, but the aura of isolation he'd worn was gone.

A cool breeze and warm sun followed us to the front door. An elderly man helped his wife up onto the porch. I held open the door while he maneuvered her and her walker inside.

"That was very gallant of you, Grant." The normality in Morgan's voice washed away my lingering apprehension. He cut around me and I followed him.

Salt, buttermilk, and a hundred years' worth of aged wood saturated the air. Pale blue walls reflected the unrestricted light pouring in from the windows across old rickety tables and mismatched chairs.

And they say time travel isn't possible.

Even some of the patrons looked like they'd fallen out of the early 1900s, dressed in overalls, flannel shirts, and floral print dresses. The sprinkling of young people with more modern taste were the only cracks in the illusion.

A sign at the front read *Seat Yourself.* I scanned the room. Some people looked up from their meals. It wasn't the quick kind of glance, but one of those *I've seen you before but where?*

"There are empty spots over there." I tipped my head in the direction of the vacant tables.

Morgan flicked thoughts. "Won't work." Before I could ask why, he yelled out, "Miranda." One of the waitresses glanced our way, then went to the back.

Morgan rocked on his feet.

"You sure you want to do this?" I said.

"Yes."

"Miranda." Morgan didn't seem to give a shit just how loud he yelled.

Two men in bright orange vests gave Morgan a dirty look. I caught the redhead's gaze. The battle lasted all of three seconds before he went back to picking at his ham and eggs.

"Miranda."

"Is she in the back?" I said.

"Miranda."

"Do you want me to go look?" I took a step, and Morgan grabbed my arm.

He started to yell again when a dark-skinned middle-aged woman came barreling in from the back. "Hold your horses, Morgan Kade." She took him by the elbow and led him around the tables.

"What took you so long?" Morgan said.

"I was up to my elbows in dough."

"You shouldn't take so long."

"And you should'a called. We've had this conversation before. You call, I'll meet you out front, and you won't have no need of yell'n your lungs out." She looked over her shoulder at me. "You must be Grant."

"Yes, ma'am." I wasn't one for forgetting a face, and I'd never met her.

"I'm Miranda Cane." She cut me a sly smile and ran a look over me. I had the sudden urge to make sure I hadn't forgotten to zip my fly.

A waitress handing out plates to customers paused and watched us go by.

Three elderly women sitting at another table had stopped eating. They tracked us until we reached a hall going—I had no idea where.

The narrow space took us to a back room where the tables were long benches and the chairs plastic. There was a snack machine and a microwave on a small piece of counter against the wall.

"Have a seat." Miranda gestured to me. "I'll go get you a menu, unless you know what you want."

"Biscuits," Morgan said. "Gravy, two eggs scrambled, three pieces of bacon, and orange juice."

"I was talking to your boyfriend, Morgan. Everyone knows what you want."

116

She batted her eyes at me.

"Uh, a menu. Thanks."

"Coffee?"

"Sure."

She left, and I sat. "Is this the break room?"

Morgan scanned the room. "I hadn't noticed."

"You didn't…" I caught a glimpse of his smile. "Quit yanking my chain."

"But you're so easy, Grant. Not that I'm complaining." Morgan's shoulder jerked. "Yes, it's the break room."

"Is there a reason we're back here?"

He fluttered his fingers. "It can get too crowded out there. Loud. Bright. Too much going on. Quieter back here."

"You work at Toolies when it's crowded."

He nodded. Then he tapped his ear. "Earbuds. Keep the music loud enough to drown most of it out. It helps I'm there all the time. But sometimes when there are a lot of new people, I stay in the back and wash dishes."

Miranda returned with our drinks and a menu.

"I changed my mind," I said. "I'll have what Morgan's having."

"Sure thing." She hovered a moment at the end of the table before vanishing back down the hall.

"Is it my imagination, or is she staring at me?"

"She's staring." Morgan moved the napkin dispenser from the center of the table to the edge. "When can you teach me to drive? I was thinking Sunday. Early afternoon. It's supposed to rain on Saturday."

I thought a moment. "Sunday should work."

"What time? Twelve would be good. Unless you want to do it earlier. I get up early, as you know, so we can do it at nine if you want. But if you don't, I can work on a few sculptures till you come over."

"Nine works for me."

Morgan nodded. Then he moved the napkin dispenser to the opposite side.

I picked up one of the straws Miranda left behind. "Want one?"

"Thanks." Morgan took it. "Since you're retired, what are you going to do this week?"

"I have a kitchen sink needing to be plumbed." Just one of many unfinished projects. Thing was, I really didn't care if I went back home or not. I could have spent days locked up in a room with Morgan. I wouldn't even need food and water as long as I had a bottle of lubricant.

"Get your head out of the gutter, Grant."

I laughed. "You a mind reader now?"

"Don't have to be."

"Then how would you know when I was thinking dirty?"

"Your eye twitches."

"My eye twitches?"

"Yeah."

"Should my bullshitamometer be sounding off?"

"Don't know. Might wanna check into getting a new one when you replace your watch."

117

I threw an unopened creamer at him, and he ducked. With his head down, I don't even know how he saw it coming. Then again, this was a man who could *hear* light.

And just like that, I felt unworthy of his presence. It was silly, 'cause I knew damn well Morgan would never think such a thing. Which made it all the more difficult to feel any other way.

I took a sip of my coffee. It was perfect.

"Grant."

"Yeah?"

"I—"

Miranda walked in with our food balanced on her arm. "Here you go." She set a plate in front of me, but Morgan's plate she turned putting the bacon on the right, the eggs on the left, the bowl of gravy at the top, leaving the two biscuits lined up in the center.

Morgan stared.

"Oh, honey, what did I forget?"

"It's all wrong."

"Wrong? How could it be wrong? I put everything just like you like it."

"That's on Tuesdays, today is Thursday."

Her mouth fell open. She looked at me. I have no idea why. It's not like I knew.

Miranda exhaled defeat and started to reach for the plate. Morgan tipped his head just enough to flash a smile. He fluttered a hand at his temple, and she slapped him on the shoulder.

"Wise ass."

"Not my fault you don't pay attention."

"Eat your breakfast."

Morgan held out a hand.

"What?"

"Silverware."

Miranda patted down the pocket of her apron and came back with paper wrapped eating utensils. "I ought to make you eat with your fingers, but I don't want to have to clean up the mess." Her tone was serious, but her eyes laughed. To me, she said, "I sure hope you can keep him in line. He gives me more gray hairs than my kids ever did."

Before I had a chance to reply, she was gone.

"That was mean." But I still grinned.

"She's used to it."

"Do you make a habit of picking on waitresses?"

"Nope. Just Miranda." He ate his eggs.

"You two must go back a ways."

His shoulder jerked and he lost his bite of eggs onto the table. Morgan didn't miss a beat. He scooped them up and popped them in his mouth. "She and Lori used to work together as housekeepers for some folks. After Lori quit, Miranda would come by to help out. You know, clean house, help do the shopping."

From what little I'd learned about Morgan, I was pretty sure why. What Morgan said next confirmed it.

"I was a lot of work. Lori never said so. But I know I was."

"She sounds like she was a remarkable woman."

He nodded.

I ate, and Morgan ate. I couldn't help but wonder how Lori paid the bills. Most folks didn't clean other people's houses for fun. So she probably didn't have a savings or some kind of inheritance to live off of.

Morgan used a knife to dissect his biscuit. He ate the outer crust first, then the soft insides. Each bite was paired with a dab of gravy and a bit of bacon.

When he was halfway done, he put down his fork. The tic in his shoulder was accompanied by a flutter of his hand next to his temple. I waited for him to gain control. It didn't take as long as it did in the truck.

Another few moments went by before he spoke. "I met Dillon when he came into Toolies. I think I was in love with him before he even sat down in one of the booths. Lori asked me not to leave with him, but I did. It didn't take me long to figure out I was just a hole for him to fuck. It started small. First he complained about how I embarrassed him in front of his friends, then he accused me of sleeping around, then he hit." A whine ticked out of Morgan's throat. It stopped. "I wanted to go home. I would have called Lori, but he didn't have a landline and always took his cell with him. Things went really bad when he caught me trying to sneak out." Another series of muscle spasms assaulted Morgan. "He dragged me back up the stairs. I screamed for help, and no one opened their door. He turned up the music to drown out the rest. They said it was three days or so before anyone found me. And only because he'd left the music on and the landlord couldn't get anyone to answer the door. But I don't remember any of that because I went away."

Went away. Last night in the grips of that dream Morgan had went away. It seemed too simple of an explanation, but I couldn't think of a better one.

"He would have gotten more time if I could have testified. But I couldn't, so they let him plead out." He took a bite of his eggs. "That's what happened. Now you don't have to ask."

What did I say? Thank you for telling me? It felt like an insult.

The thought of Morgan lying broken for three days did something to me. I don't even know what, but it was a physical shift as loud and hard as the truck's transmission.

"Will you do me a favor?" Morgan took a sip of his orange juice.

I nodded because I didn't trust myself to speak. My mind was still rolling over the things he'd told me. And I'd seen enough beatings in my life to fuel my imagination.

"My order of bottles will be at the post today. I found red ones. Not the brown red or the orange red, but real red, like cherries. I've never had glass that color before. I ordered a dozen, so the box will be big. Usually I ask Jenny to pick them up, but I thought if you were going to be in town—"

"Yes." My voice didn't even crack.

Morgan nodded again. "You can bring them by whenever."

"Sure thing." I forced myself to take a few more bites, but the food had lost its flavor and I'd lost my appetite.

Years ago, when I first got into the business, Eugene told me every man has a limit. No matter how hard you try to be respectable. After twenty years of smuggling, I'd never hit mine. I got out because I didn't want to discover what it was.

Who would have thought I'd find it in a Podunk town in the middle of nowhere, in the form of a beautiful man with the most incredible eyes? Thanks to Durstrand, that monster I'd tried so hard not to become would finally win.

The scary part was, I had no desire to fight it. If anything, I embraced the cold hate. I

119

could only hope the bastard did not get out. If he did, he and I were going to have a talk.

And only one of us would walk away.

****

After I dropped Morgan off at home, I called Harriet. She was in court so I left a message with her secretary.

It wasn't until I pulled into the post office parking lot it occurred to me they might not give me Morgan's package without some sort of slip. I decided to go see before making a trip back to Morgan's.

There weren't many people waiting in line, but the tight confines of the squat building forced everyone shoulder to shoulder. The old man trying to get his mail out of his post office box had to stand sideways. He still managed to clock himself in the head with the door when the lady with the baby on her hip bumped it with her shoulder.

I grabbed the door to keep it from closing again and smashing his fingers. "Thank you," he said.

"No problem."

He squeezed his way back through the group of people to the door. I stepped in line behind the lady with the kid. What looked like strawberry jam made a circle around the infant's mouth.

Two older ladies worked the front desk. In between transactions, they exchanged updates about their lives with the people as they got to the counter. What should have taken ten minutes tops, five if they hadn't stopped to bicker in between every other customer, turned into a half hour. The young man wearing overalls said his good-byes and squeezed his way back through the line to the door.

I stepped up to the counter beside the woman with the infant exchanging small talk with the other clerk.

"And how can I help you?" The woman was short, round, and had enough smile lines to suggest she rarely did anything else.

"I'm here to pick up a package for a friend, Morgan Kade."

The woman raised her eyebrows. "You're the fella who bought the old Anderson place?"

"Yes, ma'am."

She exchanged a look with her short friend who hurried into the back. Then she resumed staring. The smile on her face turned into a grin. "So, where you from?"

The casual conversation going on between the other townfolks standing in line stopped and an odd hush filled the room. I glanced over my shoulder. They all stared at me.

"Uh, Chicago."

"You don't talk funny."

"Originally from Alabama. Guess I never lost the accent."

An elderly lady to my right barked a laugh. "Well that explains it. He's one of those corn-fed boys." There was a murmur of agreement.

"How you do you like living in Durstrand?" the post lady said.

The weight of a dozen or more stares continued to beat at my back. "It's quiet." And suddenly somewhat scary.

There was a shuffle from around the corner and the other clerk came back with a box and a tray balanced on top. She put everything on the counter.

"You think you could take these with you too? Morgan won't pick them up." She put down the tray. A pile of certified letters threatened to spill over the side.

"He'll have to sign for those." That from the little old lady. She was so close now her exhale brushed my arm.

"Marge." The clerk huffed. "I know how to do my job."

Marge tapped my shin with her cane. "You sure'a sturdy fella."

Someone in the back laughed. Before I could look, the woman with infant said, "You single?" She pushed back a lock of mangled hair. It slid back into place and her kid resumed chewing the knotted ends.

"He's gay, Beth," said the short clerk in the matter-of-fact tone of someone pointing out the obvious.

"So?" Beth continued to watch me with doe eyes.

"That means he don't like the ladyfolk."

The old lady tapped the back of my knee with her cane. "Definitely sturdy."

"Here." The clerk gave me a pen. "Just sign these right quick."

Quick? There had to be twenty or more. I started to inch down to the end of the counter so the guy behind me could get his stuff.

The clerk patted my hand. "You're fine right here, honey."

"I don't want to hold any one up."

"I ain't got nowhere to be." That from the guy behind me. "You just take your time there, son."

"Besides, there ain't no room down there anyhow." The old lady beside me nudged the boy behind her, and he moved into the few inches of space and propped his elbow on the counter. "See?"

No one had pitchforks or matches out, so that was a good sign. Thing was, I didn't get a single aggressive vibe from any of them.

I set to work signing the cards. All the while the crowd of people grew one by one. A ripple of whispers traveled to the back of the line, cutting off any questions the new arrivals asked.

Until one guy. "Like I give a shit. Tell him to get out of the way, I've got better things to do than stand around watching some faggot pick up another faggot's mail." Everyone turned to look at him.

Pretty sad when that kind of reaction unnerved me far less than the silence.

"Chad Grizzle," the old lady with the cane said. "You watch your mouth."

"Guess what, Mrs. White, I ain't in the third grade anymore so you can just shut your flap."

I would probably regret it, but I did it anyhow. I turned around. I was one of the taller men there so I had no problem spotting the greasy headed blond. "Hey, you don't talk to a lady that way."

"Lady?" He laughed. "That bitch ain't been a lady since the Stone Age."

I handed the clerk her pen. "Hold that for me for a moment." I maneuvered my way to the back.

The cocky grin on Chad's face wilted with every step closer I got.

He couldn't have been more than twenty-five, but was going on fifty. Between his dirty clothes and unkempt hair, he looked like something scraped out of a Chicago alley.

Smelled about as fresh too.

I nodded at the door. "You mind if we step outside for a moment."

"What for?"

"Because I think you and I have a few things to discuss."

"News flash, faggot, I ain't got shit to say to you, or that old—"

I snatched him by the arm, spun him around, and cranked his elbow back. Chad screamed like a little girl. In my experience, most bullies did.

The black man standing next to the door held it open. "Thank you." I shoved Chad out front.

"You mother fucker, I'm gonna kill you. You goddamned—"

I pinned Chad against the brick wall hard enough to knock the wind out of him. The whites showed around his blue eyes.

"Now, look." I leaned in close to his ear. "If you gotta problem with me, fine, but leave other people out of it."

"Yeah, and what are you gonna do about it?"

I cranked his arm higher between his shoulders. Pain stripped the anger out of his features.

"You may think you're tough, you may even think your scary, but I promise you, you are nothing but a skid mark compared to the men I've killed."

I held his gaze and watched the doubt in his eyes evaporate.

Chad swallowed several time. "Please, don't hurt me."

"I don't think you understand, Chad. I won't hurt you. I will kill you. There is a distinct difference. Do you understand what that difference is, or do I need to give you a demonstration?"

He tried to shake his head and only succeeded in scraping his cheek on the brick.

"Good." I eased off the pressure on his arm. "I'm going to let you go, and you're going to walk in there and apologize to everyone."

A nasty retort formed on his lips. Before he could spit it out, I shoved him back against the wall.

"I'm sorry, were you about to say something?"

His breath shuddered out. "No."

"No, what?" I twisted his thumb. Tears sprang up in his eyes.

"No, sir."

"That's better." I eased off again. "Now, as I was saying. You're going to go back in there and apologize for being rude, then you're going to go home and reflect on your behavior."

He wanted to challenge me. It was right there in his expression. A dark cloud wavering underneath the fear. But he believed me. Or at least he believed me enough.

"Okay." Again he tried to nod. "Okay, okay. I will."

I turned him around. The black man opened the door again. Nothing but silence greeted us as we stepped into the stuffy room.

I let Chad go. He glanced back at me, rubbing his arm.

"Go ahead."

"I'm sorry."

I thumped him on the ear. "Not me, everyone else." And I'm pretty sure he would have rather eaten his boot. "Now."

Chad stared at the floor. "I'm sorry." He started to turn.

"Not so fast." I motioned him back around with a finger. "What do you say to Mrs. White?"

"I'm sorry."

"And what else?"

He gave me a confused look.

"And you promise this will never happen again."

He opened his mouth, then shut it. Chad slumped. "I'm sorry, Mrs. White, and it will never happen again."

"Good boy." I stepped out of his way, and he dove for the door. Chad ran across the parking lot without a look back.

I waded through the clump of people to the desk. Mrs. White patted me on the arm as the clerked handed me back the pen.

"You're such a good man."

I wasn't, but I didn't want to pop her bubble. I finished signing the slips.

The short clerk pushed the box over. Morgan was right, it was heavy. I stacked the mail on top, but the envelopes kept sliding to the edge.

"Here," she put the mail back into the tray. "You take it with you, and bring it back next time you come in."

"Thank you. I will." I nodded at the guy crowding my back. "Pardon me." He stepped aside. Or at least stepped as far as he could.

"Can I ask you one thing before you go?" the clerk said. Her short friend watched me over the edge of her glasses.

"Sure."

"Are you and Morgan going to the movies again anytime soon?"

I swear every person in that room leaned closer.

"Uh…"

"Mr. Newman is gonna be showing the cows The Sound of Music next Friday," Marge said. Then I'll be damned if she didn't grin.

What the hell did I say? Because they sure were waiting for me to say something. "We'll see."

Marge patted me on the arm. "Well, you just let us know."

I faced some scary people in my life, had guns shoved in my face, seen the results of a disgruntled colleague's handiwork, and never ran. Apparently a room full of Durstrand locals could do what bullets had failed at.

I set the box of bottles on the floor on the passenger side of the truck and cranked it up. Everyone in the post office watched me out the window. Even the two mail clerks had squeezed up front. About half of them waved.

With my face on fire, I fled the parking lot.

****

123

A trip into town was the last thing on my list, but I was out of plumber's glue, finishing nails, joist hangers, and just about anything required to hold something together.

I tried sitting around, which led to thoughts of Morgan, which reminded me I was almost out of lubricant. I figured I should probably give my hand a rest and put my ass to work, which meant going back into the shark-infested waters.

If only it was sharks.

There were a few cars in the parking lot, but the inside of the hardware store was a ghost town.

Thank God.

"Well, look what the cat dragged in." Then Berry gave me the look. The same one everyone in the post office had. Come to think of it, so did Miranda, and those people at Fran's.

Shit. Was there anyone who didn't know?

I pointed at him. "Don't start."

He glanced around. "Why, Grant, I have no idea what you're talking about." His attempt to keep a serious face was overrun by his smile.

"Jesus, there wasn't that many people at the drive-in."

Berry laughed. "Don't need to be, son. Word travels fast. Especially now in the age of cell phones."

Aw fuck. It hadn't even dawned on me.

Did I really need supplies this bad? I mean, I had a working sink in the bathroom, and the toilet was good to go. The shower too. And surely those sagging floor joists would hold another six months. Maybe even a year.

But I knew from experience small town memories rarely faded and unless I planned on driving to a whole new place, I needed to buck up.

I took a breath and walked to the counter.

"Here." I took out my list and slid it across the counter. Berry picked it up. I said, "How bad is it?"

The gleam in Berry's eyes went blinding. "You check out YouTube lately?"

Goddamn it, why couldn't I just have gotten shot or something?

"Don't worry, it was too dark to see, and the movie was too loud to hear," he snorted, "...much."

I was not even about to ask just how much could be heard or worse, seen. "Something tells me it's going to be a long time before I can show my face in town."

"Aw, Grant. It ain't that bad. If people can get over Reverend Paul Harley running across the football field wearing nothing but a diaper, they can get over the escapades of young love."

I laughed. "A diaper?"

"Yeah, apparently someone spiked his bottle."

I blinked several times. "Excuse me?"

Berry held up a hand. "You don't want to know." He scanned my list. "C'mon, let's get your stuff."

I followed him to the back.

"So, I guess things are pretty serious between you and Morgan."

Were they? I had my island picked out, my plans of a nice little place with a perfect oceanfront view and sunsets over clear blue water. A future Morgan wasn't a part of.

Berry held open the door to the outside lumberyard.

"I suppose." How did two words feel so incomplete?

"You suppose?"

"Morgan's young. I'm sure he'll get tired of me."

Berry stopped so fast I almost ran over him. "Morgan will get tired of you?"

No, he wouldn't. I don't know why that was so easy to believe. It had to be the way he looked at me. Or how I thought he looked at me. I counted the two by fours stacked on the shelf to my right.

"We've only known each other for a few weeks." Because I'd done my damnedest to avoid him.

I counted the two by sixes, all the while Berry stared.

"Ah hell, Berry, I don't know." There. I said it.

He shook his head at me and continued down the aisle to the back wall where plastic bins were stacked with every kind of joist bracket known to man.

"You need two by sixes or two by eights? You didn't specify on your list."

I picked up one of the brackets. "What if it's a mistake?"

"Does it feel like one?"

"No. But I've been wrong before." And it almost got me killed and still might put me in prison.

"Did what you had before feel anything like what you have now?"

I thought a moment. "No."

"Then I'd say maybe this time you got it right."

"There's no way for me to know that, yet."

"'Cause you've only known each other for a few weeks?"

"Yeah."

Berry smirked. "You like chitlins?"

"What does—"

"Just answer the question."

"Not really."

"How many times did you have to eat'em before you figure out you didn't like 'em?"

"Once."

"You like pancakes?"

"I appreciate the analogy—"

"Answer the question, Grant."

"Yeah, they can be pretty good."

"And how many times did you have to eat those before you figured it out?"

"It's not the same."

"Why?"

"Because it's food. You can't compare loving someone to what you like to eat."

"Don't know." He scratched his chin. "Sounds about the same to me."

"You're kidding."

"Do I look like I'm kidding?"

"Then explain to me how eating even comes close."

Berry leaned against the bins. "Well, last time I checked, if you don't eat, you starve to death. Same thing happens when you don't love, only you starve to death on the inside instead of the outside. Either way you die. So seems to me eat'n and love'n have a lot more in common than you think."

And Morgan satisfied a hunger I'd never been aware of. Three years was more than enough time to decide whether or not we were right for each other. Thing is, I didn't need three years. I don't even think I needed three more days.

Could any Seychelles sunset be nearly as beautiful as him?

"Two by eights." I dropped the bracket I held back in the bin. "Better double the count. I'll probably be ready to replace the back porch by spring."

"Gonna have a sale on decking sometime in January." He took a paper bag off the shelf on the wall and shook it out. "Mark it on your calendar."

"I'll do that."

"And Grant?"

"Yeah?"

"Whatever it is holding you back won't love you half as much as Morgan. Later on if you decide I'm wrong, I'm sure, whatever it is you think you'll miss, will still be there waiting on you."

****

I paid for my supplies and carried them to the truck. It was still early enough for the lunch crowd to linger around Toolies. Old cars, new cars, but mostly family cars cluttered the parking lot about a block down. A stark contrast to after dark when it was mostly trucks: pickups in the lot, semis across the street at the rest stop, a few beat-up Buicks and shiny sedans belonging to those passing through.

Would showing up seem clingy? I didn't know. But I was suddenly thirsty and seeing Morgan was the only thing that would quench it.

"That shack you're working on is starting to resemble a house." Jeff took off his sunglasses and tucked them inside his jacket.

How the hell did I miss him walking up behind me? I was losing my touch. Or getting too comfortable. Either of which could get me killed. "What the hell do you want?"

"Was driving by, saw your truck, thought I'd stop and say hello."

Don't ask me what possessed me to do it, but I stuck my finger in the air.

Jeff made a face. "What are you doing?"

"Hush, I'm checking the weather."

"The weather?"

"Yeah, pretty neat trick, maybe you should try it."

He laughed. "And how the hell does sticking your finger in the air tell you what the weather is going to be?"

I shrugged. "Hell if I know. It just works. Go ahead, try it."

"No, thanks."

"C'mon, Jeff, humor me here. It's a neat trick. If nothing else, you'll have something to take back home and show the office folk."

"You cannot tell the weather that way."

"How do you know? You haven't tried."

126

He stuck his finger in the air. "This is stupid."

"Not working?"

"No."

I looked at my finger. "Don't know, seems to be working for me."

He started to lower his hand.

"Maybe you should try the other one."

"I'm not trying the other one."

"But I'm trying to teach you something, Jeff."

He stuck his other one in the air. "Still not working."

I snapped my fingers. "Ah hell, I know why it isn't working."

"Why's that?"

"I went and got my barometer and bullshitometer mixed up."

Jeff glanced up at his hand and dropped it. "You're an asshole, anyone ever tell you that?"

"Lots a folks have, but lucky for me, their opinion doesn't matter. Now what do you want?"

He waved a hand in the direction of Toolies. "Do you think we could go sit down and have a cup of coffee?"

"No."

"You need to reconsider."

"Why?"

"I got some news on Ulrich for starters."

I ran a bungee cord around the box in the back. Not because anything would be damaged if it slid across the bed, but to give me a reason to look away so Jeff wouldn't see the flicker of fear I knew showed in my face.

"Fine."

"You want to take my car?"

"It's less than a block. I'll walk." I headed across the street, and he followed. "Thought you were driving."

"Like you said, less than a block." If there'd been more cars, I might have had a chance at one of them hitting him. But the cars currently present were parked in the front of Toolies.

I jerked open the door and the bells clanged hard enough to make a few people look up. I hoped to God none of them recognized me. Then a few of them didn't look away.

Shit.

"C'mon." I found a booth in the back near the bathrooms.

Heads turned and eyes followed me across the room.

"Why are those people staring at us?" Jeff slid into the booth.

"They're not staring at us. They're staring at me."

"All right, then why are they staring at you?"

"I'm popular." I picked up a menu. I wasn't really hungry, but it gave me something to do.

A woman in the booth behind Jeff looked over the top. "Hi." She waved at me. "Uh, I know this is crazy and all, but I was wondering, can I have your autograph?"

Again, what did I say? No? I guess I could have. Maybe it was the look on Jeff's face that made me say, "I don't have anything to write on."

"Oh, I got something, just hang on." There was a rustle, then she reappeared with a book in her hands. "Would you mind?" She handed it to Jeff. He glanced at the cover before he passed it over. Lucky me, she already had a pen stuck in the pages.

"The Kama Sutra?" Jeff looked at me when he said it.

I opened it.

"No, no, the front," the lady said. "You know where everyone can see it."

I wrote my name.

"Will you put something like, good luck or with love, you know, make it personal?"

I wrote good luck and with love.

Jeff passed everything back. She hugged it to her chest. "Oh my God, my husband will be so pissed. Maybe it will inspire him, you know…" She dropped her voice. With half the restaurant tuning in, I doubt it did much good. "Spice things up a bit. Thank you so much." She kissed the book and ducked back behind the booth.

I went back to looking at the menu. Jeff pulled it down. "And what exactly did you do to get popular?"

The waitress saved me. "Hey there, Grant." She flicked a look at Jeff then back. I could practically see the question rolling through her head. *Who the hell is that?* "You want me to let Morgan know you're here?"

Just hearing his name soothed something inside me. "Sure."

"If I do, you gotta behave? This is the family hour."

"Scouts honor."

She giggled. "So what do you fellas want to drink?"

"Iced tea, no sugar," Jeff said.

"Iced tea, with sugar."

She raised her eyebrows. Apparently my disdain for my lunch date came through loud and clear. "I'll be right back to get your order." She left.

Jeff continued to watch the lunch crowd. They continued to watch us.

I folded my arms on the table. "All right, I'm here. Talk."

"Uh, yeah."

"Earth to Jeff. Start talking or leave so I can eat my lunch in peace."

He cast one more uneasy look around. "I got a call from the office. They picked up Ulrich last night."

"Where?"

"California."

"That's nowhere near here." In fact, he couldn't get much farther unless they'd found him in Hawaii.

"Yeah."

"If Lorado wanted him to kill me, then why would he be in California?"

"Don't know." He plucked packets of artificial sweetener from the holder next to the bottle of ketchup.

"How come you sound disappointed?"

"More like worried."

"Why?"

128

"Because we don't know why he was there."

"Vacation?"

Jeff rolled a look up at me. "I don't think he's the vacationing type."

"Well if he's on the opposite coast, then it's unlikely he's taken any kind of job concerning—"

Our waitress came back with our drink. "You want something to eat, Grant?"

"Hamburger. Fries."

"Everything on it?"

"Yes, ma'am."

She pinched my cheek. "You're so sweet, no wonder Morgan *likes* you so much." She flicked Jeff a strained smile. "Be right back with your burger."

"Excuse me," Jeff said. "I'd like a burger as well."

She gave him another one of those looks. "Sorry, we're all out."

"He just ordered one?"

"Last one. Lucky man." She sauntered off.

I bit the inside of my cheek to keep from smiling.

Jeff turned his confused expression on me. "What just happened there?"

I shrugged. "They ran out of burgers."

"Yeah, right." Jeff sprinkled his packs of sweetener into his drink and stirred it with his straw.

"You were saying?"

"Yeah. Airport security picked Ulrich up on a flight from Mexico."

"I didn't think smuggling was in his job description."

"He wasn't smuggling anything."

"Then why did they pick him up?"

"Homeland Security. They can detain anyone who looks suspicious. I doubt they'll get to keep him long. As soon as his lawyer finds out, he'll be on a flight home." Jeff took a sip of his tea and abruptly spit it back out into the glass. "Jesus." He grabbed a couple of napkins and gagged into them.

"What's wrong?"

"It's practically saltwater."

Our waitress whisked by. Jeff waved at her, but she turned her back.

"Who the hell runs this place?"

I pointed to Jessie at the bar. "Him."

"He needs to have a talk with his help."

"I'm sure she just missed you."

Jeff pushed the glass of salty tea away. "And that?"

"Sugar and salt are both white. Maybe they got it mixed up." I caught our waitress's eye. She came right over. "What'cha need, honey?"

"I think they messed up on his drink."

The look of surprise on her face was so fake it might as well be painted on. "Oh, gee. I'm sorry about that. I'll bring you another."

Before she could go, I motioned her closer. She leaned down. I whispered, "Go easy on him, he's a prick, but he's just doing his job."

She pinched my cheek again. "Like I said, so sweet." She sauntered off.

"What did you say to her?"

"That—"

"Hey, I know you. You're that guy on the video." The kid couldn't have been more than sixteen. He grinned and shook his finger at me. "Yeah, yeah, oh man." He snatched his hat off his head. "Will you sign this for me?"

I took the cap. "I don't have pen."

The lady in the booth behind Jeff popped back up. "Here ya go." She gave the pen to the boy, he gave it to me.

"Brady Johnson," A woman in a floral dress pushed her way between the tables.

"Look, ma, it's—"

She grabbed him by the ear. "What the hell do you think you're doing?"

"I just wanted his autograph."

She gave me a wide-eyed look. Her gaze fell to the hat in my hand, and she snatched it away. "Get out there to the car, right now."

The kid ducked but not quick enough to avoid a slap to the side of the head with his hat. "Ma…"

"Don't ma me. You have no business consorting with the likes of him. And this Sunday, you are going to church." The clang of the bells followed her out the door.

A middle-aged carbon copy of the kid in jeans and T-shirt stopped by. He was too old to be the kid's brother, so there was only choice left.

He watched his wife shove their son across the parking lot. "You still got that pen?" The toothpick in his mouth went from one side or the other.

"Uh…"

He took off his hat. "Put 'To Bill.'"

I did.

"And a bunch of X's after your name. You know, like Xs and Os."

With great reluctance, I did that too. He took the hat and put it on. Then he left.

You could hear the lady scream all the way from inside the restaurant.

Of course, the place going dead silent didn't help.

The lady behind Jeff said, "Can I have my pen back?"

I handed it to Jeff; he handed it to her.

The guy wrestled his raging wife into the car and they drove off. Everyone turned back to their meals, and the hum of conversation resumed.

"What the hell was that?" Jeff turned back to me.

I drank some of my tea.

"Grant?"

"You don't want to know."

"Uh, yeah, I do."

"Do you have anything interesting to say about Ulrich, or are you just wasting my time again?"

He blew out a breath that popped his cheeks. "Nothing other than we have no idea why he was in California."

"So you're wasting my time?"

130

"No, I was hoping you might have some ideas about what kind of business Lorado would send him there for."

I had a few. But hell if I was going to share them with Jeff. "No idea."

"Grant."

"Do you need me to spell it out for you?"

Jeff leaned in close. "Look, I'm trying to watch out for you. I can't do that if I don't have information on the guy who's coming after you."

"If he's in California, he's not coming after me."

Jeff sat back.

Our waitress arrived with food and drinks. She put a plate in front of Jeff. "I thought you said you were out?"

"My mistake." She handed him his drink. "Burger with everything." She handed me mine.

"Looks great, thanks."

"Morgan will be out in a minute, he's finishing up the dishes." Jessie called for her. "Oops, gotta go, boss needs something."

Jeff sipped his tea.

"Is it all right?" I squeezed some ketchup out on my plate.

"Yeah." He picked up the bun on his burger. Poked at it. Looked at the underside.

"Problem?" I ate a fry.

"Just making sure they didn't make another *mistake*." He poured a new packet of sweetener into his tea. "Who's Morgan?"

I took a bite of my burger, stalling. But why? The answer was obvious. I knew Jeff would have the same first impression I did. The knowledge pissed me off. Not at him, but at myself.

Because I had nothing to be ashamed of. And neither did Morgan.

"The guy I'm dating."

"You're dating?"

"Yup."

Jeff watched me over the edge of his glass while he took a drink.

"What's that look for?"

"I don't know. I just didn't think you'd get into another relationship, seeing you don't plan on sticking around."

I pointed a fry at him. "And who says I'm going anywhere?"

"C'mon, Grant." He laughed. "We both know as soon as the heat dies down, you'll be on a plane to some faraway island where Uncle Sam can't reach you."

"Really?"

"Yeah, really."

"Is that why you guys are following me around? Because you think I'm going to disappear?"

"Not think, know."

I bit the fry in half. "In case you missed it, I bought a house."

"A shack."

"When I'm done restoring said shack, it will make your downtown apartment look like a shit hole."

"We know about the money."

I held his gaze. "What money?"

"The offshore bank accounts."

"I have an offshore bank account?"

"*Accounts.*"

"You make it sound like there's more than one."

"Stop playing dumb."

"You wouldn't happen to have account numbers would you? 'Cause if I've got money out there, I sure could use it. Do you have any idea how much a two by eight costs?"

"Stop it, Grant."

"Not to mention wiring. The price of copper has gone through the roof."

Jeff hit the table with his fist hard enough to slosh our drinks. "I'm trying to help you, all right? If it wasn't for me, you'd be in jail right now. I've convinced the higher-ups you'll cooperate. That's the only reason you aren't in cuffs." Every word came out on a hiss.

"First off," I pointed a fry at him. "I haven't done anything to get arrested for. Second, you don't have that kind of pull. If your superiors wanted to arrest me, we'd be in a little gray room with a one-way window right now." I popped the rest of my fry into my mouth and chewed. All the while I smiled.

Jeff flopped back into his seat and proceeded to stab the glob of ketchup on his plate with a french fry.

Morgan walked up and slid in next to me. His wayward hand fluttered by his temple.

Jeff's cursory glance turned into an all-out stare.

"Jeff, Morgan, Morgan, this is Agent Jeff Shaldon with the FBI. He and I go way back." Morgan didn't look up. He stole a fry from my plate and ate it.

"We still on for tomorrow?" I said.

Morgan tipped his head. His smile was subtle but still blinding. "Don't be late."

"Wouldn't dream of it."

A tic pulled at Morgan's shoulder.

"Grant?" Jeff flicked a look from Morgan to me. "You two are dating?"

"That's what I said."

Jeff propped his elbow on the table and messaged his temple.

"Something wrong?" I narrowed a look at Jeff.

"You really have to ask."

"If I didn't, I wouldn't have."

"Do you think dating this…" He glanced at Morgan. "Young man, is appropriate?"

"He's twenty-four, well over the legal age."

"Twenty-five next month." Morgan snapped his fingers, then tossed thoughts.

"You didn't tell me you had a birthday coming up."

"You didn't ask."

"I didn't know I was supposed to."

"Well, now you know." Someone yelled for Morgan in the back. "I better go see what they want. Tomorrow, nine sharp Driving lessons. My place. Set your watch. Might want to get a new one."

"I won't be late. Go."

Morgan flashed me a wicked grin, then slid out of the booth. I couldn't take my eyes off him until he was gone.

"Grant."

"What?"

"You're sleeping with him?"

"That's a bit personal, don't you think?"

"What the hell is wrong with you?"

"Nothing that I'm aware of."

"What do his parents say?"

"He doesn't have any."

"Then whoever takes care of him."

I shook my head. "Lives alone."

"Is that why you think you can take advantage of him?"

"No one is taking advantage of Morgan." I reached for my burger, and Jeff pulled my plate out of reach.

"You're having sex with a mentally disabled kid."

"Sorry to interrupt." Our waitress raked a look over Jeff. "I thought I would drop by and see if you needed anything."

"More tea." Jeff pushed his glass over.

She turned to me, and her cheery voice was back. "Need anything?"

"No, thanks, I'm good."

She left without taking Jeff's glass.

He frowned. "What the hell is with her?"

"Must be something in the air." I pulled my plate back over. "Your burger's getting cold."

Jeff propped his elbow on the table and held his chin. His frown peeked at me from between his fingers. "I don't know what's happened to you, Grant, but it isn't good."

"What do you mean? I feel great. Nice town, friendly people." I leaned across the table. "Best sex I've had in my entire life. I mean Morgan does this thing with his tongue…"

"Jesus." Jeff jerked back. I wanted to be pissed for the look of disgust he gave me. But six weeks ago, I probably would have reacted the same way. Of course six weeks ago, I still had visions of pristine beaches and living the highlife.

Every passing second, oceanfront scenery seemed less and less appealing.

"I appreciate everything you've done." I said. "Keeping up with Ulrich and letting me know where he is. It's a relief to know it isn't here. As for why he's in Cali?" I shrugged. "I've got nothing to tell you, and even if I did—"

"You wouldn't."

"Yup."

Morgan came out from the back with a box tucked under his arm.

Jeff's angry expression turned to pity. "And I hope you at least come to your senses."

He stood. Morgan held out the box. "Take it."

Jeff did. "Why are you giving me a box of toothpicks?"

"Well, I know you don't think I'm smart."

"That's not what I…"

"No, it's okay. I just wanted to show you what I can do."

"And what's that?"

"I can count toothpicks." Morgan waved at the box. "Go on. Open it."

The woman behind Jeff was back to peering over the booth, the people beside us turned in their chairs. Pretty soon the entire restaurant watched.

"That's okay you don't have to." He tried to hand the box back.

"No, no. Please. I'd love to show you."

Jeff cast an uneasy look at the room full of people. He opened the box.

"Take out a handful," Morgan said. "Count 'em. Then dump the rest on the floor. I'll tell you exactly how many are left."

I coughed to cover up a laugh.

"There are fifteen hundred toothpicks in this box."

Morgan gasped. "Really? Is that what all those zeros mean?" He tipped his head and looked at the box. "Wow. That's a lot. But that's okay. Go ahead. I can do it."

Jeff took out a few toothpicks.

"Now don't let me see them." Morgan covered his eyes. "Make sure you count 'em right. I don't want you to think I got the number wrong."

Jeff looked at me.

"He did it for me," I said. "And let me tell you, it's pretty damn impressive."

Jeff counted the toothpicks.

"When you're done, dump the rest out."

Jeff hesitated. I gave him a thumbs-up. He dumped the box of toothpicks, and they covered the floor beside the booth.

"Okay, they're dumped."

"All of them?" Morgan parted his fingers.

"Yeah." Jeff shook the box.

Morgan dropped his hands.

Jeff watched. I watched. Everyone in the restaurant watched.

"You sure…"

"Shhh—" Morgan held up a hand at Jeff. "I'm counting."

Someone slurped their drink with their straw. It was the only sound other than dozens of people breathing.

"Look," Jeff said.

"Give me a minute."

He did. Then another. And another.

"Okay, I'm done."

The tension drained from Jeff. He even managed a smile. "All right, how many are there?"

Then Morgan gave him the look. That stone cold, sharp as a razor, predatorial, cunning, flash leaving you with no doubt you'd just been played. And not just played, but rolled in shit and stuck out in the sun to dry, played.

"Fuck if I know, asshole, but you got yourself a mess to clean up." Morgan tugged me out of the booth.

The guy in overalls at the table beside us pointed at Jeff with his tuna sandwich. "I gotta nice stretch of beachfront property in Arkansas I'm looking to sell. You interested?"

Our waitress squeezed past Morgan and me. She held a broom and dustpan out to Jeff. "Here ya go, hon. That ought'a help."

The look Jeff gave me almost made me feel sorry for him.

Almost.

Morgan towed me through the kitchen and into the back office. He shut the door. Locked it.

"What are we—"

He met my gaze, and the heat in his eyes practically set my boxers on fire.

"Morgan?"

He shoved me into the wall.

"I don't know what you think—"

"Shut up, Grant."

"He was asking questions about—"

"Grant." Morgan grabbed the front of my shirt. "I said shut up." He attacked my mouth. I barked out in surprise, but it quickly turned into an agonizing groan. I slid my hands inside Morgan's jeans and cupped his ass.

He pulled away and bit my earlobe. "Fuck. Morgan... Whatever you think was going on—" He covered my mouth.

"I don't think you were trying to cheat. I don't even think you like him all that much. But I want to make sure you know there's nothing he can give you I can't."

I held Morgan back. "That's where you're wrong." He quit moving. "You can never give me what he can." With a hand on each cheek, he could not look away. "And you can't because he has nothing I want. Do you understand? Nothing."

I didn't have to worry about Morgan believing me. He'd see the truth. He'd peer right into my soul and know I meant every word I said.

He caressed my jaw, my cheeks, my ears. He dragged his touch to my neck. His fingertips were cold, but the skin to skin contact burned. Morgan hooked a leg around my hip and pulled himself up my body until he looked down at me.

Like the fragments of light he chased, he mapped my features with his touch.

"There will never be anyone like you, Morgan."

He closed his eyes for a moment.

"Never, not in a million years or a million lifetimes, will there be anyone else who has what I want."

He kissed me again. Slower. Deeper. Stroking the inside of my mouth with his tongue and drinking my sigh.

The distinct sound of muffled voices came from the other side of the door. Morgan gave me a questioning look. I lowered him to the ground.

Shuffling and someone whispered something.

I pointed at the door. Morgan nodded.

The lock was one of those push button kinds so I only needed to turn the handle to disengage it. I opened the door.

The waitresses, the kitchen staff, and fucking hell, I'm willing to bet half the customers had squeezed into the tiny space between the rack of pots and pans and office door.

We stared at each other until a lady with snow white hair held out her handkerchief and said, "Can I have your autograph?"

****

I had exactly two minutes to spare when I pulled into Morgan's driveway. He was already on the porch and had on a bike helmet.

I barely had the truck stopped when he skipped down the steps and opened the door.

"See, I'm not late."

Morgan flicked thoughts. "Only because you're early." He waved me over. "If you're gonna teach me how to drive, you're gonna have to move."

"At least let me get stopped first." I put it in park and scooted to the passenger side. "Where do you want me to put this?" I picked up the box from the floorboard.

"Just set it by the gate." I left the letters and box beside the footpath leading to his house, then got back in the truck.

"Okay, I'm ready." Morgan bounced in the seat.

"What's with the…" I tapped the helmet.

"Safety first."

"But this is a truck."

"Yeah, Grant, it's pretty obvious this is a truck."

"You don't wear a helmet when you ride your bike."

"Why should I? I know how to ride a bike, and besides, do you have any idea of the statistical difference between my chances of wrecking my bike verses crashing a car? Or in this case, truck?"

"Not really."

"Astronomical. A good five hundred to one. You have a greater chance of being hit by lightning while being eaten by a shark."

I attempted to do the math. Made sense. Sort of. How many bike wrecks did I see on the road? Excluding motorcycles? None.

I glanced at Morgan, and his mouth twitched.

I propped my elbow on the door. "You're doing it again, aren't you?"

"Yup."

"Damn it."

"Had you going, didn't I?"

"Nah."

He held up a finger.

"Okay, fine maybe a little."

"Good to know what they say isn't true."

I'd never learn. "And what's that?"

"You can't teach an old dog new tricks."

I gave him my best go-to-hell look, and he laughed.

He gazed through the windshield up at the trees before dragging his attention back to me. "Okay, what's first?"

"You're still wearing the helmet."

136

"Very observant of you, Grant."

"Why are you still wearing it?"

"In case we wreck."

"Wait, I thought…" I scrubbed my hand over my mouth. "You wouldn't happen to have a spare, would you?"

"Nope. Gonna have to get your own."

I huffed. "That's not very reassuring."

"Wasn't supposed to be." He patted the steering wheel. "Ready when you are."

"You sure you want to learn to drive?"

He flopped back in the seat. "Do you really have to insult me by asking me?"

"Point taken." I gestured at the dash. "Let's start there. P means park, which is where you are now. D, drive, and R is reverse."

"What about the D2 and D3."

"Ignore those for right now."

"But what if I need them?"

"Hopefully, I'll be driving." I pointed to the pedals on the floorboard. "Right is the gas. The one to the left of it is the brake."

"I can't tell right from left."

I'd forgotten. "Okay then. The skinny rectangle is the brake. The square one is the gas."

Morgan shook his head. "Technically they're both rectangles."

"What?"

"The pedals. Two sides one length, the other two a different length. Squares are even all four sides."

"Are you messing with me again?"

"You should have learned this in kindergarten. Or didn't they have kindergarten when dinosaurs roamed the earth?"

I glared.

"Maybe you should have studied those cave paintings harder."

"You know it's gonna be real hard for you to learn how to drive if you don't have a truck to borrow."

He flicked one hand and held up his free one in defense.

"Okay, back to the rectangles." I pointed. "The right… never mind. Take off a flip-flop."

"Why?"

"Don't ask questions. Just take one off."

"Which one?"

"I don't care."

Morgan did. "Now what?"

I checked to see which one he'd taken off. "Okay, your bare foot is responsible for that pedal." I pointed to the gas. "Your flip-flop is responsible for the other one."

Morgan grinned. "You're getting good at this, Grant. I'm impressed."

"Don't push your luck." I tapped his right knee. "Bare foot makes the truck move. Flip-flop makes it stop. Just make sure you don't push the pedals at the same time."

"Why?"

"Because."

"Because why?"

I made a face. "You ask too many questions."

"You don't know, do you?"

"Yes, I do. You can't go with the brake on; it just revs the engine and wastes gas. Satisfied?"

"Yup."

"Now put your flip-flop foot on its pedal and push down."

He did.

"Move the gear shift until the red line moves from the P to the R."

"And R is reverse, right?"

"Yes."

Morgan shifted the truck into reverse.

"Now ease off the brake, I mean flip-flop."

The truck crawled backward.

"Now, when you're far enough back, step on the brake again." The edge of the woods came closer. "Good. Just a little more." We went another few feet. "Okay, stop." The truck kept going. "Brake Morgan."

"Which one's the brake?"

"Left, I mean, flip-flop." The truck jerked to a stop. I slammed my hand against the dash to keep from getting thrown around.

"You're not a very good copilot, Grant."

"You're not a very good pilot."

"That's because I don't know how to drive." Morgan flexed his hand on the steering wheel.

I counted to ten before saying anything. "Now you need to put the truck in drive and make a right... I mean bare foot." The truck shot forward. "Stop, Morgan. Stop. Flip-flop." It jerked to a stop hard enough to dump me into the floorboard and crack my head on the dash.

"Fuck." I struggled to get back into the seat.

"Should have brought a helmet."

"If I'd known you were going to try to kill me, I would have."

"You're the one who said bare foot."

"I meant direction."

"We didn't discuss direction, just flip-flops and bare feet."

I touched the side of my head. It wasn't bleeding. Considering how bad it hurt it should have. "Okay, direction." I pointed at the passenger window. "Right will be passenger side." I pointed to the other way. "Left will be driver's side. Clear enough?"

"Yeah."

"Okay, let's back up again."

He did and managed to stop right on cue.

"Good. Now, passenger side."

Morgan turned the steering wheel.

"Ease off the flip-flop."

The truck crawled down the driveway.

"When do I get to use barefoot?"

"Let's wait till we're actually on the road."

"At this rate, it will only take a week."

"It will not."

"A day at least."

"Morgan."

"Oh look, we were just outmaneuvered by a leaf."

"Okay fine, but just a—"

Gravel shot up into the wheel well and the truck slid sideways. Then before I could blink, we were heading across the pasture in front of Morgan's house.

"Brake." The frontend dipped into a rut and the force tossed me close to the ceiling. "For God's sake, flip-flop, flip-flop."

The pickup cut ruts in the wet ground, spun halfway around on the grass before coming to a halt.

Somehow I'd wound up with my ass on the floorboard again and my legs on the seat. I glared at Morgan. The flush in his cheeks glowed against his pale skin.

He swallowed several times. "Well, at least it went better than last time."

"Jesus, how could that have been better? You almost killed us."

"I didn't catch the truck on fire." He fluttered his hand next to his temple. "Or drive into the pond."

"Where the hell is a pond?"

He pointed. "Through the fence and down the hill."

"Fucking hell, Morgan."

"Told you I couldn't drive."

I struggled back into the seat and put the truck in park before he could take us on another go-round.

"Guess I should cross driving off my list, huh?" He laid his forehead on the steering wheel.

"Depends on how long you want to live."

He laughed, then scrubbed his face. A tic in his shoulder knocked his hand against the bike helmet. "I suppose you want to call it quits."

The defeat in Morgan's expression broke something inside me. Here was a man who defied all odds, lived by himself, worked, created beautiful art. A complex mind stumped by some of the simplest tasks.

If he could, he would keep trying until there was only absolute failure or success.

How many people could say that?

I took a breath. "Go ahead and flip-flop."

Morgan jerked his head up.

I nodded. "C'mon, flip-flop, then reverse. Turn to the passenger side and head for the road."

Morgan did as instructed, easing into reverse, then turning the truck around.

"Easy on the bare foot."

"Kinda hard to judge." He changed gears.

"Feather light."

The truck ambled across the field toward the road. Then the pickup made the slow climb up the gully to the shoulder.

"Cut it tight, passenger window."

He did.

"Now straighten it out." The bumpy ride over rough ground turned into the smooth glide of asphalt.

"I can't believe this." Morgan rocked in his seat. "I'm driving."

"You are, but let's keep it below fifteen miles per hour."

"I'm driving, Grant." He laughed. "Holy shit, I'm driving. I could hug you."

"Please don't."

"Why?"

"Because you'd have to let go of the wheel."

"Okay, later then."

His dopy smile was contagious. "I'll hold you to that."

****

I had no idea teaching someone to drive could work up such an appetite. 'Course, it could have been the near death experience had made my body desperate for one more taste of food before it lost the chance.

"I think I'll take your advice."

"What advice?" Morgan picked up the box of bottles and tray full of mail.

"Get some seat belts put in the truck."

He laughed. "So when's my next lesson?"

"As soon as I get those seat belts."

"You should get Jenny to order you some. Her parts guy is pretty quick. Not sure how long it will take to find some to fit this model."

"I'm not even sure if they ever made any to fit this model."

"If they don't, she can rig 'em." He grinned. "You might have me back in the driver's seat in the next two weeks."

I'd call Jenny, but I'd ask her to take her time. I wasn't sure I was ready for another near death experience. Although, the smile, the joy, the pride Morgan exhaled because he'd managed to circle the block made my head fill up with the most wonderful feelings. I think for the first time I understood why some people got hooked on drugs after just one use. 'Cause I was hooked on Morgan.

Okay, maybe I would ask her to hurry. And if by some chance she couldn't pull off a miracle, there was always Alabama Chrome.

Duct tape.

I followed Morgan inside. He sat the box by the back door and emptied the tray into the garbage.

"Aren't you going to open those?"

"If I was, I wouldn't have thrown them away." He got out the bread. "You want chicken salad or a ham sandwich?"

"Chicken salad is good."

He nodded. "One or two?"

"Just one." My stomach disagreed. "Better make that two." He'd already gotten out the extra slices of bread and laid them on the plate. As I passed by the garbage can, I glanced down. Keller and Associates was on the return address on every visible label.

"Reading other people's mail is rude."

"Sorry." I walked over. "Want some help?"

"You can get the chicken salad out of the fridge. Green bowl. Top shelf."

I did. "What if it's important?"

"It's not."

"How do you know? You haven't opened them." There had to be close to a dozen. "How long have you been avoiding those letters?"

"Obviously, not long enough. They're supposed to send them back after ten days."

"Want me to get the drinks?"

He nodded.

"Tea?"

"Sure."

I got the glasses. Morgan made quick work of our sandwiches. He cut them into squares and put them on plates. I followed him back to the table with our drinks.

I handed him his tea, and he put my sandwich on the table. "Why don't you want to open them?"

Morgan flicked thoughts while he picked the crust off one square and ate it.

I drank my tea.

He ate the square.

I propped my elbow on the table.

"There's no need for me to." He snapped his fingers. "I already know what they say because it's always the same."

"And what do they say?"

"I don't want to talk about it." His shoulder jerked hard enough make him slosh his tea. I started to get up and grab a towel. "I got it." He went back in the kitchen and returned with a roll of paper towels.

"You know you can—" My cell phone rang. I checked the number. It was Price. "Can you excuse me? I need to take this."

Morgan nodded, and I went out front.

"Hello?"

"Good afternoon, Mr. Kessler. I got your message."

"Since when did I become Mr. Kessler to you?"

She laughed. It was a thick hearty sound belonging to a man not a woman of eloquent beauty. "I figured since I haven't heard from you in a while, that we'd gone from good acquaintance to strict business associates."

I leaned against the post. "You haven't heard from me because I haven't been in need of your services."

"Until now." There was a bit of a chill to her tone.

"It's nothing serious. Retired life is working out better than I hoped."

There was movement in the background. "I'm glad to hear. Real glad. Now tell me about your not-too-serious problem."

I gave her a rundown on Dillon, the parole hearing, and Morgan's fears of the man coming back. When I was done, Price sighed in a way I knew things were not in my favor. Or in this case, Morgan's favor.

"Even dirt bags have a right to parole."

"Can't you petition the court, or whatever it is you lawyers call paperwork now days?"

"It would be better if Morgan could show up."

"He can't." The gentle melody of classical music drifted from inside the house.

"Grant?"

"I'm sorry I got distracted. What were you saying?"

"I said, why not?"

How much could I tell her without hurting him? I settled on vague. "It's personal."

"All right, I'll make some calls and have an associate attend the hearing."

"You can't?"

"I'm not licensed in Georgia. That and I have an important trial to prepare for."

Important was Price's code word for very wealthy and usually criminally connected client. I wish I could say she'd never used the word with me. At least it wasn't for killing someone.

"But other than the snafu with your friend, things are good?"

"Yeah." I picked at a splinter on the railing.

"Sounds to me, they might be better than good."

"They are." A soft wind pushed leaves from the branches stretching out over the front of the house. Flashes of gold cut the sunlight. The bottles around the picket fence were almost lost among the fall colors piling up around them.

Could the sands of a beach be any more magical?

Probably. But the beach didn't have Morgan.

I cleared my throat. "I need you to do something for me."

"All right."

"I'd like to change some of my financial arrangements."

"Money problems?"

"No, no, not at all. But I'd like to extend the deposits."

"You make it sound like your three year plan just got longer?"

"Hopefully infinitely longer."

I could practically hear her smile. "Those plans have anything to do with your friend?"

"Yeah."

"Wow, Grant. You're just full of surprises." She laughed again, this time it was softer and as feminine as the average woman. Only there was nothing average about Harriet. At six foot, skin so dark it was close to blue, and eyes black as onyx, she was the epitome of beauty but nothing close to fragile.

No, Harriet bled strength and confidence.

"Why do you say that?" I said.

"Because it's hard for anyone to forgive. And it's twice as hard for you to forgive."

"You can't forgive a rattlesnake for doing what come's natural."

"Not Jeff, yourself."

I pushed a leaf off the porch with the toe of my shoe. "Yeah, I guess I surprised myself then."

"I'm glad." Someone spoke in the background. "I've got to go. I'll make those calls and let you know what I find out. Tell your friend not to worry, if anything can be done, I'll do it."

And she meant it.

We said our good-byes and hung up.

Violins and flutes sang in chorus with cellos and clarinets. The flow of music matched the afternoon perfectly.

Back inside, I froze in the doorway. Morgan had moved the dining room table up against the wall, clearing a space. He stood on tiptoe, arms up, body curved, then dropped with the fall of the music, tipping forward and lifting his leg toward the ceiling. His flip-flops and shirt were gone, leaving his raggedy blue jeans and miles of perfect skin.

The music filled him, turning him liquid, twisting his body in the most beautiful ways.

I admit, I didn't know jack shit about ballet, but it didn't take an expert to see he was flawless or damn well close to it.

Those people at the dance school had truly missed out.

He switched feet, arching back over a curved leg. His eyes were closed, and he wore a blissful expression. One I'd seen when he watched the light, or when I made love to him.

There wasn't enough room to leap, but I knew just by watching how he danced from one foot to the next, he'd jump like a deer.

The most amazing thing was the lack of tics. They were just gone, leaving behind a gorgeous man who would never be normal. Not because of the autism, but because he was too extraordinary.

I didn't want to disturb Morgan, but my feet weren't listening. In just a few steps, I found myself close enough for the current of air to brush my skin as he moved. He didn't open his eyes when he lifted my hand and pirouetted so fast he made me dizzy.

Then he stopped and looked at me.

It was then I knew. Staring into those eyes. Eyes that saw where no man could, I was falling for him. I take that back. I'd already fallen for him. I couldn't say when it happened or how. There at the doorway, before in the truck, at the diner, at the movie, but it didn't matter.

My heart was his.

I seriously began to wonder if it ever wasn't. That he'd always held me and I just didn't know it. Like seeing the light in a way I couldn't, he'd seen a love that hadn't happened yet, but knew it would.

Of course it might have all been in my head. But it wouldn't have surprised me if it wasn't.

Morgan ran his fingers from my chin to my throat. A shiver danced down my spine becoming an electric heat as it spread over me. I leaned down, but instead of taking my mouth, he brushed his lips against mine and drank my exhale.

His brow crinkled.

"What are you worried about?" I cupped the back of his head. Morgan continued to search my face. I wished I knew what it was he looked for. Or what he saw when he found it. Sometimes it happened in seconds, sometimes in long aching moments.

Morgan tugged on my shirt, and I helped him pull it over my head. He kissed my shoulder, the center of my chest, then he dragged his teeth back up to my jaw.

I didn't even try to suppress the shudder.

143

His caresses flowed down my ribs and traced the edge of my jeans. I was already hard by the time he pulled down the zipper.

Morgan continued to sigh against my skin. Sometimes it was my cheek, or my ear, but mostly my lips. All the while he held my gaze. I had a feeling it was the longest he'd looked at anyone.

I was willing to bet he'd never wanted to before.

My jeans fell to the floor. I stepped out of them as I pushed Morgan closer to the wall. He tugged on the zipper of his pants, and I knocked his hands away so I could take over.

A devilish smile flashed on his lips, but it vanished into an open mouth gasping as I gripped his freed cock. He avoided my mouth again by turning his head. My confusion must have shown in my face because he shushed me.

I pressed Morgan against the wall, and he used the newfound leverage to climb to my waist. His exhale heated the tender flesh on the side of my neck.

I ran my thumb over the head of his cock, and he thrust his hips, sliding the crack of his ass over my dick.

"Do you want me, Grant?"

As if he needed to ask.

Morgan peppered my jaw in light kisses. "I think you do. I think you want me. I think if I asked you, you'd fuck me right here."

I would. God help me, I would.

"I'd like that." He raked his nails up my back. The sharp lick of pain pulled a groan out of my chest. "I think you'd like it too."

"No lube."

"Don't care."

"I do. I don't want to hurt you."

"I'm tougher than I look, Grant. Haven't you figured that out yet?"

"I have no doubts about how strong you are." Not anymore.

"Then go slow." Morgan slid around me until he was at my back. In long slow strokes, he milked my cock until it ran over his fingers, turning them shiny. I have no idea how he coaxed so much fluid to the tip.

"Still won't be enough."

He twisted his wrist as he moved to the tip and the combination threatened to push me over the edge. A thick line of precum stretched from the tip. He caught it and smeared it over the head.

"Morgan." Oh god, I did not want him to stop. I couldn't even jack my own dick with the same kind of skill. "There's oil in the kitchen." It was only a few feet away. He made the move again, and I bucked back. His cock slid between my legs. I closed them to give him friction, but he was already in motion again. One leg hooked around mine, his arm over my shoulders. He swung using me like a pole and faced me before I could even turn my head to watch him move. His jeans were gone now, and nothing restricted the flexibility of his legs.

"I want you to fuck me, Grant." He held himself up with just one arm around the back of my neck. I found his hand at his back, his fingers buried in his ass. Three, stretched him wide, and the puckered flesh around his digits was wet. The saliva wouldn't stay for long. We needed lubricant.

"Just let me—" He yanked my hair hard enough to cause me to stumble back. My hip hit the table, and his mouth found mine. I begged him to kiss me, but he only played with my lips and tongue.

"Sometimes I like it to hurt." He bit my lip. "I promise, go slow, and I'll be fine."

"Condom." Maybe he had one in his pocket.

Morgan breathed against the shell of my ear. "I want to feel you. All of you. Your cock, your cum, your heat. Fill me, Grant, please."

I'm not even sure at that point I could have told him no. I leaned forward, resting his ass on the edge of the table. My cock was already at his opening as if it had a mind of its own. I gripped my length, rocked my hips, and milked myself for every drop of precum I could to smear over his opening. He'd prepped himself, but every time the tip of my dick touched the ring of puckered flesh, it tightened. There was no way, no way, I wouldn't tear him. Maybe if there was a little less of me.

Morgan inhaled deep, and from head to toe, the tension in his limbs bled away. "Now."

I hesitated.

"Grant." He moved his legs higher and locked his heels behind my back. "Now."

I pushed, and between his control, and the precum, the amount of resistance I expected wasn't there, but the friction brought a whole new element I'd never experienced. Every crease of his entrance rubbed every inch of flesh on my cock. Slick with lubricant, those details were always blurred, but not now, every nerve ending reacted.

In one long stroke, I took him, then the breath I'd been holding whooshed out on an agonizing moan. Morgan panted in my ear. I wanted to move, I needed to move, especially before the precum dried too much. But it felt so good to be there, like that, wrapped in heat, our bodies pressed together, his leaking cock crushed between us.

I kissed his chin, went for his mouth, he turned his head just enough to make me miss.

"Why won't you let me kiss you?"

Morgan smiled as he brought his lips back to mine. I tried again and got the same result. The third time, I made no attempt to take his mouth, and he claimed mine.

There was no gentleness in how he thrust his tongue or the weight he put into the contact. Our teeth scraped together, his caught my lip, blood smeared across his chin when he yanked back only to dive at me again.

I didn't realize I moved my hips in rhythm with his attack until the table hit the wall hard enough to knock a picture loose.

"Don't stop." Morgan pulled my hair and crushed my ear against my head. "Fuck me, Grant. Hard."

I pulled to the tip and shoved deep. His body clamped down around me with enough force to break my rhythm. I reached between us, and he pushed my hand away.

"I want you to come."

The fire in his eyes darkened. "Make me."

I huffed a laugh. "I'm trying."

"Try harder." He bit my jaw. The shock of pain made me jerk hard enough to pop the table off the floor. "Like that."

"If you want me to fuck you that hard, we really need…" I don't know what Morgan did or how he did it, but his entire body rippled, every muscle dancing in a long slow wave to where we connected and practically pulled me deeper.

Again he tightened around me, squeezing my cock with his hole like someone could with a hand.

"How the fuck do you do that?" Without my consent, my hips were moving again. I kept my thrusts short and deep, angling myself in hopes to hit his prostate. Morgan helped by drawing his knees up. I knew I found it when his eyes fluttered closed and his mouth fell open in a silent howl. The position also left his cock vulnerable. I stroked him faster than I fucked him. "Want you to come for me."

He grinned at me through the veil of euphoria. His breathing hitched, and I waited for him to blow his load, but he held on.

Sweat ran down my neck, made droplets on his chest, my hair slid into my eyes. A cramp started in my big toe, but any attempt to work it out would have forced me to break rhythm.

Under me, Morgan made small deep sighs and a flush spread over his skin, making him look sun-kissed. I lapped at the hollow of his neck, ran my teeth to his jaw, and when he tried to control the kiss, I begged him to deliver, it was my turn to deny the contact.

"Two can play that game." I huffed against his lips. "Come for me, Morgan."

"No." His entire body shuddered, and more precum bled from his slit until the foreskin squelched.

"Please."

He shook his head until his curls were a blur. Morgan arched his back and keened. I was so sure he'd lose it then, but unlike the tics controlling him, he was able to rein in his climax.

I'd been with a few who edged, taking themselves to the height of an orgasm then stopping. Some did it because it was just a kink, others because they liked how it built up the end, a few to increase their stamina. But what Morgan did, was nothing like I'd ever seen.

And while he might have been able to hold back, my body rapidly reached its limit. The fire in my muscles turned into an electric crawl. The rush pulled my nuts tight and yanked me to my toes. I barked out a cry that became a series of grunts as my body seized up and pulse after pulse rippled down my cock. I emptied everything I had, and Morgan undulated against the table as if the sensation of cum filling him was a whole new pleasure.

"Love that," he gasped. "Love how that feels." He was still hard in my hand. Morgan held me in place with his legs, humming while he rolled his hips. Cum leaked from around my softening cock. If I'd been ten years younger, I would have been pounding him again, working my cock until it was rock hard and stretching him to his limit, but my recovery time was a bit longer now.

I didn't care, watching him was enough.

Morgan put his hand over mine. One at a time, he pulled open my fingers until I released his dick. It slapped it against his stomach, all swollen, angry, and weeping.

"Why did you hold back?" I didn't realize just how much it hurt my ego, but the tone of my voice said everything I wasn't willing to admit.

"Want you to suck me." He sat up on his elbows. "Want just your mouth, Grant."

I wasn't quite sure what he meant until he pushed away any attempt to hold him. I wound up with my hands on the edge of the table so I could balance myself. Morgan gripped the back of my head and pushed me down. He didn't cram himself to the back of my throat, just deep enough to take half his cock. I started to bob my head, but he pulled my hair.

"Be still."

I did. Even though it made me feel useless, I stopped moving and stood there while Morgan watched me. Then slowly he began to move. First it was just a roll of his hips, then he pulled his feet up to the edge of the table and it became an all-out face-fucking.

Head back, one arm holding him up, the other hand buried in my hair, he held me in place. Even if I'd wanted to pull away, I couldn't have. Not with the image of his glistening body weighing down my mind, the scent of musk and clean sweat in my nose, the taste of precum, the anticipation for more, and the animalistic sounds he made with every thrust.

I think I would have stayed there forever if he wanted me to, but once in control, the constant tension in Morgan's body didn't return, and he simply rode out the crash and ebb of pleasure until one final thrust had him shooting down the back of my throat.

I swallowed, but it wasn't quick enough to keep the stream of cum from backing over my lips and making lines down his cock and leaving droplets in his golden hairs.

Morgan pulled me forward until we were nose to nose, chin to chin. He licked the cum from my lip. His dark gaze was on me and at the same time far, far away.

He didn't resist when I molded my body to his and wrapped him in my arms. The heat of his flesh, the curve of his muscles, the strength in his body, nothing had ever felt so perfect in my life.

Morgan peppered my shoulder in kisses. "Gonna have to get a new table."

My mind was still fifteen seconds behind. "What? Why?" We hadn't damaged it.

"'Cause I'm never going to be able to keep a straight face if Aunt Jenny comes over for lunch."

I laughed, but it died too quickly. Like I said, my thoughts lagged.

"What's wrong?" Morgan tilted his head. A small tic pulled his shoulder and his hand went to his temple, but I caught it and kissed his palm. The involuntary pull fell slack and his fingers opened. I did it again.

"Grant?"

I pushed one hand behind his back, but when I reached for the other, he eluded my grasp.

"You want an encore, then we're gonna have to get the lube." The warmth of his gaze didn't match the sudden edge to his words. It was like seeing two men. One on the inside who wanted me, trusted me, then another on the outside who couldn't lose control.

I took his hands again. "I won't hurt you." I brushed my lips against his. "I swear to you, Morgan, you can trust me. I'll never hurt you." His lips parted, and his breath huffed in and out.

"What makes you think I don't trust you?" He pulled out of my grasp again, but I regained control before he got very far. His gaze slid away, and some of the color left his cheeks.

"I think you know why." He really pulled then. I let him go because it was either that or leave bruises. Then he was off the table, grabbed his jeans off the floor, and headed toward the bathroom. Cum left a shiny streak across the back of one ass cheek and thigh.

"I gotta get ready for work."

"I'm not him." I don't know why I said it.

Morgan froze in the doorway. The muscles in his shoulders bunched.

"And whatever it is he did, I won't."

His hand flexed on the doorknob. "I know you're not Dillon. And I know you're nothing like him."

"Then why don't you trust me?"

Morgan turned. I swore there were tears in his eyes, but when his hair slid out of the way, as me met my gaze, they were gone. "It's just sex, Grant. It's not like we're married. Three years, remember? You know, to fill the space, because it's better than crossword puzzles."

I took a step, and he withdrew. I couldn't be sure, but I don't think he realized he did it.

"What if it's not?"

Morgan laughed, but it fractured. "C'mon, Grant, when's the last time a crossword puzzle made you growl like a rutting bull when you come?"

"I don't..." Okay, I did make a lot of noise. Maybe not like a rutting bull. But honestly, I don't think I'd ever heard one before. I took another step, and this time he held his ground. "Maybe I don't want to be with you to fill the space anymore."

"So you want to watch TV instead?" His gaze slid away and his wayward hand flicked thoughts.

"No. I want you. Next to me. Every night."

Morgan dropped his jeans in the dirty laundry pile inside the bathroom door. Then he turned on the shower and tested the water for a lot longer than he needed to before he went to his room and came back with some clean clothes.

Again he stopped at the door. "I know you've got some things to do, but would you like to stay the night?"

"You know I would."

"I was thinking about cooking dumplings."

"Sounds perfect."

He nodded once, then twice, before stepping into the cloud of steam and shutting himself inside.

****

The skill saw screamed through another two by four. Even with earplugs, it left my head ringing. After you run one of those things for so long, there's just no escaping the sound. It echoes in your bones and occupies any moment of silence in between daily noises.

No, the only way to get that irritating screech out of your head was to replace it with something louder and far more memorable. Morgan would be leaving Toolies around eight. He wanted to ride his bike home, but I was going to pick him up. If he complained, I'd make it up to him in any and every position possible.

I picked up my shirt from the railing and wiped my hands before carrying the stud inside. While rewiring an outlet, I discovered a soft spot in the wall. The soft spot turned into a patch, and the patch turned into an all-out nightmare. A lot of old home places are built on stone foundations. Not concrete block, not brick, I'm talking rock. The kind you dig up out of the garden and toss off to the side. Depending on the age of the house, sometimes that rock isn't even held together with mortar, just stacked and glued with luck.

The Anderson house had a stacked rock foundation. Whoever had done it had been a master at fitting those rocks together. Whoever tried to do the repair job caused by time, erosion, someone backing his car into the corner of the house, had been an idiot. Instead of taking the time to shore up the spot and fit the stones together, they'd slapped some globs of mortar and tried to paste the rocks in place like macaroni on a kindergarten paper plate project.

And see, the thing about mortar is, it's porous. It sucks up water like a sponge, and badly mixed mortar will not only suck up that water, it will crumble. The fact the floor wasn't sagging was a miracle and a testament to the skill of the original builder. Unfortunately there had been enough rain over the years to soak the mortar until it hit the wood and the wood had done the rest, drinking up Mother Nature's offering until the oak had blackened and turned soft as a sponge.

What was left of the insulation had been tunneled into one of the nastiest black ant infestations I'd ever seen in my life. With a liberal amount of Borax and a new section of wall, I could convince them to move on. If it had been fire ants, I would have had to burn the place down and collect on the insurance.

It took me two days to rip out the wall, remove the window, shore up the floor and restack the stone. I had no illusions regarding my rock stacking skills, so I cheated and used concrete block to brace the spot and covered it up with the original stone.

I'd had to build up the foundation from under the house and despite long sleeves, coveralls, and a box of Borax, the few remaining ants had fought well.

With the last stud in place, I was ready to reinsulate the wall. Looking at the roll of pink fiberglass, I couldn't help but wonder what would itch worse by morning.

I made a mental note to grab some calamine lotion on the way home.

Age had turned the oak of the outer wall planks into the consistency of concrete, so I'd been able to save all but a few. Now the sun broke through the small spaces in the slats, scattering irregular shapes on the dark floor. They lay there like puzzle pieces waiting to be snapped together, and I couldn't help but wonder if I stared at them long enough, I'd eventually see the picture they made.

If there was a picture at all.

According to Morgan, the light held more than just pretty colors and patterns, it spoke. If his sculptures were anything close to what he saw when he watched the sun break through the trees, then I could only imagine what kind of music it made.

Maybe I could have imagined. I don't know. I wasn't sure if my mind could even stretch that far. Part of me really wanted to know what it was like, another part was terrified by the prospect.

Not because I feared what I'd see, I feared I'd never want to come back.

I didn't even hear the car drive up. Like I said, the ring of a skill saw sticks with you for a while. The scent of Old Spice cologne drew my attention. Jeff stood at the front door in his suit, sunglasses in his front pocket, smirk—although subtle—on his face.

On any other man, Old Spice was Old Spice, but on Jeff, it morphed into a rich flavor saturating the air. It wasn't because he wore a lot of it, honestly it only took a few drops, but there was just something about his body chemistry that transformed it into some sort of Spanish Fly.

At least it used to. According to my dick, it still did.

"Been busy?" Jeff ran a look over me from head to toe. Covered in dirt, Borax, sweat, and ant bites, I'm sure I was regular Kodak moment.

And my deodorant had long ago gone by the wayside, washed away by hours of sawing, hammering, and crawling around on my belly under the house.

"Are you ever going to stop?" I made myself busy picking up tools. The air stirred, and his shiny black shoes came into my periphery.

"Grant—"

"No." I closed the toolbox.

"You haven't even heard the question."

"You're a broken record, I don't need to." I stood, and suddenly he was too close. Only the toolbox kept space between us. And it wasn't nearly enough.

"I was going to ask you how you did it." For once, I had no idea what he was talking about. It must have shown on my face because he added. "The warehouse."

Maybe it was his cologne, the heat of his body, or how he searched my face, pausing on my lips, sliding to my throat, then making no attempt to hide the slow drag down my chest to my groin, but my brain still skipped.

"It was empty," he said.

Warehouse. Empty.

Then it hit me. Jeff brought his gaze back up and I could practically see what he was thinking about, and it had nothing to do with my warehouse near the old carpet mill where I'd stashed some of my most valuable personal items under lock, key, and concrete.

"I have no idea what you're talking about." I said it so smoothly even I would have believed me.

But Jeff knew me way better than most. "We had that place under twenty-four hour surveillance. No one in, no one out, and it was empty."

Empty.

Not just empty of the documents containing information on Rubio's family but empty of everything.

I knew Rubio was good but... damn.

"You mean I've been robbed?" I pushed past Jeff and carried the toolbox into the kitchen. When I turned to go back for the rest of the tools on the porch, he blocked the way.

Once again, too close. He took a step, and I wound up with my back against the fridge. "Do you mind?"

"What's wrong? You seem a little jumpy?" He exhaled a mint-flavored breath.

"No, I've just been informed my storage building was broken into and my belongings were taken. I probably should make a police report, I don't suppose the FBI could do that for me, can they? I mean, since you're already in town and you don't have anything else better to do."

Closer, head to toe, we were less than a hair apart. Jeff put a hand against the fridge on either side of my head. He was only slightly shorter than me, but he'd always been wider in the shoulders and he used that width to box me in.

"You definitely took the wrong career path," Jeff said.

"Really?"

"Yeah. With the way you can make things disappear, you could have been a world-famous magician."

"Maybe I'm not after fame."

"Wealth." He smirked. "Now I know you're not going to tell me money doesn't interest you."

"What do you want?"

"What was in the warehouse?"

"Personal items. If you get out a piece of paper, I'll make you a list so I can turn it into

150

the insurance company. I'm going to need a copy of the report of course. And my lawyer will want to see the search warrant. You did have a search warrant, right? If not, the insurance company might put you on the list of who to interview."

"Insurance companies don't interview people over stolen property."

"Considering how much some of those paintings were worth, my agent is apt to get a court order colonoscopy for everyone on your team."

"Anything else special in there you want to tell me about?"

"Why do you care?"

"I thought we've been over this." Any closer and he was going to get dirt on his vanilla colored button-up. "I'm trying to help you."

I rolled my eyes. "Oh, yeah, that's right. From a would-be hit man, and Lorado's wrath. C'mon, Jeff, you know as well as I do I have nothing he wants. We dealt in two different worlds." Lorado: guns, drugs, and misery. Me? Things people liked to look at. Sometimes they drove it around, sometimes they hung it on their walls, sometimes they hid it in their wall safe. "You lied to try and scare me into telling you what you failed to get after four years of playing the part of Jeff Myers. Even standing over me while I arranged a shipment, you couldn't find one illegal speed bump."

"What about the job you did for Mr. Avner?"

Ah, my one almost slip-up. Jeff walked in on me while I was gluing the last of the wax-dipped coins to the foot of an antique school desk. "You mean the gold collection three SS officers dug out of his father's floor safe before putting a bullet in the man's head, then hauling Avner and his mother off to Ravensbrück. Yeah, I recall that one. I also recall the unwillingness of the so-called victim to file charges. Especially when he realized he'd have to prove how he acquired the coins." The part of the collection belonging to Avner I'd returned gift-wrapped. The rest of the collection, taken from the unwilling seller, had been moved overseas to a collector with the understanding if the real owners ever showed up he was to hand them over. I'd reimburse him of course.

So far no one had come forward to claim a single coin out of the three million dollar collection. Even Avner hadn't been able to turn up survivors.

It was probably the only deal I wished I could give a refund on.

"I didn't steal anything. I just returned a lost item to its rightful owner."

"So you're what? Robin Hood now?"

"No, Jeff. Not by a long shot."

"What was in the warehouse?"

"I told you I'd make a list for my insurance."

"There is nothing you'd put on an insurance claim important enough for you to risk moving it while under surveillance. The job was clean, and none of your usual associates were involved. But you had to have help, so who was it?"

I winked at him. "A magician never reveals his tricks."

"Grant, the Associate Deputy Director wants me to bring you in. If you don't cooperate, I won't be able to keep them from doing it."

"More threats, Jeff?" I tried to shove past him, but he knocked me back into the fridge hard enough to make the ancient metal casket rattle. His mouth hit mine and he sank his hands into my hair. For a split second, it was just like old times at the loft overlooking the docks. Jeff would walk in, shove aside whatever it was I had in my hands, and draw me in.

Half the time, I wouldn't even bother with getting undressed, I'd just get his jeans out of the way and fuck him against the first available piece of furniture.

I yanked my mouth away and dodged another attempt. "No, Jeff."

"No wires, I swear, it's just me." The desperation and hunger in his words left no room for a lie. And any doubt lingering in the back of my mind disintegrated when I met his gaze.

"Does your team know you're here?"

"No."

"Hines?"

He shook his head. "They gave me your case. It's just me." So even his former boss didn't know he'd gone off the grid.

Jeff raked his teeth across my jaw and down my neck. Sweat and grime made tracks on his shirt. He shrugged out of his jacket and began pulling at his tie. It made enough space for me to escape. The memory of his body pressed to mine crawled over my skin. How many nights had I held him, kissed him, loved him?

But it wasn't desire welling inside me. I can't really give what I felt a name. Something like shame, but closer to remorse. The kind of loss you feel when someone you knew died. Not someone you were close to, but had known just enough to shave off a bit of your life and take it with them when they were gone.

Jeff came at me, shirt half unbuttoned, and his cock practically crawling down his thigh. I kicked a sawhorse into his path, only then did he stop.

Confusion took some of the heat out of his eyes, and the color from his cheeks.

"Go home, Jeff. Or go back to your hotel. Or wherever the hell you're staying while you stalk me."

"You're serious." He flicked a look over me. For some reason, it made me realize I wasn't even hard. If anything, my nuts had crawled a few inches higher in an attempt to escape.

"It's over. Everything. Your lies about Lorado, your BS scare tactics." His chest continued to rise and fall. "And us. Especially us."

"I told you I'd do everything to keep you from going to jail."

"Do you really have that kind of authority?" For a second or two, there was a dark flash in his eyes, whispering of secrets untold. "Out of curiosity, Jeff. What are you not telling me?"

He wiped his mouth and turned away.

"At least tell me why Hines is so hot to have my client list. It won't do him any good. You know that."

I don't know if Jeff meant to, but he nodded. "So when are you going to tell him?" He buttoned his shirt.

"Who're you talking about?"

"The kid you're fucking." It was the way he said it. Like I was doing something obscene.

"What the hell does Morgan have to do with anything?"

Jeff brushed at the dirt stains on his shirt. "You know being a thief is one thing, but having sex with a—"

I didn't even know I'd shoved him into the wall until I was there, our faces inches apart, and a rage so deep I was less than a hair away from wrapping my hands around his neck and breaking it. I've been angry in my life more times than I could count, but what boiled inside me then wasn't something I'd ever experienced. I think it caught Jeff off guard too because he reached for his gun, but it wasn't there.

"I'll ask you one more time." My voice warped into something thick and dangerous. "Why are you bringing up Morgan?"

Jeff stepped aside, and I didn't stop him. "Touchy, are we? A little bit of guilt maybe?"

"For what?"

"I just wanted to know if you've told him."

"And what is it I'm supposed to tell him?"

"That you're not going to stick around. How in two maybe three years you'll be in some far off place where the US government can't touch you, enjoying the millions your *business* has made you."

"Who says I'm leaving?"

Jeff laughed and shook his tie at me. "Oh, now that's a good one."

Thing is, now I'd said it, I meant it. I mean, the thought had been there, every morning I got to wake up next to Morgan and every night I got to fall asleep with him at my side. I could see beautiful beaches in pictures, but I'd never experienced anything like him. There was no sunset, no sunrise, no virgin stretch of coast worth losing the opportunity to look him in the eyes, to know I was worthy of the opportunity.

Something must have shown in my face because Jeff left his tie half looped and shoved on his jacket. "What the hell has happened to you, Grant? You used to be…"

"What?"

"Normal."

Now I laughed. "And somehow I'm not?"

"Normal people don't take advantage of mentally impaired people."

"Morgan's not mentally impaired."

Jeff headed toward the door but not quick enough to hide the look of disgust on his face. I snagged him by the arm of his jacket. "He's a grown man, capable of making his own choices."

"I'm not talking chronological age here."

"Neither am I."

"He isn't normal."

"Doesn't mean he isn't smarter than you are, or me, for that matter." Jeff's expression didn't change. "Look, I thought the same thing you did when I first met him. But I was wrong. He's different, I'll give you that, but the way he's different isn't a bad thing."

"Whatever." Jeff pulled away. "The least you can do is tell him you're not sticking around. Maybe by the time you ship off he'll realize what that means."

"The relationship was his idea."

Jeff paused with his hand on the doorframe. His knuckles whitened with the flex of his hand.

"He thought it would be more entertaining than crossword puzzles. He knew my plans were temporary."

Jeff watched me from the corner of his eye.

"Yeah, *were* temporary. Not anymore. I mean it, Jeff, I'm staying here as long as Morgan will have me."

Then there it was. Defeat flashed through Jeff's eyes so quick and fleeting I could have imagined it, only his body betrayed him. It was like all the fight drained from him, pulling his shoulders down until he was almost a shell of a man.

And I still didn't feel anything for him even though I thought I should.

"I'll fax a copy of the search warrant to your lawyer. If I were you, I'd seriously reconsider the ethics of your clientele. I need those names, Grant. Even if it's just a few. I need dates, times, and route. We both know you're nothing but a common criminal, not Robin Hood, not some self-proclaimed equalizer. You help people move stolen goods. That makes you as much of a thief as they are.

"Until you do something to right that, you're never going to be rid of the FBI. We're going to watch everything you do, every place you go, and search every piece of trash you throw away.

"Eventually you'll fuck up. And when you do, I'll be there."

He headed down the steps to the trunk of his car. There he changed his shirt and tie both. Didn't surprise me one bit he kept a spare. Jeff the FBI agent kept his closet color coded, his sock drawer like a file cabinet, aligned his shampoos in alphabetical order and his cologne by engagement.

I knew a lot about him he didn't realize, for reasons I was ashamed to admit.

"While you're here, you should try the biscuits over at Fran's. They make them fresh every morning, but you have to get there early or they run out."

He fixed his tie and slipped on his glasses. "I will not give up, Grant."

"Like I said, early."

"I'm done trying to help you."

"Ask for Miranda, she'll fix you right up."

"Eventually, you will go to prison. Maybe some time in an eight by six room with nothing but a brick wall view will loosen your pride and you'll realize just how generous I've tried to be." Jeff slammed the trunk shut. New shirt, tie in perfect order, you would have never known just minutes before he was ready to go down on his knees and suck my dick.

A cloud of dirt followed his sedan to the main road. It paused at the stop sign a lot longer than it needed to. Just when I began to worry he might turn around and come back, he made a left and vanished beyond the stretch of trees and farmland.

****

I arrived at Toolies about fifteen minutes before Morgan's shift was due to end. It was Tuesday so the only ones still hanging around were the regulars who practically had name plates on the seats they occupied.

I don't know why, but it always made me sad to run up on patrons who were committed to wasting the evening of their life perched on a vinyl stool with a beer mug in one hand.

Jessie smiled at me and tossed the towel he held over his shoulder. "Look what the cat dragged in."

I parked it at the corner.

"Thirsty?" He had a mug on the counter in front of me before I could answer. I took a sip. Shit got better every time I tried it. "So what's new?"

I shook my head. "Not a whole lot."

154

"Well, you need to hurry up and find something."

I raised an eyebrow.

"I have to tell the blue-haired ladies something when they ask about you."

"Blue-haired ladies?"

"Yeah, your fan club."

The heat in my cheeks had nothing to do with the alcohol.

Jessie laughed. "I was thinking maybe we could get a couple of glossies made, you sign them and I could sell 'em. Split it fifty/fifty."

"Remind me to kill the SOB who invented camera phones." I drank my beer and tried to push aside the fact people still gave me the look. The one they got the moment they realized where they'd seen me before.

But every time I went to Berry's store, he reminded me it could have been worse.

I didn't even want my imagination to wander in that direction.

"I thought Morgan was riding his bike home."

A clump of foam stuck to my lip. I wiped it away. "He was. I just kind of showed up hoping he'd let me give him a ride back instead."

Jessie clicked his tongue. "You got it bad, my brother."

I did.

"But it looks good on you. Good on Morgan too. Been a long time since I've seen him this happy."

I drank some beer to try to cover up the stupid grin on my face. I don't think Jessie was fooled. Personally, I couldn't remember if I'd ever been this happy.

The door to the back swung open, and Morgan came through with a bin on his hip. He paused for a second before rushing past to the last dirty booth. After he cleaned it, he wiped down the tabletop until it gleamed. Then he was gone, without a word.

Jessie collected money from one of his customers. When they left, to me, he said, "You two argue?"

"Not that I'm aware of." But by all his actions, it was as if I hadn't even existed. "You mind?" I threw my thumb in the direction of the back.

"Naw, sure, go ahead. He'll leave out the back anyhow."

I left my beer half empty and made a dash through the kitchen. Morgan was rinsing his hands in a large sink close to where they washed the dishes. Clean pots and pans hung neatly on the hooks overhead.

"Hey," I said.

He turned off the water and took out a paper towel from the dispenser, used it until it was too wet to be useful anymore, folded it up, threw it away, pulled out a second, and repeated the process.

"Is everything okay?"

"Everything's fine, Grant." The deadpan reply was worse than any scream. And the fact he wouldn't look at me?

"Talk to me, Morgan."

He hung his smock up on one hook next to his jacket. The nights were getting colder now, and honestly the windbreaker wasn't enough, not with just a T-shirt underneath. I was glad I'd made the decision to come pick him up. The last thing he needed was to get sick, cause he'd never go to a doctor. Luckily his feet had healed with minimal care, but pneumonia was a whole other story.

I could see me trying to get medicine down his throat. It would be like trying to bathe a feral cat.

Morgan took a sweatshirt with the store logo from another hook, slipped it on, then picked up his jacket.

"Why are you here?" He put on the windbreaker and zipped it up.

"I wanted to give you a ride home."

"Why?"

"Because it's cold."

Morgan pulled a stocking cap from his coat pocket and put it on. "I told you I was going to ride my bike home."

"I know, I just thought—"

He tucked back waves of blond hair with his beautiful fingers. "I can take care of myself, Grant. I've been doing it for a long time."

"I never said—"

"When I tell you I can ride my bike home, I mean I can ride my bike home." He flicked thoughts, and his shoulder jerked.

"It's colder than you thought—"

"It rains sometimes too. I get wet. I use a towel to dry off."

"Morgan, that's not the—"

"I don't need you making decisions for me."

"I'm not, I—"

"I'm perfectly capable of—"

I grabbed him by the shoulders. "Will you shut up for a minute and let me finish? I'm not," I tried to catch his gaze and failed. "I'm not here because I thought you shouldn't ride your bike home. I'm here because I wanted to give you a ride home."

His body jerked with a series of tics. I held on. "What's the diff... difference?"

With the sock hat on, his bangs were corralled back and there was nothing to hide the anger blooming in his cheeks or how his gaze darted around, going everywhere but to me.

"One, you do because you're worried the person might be making a bad decision, the other, you do because you miss them. You care about them and you want to be with them." Morgan dropped his chin to his chest. I cupped his face, and he didn't fight meeting my gaze. He had such beautiful eyes. Surrounded with dark heavy lashes, the brown was made all the richer. Just the tiniest flecks of mossy green surrounded his iris. But what took my breath away were the moments he focused on me. It was like having my soul examined, but in a good way. Scary, but good.

His fingertips were cold on my jaw. He drew a path down my neck to my shoulder. He retraced the path up my neck to my jaw. His touch reached my lips. There he rubbed the dip at the top of my chin. The only place I never seemed to grow hair. I wasn't sporting much of a beard, maybe a few days of a shadow, but it was all it took to make the bare piece of skin stand out, giving me the illusion of a cultured pattern.

Morgan rasped a thumb over my chin. Chills raced down my chest turning into a heavy weight when they reached my stomach. My skin warmed head to toe, my muscles tightened, and my cock hardened enough to threaten a slow crawl out of the top of my jeans. I hoped Jessie would stay busy up front. I didn't need more videos on YouTube. Although, at the moment, I don't think I cared.

"Yesterday, you said you didn't want to fill the space anymore. You wanted to be with me."

Morgan touched me again, and the effect echoed twice as loud.

I tightened my hold on him. "Yes."

"Why?"

Why? It was a simple question, and there were a thousand things I wanted to say, but none of them felt good enough.

Good enough for Morgan.

I let him go and stood there with no answer. No way to put into words how he made me feel. How touching him connected me to the world. How tasting him breathed life into my lungs. How I hadn't been alive until the moment I saw him and even then I'd resisted, afraid of what I'd felt, fighting what I feared.

How I thought I knew what love was only to realize, standing in front of him, I knew nothing.

Morgan waved a hand at the back door only to follow up with a string of flutters and snaps. "I heard from a pretty reliable source it's a lot colder than the weather man said it was going to be. I didn't put on any long underwear, and only one pair of socks. Do you think you could give me a ride back to my place?" He shrugged. "I mean if you have the time. If you don't..."

All I could do was nod.

Morgan led the way out the back door. It occurred to me I hadn't paid for my beer, but I'd make it up to Jessie next time I was in town. I didn't know what was happening between Morgan and I at the moment, but I wasn't about to break it. He pushed his bike over to the truck, and we lifted it in the back. He made a few adjustments, wedging it into the corner and turning the wheel until the pedal acted like a brace, before getting into the passenger side.

Morgan didn't speak until I parked the truck and asked, "Do you mind if I come in?"

His shoulder jerked and he snapped his fingers, then there was only silence.

"Please talk to me."

"Did you have sex with him?"

I squinted at Morgan. "What are you talking about?"

"I'm assuming it was the FBI agent, Jeff."

What the hell had Jeff gone and done? "Did he tell you that?"

"No." Morgan sat back in his seat. His wayward hand made an escape attempt, but he tightened his hold on his wrist. His knuckles turned ghostly.

"Then why would you ask me that?"

"But you saw him today. Was it at your place or in town? My guess is at your house. It would have been private."

"Yeah, he came to the house."

"You weren't expecting him?"

"I'm never expecting him; he just shows up. Why would you think I had sex with him?"

"I don't think you had sex with him. That's why I'm asking. I didn't know." Morgan nodded. The fingers on his wayward hand opened and closed. "So did you?"

"No."

His shoulders fell.

"Now will you tell me—"

"You have scratches on your neck, and your chin."

"I'm covered in scratches and about three layers of calamine lotion. I've been crawling under the house all day and fighting off army ants."

"We don't have army ants, Grant. Just black ants. Sometimes farther south you see fire ants, but not often. Army ants or they're sometimes called Legionary Ants don't really have nests, and you'd only run into them in Africa or parts of Central and South America." He took a breath. "You have teeth marks on your collarbone. Even army ants don't have teeth."

I'd looked myself over in the mirror a good twenty minutes after I showered. Not because I wanted to make sure Jeff hadn't left evidence but because I wanted to make sure I hadn't missed painting any of the ant bites. Sure I'd seen the scratches, but they'd just been scratches.

I turned on the cab light. Maybe it wasn't bright enough, but I still couldn't see teeth marks in the rearview mirror. "Something tells me any attempt at a surprise party would be a waste of time."

Morgan wrinkled his nose. "Surprise party? What does that have to do with anything?"

"You see everything even when there's nothing to see."

He dropped his gaze and reached for the door to get out. "Not always. The last time almost got me killed. That's why I asked."

I stopped him. "I swear nothing happened but not because he didn't try. He came on, hard, I turned him down, but it took some pushing, shoving, and parking a sawhorse between us."

"Did you want to?"

I paused only because I wanted to make sure I didn't lie. "Yes and no."

"Why yes?"

"Because we'd been together a long time. There are a lot of memories and they don't like to stay buried. That and sometimes my dick has a mind of its own." Morgan snorted, and I chuckled. "Don't pretend you've never noticed."

"And the no?"

"Because I only want you."

"But you can't tell me why?"

"It's not that I can't, I just don't know how. I was never good with words." I could have told him I loved him, but my throat tightened. How many times had I whispered those three words to Jeff? How many times had I called them out when making love to him? They were just three words, but they felt tainted because I'd already given them up once to another man.

Saying the same thing to Morgan felt like re-gifting hand-me-downs.

Morgan got out of the truck. He went right to his house so I followed. He paused at the bottom of his porch steps, and I wondered for a moment if I'd called it wrong, but then he took my hand, unfolded my fingers, and pressed my palm against his heart. Strong, rhythmic, a bit fast, as if something worried him or excited him. Or maybe even frightened him.

He traced my fingers. Counted my knuckles. Then petted the back of my hand.

"I need you in my life," I said.

He continued the ritual, mapping my digits like he did fragments of light.

"Permanently, or at least as long as you'll let me."

"You said three years, maybe four."

The tightness in my throat moved to my chest. "I know."

"You were going to Seychelles, remember? Where the beaches are perfect and the water's clear. There are some really neat shells there. I've always wondered what sand would feel like between my toes."

"If you want to go, I'll take you."

"I can't."

"You haven't tried."

Morgan stopped moving. "I left once and I couldn't get home because I had to leave the apartment. There were too many people. Too much noise."

"The beach would be quiet."

"The beach is even farther away. What if we got there and I had to come home?"

"Then we'd come home."

"And you'd never get to be there."

"We'd try again."

"And what if I couldn't?"

"Then we wouldn't go."

Morgan raised his head. His stare flittered near my shoulder. "Three or four years. That's what you promised."

"Can't I change my mind?"

He nodded.

"Then let me make it longer. Let me make it forever."

Morgan let me go and headed up the steps. Again I followed. Just inside the front door, I trapped him against the wall near his bedroom.

"Please trust me," I said. "Please, please, just for once. Trust me. I can only imagine what you went through. I can only imagine what you're afraid will happen, but I will never hurt you, Morgan. Never. Not in a million years. I'll make mistakes, I'm sure, but I'll do my best to make them right. I'll—"

He stopped me by meeting my gaze. Full on, no shield, the stocking cap holding his bangs back so I didn't even have to push them away.

"I know." He said it so matter-of-fact that I took a step back. "I've always known you'd never hurt me."

"Then why would you ask about Jeff, or think I was going to leave?"

Morgan's smile was subtle. "Because you're the one who doesn't trust. Me, yourself, even your faraway island. You doubt everything. And people who can't trust, eventually run." He took a step forward, and even though I didn't mean to, I took a step back. "You don't believe in yourself. You're scared of getting lost. Getting hurt. Being trapped."

I bumped the coffee table, stumbled, and wound up sitting on my ass. Morgan pushed his way between my knees and cupped my face. He continued to hold my gaze. Never had he looked at me with so much knowledge of who I was shining in his eyes.

"Love is easy." He traced my eyebrow with his thumb. "Trust is what's hard. Broken hearts can be fixed. Broken trust?" His touch followed a tear down my cheek to my lips. "Trust doesn't heal. Your parents broke your trust when you were really young, it changed you, it took something away. Then the one time you let trust grow, you thought it had been broken again. That's where it can be tricky, because sometimes trust feels broken when it's only a little dented

159

up.

"But it still feels like you're losing bits and pieces of yourself." Closer, his exhale ghosted my lips. "Now you're scared to trust me because you might lose everything you have left."

How did he know? I didn't. All this time, I thought I'd left Chicago to escape the business, get out while I could, enjoy life. Leave behind who I'd been, a criminal, a man I thought I'd loved, and go somewhere no one could possibly know me. No one would want to know me. I'd just be a stranger, a momentary pause in their way of life, then I could escape to nowhere, and I'd never have to risk anything again. I could live, grow old, die, safely in my cocoon of detachment. My heart safely guarded, my trust locked away where no one could touch it.

All the while, I would lie to myself the beauty of a faraway place would feed my soul everything it needed, when in fact it would starve. What I craved, what I needed to live, existed in connections with other people.

Not the kind formed from desperation or in the heat of lust. The kind cultured and cared for. The kind of trust Morgan offered me because no one I'd ever known or met was more open, real, and unguarded. His flaws made him who he was even though he fought them.

A battle he never won, but continued anyhow.

Morgan pulled me to him and my tears soaked his jacket. He shushed me. He rocked me. He kissed my ear.

"You can trust me, Grant. You don't have to run. You don't have to hide."

The need to feel him had me clawing at his jacket and tearing off his shirt. His stocking cap was lost in the pile of clothes. Static made his curls stand out. The halo they created was so appropriate.

I seized his mouth and plundered him with my tongue. His lips were slightly salty. Had he eaten french fries for dinner? An enhancer he didn't need but drove my hunger higher for the taste that was all him.

Morgan pulled me to my feet and dragged me toward his bedroom. Halfway there, he wound up with his legs around my waist and me carrying him. My shirt disappeared, and he bit my right nipple. When he brought his mouth back up, calamine lotion painted the bottom one pink.

I couldn't help but laugh as I rubbed it away. "Not sure how much of that you can ingest before you wind up sick."

"Then I'll have to make sure I only lick where the ants didn't bite."

I dropped him on the bed. He shimmied out of his jeans and boxers. As mine reached my knees, he grabbed my arm, yanking me off balance. I wound up on my stomach with Morgan straddling my hips.

His hot tongue and burning lips drew nameless pictures down my spine. He reached my ass crack. I glanced back as he parted my cheeks and dipped his tongue into the cleft. From the soft spot behind my balls, he lapped his way to my hole. Then the wet fire circled the ring of muscle, shoving a bark of surprise from my chest.

Morgan grinned at me over the curve of my ass as he did it again. I'd only been rimmed a few times in my life. It was never Jeff's thing unless he was drunk. But somehow Morgan made it different. There wasn't just the electric spiral that pulled my nuts tight. The pleasure he created by tracing my opening with the tip of his tongue, then his teeth, released an inferno in my gut that spread out over my skin.

Against my will, my hips pumped against the mattress. I didn't want to come yet; there were so many things I wanted to do to him, but in that moment, I was his to control.

Just as the head of my dick began to ache with the rise of release, Morgan stopped. I buried a cry into the mattress only because I didn't want to sound so vulnerable.

He stripped off my jeans and my shoes went with them. Then he urged me higher onto the bed. I started to roll over, but he lowered his weight, blanketing me with his body. His exhale was spiced with the musk of sex. He leaned close enough to kiss the corner of my mouth.

"Why?" His question was almost buried by my heavy breathing.

I think I understood the question now. I could only hope I had the right answer. If there was one.

"Because I want to trust, be trusted. I want someone I can count on, someone who can count on me. I want somewhere safe. I want a home. But that can only happen if I'm with you."

"I'm never going to be like other men, Grant."

I wasn't sure what he meant until I turned enough to see his expression. The knowledge in his eyes spoke of those places he looked into. The windows or portals he disappeared into when he followed the light.

"I can give you what I have, but I can never give you everything." It wasn't Morgan didn't want to, he couldn't. I could see that too. He could never give me all of himself because he didn't control everything he had.

Could I live with that?

Morgan nipped my ear, kissed the back of my neck. His touch burned trails down my ribs to my thighs. I raised up enough to reach his mouth and held him there, trapped by the need to taste one another, to feed each other the air we needed to breathe.

I reached back and gripped his cock. A small sound escaped Morgan's chest as he rocked into my fist. The position was awkward, but I didn't want the moment to end. Then he stopped and we wound up tangled chest to chest—arms, hands fighting for a place to grip, and legs entwined. His body against mine, rocking in fluid movement. Precum painted our cocks, our stomach, saliva made our lips shiny, and the kissing left mine swollen and aching.

I was about to slide down and suck him off when he rolled me onto my back. Morgan bit my left nipple hard enough to make me jump. His wicked grin softened and he followed the line of hair to my navel, there he lapped at the dip like he had my hole. The shock of pleasure made my cock jump. Lower, Morgan licked my weeping slit, one slow stroke of his tongue.

I was so busy watching him tease me I didn't realize he'd slid a hand between us until a fingertip pressed against my hole. There was just enough saliva left for him to push in. Even with delicate hands, the increasing width of each knuckle rekindled the burn. He found my prostate and the rolling euphoria exploded in a sudden burst. Tremors ran down my legs. I eased out a breath, focusing on the occasional slide of heated silk up the length of my dick.

"If you'll…" He pushed in another and my words turned into a groan. "If you'll turn around I'll…" Another deep growl rolled out of me. I'd had fingers in my ass while getting sucked off on more than one occasion. And I'll admit, it always made me nervous because I know when I did it to a lover, my dick was usually next.

Morgan took my cock to the back of his throat, working his throat muscles, swallowing around me, while at the same time massaging me with his tongue. I'd never known a guy who could suck cock like him. Zero gag reflex and every part of his mouth to his throat working in sync.

I stroked his head. "God, Morgan…" Whatever else I said, I couldn't remember. Or maybe it was nothing and just one of those guttural noises. A rutting bull. Yeah, maybe I did sound like one. "Don't want to… yet." Ah hell, I was well on my way to losing the battle. Then he pulled out his fingers and reached for the bedside table.

The sound of the drawer opening tempered my rising release. I tracked the movement of his hands as if he held a weapon instead of a bottle of lubricant.

"I'm going to fuck you, Grant." Morgan kissed the head of my cock. Any attempt to flag was thwarted.

Did I tell him I'd never been topped?

Well, that wasn't completely true, Cody tried once. He'd been average sized but impatient. He wanted to just cram his dick in and go. The surprise and the discomfort of having something trying to go into a place that, in my mind at the time, was only an exit, had me clenching so hard he couldn't even get inside me with enough lubricant to thread a camel through a needle.

He gave up and wound up rubbing off between my ass cheeks. The friction left my hole raw and me determined to never give him the opportunity for a future attempt.

I won't say I was any more attentive, especially the first few times, but he seemed to like it rough. I probably never would have learned to work him with my fingers if he hadn't been so easy to make come. Half the time, he'd lose his load before I could even get started, then I'd have to convince him to stay long enough to let me finish, by working him up again.

It was terrible sex, and half the time one-sided—his side—but I was young, dumb, and horny and didn't care. In all of its awkwardness, it taught me a lot about how to find erogenous zones. Most of the lovers I'd taken to my bed didn't expect long drawn out foreplay, but then neither had I.

Until Jeff. Then it became something else more important than getting off, it became pleasing someone, giving them something, showing them through the time I took with their body how much I appreciated them.

And with Morgan? It became something beyond a connection of bodies. Sex wasn't even close to what he did with me.

Morgan returned to the tip of my dick. He watched me over the plane of my body. A small tic pulled his shoulder. He popped the cap, and paused again.

"Would you rather me ride you?" Morgan sat back on his knees and his beautiful cock jutted out. He wasn't quite as long as me, but just as thick, and curved. Hard, the foreskin all but disappeared behind the swollen head. "Grant?"

"No… I…" All I had to do was say it. Morgan abandoned the bottle of lube next to my thigh and climbed over me. He held my face, searched my eyes, then his bangs slid down and I had to push them back so I could see him. "Don't stop."

He exhaled a sigh against my mouth. "If you'd rather—"

"No. Keep going. I'll be fine."

The pupils of Morgan's eyes expanded, he pressed his cheek against mine hard enough to make a rasping sound. "I've wanted to be inside you since I first saw you." He picked up the lube. When he dropped it again, the lid was shut but slick as if he'd spilled some down the side. He reached around his back and his touch slid between his legs, past my cock, and his fingers were at my entrance again.

I tried not to startle when he pushed in because I was afraid he'd stop. But Morgan didn't, not until he was knuckle deep. My cock slid against his ass, rocking his entire body as he pumped

162

his fingers in and out. Again he found my prostate and the deep movement turned into a slow massage.

"Ah, hell..." Sweat ran down my neck and ice crawled through my veins. I lifted my hips, searching for just a little more pressure. I'd never come hands-free, but I knew without a doubt Morgan could make me.

A third finger stretched my opening until it burned. The discomfort was too close of a reminder of the first time, but the way Morgan worked me from the inside made it irrelevant. The growing ache seized my muscles. Just as I reached the edge, knowing I was going to fall, his fingers were gone and I was left writhing in the sheets.

"Damn it." I heaved for breath. Morgan scooted down between my knees and lifted one of my legs to his shoulder, pushing it toward my chest. Almost immediately my hip protested. "I don't think I'm as bendable as you."

He pulled down the pillows. "Here. Raise up." I did, and he packed them under my back until my ass was off the mattress. "Comfortable?"

More like vulnerable. Morgan licked the head of my cock and pushed his fingers in again. The liquid squelched, and for some damn reason, I laughed.

"Here." He picked up my hand and poured some lube into my palm. "Slick me up." Morgan leaned forward enough to present his cock. The lubricant turned the velvet flesh into oiled fire. He flexed his hips, pushing into the tunnel of my fist, undulating against the air. Bodies just weren't supposed to move that way, at least not without aches and pains to pay for it.

"You like watching me." He bit his lip.

"Who wouldn't? You're beautiful, Morgan." He averted his eyes, but not in the way he did when he looked beyond. I pulled him down until our foreheads touched, until he was forced to look at me or close his eyes. "You are beautiful."

"Sunsets are beautiful, beaches are beautiful, not men."

"I'd rather watch you."

His fingers disappeared again, and he pushed at the back of my knees until they hung over his hips. With all the pillows under me, my ass was right there for the taking.

"Gonna have to let me go if you want to do this."

I pressed my thumb against the head of his cock while rolling the foreskin to the tip. Morgan's breath shuddered out, and I'm pretty sure the jerk of his hips was completely involuntary.

"Grant." He kissed my chin, my neck, my chest. "I want to be inside you." Morgan caressed the inside of my thighs down to my ass. He spread my cheeks apart and the cool air touched my opening.

I let him go, and his cock slapped my balls, then slid behind my sack. With my cheeks still spread wide, he rocked his hips and the head of his dick bumped my opening.

I'd topped enough guys to know to push down to relax my hole, but my body wasn't listening.

"Grant?" Morgan kissed one knee then the other.

A shiver ran down my spine. A cross between the memory of how he could bring me to the edge and the fear of not being able to get off. His cock was bigger than his fingers, curved, but he wouldn't have the same control, and I could only hope I would enjoy this.

I'd never put much thought into the idea of how some guys didn't like a dick in their ass for whatever reason. Lying right there, I realized I was probably one of those guys.

Worse was Morgan wanted me. The flush in his face, the heat in his eyes, with every nudge his breathing quickened.

He leaned over me, one hand beside my shoulder. "What's wrong?"

"Don't laugh."

"I'd never laugh."

"Last time I tried this, things didn't go very well."

"What happened?"

I scrubbed a hand over my face. "I was young, he was impatient. I wound up needing hemorrhoid cream for friction burn." Morgan didn't laugh, but I did. It was either that or cry, and damn it, I was not going to cry like some idiot.

"You like my fingers inside you." He lowered himself down. His other arm was trapped between us, and his hand brushed my ass as he pumped his dick. My own erection withered despite the slight movement of his body stroking me.

"Your dick is bigger and…"

Morgan cocked his head.

"It's your fingers, I don't know why it's different." I brushed his hair away from his face; he watched something I couldn't see. "This has nothing to do with not being able to trust you." I didn't want him to think it was. If it had been the other way around, I'm pretty sure it's the conclusion I would have come to.

"I know." His gaze returned, accompanied by a twitch of his shoulder. Fingertips rubbed my opening, making small circles, then pushing enough to enter only to pull away when the ring of muscle gave in. The tease had me lifting my ass before I realized it. He raised up on his arm again taking away all contact except for where my thighs rested on his hips and the head of his cock touched my hole. "You know it's okay to be scared."

"I am not…" Damn it, he was right. I would have gotten up and left, only it meant I'd have to stop touching him, and I didn't want to stop. I cupped Morgan's face, and he didn't resist when I pulled him close enough to kiss. What started as a soft brush of flesh turned into warring tongues. He tried to pull away, but I tangled my fist into his hair. I wanted him, but I just couldn't put it into words. There was a moment of surprise in his eyes, then his gaze darkened.

Pressure returned to my hole, and in one long push, Morgan breached my opening. The burn caught me off guard, but it was nothing compared to the sudden sense of fullness. I can't say it felt good, or bad, only strange. He drank down whatever sound I made and fed me his own cry of pleasure.

"God, Grant." Morgan arched his back and what felt balls deep went deeper. I bucked, but he didn't pull out. His exhale warmed my ear. "Do you want me to stop?"

The very wanton tone of his voice held me where I was. "No."

His breath shuddered. "You feel…" Morgan hummed and rolled his body in that fluid way, grinding against me. Whatever apprehension I'd had crumbled as an electric crackle danced over my nerve endings. "So gooood."

He did it again, and the sudden need for friction had me drawing up my legs, setting Morgan free. He took control, sitting up on his knees, pumping his hips. I had to grab onto the headboard to keep from being shoved off the stack of pillows.

Flesh slapped together and our breathing filled the room. My cock, hard and swollen again, leaked precum on my stomach. The need to come had me gritting my teeth. Morgan shifted his weight. It changed the angle somehow, and every thrust put pressure against my prostate.

My balls tightened and pleasure coiled in my gut. I started to jerk off, but Morgan smacked his body against mine and I was forced to steady myself with my grip on the rungs or lose the position that set my flesh on fire. Above me, Morgan danced, his tawny muscles quivering, his chest heaving, his mouth open. His eyes were closed, but the expression on his face was pure bliss.

"Want you to come," Morgan said. He leaned forward, balancing himself with his hands on my chest. The euphoria created by the friction condensed until it was almost pain. "Need to see you come, Grant."

I reached for my cock. The head was so sensitive the first contact made me jump. All I could do was grip the length of flesh, almost afraid to move because of how sensitive the nerves had become. Morgan slowed his thrusts and the rising tsunami threatened to recede. Desperation had me pumping my fist.

"That's it," he hissed. "That's it. Fucking hot. You are so fucking hot." He dropped his head low enough to bite one of my nipples. The sharp sting of pain added another layer of static. "You like that." His bangs parted and the wickedness in his gaze spoke of devilish thoughts. "One day I'm gonna tie you down and do this to you. Maybe do it while you're asleep, let you wake up with my cock in your ass." His pace increased and his thrusts shortened. Cords stood out on his neck and his fingers dug into my chest.

"I think you're the one who's gonna come."

"Wanna bet?" He swiveled his hips.

Lightning shot up my spine. "Oh, hell, Morgan…" Ropes of cum shot over my fist, coating my stomach, even reaching my chin. Morgan's cry of conquest turned into an agonizing groan. With every pulse of his cock, his thrusts slowed. The heat of his cum followed his moving cock and ran down my crack.

We were going to have to change the sheets before we could go to sleep. Morgan covered me with his body, still inside me, our skin stuck together with sweat. The hell with the sheets. I wrapped my arms around him, and he tucked his head under my chin.

For a very long time, there was only the sound of our beating hearts and labored breathing, then Morgan said, "I'll understand if you ever change your mind."

"About what?"

"Me."

"I won't."

"You might. Things happen."

"I'd be more likely to win the lottery and I don't even play it."

He kissed my collarbone, then traced it with his fingertips. "But just in case, just so you know, I would understand."

Chapter Five

I dreamed about the day when Jeff's solo deal went bad. When bullets got thrown around. People got shot. People died.

And for what? One sorry-ass FBI agent who'd led me on with four years' worth of lies. Lies that I was stupid enough to swallow hook, line, and sinker.

I won't lie. It wasn't the first time I killed a man, but it was the first time I'd killed a man not pointing the gun at me. It was a step down the road of violence where businessmen held grudges and got even by taking out the people you cared about. The only reason I didn't wind up with cinder blocks around my ankles was because Jeff Meyers took the blame for that killing shot. Otherwise Caruso wouldn't have been so understanding and instead of a get-well card at my hospital bed, he would have set me up with a car bomb or something equally glorious.

Don't think for a minute Jeff covered because he was trying to protect me, he had to bury his identity. See, after Jeff Meyers fucked with my reputation, I let him disappear and made no attempt to stop the rumors of his demise. It was just better for the rest of the business world to think he'd been another casualty in the house fire that erased any evidence the FBI could use to connect me to the botched job.

I wanted to blame Jeff. But the only one at fault was me. I'd let my guard down and almost died because of it. I knew the rules, and I'd broken them because I'd followed my dick.

Only that wasn't exactly true either. We had started out as nothing but sex to break the tension, but it turned into something else. I think Jeff was surprised at what grew between us, and I know for a fact he broke more than one FBI undercover rule. How he managed to keep his job, especially after that last blunder, I had no idea.

My only consolation was none of the people involved were close friends or even close associates. My people knew better than to strike up a deal with someone who was green.

Jeff might have followed me around the block and back, but he'd never learned the real ins and outs. Because I didn't let him. At least I had enough of my wits to keep him far enough back to never figure out how I moved those articles right in front of him. Otherwise I would have been in that six by eight cell Jeff threatened me with, rather than a quaint farmhouse, in a no-where town called Durstrand.

The echo of gunfire followed me from sleep, and I lay there, staring at the ceiling. I ran a hand over the cool rumpled sheets on Morgan's side of the bed. How long had he been up?

There was another crack.

And another.

The remaining brain fog peeled back, and I realized the gunfire was never in my dream to begin with.

I snatched my pants off the floor and ran through the house. "Morgan?"

One leg in, the other out. I tripped over my shoes. My shoulder hit the doorframe to the kitchen.

The shots kept going.

Somehow I got my pants up on my way out the back door. Morgan stood beyond the fire pit with a gun in his hand. On a far stone wall backed by a stack of hay bales, red glass bottles exploded in rapid fire.

If I hadn't been so caught off guard, I might have stopped to admire his stance.

"Morgan." I skidded to a halt beside him. My first instinct was to grab the gun, but I knew better.

He stopped shooting. "Good morning, Grant."

"What the hell are you doing?"

"Isn't it obvious? I'm shooting bottles."

"No, I mean, what are you doing with that?" I almost reached for the gun. Almost.

"It's called a gun. Or more precisely, a GLOCK G3OS. With a full capacity .45 Auto round count. Not too heavy. Not too light. Easy to conceal if you have to."

"Why do you have it?"

"I can't shoot the bottles with spit balls."

"Morgan." I waved his hand down, and he complied. "The last thing you need to have in your hand is a gun."

"Why do you say that?" Head down, I couldn't be sure of his expression, but his tone rang of a warning. Thing is, I don't think I cared. He didn't need a gun. Him of all people should never handle a gun.

"They're dangerous."

"Yes, they are. Which is why I took classes on the proper handling of a firearm. Or did you mean they're dangerous in a different way?"

Definitely that tone. Cold. Hard. Daring me to challenge him.

"What if you misfire?"

"I won't."

"Morgan, you wear a long-sleeved shirt when you cook for a reason."

"This isn't cooking."

"No, this is firing a weapon. It's far more deadly."

"I'm aware of how deadly it is. That's why I bought it to begin with. With this, I can protect myself."

"Who the hell do you need to protect yourself from?"

His gaze came up and flicked away, following the bits of colored light from the kinetic sculptures or simply watching something I couldn't see. When he brought his attention back to me, he clenched his jaw. "I know you think your lawyer friend will fix things. But the truth is, Dillon will get out, and when he does, he will finish what he started."

With lightning fast precision, Morgan popped the clip, put it on the edge of the fire pit, then cleared the chamber. He turned it butt first toward me.

"Do you want a turn?"

"No, I just want you to put it down before you hurt yourself. Please, Morgan. Harriet is going to take care of everything. She's good at her job. If there's a way to keep him in jail, she'll find it."

"Won't matter what she does. He'll still get out."

"You don't know that."

"Light travels at six hundred and seventy-one million miles per hour. The light we see

Adrienne Wilder   In the Absence of Light

coming from the stars is billions of years old. Most of those stars are long gone. If you could spend a day moving at that speed, hundreds of years would pass in what felt like only months. Everything, everyone you know, would be gone. Lost to the past."

"What does any of that have to do with you owning a gun?"

"I told you the light speaks, not in words but it has a language. It's already been where I haven't. It's how I know he will get out."

I didn't have even one idea where to begin to argue against what he claimed. "Okay, let's say he might get out."

"Will, Grant. Dillon will get out."

"Why would he come here? He'd be more likely to run and hide. Durstrand would be the first place they'd come looking for him, and he could wind up with a lot more time in jail." If I didn't kill him first.

"He's not going to run. He can't run."

I shook my head. "Why?"

"Because he asked me one time about the things I saw."

Morgan meant the things he saw when he went away. Hadn't Aunt Jenny warned me never to ask Morgan a question I didn't want answered?

"I told him, Grant. I told him, and because of it, he'll never stop until he kills me."

"I won't let him hurt you." I hoped he'd hear the vow in my voice if not read it from my soul.

Morgan's smile was sad. "You won't be able to stop him. Now if you excuse me, I have to practice and break the bottles."

"Can't you use a hammer?" A rock, anything.

"Why don't you just say it?" Morgan tilted his head enough for me to catch a glimpse of his eyes. I wish I could say I never saw the hurt. Maybe I didn't and just imagined it. Or felt it. "You think I can't handle a gun because I can't tie my shoes, tell left from right, or drive a car. Which I can sorta drive a car now. But you know what I mean. You think I'm incapable. That I'll hurt myself. That maybe I'll even accidentally shoot someone." He nodded. "Don't worry, you don't have to say anything. I know. But I also know you're wrong." Again, in a blur of speed, he popped the clip back in, slid back the lock, and aimed at the bottles. Staring somewhere close to my shoulder, he fired the gun.

One bottle after the next exploded into crimson shards. Morgan never once looked at his target. And he never missed.

When the last bottle lay in shards in the metal trough underneath the wall, he once again cleared the gun. Morgan slid the clip into his pocket. His wayward hand fluttered next to his temple.

"I'm cooking French toast and eggs, but I'm out of bacon, so we'll have ham."

Morgan left me staring at the empty space his targets had occupied.

If I'd been shooting at the same distance, I don't think I would have hit half as many. I didn't know of many people who could. The ones who would have, sure as hell wouldn't have been looking the other way.

I waited a few moments before I went back inside. Part of it was to get my mouth under control, the other part was to wait till my heart stopped clawing the inside of my ribs in an attempt to give me a heart attack.

168

By the time I made it to the kitchen, Morgan was wearing a long-sleeved shirt and dropping a slice of ham into the frying pan. There was no sign of the gun.

"Where did you put it?"

"It's safe."

"Morgan, please." I wanted the damn thing out of there.

"I'm not a child, Grant."

"I never said you were."

"Then quit treating me like one."

"I'm not. It's just there are some things you've got to realize you shouldn't do."

"And why is that?"

"You know why."

"Because I'm defective?"

God help me, I almost said yes. It was right there on the tip of my tongue. I wish I could have said I didn't think he was. And I guess I didn't in the way he feared. But I did think it. I should have known just letting it wander through my mind was all it would take for Morgan to know.

"Get out, Grant."

"Morgan, please."

"Get out." Morgan's arm jerked hard enough to yank the pan off the burner. He stopped it before it got very far, but not quick enough to avoid slapping grease over his hand.

"Fuck."

"Here." I started toward the sink, but he stopped me with a look.

"Just go."

"You're hurt."

"Yeah, and I'll take care of it. Now get the hell out." Spit flecked his lips. Anger turned his cheeks crimson. Morgan's entire body trembled with a kind of rage I never dreamed he was capable of.

But it wasn't the kind of uncontrolled fury unleashed by circumstance; it was the raw kind born of broken faith. Which made sense if I thought about it. He'd thought I too believed in him, and I'd shattered his belief just as efficiently as a bullet to those bottles.

I went back to the bedroom and got dressed.

Morgan came to the door as I was putting on my shoes.

"Don't come back." The dead weight of his words was far scarier than the anger. "Not forever, but not till I'm ready."

At least he left me a glimmer of hope. I stayed silent, because anything I said would have made things worse.

****

The plumbing in the kitchen took me half a day. Reinstalling the sink and a new cabinet ate up the rest. Afterward, I fixed the weak spot in the floor by putting down fresh OSB board, then pieced together slats of wood to fill the gap in the hardwood. It would have been easier to slap down some linoleum and be done with it, I mean, who the hell wants to deal with wood floors in the kitchen, but for some reason, I decided to do it the hard way.

Seemed like I did everything the hard way.

After about five days and four finished projects, the silence from Morgan was killing me. I desperately wanted to hear his voice, look at his beautiful eyes, touch him, taste him. I craved his scent and woke up in the middle of the night searching for him only to find the bed empty.

Since he'd told me he didn't want to see me until he was ready, I didn't call, I didn't go to Toolies, and after a while, I didn't even sleep. I just sat in the dark staring out the window, wondering what he was doing in that moment. Maybe he was sleeping, or maybe he was looking out his window wondering the same thing about me.

I didn't want to screw things up any more than I already had, but I had to know if he was all right. Like hadn't accidentally shot himself with the damn gun.

A gun. All this over a stupid gun.

If only it were true. All this was because I doubted him. I'd shown I didn't trust him as much as I claimed. I'd proven I was still prejudice, tainted by first impressions, spoiled by the privileges given to me because I appeared normal.

Jeff had the excuse of ignorance. I had no excuse at all. How did you apologize for something so ingrained it didn't even feel wrong? Worse. What if there wasn't a way?

I decided to drive out to Jenny's. If anything, she could punch me in the head for hurting Morgan. I found a spot beside a van and walked down the hill to the red metal building. All three bay doors were up, and cars of every make and model were being pulled apart and put back together by men in coveralls.

Jenny came around the back of an old Impala. Grease painted her arms all the way to her elbows. She had a smudge on her chin, and a Band-Aid on her forehead.

"Afternoon, Grant." She smiled, but something in her expression told me she already knew.

"What happened to your head?"

She touched the Band-Aid. "Low clearance on a Toyota hood. It'll get you every time." She took a rag out of her pocket and cleaned her hands. "If you're looking for Morgan, he's not here."

"I didn't think he was. That's why I stopped by."

"Still not speaking to ya?"

"How'd you guess?"

She jerked her chin in the direction of her office. "C'mon, we can talk over a fresh pot of coffee and moon pies."

She pulled two chairs over to the table near the wall. "Just put those magazines on the windowsill."

I did.

"You take cream and sugar in your coffee?" Jenny went around to the other side of the desk.

I followed her to the edge and propped my elbows on the countertop. "Cream is fine."

"I asked Morgan what happened between you two, but he wouldn't say."

I pressed my thumb and first finger against my eyes. "Well, obviously I fucked up."

"How so?" She fixed the coffees. Despite wiping her hands, she still left gray thumbprints on the Styrofoam.

"I made the mistake of telling him he couldn't do something."

"Oooh boy, yeah, that'll get him madder than a wet hen. Just be glad he let you keep your teeth." Jenny opened the cabinet under the desk and came up with a couple of moon pies. "Here." She tossed me one, and I caught it. "Let's go sit down. I'm not as young as I used to be, and my legs get tired." We went to the table and sat.

Jenny opened her moon pie and sipped her coffee. I just looked at mine.

"You gonna talk or stare?"

"I'm not sure where to start."

"How about whatever you told him he couldn't do?"

I scrubbed my face and peered at her over my fingertips. She ate her moon pie, all the while watching me like a hawk about to pounce on a mouse. I seriously began to wonder if this was such a good idea.

I flopped back in my chair. "Did you know Morgan has a gun?"

"Yup."

"And it doesn't bother you?"

"'Course it bothers me. But I can guarantee not for the reasons it bothers you."

"What do you mean?"

"Well," she chewed, swallowed, drank some coffee. "I'm willing to bet you're bothered by the fact the gun. Whereas I'm bothered by the fact he feels like he needs it."

I hadn't really thought of it like that. Once I did, I couldn't decide which was worse. "He's that afraid of Dillon?"

Jenny put down her moon pie. There was the barest tremble in her bottom lip, then she cleared her throat and it was gone. "I've never seen anyone get to Morgan, Grant. At all. Ever. He's taken everything the world has thrown at him. I'm not saying it didn't knock him down, but damn that boy got right back up. Then he kicked someone's ass."

"But Dillon? I don't know why or how, but the SOB broke him. He cracked Morgan open and took something out. He's not just scared of Dillon, he's terrified of him." She popped the last bite of moon pie in her mouth and ate it.

"He told me he thinks Dillon will come back."

Jenny nodded. "Yeah, I guess it's possible."

"Well if he tries anything, he'll wind up right back in prison."

She laughed. "And I'm sure that line of thinking keeps people from doing bad things all the time."

Of course it didn't. "Shit."

"You can say that."

"How much danger is Morgan in?"

"I don't know to be honest. But Morgan thinks he's in danger. That's enough to worry me. I can only imagine what the man did to break him. But I don't because I wouldn't be able to stand the nightmares."

I didn't need an imagination. I'd seen men broken before. I don't care who they are, it's never pretty. And I don't think any of them ever healed.

"Is he safe with that gun around?"

She snorted. "Is that your way of asking me if he's gonna accidentally shoot himself or someone else?"

"Yeah, I guess it is."

"Accidents can happen to anyone, even Morgan. But I'd say his chances are way down there in the ranks. You ever seen him shoot? Boy's like Billy the Kid. Except Morgan's not stupid enough to go twirling a fire arm around on his fingers."

I drank my barely warm cup of coffee.

"You want another?"

"I'm good, thanks." Well, as good as I could be considering the situation I'd gotten myself in. "I don't know how to fix this, Jenny. I'm not even sure how it fell apart. One minute, we were fine, the next?" Morgan was kicking me out with the order to not come back.

"Who's to say there's anything to fix?"

"I haven't seen him in almost a week."

She laughed. A real throw back your head belly shaker.

"What's so funny?"

"You, Grant. You." She wiped the tears from her eyes with her thumb. "Pining like some love struck school girl."

I opened my mouth to argue, then shut it. She was right. Then the last thing I wanted to say fell out. "I think I'm in love with him."

I glanced up at Jenny who smiled at me while she drained her cup. "'Course you are. You'd have to be deaf, blind, dumb, and dead to not be." She reached across the table and ruffled my hair. "Now eat your moon pie." Jenny took her cup over to the coffeemaker.

The moon pie wrapper split with a loud crinkle. I broke off a bit of cookie and ate it. "I can't remember the last time I ate one of these." The bad part was that I couldn't even decide if I liked them.

After a couple of bites, the taste grew on me and I was able to make short work of the cookie. Then I only had that sad plastic pouch with its lonely crumbs. It might as well have been an analogy of my life.

Jenny leaned on the table and regarded me over the edge of her cup. "If it's any consolation, he loves you too."

"Maybe under different circumstances it would be." Right now it just made things worse."

"You wanna know his secret?"

Sure, I did. I was just afraid I'd slip and fall on it. "Is it going to make things worse than they already are?"

"Only if you misuse it."

"I wish I could promise it wouldn't happen."

"As long as you try not to that's all that counts."

I folded the wrapper into a neat square. It spread back out as soon as I let go, looking almost as perfect as it did before I'd creased it. "All right. Tell me."

"Morgan lives every day on the edge of a prison. He's helpless against his body and mind, and he has to fight continuously not to drown. So he seeks control in everything from how he arranges his food, to riding his bike to work. Even those kinetic sculptures he builds is his way to control the light inevitably controlling him.

"And it's exhausting, Grant. He needs you, Grant, and I think it scares him. Especially after Dillon."

"Then how am I going to help him?"

"You're going to have to convince him to let you. And he'll fight you, Grant. He may even hate you. But if you can do it, I think Morgan will find the kind of peace he hasn't had since Lori died. He might even find more." Jenny stood. "But just in case I'm wrong, you might wanna look into getting some dental insurance."

****

They say, be careful what you wish for.

I sat for another two days trying to come up with a plan. Even in my head, every scenario ended up less than favorable. How the hell did I convince a man, who wouldn't so much as let me make him come, he could rely on me?

Mulling over the things Jenny said made me realize something else too. Morgan fought for control, but he didn't always win. And I'd made it all the more humiliating by telling him he couldn't—shouldn't—do something because he wasn't capable.

Since I failed to come up with a plan, I decided I'd just show up and hope for the best. I was just about to call Toolies to see if he was there when the phone rang.

"Hello?"

"Grant." Jessie.

"Just the man I wanted to talk to."

"You'll have to save it for later." Tension strained his voice.

"What's wrong?"

"The FBI is here, Grant. One of them's that guy from the other day. He wants to arrest Morgan."

"What? Why?"

He made an angry sound. "Something about money, fraud, extortion, and a whole other list of accusations that honestly sound like bullshit but I'm not no lawyer."

I stomped on my shoes and grabbed my jacket. "Have you called Jenny?"

"She's out of town. She told me to call you. Morgan's not handling it well. Deputy Harold is here. He's trying to convince this asshole FBI guy to let the local boys handle it, but I don't think he's going to win the argument."

The screen door slapped against the frame behind me. "I'm on my way."

I shot out of the driveway fast enough to spray gravel across the asphalt. Driving more than forty-five in the dark was stupid. Especially with all the deer crossing the road. The speedometer hit seventy on the straightaway, and I could only hope Bambi wasn't in the mood to play Kamikaze.

There was no way Morgan was involved with whatever bullshit Jeff had dreamed up. He was just pissed. I knew he could be a vengeful shit when he wanted to; I just never imagined he'd use Morgan to get back at me.

Two sedans were parked at the front of Toolies with a police car between them.

I'd hoped this was Jeff trying to bluff his way into getting me to talk, but a second car meant he wasn't alone, and he might not even be in charge.

Angry voices carried out into the parking lot.

Yelling meant people were losing their cool, and when that happened, they got stupid. An affliction law enforcement was not immune to but twice as dangerous for them because they thought they were.

I yanked open the door. The three men in suits and Deputy Harold looked up. In the sudden silence, there was only the high-pitched keen from Morgan coming from somewhere in the back.

"He's locked himself in the bathroom." Jessie nodded at the three suits. "And these assholes want to break down the door."

I pointed at Jeff. "This is low. Even for you, this is low."

"Believe it or not, this doesn't concern you."

I barked a laugh. "Yeah, right. You've only been following me around town for over a month because you like the scenery."

I ran down the hall. The pain-filled sound Morgan cried cut deep.

"Morgan?" I knocked. "Morgan, it's me." There was a stutter in the constant wail. "Please open the door."

"If he doesn't open the door, we'll go in after him." I didn't recognize the FBI agent who'd stopped at the end of the hall. Jeff stood beside him. But his partner, I'd seen driving the Bronco a few weeks ago.

"Both of you, get back."

"That's not your call," Jeff said.

"The hell it isn't. You're playing a game here and could get someone hurt."

"No game. Mr. Kade has committed some serious crimes."

"Extortion? Fraud? Bullshit. I think they've had you locked up in a surveillance van so long you've suffered oxygen deprivation. Or maybe you just have your head shoved that far up your ass."

Jeff pulled an envelope from his jacket. The remnants of a certified mail sticker stuck to the back.

"What gave you the right to go through my truck?"

"The fact you're under investigation."

"Did you have a warrant?" I met him toe to toe. "Last time I checked search and seizure required one."

"What do you know about Morgan Kade?"

"Enough."

"I don't think so. I don't think you know jack shit about him." Jeff slapped me in the chest with the envelope, and I snatched it away.

He nodded once. "That's a letter from a lawyer who's been trying to contact your friend in there quite some time. Apparently they discovered an unauthorized transaction being deducted from a client's account on a monthly basis for the past five years. They wanted to settle this without involving the authorities, but Morgan has refused to cooperate."

I skimmed the letter. It confirmed everything Jeff said. I still didn't believe it.

"We're not talking small change here, Grant. He's taken more than a hundred thousand dollars." According to the letter, Morgan threatened to disclose personal information on the client's wife.

"This makes no sense." I folded the letter back up and crammed it in my pocket. Jeff scowled, and I said, "I'm returning it to its rightful owner. And if I were you, I'd start praying he doesn't sue you for violation of his civil rights."

"There was no violation, Grant. See, I have a warrant for you. I can look through everything you own, at any given time. Which means I could look in your truck and collect anything I deem pertinent to your case. The letter from the lawyer just happened to be a bonus. You see, we contacted the lawyer, his client filed charges yesterday. Since we were already here, we just saved them the trouble of having the locals pick him up. And since this happened over state lines, it puts the case in FBI jurisdiction."

Jeff's cocky expression said it all. He couldn't get to me, so he was going to make Morgan's life a living hell. "Let me go talk to him."

"He's resisted arrest, assaulted an agent, and you want me to let you go talk to him?"

"He doesn't deal well with change, and if he hit one of you, you probably deserved it." I should have kept my mouth shut about the second part.

Jeff flexed his hands, making his knuckles pop. I knew from experience he only did it when he was a few steps past angry and you're chances of reasoning with him were running thin.

"I'll go talk to him. Then we'll sit down, here, and figure this out."

Jeff raised his eyebrows. "We will, huh? And why would I do that, Grant? Why would I even entertain the idea of trusting you with getting him to cooperate, when you're nothing but a criminal yourself?"

I glanced back at the door. Morgan was quiet now, but the lack of sound didn't comfort me. "You'll let me." I turned back to Jeff. "Because I have something you want far more than anything Morgan has to offer."

Victory shone in his eyes. He'd played his hands, and I'd folded. To Jessie, I said, "Do you have a key?"

He pulled one out of his pocket.

Jeff shot him a dirty look. "I thought you didn't have one."

Jessie shrugged. "My mistake."

"Go sit down." I went back to the bathroom door. "We'll be out in a minute."

"We haven't agreed to anything."

"Yes, you have. Now go."

There was a tense moment where I was afraid Jeff would refuse just for the chance of punishing me. But I was right. He wanted what I had far more than the stupid charges brought up against Morgan. Him and another agent put their heads together. Then the one I didn't know nodded.

"You've got ten minutes." Jeff and his buddies vacated the hall.

"Grant, he's not going to go," Jessie said.

"He will."

"If they try to arrest him, they'll wind up hurting him." The look in his eyes said they might even wind up killing him. Because he was right, Morgan would not go without a fight. He would not let someone take control of him and decide his fate.

"We'll figure something out." I waved a hand toward the dining room. "Would y'all mind sitting down in there with the Three Stooges?"

"If they insist on taking him in, we'll go to the station," Harold said.

"Let's hope it doesn't come to that." I waited until they left before I opened the door. Morgan stopped pacing when I turned the deadbolt. His wayward hand threw thoughts in rapid fire, and the tic in his shoulder continuously snapped his torso to the side. Even with his head down, I caught a glimpse of the torment on his face.

"It's just me."

He nodded. Then he walked over and pressed himself to me. I wrapped my arms around him. His muscles continued to spasm.

"Everything's going to be okay." He made a sound, almost a word, but it broke into a rough whimper. "I'm sorry. I didn't think Jeff would involve you in this."

He nodded again. I petted his hair. Slowly the worst of the tics died down.

"I didn't do it."

I don't know what made me feel better. Him saying he was innocent, or him just saying anything at all.

"I know you didn't."

"I never wanted the money. I told her that. But she wouldn't listen."

I kissed his temple. "And who's she?"

He shuddered and buried his face into my neck.

"I know this is hard, but I need you to talk to me and tell me who this woman is."

His answer wasn't much more than a sigh. "My mother."

****

Morgan stalled out at the end of the corridor when he saw Jeff and his fan club occupying a booth near the door.

"Afraid we'll run?" I said.

"Nah, even you aren't that stupid."

I squeezed Morgan's shoulder. He fluttered a hand near his temple. All three agents wore the same confused expression.

To Deputy Harold, I said, "Can you move one of these tables closer? Just make sure to leave some space."

Jeff started to stand.

"Stay there, I said."

"This is an interrogation, not a family gathering."

"This is a circus, and for once, you'll just have to talk out of your mouth and not your ass. Sit, Jeff."

His cheeks reddened, but he sat.

"I'll go get us some coffee," Jessie said.

"I'll take mine black," Jeff said.

"I said, *us*. Not you." Jessie went to the back. Thank god, I managed not to smile.

"Is he on something?" The Bronco-driving agent stared at Morgan.

"No," I said.

"Then what's wrong with him?"

"Nothing's wrong with him."

The guy opened his mouth to argue, but his partner gave the slightest shake of his head.

I walked Morgan over to the table. He stopped again a few feet away.

"They aren't going to hurt you. They aren't even going to touch you." I shot Jeff a look, daring him to contradict me. I pulled out a chair, and Morgan sat. I stayed standing with my hand on his back, making small circles. He tilted his head up at the light, rocked, and fluttered his hand.

"Go ahead," I said. "Ask your questions."

"Tell me about the money in your account at Mountain Trust Bank."

"It's not my account."

"It has your name on it."

"She set up the account and put the money in there. I never wanted it. I told her I didn't want it."

"So Mrs. Day just gave you over a hundred thousand dollars out of the goodness of her heart?"

"I—" Morgan's face contorted with the effort to control the tic in his shoulders. "Still not mine. I never wanted the money. She opened the account, not me."

"There were over sixty deposits made into that account by Mrs. Day over a five year span. Why would she do that?"

Morgan shook his head.

"Her husband says you threatened to blackmail her."

"Not true."

"You have an awful lot of money in an account that suggests otherwise."

Jessie came out with a cup of coffee for me and hot chocolate for Morgan. "Let me know if you need anything else."

Nope, Jeff definitely wasn't happy about the blatant shunning. He tossed his chin at Morgan. "Answer the question."

Morgan dropped his head and nodded. I continued to rub his back and after a few deep breaths, he quit rocking. "She wanted me to take the money because she felt guilty."

"For what?" Jeff said.

"For letting my father talk her into getting rid of me."

Jeff sat forward. "You make it sound like—"

"They're my parents. When my father found out I wasn't—" Morgan balled up his fist. "Found out, I…"

"They didn't want him," I said.

Jeff glanced at me. Then he did the one humane act that moved him up on my shit list from cesspool to bottom of my shoe. He didn't ask Morgan to elaborate.

"Lori worked for them with Miranda."

"Who's Lori?" Jeff said.

"She was one of their housekeepers. My father wanted to put me in an institution. My mother asked Lori to take me instead. Mrs. Day gave Lori some money to help out because she didn't want my father to know. "

"You're saying Lori kidnapped you?"

Morgan snapped his fingers. "No. Mrs. Day wanted Lori to take me. She made it so she could adopt me."

"Do you have any proof?"

"Like what?"

"A legal agreement? Adoption papers?"

"They're probably somewhere in Lori's old things but my parents' names aren't on them."

"Why not?"

"Mrs. Day didn't want Mr. Day to know I wasn't in a hospital somewhere."

"Did you ever try to contact her?"

Morgan shook his head. "She was the one who wrote me letters."

"Really?"

"Where are those letters now?"

"I threw them away."

"Why?"

"Because I didn't know her."

"Do you remember what the letters said?"

"I never read them."

"I find it hard to believe, if she sent you letters, you didn't at least read them."

"If you doubt him," I said. "Ask the woman." If she had a guilty conscience, then surely she would back him up.

"We can't," Jeff said. "She died about a year ago from cancer."

"I thought you said the transfers were recent." And money didn't just jump from one account to another without prearrangements set in place.

"Automatic draft?"

"You don't sound very sure."

"We're looking into it."

"I'd think getting your facts straight before tearing up someone one's life would be on the top of your priority list."

"Why don't you shut up and let your girlfriend finish answering our questions?" That from the FBI agent I didn't know.

I ignored Mr. Unknown, and to Jeff, I said, "Have you checked with the bank to see what kind of arrangements were made?"

He gave me a bored look. "I know how to do my job, Grant. And as soon as the sun is up and people are awake, I'll start making the calls."

"What about Mr. Day?"

Another one of those looks. "What about him?"

"Why did he wait so long to file charges? If his lawyers have been trying to contact Morgan for a year, then he's known about the withdrawals for at least that long." My bet was probably longer.

Jeff exchanged looks with his two cohorts.

"You've already asked yourself the same question, haven't you? Have you asked Mr. Day?"

"We spoke to his lawyer; he said the reasons were personal." Jeff nodded at Morgan. "After what Morgan has said, I think Mr. Day might have been trying to spare him the embarrassment."

I laughed. It was a cold ugly sound. "You mean the guy was trying to save face. Now he has to admit he's Morgan's father."

Jeff shook his head. "Either way, it doesn't matter. The money is in an account with Morgan's name on it, transferred from an account by Mrs. Day under duress."

I put my hands on the table. "So says Mr. Day. I call bullshit. No one waits a year to involve the authorities when thousands of dollars are being removed from their accounts unless they are doing something illegal or they're trying to keep something hidden. This guy waited because he had to, not because he gave a shit about Morgan."

"All right then, maybe he was just that desperate to keep the relationship between him and Morgan hidden."

"Yeah, and if he was, why not just walk away from the money."

"Because it was a lot of money."

"If it took him that long to do something about the deposits, it couldn't have meant that much. Not to mention the fact he stopped the transactions. There was no more money going out, so why not just sweep it all under the rug?" It's what I would have done. Had done. Many times.

When a deal went bad, you had to be able to let the money go.

The main reason the FBI could never catch me. I didn't live the high-maintenance life others did. To me, fast cars, high-rise apartments, fine clothes, meant nothing. Besides, it's kind of hard to enjoy those things from the inside of a cell. And my low overhead made it possible for me to walk away from millions without putting a hitch in my lifestyle.

Jeff stood. "We'll get the details worked out after we get Morgan settled in a holding cell and arrange a meeting with Mr. Day and his lawyer."

Morgan slammed his fist on the table, making everyone jump. Jeff put his hand too close to his gun.

"I didn't blackmail her." Morgan hit the table again.

I knelt beside him. "Do you know why he waited?"

Morgan rolled his gaze toward the light. I cupped his cheek. His eyes focused on me. He swallowed several times.

"He thinks I want to take the money from his company Day Enterprises."

Now I knew why the name struck a chord. The guy had written software for a company and became CEO after he married the owner's daughter and the father died.

"What would make him think you want his money?"

Tendons drew white lines down Morgan's neck. His Adam's apple bobbed with the high-pitched whine ticking out of his throat.

I kissed his temple. "Talk to me, Morgan."

He nodded, but there was nothing but another stretch of silence. One of the FBI agents stood, and I shot him a look. I think he would have ignored me if Jeff hadn't given him a nod.

"Why does Mr. Day think you want his money?" Jeff said.

Morgan dropped his gaze and tossed thoughts.

"If you know, please tell him," I said.

Morgan stopped moving. "Because when Mrs. Day died, she left everything to me."

You could have heard a pin drop in the room—from the next county over. She'd left everything to Morgan. Now it made sense. It also meant things could get ugly. Money could bring the devil out of anyone. The kind of money a billion dollar company made would drive any man to the edge.

"C'mon. Let's go." I stood and so did Morgan.

"Whoa, where do you think you're going?" Jeff held up a hand.

"Home."

"I don't think so."

"You asked your questions; you have your answers, and they make a hell of a lot more sense than any of Mr. Day's vague excuses."

"I appreciate Morgan cooperating, but he needs to be taken into custody until we verify everything he's said."

"No, what he needs is to go home. While he's at home, you verify everything he said." Jeff clenched his jaw. "Get out of the way, Grant."

"We're going home. You verify his information, and if it doesn't add up, we'll come to the sheriff's office in the morning."

"And you expect me to believe you won't jump ship."

"Morgan can't leave—won't leave—Durstrand, and if he won't go, neither will I."

"That's supposed to convince me?"

I pushed past Jeff. Just outside the door, Jeff grabbed me by the shoulder and spun me around. "I think you're forgetting who's in charge here."

I knocked his hand away. "No one's in charge. That's the problem. You and your boss have a personal problem with me, and no one holding the reins. All of this is bullshit, Jeff. Nothing more than the FBI's version of a dog and pony show."

"I've given you a lot of leeway. Way more than anyone ever would."

"Only because you don't have a pot to shit in. And because you have nothing, now you bring Morgan into your case-file fantasy land. Well, I've got news for you, Jeff. It's going to stop. Morgan didn't steal anything, and you damn well know it. This Mr. Day is pissed off about a will."

Money did strange things to people. I didn't need to tell Jeff how money did strange things to people. We'd both seen it. How a magical piece of paper or bank account number could turn the sweetest of little old ladies into pit vipers from hell.

"Even if Morgan's side of the story checks out, he's still facing assault charges."

I opened the passenger door on the truck. Morgan got in. I headed for the driver's side. Jeff stopped me. Toe to toe, we stood facing each other just like we had back in my kitchen, only this time nothing but pure anger stirred inside me.

"I can still bring him in," Jeff said.

"You don't care about filing charges against him. Besides, you don't even have a bruise to show for it. You're just pissed because you can't have your cake and eat it too." I leaned close enough to brush my lips against Jeff's ear. "You're jealous, Jeff. And if you keep singing this song, I'm gonna tell everyone who will listen that this is nothing more than a personal vendetta because I won't stick my dick in your ass anymore."

He turned his head, putting our mouths dangerously close. Lust showed in his eyes and he licked his lips.

"Sorry, Jeff. You'll just have to keep dating your right hand."

I went to get in the pickup and yanked open the door. He caught it. Our gazes clashed again. There was still desire swimming in those baby blues of his, but there was triumph too. "You're leaving because I'm allowing it." I got in, but he wouldn't let go of the door. "His freedom in exchange for information, that's the deal."

"Go fuck yourself."

"Don't think I won't make his life hell."

"Because of me?"

180

"Because I'd like to turn this backwards dirt hole into a memory that's not even worth forgetting but I can't go back to civilization until you give me what I want. And you will give it to me, Grant."

"Only because your bullshit fairy tales about me being on Lorado's hit list didn't work."

"But now I know what does and don't think for a second I won't use it."

"I don't." Not now anyways. At one time, I might have thought him a bigger man, but not anymore.

"We're staying in Maysville at the Hyatt. I'll reserve a conference room for us to meet in. Will noon give you enough time to get your lawyer on a plane?"

I yanked on the door. This time hard enough it was either let go or get his fingers slammed.

He tapped on the window. I should have just run over his ass, but he wasn't worth tearing out the oil pan.

I cracked the window. "What do you want now?"

"Two words, Grant. Homeland Security. You'd be amazed at the creative ways you can apply the law. So don't stand me up." Jeff tipped an imaginary hat at Morgan. "You have a nice day, Mr. Kade. Try not to lose any sleep."

I cranked up the truck and backed out of the parking spot. Then I hit the gas, hard enough to swing the rear of the truck. Jeff had to jump back to avoid getting clipped by the bumper.

****

There are some perks to having a high-priced lawyer.

They have two numbers. The office, where you call when it's important, and their personal cell phone, when it's a matter of life or death. Or in most cases, freedom or life in prison.

Harriet answered on the third ring. Laughter in the background almost drowned her out.

"Sorry to bother you, but I have a situation."

"Hang on a second." Muffled voices grew dim until it was almost silent. "What's wrong?"

I told her about the accusations against Morgan, making sure to include every detail. This was not a situation where the abbreviated version would benefit anyone.

Through the front door window, I watched Morgan at the table, sipping a cup of coffee. He said nothing on the way back to his home and his silence had yet to recede.

"What I don't get is if this guy really believed Morgan was blackmailing his wife, then why did he wait so long to do anything? And if he was so worried about people finding out he was Morgan's father, why didn't he just let him have the money and turn away?"

"Rich people have some funny habits, you know that."

Yeah. I did.

"But I think you're right. A man who wanted to keep a secret like this would have walked away."

"Why didn't he?"

"My guess would be, he couldn't."

I walked over to the porch railing and propped up against the post. "I don't follow."

"Wills can take a while to probate. When he found out about Morgan being the sole

181

beneficiary, he probably tried to go the legal route and have his name removed. Proving the will was changed under duress would make for a great argument. And getting Morgan charged with extortion could be used to support his claim."

"Then, what do we do?"

"Depends on what Morgan wants to do. He's entitled to the money. Every cent. He also has the grounds for a civil suit against Mr. Day for the false charges and harassment. Basically this could cost the man more than he would have lost in the will." Which was everything.

A light mist sprinkled the edge of the porch and left a cool kiss on one side of my face. "I don't think Morgan wants anything of Mr. Day's."

"Well, we can leave out the lawsuit."

"No, I mean, I don't think he wants any of it. Not a lawsuit, not the money from the will, he doesn't even want the money in the account in his name."

Harriet laughed. "I don't know of anyone who would walk away from millions of dollars. Especially when it's a hundred percent legal money."

"You don't know Morgan." I would have liked to think I did. But I had a feeling I hadn't even scratched the surface on him.

"You're kidding."

"I'm not."

She made a thinking sound. "Well, that complicates things in a way I hadn't anticipated."

"I would think it would make things easier."

"It might, it might not. Do you know if Morgan informed Mr. Day's lawyer that he didn't want the money?"

"He said he told him he didn't want the money in the account, so I'm going to assume so. Why?"

A shuffling sound rattled the speaker, then a door clicked shut in the background. When she spoke again, her voice didn't carry the same.

"Harriet?"

"I'm here. I just needed to get to my office."

"Your office? Do you normally throw wild parties at your office?"

"Every time I win an impossible case."

"Must have been some case."

"You have no idea. Nor do you want to."

Considering some of her other clients, she was right.

"Okay," Harriet said. "I'm going to make a quick note of everything we talked about." She relayed each point as she wrote them down. "Does that sound about right to you?"

"Pretty much." I went to the front door again. Morgan was no longer at the table. The living and dining room were empty, but the inside of his bedroom and the kitchen weren't visible.

"I'll make some calls," Harriet said. "And we're going to cross our fingers."

"You sound worried."

"Just a little. Morgan's willingness to give up the money should have solved the problem. For some reason, it didn't. And the list of possible reasons is very short."

"What should I tell him?"

"To stay calm. Let me handle it. Eat some chocolate ice cream."

I chuckled. "What's eating ice cream going to do?"

"Does wonders for me when I'm having a bad day. Nothing like a sugar high to smooth things over."

"Ice cream, I'll remember that."

We said our good-byes.

I found Morgan sitting on the steps of the back porch. "Do you mind if I join you?"

He didn't answer so I did.

Morgan's wayward hand fluttered next to his temple. The movement was slower than usual. Like even the tics had been worn out by the day's events.

Except for the weak light coming from the house, the night surrounded us. Crickets chirped and tree frogs sang. It was getting late in the year for both, but the night was warmer than usual, so I guess they figured it was safe to spend one more evening out.

For a very long time, there was just us, the stars, and the darkness.

When Morgan finally spoke, his voice was barely above a whisper. "I thought I told you to not come back."

"You did."

He nodded. Then he found my hand and held it. "Thank you."

I kissed his knuckles. "I didn't mean to hurt you. I should have thought about what I was going to say before I said it. I should have never said it."

He tightened his grip. His fear, his worries, his desperation sang loud and clear in that simple contact. If I'd only had words to comfort him.

"I don't know what to do." Morgan drew his knees up. "I don't even understand why I should have to do anything."

"I know. And to tell you the truth, I don't understand it either. But I'd still like to try to get you some help."

"Your lawyer friend?"

"Yeah." I rubbed my thumb over the back of his hand. "Is that okay with you?"

Morgan nodded, then after a long stretch of silence, he said, "That FBI guy, Jeff."

"You mean the douche bag in a suit?"

"Yeah, him." Morgan snorted. "He did this to get back at you for something, didn't he?"

"Pretty much."

"What?"

"He wants me to give him information on my clients so he can build a case against them."

"Why?"

"He's probably hoping threatening them with jail will get him to some bigger, more important people. Then he can arrest them. Get his picture in the paper. Further his career. Hell... I don't really know."

"You loved him." Morgan made it a statement.

I let go of his hand. Not because I wanted to but because holding him when thinking about Jeff, or more precisely what we'd had, felt wrong. "Yeah, I think I did."

"What about now?"

"No." I didn't even have to think about the answer.

"He's still in love with you, though."

If anyone else had said it, I would have told them it was a figment of their imagination, but Morgan didn't see things not there. He just saw things no one else could. "He's got a funny way of showing it, doesn't he?"

"Are you going to do it?"

"What?"

"Give him the information."

I leaned back on my elbows. A vast carpet of stars made bright points on a black sky. "I don't think he's going to give me much of a choice."

"Because he'll arrest me if you don't."

I didn't answer because I didn't want to feel like I was putting the blame on Morgan. It wasn't his fault. It wasn't even my fault. Not really. But Morgan was in the middle so Jeff decided to use him.

"Don't," Morgan said. "Don't tell him."

If I didn't, Jeff would make Morgan suffer. I knew the charges wouldn't stick. A half-assed lawyer could make the whole incident look like a joke. But Jeff would make good on his word and take Morgan in. For any other person, it would've been an inconvenience. For Morgan, it would've been devastating.

"I'll try to think of something." I had a few aces up my sleeve, but they could easily detonate and take me with them. "If I can't, then I'll have to tell him."

"But if you do, something bad will happen, won't it? That's why you don't want to tell him."

Bad was probably the best case scenario. "A lot of people have trusted me to help them with some very private… situations. I'm less worried about the FBI finding out what some of those things were, than I am private interested parties, who might have had a financial loss due to those situations."

Morgan sighed.

"Don't worry. It'll work out. We just need to concentrate on this problem with Mr. Day."

Morgan moved closer so I took it as an invitation and wrapped an arm around him. He rested his head on my shoulder. "She started sending me letters after she was diagnosed with breast cancer. I recognized the name on the envelopes because Lori had told me about her. But I never opened the letters."

"Why not?"

He shrugged. "Because I didn't want to know her." Morgan touched my jaw and danced a path to my chin, around my lips, to my forehead with small taps of his fingers. "Then one day, she showed up at my door. She was very sick. All her hair was gone. Her clothes looked too big. But she'd driven for three hours to come see me. She came alone because she didn't want my father to know. We sat at the table and drank iced tea. She told me she was sorry and begged me to forgive her."

He danced his fingers to the empty space in front of me. Pale highlights turned each digit gray and the movement blurred in the darkness. When I stared hard enough, shapes emerged from the shadows like those born from clouds.

"I told her there was nothing for me to forgive. She said she gave me up, that she'd abandoned me. She was so angry with herself for it. But she didn't abandon me. She gave me to Lori." He dropped his hand to his lap. "Mrs. Day gave me a folder with some bank information. Then she left and I threw it out. A week later, her lawyer called me and told me she'd died."

"I waited for days to feel something. Anger, sadness, anything. But it wasn't there, not like it is when you lose someone you know and I still didn't know her. I didn't even regret not knowing her."

"Why not?"

"If I'd regretted not having time with her, then that meant I regretted my time with Lori. And I didn't. Not one second."

"A lot of people wouldn't feel that way about being given up."

Morgan shrugged.

"They'd be hurt by the idea."

He returned his hand to his temple. The tossing movement was slower. "But if Mrs. Day had kept me, if she hadn't done the right thing and given me up, I wouldn't be who I am. I'd still be lost."

Morgan was right, and the idea of never knowing him left behind a chill.

"You cold?" He scooted closer.

"I'm good."

"You're a terrible liar, Grant. A terrible liar."

"I'm not cold, at least, not on the outside."

Morgan sighed. "The inside cold is always worse."

"Why do you say that?" I laid my cheek against the top of his head.

"Because you can put a coat on to stay warm, but there isn't much you can do for your heart."

I hoped one day I'd be as wise as Morgan.

****

I stayed the night at Morgan's place.

He didn't ask me, but he didn't tell me to leave either. So when he headed for bed, I followed him. Morgan undressed. I undressed. Then we slipped under the covers. He held me. I held him. And the tree frogs trickled away as the night grew colder.

It would be winter soon. For the first time in a very long time, I actually thought about Christmas.

What would Morgan like?

I didn't have a clue. I thought about getting him a computer, but I didn't know if he chose not to have one or if he couldn't use one in the same way he couldn't drive, tie his shoes, or tell left from right.

I had a feeling it was the former. Although I can't say why. Maybe it was because he didn't even own a TV.

Somewhere between petting his back and fondling the locks of hair at the nape of his neck, I fell asleep. I rarely remembered my dreams, but that night the strangeness of the images in my head stuck with me.

Light surrounded me. Not like the nontangible source of energy I was used to, but solid pieces hanging in the air like bits of glass. All shapes, all sizes, but always geometric and never three-dimensional. As each shard turned, it would disappear only to reappear as it completed a rotation.

185

Nothing held them up, but they were unmovable. And there was no space for me to get through.

In the gaps between the twirling light, Morgan stood at the edge of the world. I don't know how I knew what it was. There was nothing to suggest it was the edge of the world. Just a flat surface ending at a horizon of black.

Seeing him there filled me with a kind of fear I'd never known, and I was overwhelmed with the need to get to him. If I didn't, something terrible would happen. But the twirling fragments wouldn't move and when I tried to get past them, they left behind deep cuts.

Then my fear coalesced when Morgan looked at me and the sadness in his eyes sent me to my knees.

Morgan gave me an apologetic smile, as he stepped off the edge.

I think I woke up crying, although I couldn't be sure because I was soaked head to toe in sweat.

The cold chill that had run through me that evening turned to ice.

****

I woke up before dawn, even before Morgan, and snuck out.

There wasn't going to be a happily ever after if I gave Jeff what he wanted. I'd wind up running for the rest of my life, either from people I betrayed, people I put under the FBI's radar, or the FBI.

There was only one solution to the problem. I had to make Jeff go away. I had to make him want to go away. I had to make the threat of opening Pandora's Box so real it bypassed even his ingrained sense of self-preservation and went straight to the soul.

I needed him to know real fear.

Because fear is a powerful motivator. And for the first time, I knew just how powerful it could be. Not because I could lose everything—my freedom, my life, my money—but because I could lose Morgan.

Without him, the rest was meaningless.

I found a convenience store about fifteen miles outside of town and grabbed two disposable cell phones, then hid in their bathroom to make the first of two calls.

It rang twice, and Rubio's sleepy voice answered. "Hello?"

"I'm changing my plans."

He grunted, and sheets rustled in the background. "Good or bad?"

"Good."

"Then you call because it's bad."

"Yes."

"Do I need to get you a lawyer?" Rubio didn't mean the law book quoting kind.

"No. It's bad but not that bad." Yet. It didn't need to be said out loud. He'd been in the same dark corner I'd occupied more times than any man should.

"But bad enough." As in bad enough to call him.

"Yeah."

"Who do they have?"

"A friend."

186

"Is that why you've changed your vacation plans?"

I chuckled.

"Perhaps you could bring him to visit sometime?"

"He's not the traveling type."

"Then I will miss getting to see you and kick your ass at chess."

I laid my head against the bathroom door. My fear, frustration, and worry must have carried on my exhale. Or maybe Rubio just knew. He always seemed to know.

"What has the FBI done to your friend?"

I told Rubio what happened.

"Then things are getting dangerous for you."

"I know."

"Are you sure this is what you want to do?"

"You know it's not."

"What is your alternative?"

"You mean what can I do, besides kill him?"

Rubio sighed. "Even honorable men sometimes have to do not so honorable things."

"If I thought…" What? If I thought it would solve the problem, I would? I feared the answer. I feared the truth in that answer. I'd play my last hand before I went that route. "Do you remember the file I sent you for safe keeping?"

"You mean the file you sent me so you wouldn't do something you would regret?" There was laughter in his tone but no happiness in it.

"Yeah."

"What about it?"

"There's a family photo in there. I need you to fax it for me." I told him where and when. "Make sure it gets to Agent Jeff Shaldon, and only Jeff. And make sure the number can't be traced."

"And if it doesn't get his attention?"

"Then he's less of a human being than I ever pegged him for."

"And?"

"It will work. It has to. It's the only way out I have left. It's the only way to save what I have."

Rubio would know what I meant by that. Not the exact details, but we spoke the same language. We just learned it from different sources.

"It is good to know you are happy. I will be sure to let everyone know you won't be here for the holidays."

"Thank you."

"Call me, Grant. When."

He hung up.

I flushed the sim chip and smashed the phone under my heel. Anything that looked like a memory board was also flushed. The rest went into the garbage. The young guy at the counter didn't even look up from his e-reader when I walked out.

By the time I got back to Durstrand, pink and blues traced the horizon. There was a small shack on the county line advertising homemade breakfast. I stopped and bought four biscuits, as well as a cup of coffee.

187

While I sipped my drink, I thought about everything that had happened. Between Morgan and me, my past clients, Rubio, and Jeff.

I didn't want to admit it, not to anyone, not even to myself, but I had loved Jeff. Really loved him. If anything makes you sloppy and stupid, it's love. Kills brain cells faster than alcohol and annihilates your instinct for self-preservation.

There is one good thing that comes from loving someone. Your courage shoots through the fucking roof. Which honestly isn't always a good thing when you're thinking like a dumbass. Only one other emotion can come close to the power of loving someone and it's not hating them. It's revenge.

Seems the same thing as hate, I know, but it's not. Revenge is calmer, cold, and calculating. It has a plan. It's willing to wait. Sometimes it only has to simmer for a couple of days, sometimes weeks or months. The longer revenge cooks, the more potent it becomes. Unleashed at a toxic level, it can take the carrier with it.

When Jeff did what he did to me, revenge set up a cancer in my soul. I had every intentions of destroying him in a way I'd never wanted to do to a person.

After two months, I knew everything there was to know about Agent Shaldon, right down to work evaluations. I mean, I already knew his intimate habits. But he'd been Jeff Meyers then. A petty thief with a short rap sheet and an easy to read history. Not too easy, mind you. The FBI had made me work for my breadcrumbs, but I'd still failed to realize that's what they were.

In my defense, Jeff Meyers was a real person. So was everything about his life, right down to his high school report card. Even his ninth grade photo looked like a younger version of Jeff.

The FBI might suck at a lot of things, but they are master liars.

What I failed to realize was Jeff Meyers had been dead for five years. A fact I'd missed because he'd died in Canada and he'd gotten there on a fake passport.

Time is funny. While it usually festers the negative, on occasion it gives the body time to heal. As I dug through Jeff's life, my revenge cooled to anger, then the anger cooled to humiliation.

I could practically hear Eugene's voice in my head calling me a dumbass. Even as a memory he was right. I'd fucked up. I'd broken the rules. I'd gotten stupid. And I'd survived.

Instead of testing fate again, I'd chosen to walk away. To not become the thing I hated. I left Chicago to find paradise, only to my surprise it wasn't the island of my dreams.

Facing the darkness again was no longer a matter of pride; it was a matter of Morgan. It my last-ditch effort to remain the man I was so I could be who he deserved. Or at least as close to what he deserved as I was able to give.

Between sips of coffee, I dialed information, found the number for the Hyatt and rang Jeff's room. I could have called his personal cell, but doing so would bring things too close to home. I needed to detach myself, and I needed Jeff to feel the rift expand right under him.

The phone rang, and I hoped to God Jeff was having the best fucking dream of his life.

He answered with a barely intelligible, "Hello?"

"Late night?" He'd always been a night owl. If he was following his usual sleep schedule, he hadn't been in bed more than two hours.

There was a clank in the background, then a thump. "Shit."

"I hope whatever you broke is irreplaceable."

"Nothing broke. I just knocked the clock off the night stand."

"Pity."

"Is there a reason you're calling me at… six a.m.?"

I checked my watch. "Six fifteen a.m. and yeah, there is."

"We had an agreement."

"Who says I plan on breaking it?"

The relief in his sigh was tangible. If this worked, it wouldn't last. No, Jeff would learn a new me, hell, even I would learn a new me.

"What's going on, Grant?"

"Nothing yet, but sometime this afternoon I'm going to wind up in a little room with some FBI men who have an interest in my business log. They want me to hand over names, dates, times, you know, information that was entrusted to me in confidence."

"No one will…"

"Save it, Jeff. I don't have any interest in your lies or the promise of your lies." I blew away the trails of steam curling from the surface of my coffee. "I just need you to listen and think." I gave him a moment for his sleep-addled brain to catch up. "I don't know why you think the information in my so-called little black book will do the FBI any good and I really don't care, but there's something you need to know. There are people out there equally interested in knowing more about our mutual friend Mr. Jeffery Meyers. You remember, small-time thief with a penchant for pretty baubles. The little prick who followed me around like a lost puppy begging to suck my dick. The coward, the manipulator, the sad little excuse of a human being who pissed off a lot of people the day Caruso got shot, and his brother wound up dead because he wasn't quite as fast as I was on the trigger."

"Are you threatening me?" His words came out on a snarl.

"No, Agent Shaldon, I would never in a million years threaten an FBI agent. I'm just making sure you get in touch with Mr. Myers so he's well aware of the situation. He might even want to voice his opinion on whether or not my measly client list is really worth the risk. Because I'm betting he won't agree with you. Not after he realizes I know who he is. Really is. Where he grew up, where he went to school—go Lions—how he fell off his bike when he was twelve and broke his right arm. Oh, no wait, he didn't fall off his bike, he told the ER nurse he did, but the real truth is his old man got drunk and knocked him down the stairs.

"Mr. Myers weaved some sad tale about how his family kicked him out of the house when he turned sixteen and how he never knew the rest of his kin, when in reality his family, mother—stepfather, two sisters, niece, grandparents—who took a cruise last year and renewed their vows—heard it was a lovely reception—eight uncles, two aunts—and enough cousins to start both sides of a football team, get together every year in the month of May for a family reunion. But because they live all over the country, they take turns hosting it. This past year, it was Florida, Aunt Kelly wanted to show off her new house; next year, it will be Tennessee, near Gatlinburg.

"Mr. Myers needs to realize if I go to the FBI, there's a very good chance those people interested in him will find everything I know, considering my other black book with all the juicy details of his life is sure to fall out of my pocket. No telling what kind of nasty son of a bitch might pick it up." I practically got a hard-on listening to his breath shudder out. "You might want to give him a ring and let him know what could happen when the shit hits the fan. All the terrible and ugly things. You know as well as I do, the people likely to find the book wouldn't stop at him. They wouldn't even start with him." I took another sip of my coffee. "Anyhow, call me if you still think we should keep wasting tax payers dollars, otherwise I'm going to head on out and enjoy this beautiful day."

"Grant…"

There was a knock in the background.

I checked the clock. Right on time. "That'll be for you. You know. A keepsake. Your family is very photogenic by the way, but then the beach makes for a beautiful setting." There was movement and then silence. Was he staring at that photo at his feet, the one with him, and his nephews, aunt, and grandparents, all smiling and draped in sunlight?

Not a care in the world.

I think Jeff was about to say something because his breath hitched. Didn't matter, whatever it was would be pointless.

I hung up.

On my way back to Morgan's, I stopped on the side of the road and crushed the phone.

All these years I'd fought to keep my belly out of the mud. I didn't want to be like other people who had no qualms about breaking legs, or taking a life. It sickened me to think that I was inching down the icy road and any minute I could slip, finding myself full speed toward the bottom.

To the man staring at me from the rearview mirror, I said, "Proud of yourself?"

At least my reflection had enough of a conscience to look ashamed.

****

I didn't expect Morgan to still be in bed, but just in case, I tried to be as quiet as possible. His room was empty, so was the kitchen. I found him on the back porch working with red glass.

The bottles had been a beautiful crimson shade. Somehow the color was even more stunning after the fragments had been melted down into disks.

Sunlight broke over the trees and cut a path through the back porch. Fragments of color danced over everything. The glowing sections of light painted Morgan in a mottled rainbow, turning him into some kind of rare creature belonging to fairy tales.

The tics, which forced him to wear a long-sleeve shirt when he cooked, weren't present while he carefully twisted copper wire into the shape he needed to hold the glass.

I leaned against the door reluctant to disturb the beautiful sight in front of me. The stunning man who perched himself on a stool, wearing only boxers, and bedhead.

He flicked one of the extensions on the sculpture. The arm swung around, throwing a collage of geometric shapes.

Morgan huffed a breath and sat back. "It's still not right." It was no surprise he knew I was there.

"What's wrong?"

"The rhythm is off." He didn't look at the wall where the kaleidoscope shifted in a series of golds, reds, and oranges, when he said, "See the break?" He pointed to the rotating arm lined with carefully arranged disks of glass.

"I don't, sorry."

Morgan nodded. "I can't figure out why it doesn't work."

"If I knew the answer, I'd tell you."

"It's right there." He stopped the arm and tipped his head. "It's right there, Grant, but I can't get it to play." Only then did he look back at the wall. The starbursts of color had stopped. Without the movement, it became a disjointed series of colored shapes.

Morgan held up a hand and wiggled his fingers through the rays of colored light. His gaze softened as it shifted from here to wherever it was he went.

"Are you hungry? I picked up some biscuits."

He danced his fingers.

"I got egg and cheese, bacon egg and cheese, sausage egg and cheese, and a ham egg and cheese. I figured one of them should hit the spot."

Morgan tipped his head the other way.

I'd be a liar if I said that blissful expression he wore didn't disturb me as much as it intrigued me.

Then he returned. "Where else did you go, besides the biscuit shack? It's only a half-mile inside the county line, it would have only taken you forty-five minutes if it was busy, but you were gone for almost two hours. You went farther out, but not far enough you couldn't come back and stop to get the biscuits." Morgan fluttered his hand next to his temple. "If you don't want to tell me, I understand."

"C'mon, let's go sit down."

He got the plates. There was already a pot of hot water with a teabag of coffee grounds on the counter. I poured me a cup, and Morgan got a glass of orange juice. We met at the table.

He took two biscuits and sat. I did the same.

While Morgan dissected his food, I said, "I made some phone calls."

"More than one? So someone other than Agent Shaldon."

"A friend."

"Friends are good to have. Is he going to help you?"

"It was more about making sure he had a heads-up to help himself."

Morgan combined all the meat and eggs onto one biscuit. "But you did call Agent Shaldon." He ate and drank his juice.

"Yeah. I did."

"You're going to tell him, aren't you?" Morgan put down his food.

"Only if he decides it's worth the risk."

"Napkins. I forgot them. Do you want one?"

Before I could answer, he was gone. A cabinet door opened and shut. There was a long pause. I was about to get up and go check on Morgan when he returned.

"Here." He held out a paper towel.

I took one.

He folded his own into a neat triangle. "What's the risk? To him? I mean it has to be a risk to him because he wouldn't care about a risk to you. If he did care, he wouldn't have asked you to give him the information."

It was more like Jeff didn't care what happened to Morgan, but I didn't bother to point it out. I'm not even sure I needed to. There was no way Morgan hadn't caught on, so either it bothered him too much to say it aloud, or he was hoping I hadn't come to the same conclusion.

Considering I'd stood in a grocery store with my finger in the air for a good ten minutes, it wasn't an out of the realm deduction on his part. After that little stunt, I'm sure it surprised him I knew how to find my way out of a wet paper bag.

I have to admit, once I thought about it, I did wonder how I managed to survive this long.

I told Morgan what I said to Jeff. He ate, giving all the appearance of a person who had absolutely no interest in what I was saying. Between bites, he would turn his glass, sometimes trace the distorted bend of light it reflected onto the table, or simply stare at nothing.

When I was done, he stayed quiet until he finished his biscuit and drank the rest of his OJ. "That was a very dumb thing to do." Morgan looked at me then. His intense gaze softened with a smile. "And also very clever."

"I think it's more along the lines of desperate."

"If you were desperate, you would have left."

He was right. A desperate man would have fled. And I wasn't desperate, I was in love.

"I did fall for the toothpick trick."

Morgan laughed. "Everyone falls for the toothpick trick. And the more intelligent a person is, the harder they fall."

"Wow, I never thought being stupid could make me feel so smart."

He looked at me again. This time his expression was more than just soft, but grateful. Morgan held me in his gaze, and all the things waiting to be said were there. Spoken in silence. Conveyed between space-time.

Forget feeling intelligent. It was nothing compared to what it was like to be the center of someone's world.

Chapter Six

I had just finished ripping out the old aluminum wiring in the kitchen and replaced it with copper when my cell phone rang.

I answered it.

"It's Harriet."

"Why do I have a feeling if you're calling me, it's not good?"

"Nothing of the sort. Well, at least not completely."

"I knew it." I pulled out a chair. With all the possible negative scenarios, I needed to sit down. "Okay, let's have it."

"You sound like you're getting a finger lopped off."

I laughed. "You tell me. Am I?"

"No."

"That's refreshing."

"I scheduled a meeting with Roger Amber, Mr. Michael Day's attorney, for him to meet with Morgan."

I scrubbed a hand over my face. "He can't leave Durstrand."

"I know. Which is why Morgan is picking the meeting place and I'm sending a colleague of mine. She's local, she knows the territory, and she's mean as a rattlesnake."

"The good ones always are." A plus when you needed one, not so great if you were on the wrong side. I'd been lucky not to have that problem. Thanks to Harriet.

"Her name is Abigail Reynolds. Give her office a call so you can tell them where you want to meet. If Morgan has any questions, that would be a good time to ask." There was a shuffling sound, then Harriet's voice lost some of its sharpness. "Is Morgan sure this is what he wants? That's a lot of money to give up."

"Yeah."

"Once it's done, there is no turning back."

"I don't think he cares."

"Well, I made it a point to arrange for him to at least keep what's in his account."

"He'll never touch it." Only man in the world who'd turn down free money. Except for maybe Buddhist monks.

"Well, it can stay there, draw interest, maybe one day he'll change his mind. Then if for some reason he needs it, at least it will be there waiting on him."

"I'll let him know."

"Good."

I started to stand up, but decided it was safer to keep my ass in the chair. You know, just in case. "Is that it?" I knew it wasn't.

"Has Morgan talked to you about Dillon?"

I propped my elbows on the table. Across from me, copper wire hung from a hole, waiting to be hooked up to the new plug on the counter. "Some."

193

"Did he tell you what happened?"

I told him what I saw. "Not really."

"If you decide you want to know, I'll make arrangements to get you the notes I have on his case."

"I could always look up the police records."

"I'm not talking about the police records. I'm talking about his psych evaluation."

"Why did they have a shrink talk to him?"

"Because when they arrested Dillon, he was displaying signs of extreme psychosis. They weren't sure he was competent to stand trial and needed proof he wasn't legally insane at the time of the attack."

"What was he on?"

"They never found out. Dillon admitted to using drugs so they said it was probably a flashback of some kind and figured that's why he attacked Morgan. Either way, it's ammunition to keep him jail."

"If it can keep him in jail, then why did he only get seven years?"

"Dillon pled out. There was no need for the DA to use the evaluation."

"And now there is?"

"I spoke with Dillon's psychiatrist. He agreed to go before the parole board and testify Dillon is an extreme risk to Morgan's well-being. He's going to suggest they move Dillon to a high security mental hospital where he can get treatment. He said Dillon never belonged in prison, but a hospital."

"As long as it keeps him locked up, I don't care where he is."

"If the doctor wins his petition, it's highly unlikely Dillon will ever get out."

"Jesus Christ, what the hell was in the report?"

"Nothing you want to read if you plan on eating in the next twenty-four hours. Did you know when the police went to the apartment, they called the scene in as a homicide?"

"They thought Morgan was dead?"

"Yeah. If you saw the crime scene photos, you would understand why. It wasn't until the coroner got there that they realized Morgan was still breathing. The DA documented Morgan's injuries. He had to have three surgeries to correct the damage to his jaw and orbital socket. His collarbone was broken in multiple places, his hips shattered. The kind of damage that happens in car wrecks, not when someone gets beat up."

It wasn't until spots danced in front of my eyes I realized I was holding my breath.

Papers shuffled in the background. "Tell Morgan not to worry. I have a few more people to talk to, but considering the circumstances, I can guarantee you Mr. Barnes will not be getting paroled. Not without an act of congress."

"I'll tell him."

"Now, here's Abigail's number."

"Hang on." I searched for a pen and paper and of course couldn't find one. I wound up writing it in pencil on a two by four propped up against the wall. Harriet also gave me the date and time we'd be meeting with Mr. Amber.

Great. "I appreciate all this."

"You're welcome. And tell Morgan I said good luck." Hopefully he wouldn't need it.

"I'll do that."

194

****

Abigail Reynolds told Morgan to pick a public place he was comfortable with. Somewhere he felt the most at ease and had the most support.

He chose Toolies.

We were going to take up a booth in the corner, but when Jessie caught wind of what was happening, he insisted we meet in the back. Morgan was going to be under enough stress and the last thing he needed to worry about was a crowd of people trying to listen in, or the constant distractions created by business as usual.

The meeting was at six. We were there by a quarter till. I knew immediately the short squat woman in the business suit was Abigail. Not because of the way she was dressed, but the aura she gave off. If she'd been introduced to me as a potential client, I might have worried she would've killed me if I declined her business.

She extended a hand to Morgan. "Pleased to finally meet you. I'm Abigail. You can call me Babs for short."

Morgan shook her hand. His shoulder jerked, but she didn't acknowledge it.

"You must be Grant."

Her grip was as firm as any businessman I'd ever met. This was definitely a lady to respect. "Yes, ma'am, I am."

To Morgan, she said, "Do you want Grant to join us?"

"Yes." Morgan tossed thoughts. His shoulder jerked again and a small whine ticked from his throat.

"You have nothing to worry about Morgan," Abigail said. "And if at any time, you feel uncomfortable, we'll call it off."

"I just want to get this over with."

"I know. But if this becomes an inconvenience to you, we'll end it, and they can make the three hour drive another day."

Yup, I definitely liked her.

We went inside, and Jessie came from around the corner. A few people looked our way, but their gazes didn't linger. He ushered us through the kitchen and into the office. Extra chairs had been brought in, and shelves taken out to make enough room for everyone to sit.

"You need me to bring you anything to drink?" Jessie said.

"Water." Morgan tapped off his fingers on the palm of his hand. "In a bottle, in case I knock it over."

"Water sounds fine." I nodded at Abigail.

She said, "Same for me."

Jessie left, and Abigail put her briefcase on the desk. I sat on the same side with Morgan between us.

"Are you sure you want to sign off on everything?" She laid out a folder and pens.

"Yes." Morgan tried to corral his wayward hand. It wound up in a fist next to his temple. The tendons in his wrist stuck out in white lines. "I never wanted her money."

"But she wanted you to have it."

"Please. Just…" Morgan tilted his head enough for me to catch a glimpse of his eyes. The

195

message was clear.

"He doesn't want the money," I said. "Let's just sign whatever needs to be signed so we can go home."

Abigail pursed her lips. "Very well." She closed her briefcase.

Jessie walked back into the room with bottles of water tucked in the fold of his arm. "I think they're here." He handed out the bottles. "Do you need me to keep them out front for a few more minutes?"

"No," Morgan said. "Just send them in. I'll sign whatever it is they want me to sign."

I wondered if I wore the same defeated expression as Abigail. Jessie nodded and was gone again. I held out my hand to Morgan and he took it. The tics assaulting his body slowed.

Muffled voices came from the other side of the door, it opened, and two men and a woman walked in.

They were dressed so stiff I wasn't sure who the lawyers were until the man with salt and pepper hair and the woman spoke.

"Mr. Kade." The woman looked at me when she said it.

"Kessler."

Her gaze slid to Morgan, and her smile dimmed. She glanced at the tall blond dressed in a dark blue suit. He had Morgan's beautiful face, only his features were hardened by age. There was no kindness in his eyes, and I couldn't decide what burned brighter shame or revulsion.

"Yes, I can understand you." Morgan snapped his fingers. "I can even read, believe it or not."

"Yes. Well." She fumbled with her briefcase. "My name is Lucy West; this is my associate, Greg Smithson, and our client Mr. Day."

They each took up a chair across from us.

"I thought we would be meeting with Mr. Amber this morning," Abigail said.

"He had an emergency court appearance come up." It was Morgan's father who answered. And he said emergency as if it had been a planned personal insult.

"So you must be the two new partners in Mr. Amber's law firm." Abigail gave both lawyers a warm smile. "Congratulations."

I think they were about to thank her, but Mr. Day jerked out a chair and sat between them, sending the chill in the air to artic proportions.

Greg cleared his throat while he set up his briefcase. "I suppose your lawyer has explained why we're here?"

"No." Morgan tossed thoughts. "I told my lawyer why I wanted to meet with you. She agreed to arrange it for me."

Mr. Day continued to stare at Morgan.

Greg extracted a ream of paperwork from his briefcase. Lucy added a file and passed it to Abigail who handed it Morgan. He laid it on the table.

"These are the copies of the contracts we sent to you," Greg said to Abigail. "I take it you've gone over the details with your client?"

Morgan answered. "Yeah."

"Good." The man smiled, but it was strained. "Then I'm sure you can appreciate Mr. Day's generosity in his decision not to pursue any legal action. He's also been so kind as to make allowances for Mr. Kade to keep the money in his account at Mountain Trust Bank."

Morgan pushed the contract across the table. "No."

To Abigail, Lucy said, "I thought you were going to discuss our terms with your client?"

Morgan snapped his fingers at Lucy. "I'm right here." His wayward hand returned to his temple. A tic jerked his shoulder hard enough to make the lawyers and Mr. Day jump.

I squeezed Morgan's hand. He took a breath and the tension in his body eased with his exhale.

"There is nothing to discuss," Morgan said. "I don't want any terms. I don't want the money. Any of it. The account and whatever else Mrs. Day left me. I never asked for it, and I never wanted it."

"Here's Morgan's contract." Abigail pulled out a different set of papers. There might have been five sheets at the most. She handed it to Lucy who scanned it, then Greg.

"Is this some kind of joke?" Greg turned the page.

"No joke. It's just plain and simple. My client doesn't want Mr. Day's money. He simply wants to be left alone and wants a guarantee Mr. Day will not create any new campaigns using the authorities to harass him. The apology was my idea."

"What kind of game are you playing here, Abigail?" Greg continued to turn the pages.

"No game. It is what it is. Your client leaves my client alone and goes back to pretending he doesn't exist just like he has for the past twenty-odd years."

Mr. Day held out his hand to Greg. He gave the man the contract. The crackle of turning pages was divided by a significant length of silence. Halfway through, he closed the contract.

To Morgan, he said, "What do you want?"

"Nothing," Morgan said.

"You can't possibly think you're capable of running the company."

"I don't want your company."

"And the board would never approve of granting you a position as shareholder."

"I don't want shares either."

The hard line of Mr. Day's mouth curled into a half sneer. "The only reason Catherine restructured her will was because she wasn't in her right mind. The chemo impaired her judgment. If I wanted to challenge the will, it would never hold up and you'd be in debt for a lawyer you couldn't afford."

"I don't need a lawyer. I don't want the money, the company, anything."

Mr. Day flicked a look over Morgan. "Is it notoriety? Because there's no birth certificate with my name on it."

Greg nodded at the contract Mr. Day held. "I think—"

Mr. Day held up a hand. "I will not play your game, Morgan. What is it you want?"

He slapped his hand on the table, one, twice, three times. Two of the water bottles fell over. Luckily, they had the caps on. "I don't—" Morgan's words disintegrated into a mewling sound. "I don't—"

Abigail looked at Morgan who nodded. She said, "He doesn't want anything, Mr. Day. Not everyone's money hungry. Morgan is happy, and that's all he cares about. He didn't contact Mrs. Catherine Day; she contacted him. He didn't want her money. That's why he never took it."

"I know about her giving Mrs. Kade money." He addressed Morgan when he said it. "She seemed to have no trouble taking it."

"Because she couldn't work," Morgan said. "I can work. I don't want your money."

"You're a busboy."

"It's a job. It pays the bills. That's all I need."

"Take the contract back with you to the hotel," Abigail said. "Read it. Have your lawyers read it. There's nothing special in there. No loopholes. No arrangements for future arbitration. "

Morgan's father tossed the group of papers onto the desk. "Let's go."

"Mr. Day—"

He cut Lucy off with the same cold gesture. "I don't know what you're trying to do, Morgan, but whatever it is, it won't work. I will fight you, and I will win."

Morgan shoved himself away from the desk. He was at the door before I could even stand. Mr. Day grabbed him by his arm.

"Catherine had an affair before we were married. She didn't want me to find out. She tried to get rid of you. The doctors said that's why you're…" Mr. Day sneered. "She tried to abort you in some backwoods clinic, and it failed. Then when you were born, she threw you out with the garbage to keep her family from finding out she was nothing but a whore."

A tremor ran down Morgan's body. He pulled from his father's grasp and shot out the door. I went after him. My shoulder caught Mr. Day's hard enough to send him stumbling.

I hoped he fell on his ass.

The bells on the door clanged. "What's wrong?" Jessie came out from behind the bar as I ran through the dining room.

"I'll handle it." I grabbed the door before it could finish closing. Morgan was already by the truck, pacing back and forth. His wayward hand bumped against his temple. "Morgan?"

He pulled away. "T… t… t…" He hit the truck. "Take. Take. M… m… mmm… ee h… h…" Tears gleamed on his blood red cheeks. The rest of his words were lost under a wounded cry.

"Okay." I opened the passenger side door. "I will. Get in and I will."

He took one step forward, two back. Would he win this battle with his body? The tremors grew more fevered. Spit flecked his lips.

"Morgan." I held my hand out to him. "Morgan, please."

Pain, fear, humiliation, it turned his beautiful dark eyes into a window of hell. It was the first glimpse I'd had of the prison he lived in. A captive to the uncontrollable tics ravaging his body. I think it was then I understood the solace he found in the light. Just as it blinded the world to seeing what was there, it blinded Morgan. It tucked him away from the things he could not control and the things reminding him he was different. How he would never truly fit in. How he existed on the edge between here and wherever it was he went when the light spoke to him.

My heart broke. One sharp crack of pain. I'd never felt anything like it. And if it was one tenth of the agony Morgan felt in that moment, I didn't know how he survived.

"Take. Me. Home."

I nodded. "I will."

"Home."

"I promise, Morgan."

"Home." He moved around me and got into the truck.

I took out my keys, and the bells on the restaurant door jingled. Abigail stopped on the sidewalk. I shook my head, and she nodded once. Then I got into the truck.

Morgan didn't speak on the way back to his house, and while the knots in his body tightened, he managed to keep his hand subdued to his lap, meeting every attempt at escape with a tight grip and hard pull.

He'd have bruises tomorrow. There was no way he couldn't.

I'd barely pulled into the driveway when he threw open the door.

"Morgan, wait." I followed him around the side of the house.

He stopped, but I don't think it was because he wanted to. His hand fluttered erratically, and his gaze jumped in every direction. He tilted his head up, to the side, then back down.

Morgan rocked on his heels.

I cupped his face, and he closed his eyes.

"Look at me."

He clenched his eyelids.

"Please, Morgan. Please look at me."

Tears trickled down his cheeks. I wiped them away, but they wouldn't stop.

"Nothing that asshole says matters. Do you hear me? Nothing."

"But what if it does?" His hollow gaze met mine.

"It doesn't."

But he didn't believe me. Like a horrible stain; there it was in his eyes. This beautiful man, his incredible talent, his insight to the world seeing things no one else could perceive or were strong enough to acknowledge, doubted himself.

What frightened me more was the idea he might even doubt his reason to exist.

I needed him to know how wrong he was, but I had no idea how to do that. Give me valuables to smuggle, hide, or sell and I was a magician. But facing the battle of Morgan's self-worth, I was at a loss.

I smashed my mouth against Morgan's and swallowed the yelp that escaped him. Copper mixed with his natural flavor, but I didn't care. I kissed him until my jaw ached and lips my burned.

A few steps back sent him off balance. I chased him to the ground, trapping him under me.

Morgan worked his mouth against mine hard enough to grind our teeth together.

I shoved his shirt up and found his nipple. Pinching them earned me a surprised gasp. I twisted and the sound turned into a pleading cry. I sucked one then the other.

He pawed at my shirt.

"Grant..." Morgan rocked against me. "Oh god... god..."

The zipper on his jeans didn't want to open so I yanked the fabric until the teeth gave way. His cock found my hand. The head was already slick when I stroked him.

Morgan dug his fingers into my shoulders.

"I'm going to make you come. I'm going to make you come over and over until you can't even think." He wailed when I tightened my grip. "And you're not going to fight me. You're going to give yourself to me, Morgan. You're going to trust me because you told me you did." I dragged my thumbnail across his slit.

He hissed between clenched teeth.

"And do you know why?"

Morgan shook his head.

"Because you're perfect and for some reason you find me worthy of your perfection. Because you're a gift and I will not let you forget that." I brushed my lips against his. His dark eyes searched mine. "And do you know the most important reason?"

"No."

"Because I love you." I moved down and took his cock into my mouth. Clean sweat, his musky skin, it worked like an aphrodisiac crawling into my senses. I sucked him. I fondled his balls. I used every trick I knew, my tongue along the glans, pressing him against the roof of my mouth, going deep, shallow. His muscles turned to rocks under my hands. I bobbed my head faster, and he pulled my hair. The bitter salt of precum replaced his natural flavor, but that was all.

I gripped him again. The cords on Morgan's neck stood out. The flush was back in his cheeks. His golden hair caught the broken pieces of sunlight dancing around us and all but glowed against his skin.

"Come for me."

He shook his head.

"You will."

He shook his head again.

I yanked off his jeans, taking his shoes with them. "You will, Morgan. I won't give you a choice." I stuck two of my fingers in my mouth and descended on him again. He spread his legs without hesitation.

As soon as I pushed my fingers into his opening, he shouted, "More, please, more."

I pumped them in and out with as much force as I sucked him.

It had never bothered me this much before when Morgan refused to let go. I knew it was something he had to do. A kind of proof that he wasn't completely at nature's mercy.

But this time, it pissed me off. Not at him, but for the reasons he did it.

That would change.

I moved over him and undid my pants. Dried grass tickled the head of my cock while I milked it. I wasn't sure it would be enough so I coated the head in spit.

Morgan grabbed his dick, and I slapped his hand away. "That's mine. You're mine." He started to protest, but I shut him up by pushing into his ass.

His mouth fell open. I thought I'd hurt him until he bowed off the ground and locked his ankles behind my back.

I thrust in long slow strokes, pulling to the tip and shoving my cock deep enough to bruise my balls. Morgan reached for his dick again, and I pinned his wrists above his head.

He rolled a look up then back at me.

"I told you, you were mine. All mine, Morgan. Perfect. Beautiful."

Under the fire of pleasure in his gaze, there was a flash of doubt. "I'm not."

"What did you say?" I made two short pumps and one hard reentry.

"I'm not." His scream broke apart into needy whimpers.

"You are." I thrust faster. "You are and you're going to say it."

He gritted his teeth.

"Say it, Morgan, say 'I am beautiful.'"

"No."

"Say it." I shoved my cock into him hard enough to push him a few inches across the ground.

"Oh god, Grant, please, please, I need to come."

"Not till you say it."

"No."

"Then you won't ever come." I dropped my forehead to his. "And I will fuck you into the ground."

"Grant, please…"

I licked the tears off his cheeks. Morgan tried to kiss me, and I turned my head. He fought against my grip, but I had the advantage of body weight.

"All you have to do is say it. Tell me you're beautiful, Morgan." I should have been ashamed by the horror reflected back at me. "Tell me." Sweat dripped from my chin onto his.

Morgan pressed his lips together.

Deep in his ass, raging with the need for release, I stopped.

"Goddamn you, Grant." Morgan thrashed. "Move, move."

Unlike Morgan, my words were a whisper. "Say it."

The stubborn shield he protected himself with cracked and his expression crumbled. The sob that broke loose hurt, but I'd taken this too far to back down. I needed him to know just how much I believed the words I said and needed him to say them.

"I…"

"Louder."

"I'm beautiful."

I rewarded him with one slow roll of my hips. "Again."

"I'm b… beautiful." Another stroke and he moaned.

"That's it, baby." I found a short quick rhythm. "Now, tell me how perfect you are." He hesitated, and I slowed down.

"I'm perfect." He sobbed again. "Grant, please."

"Say it again. All of it."

"I'm beautiful. I'm perfect."

"I love you, Morgan. Tell me that."

"Grant…"

"Say it, Morgan, or I swear to god, I'll stop."

"Y… you… love me."

"More than anything."

"More than… anything." His eyelids fluttered. "Now please let me come."

"Not yet."

"I said it. I said what you wanted me to." Morgan inched his legs higher and attempted to use the closeness of our bodies to stroke himself.

I arched my back, making space between us.

"Goddamn you." He tore the grass within his reach.

"Come for me, Morgan. Prove to me you trust me and let go."

That stubborn veil tried to fall back into place, but the damage was done.

I pumped my hips. "Let me love you."

"Why?"

"Because I want the chance to treasure you. Worship you. I want to spend the rest of my life with you."

"You don't mean it." He bit his lip.

"Yes, I do." I gave him two hard thrusts. "You can feel that I do. You see it." I freed his hands. "Like everything else, Morgan, you see the truth."

201

He petted my face. Traced my mouth with his fingers. He stared at me. Through me. Then he opened himself. The beauty I'd thought I'd known was nothing compared to the glimpse he gifted to me in that moment. His vulnerability, his capacity to love, his willingness to trust. Morgan not only showed me those things, he pulled me in, wrapped me up, and whispered the secrets of his world in my ear.

I won't pretend I understood what he said. I don't think any mortal could.

Then he brought me back to the surface and said, "I was afraid you'd never tell me." And I knew what he meant.

"Forever?" He breathed the question against my lips.

"Yes."

"No matter what?"

"No matter what."

Morgan undulated in fluid movements, meeting my thrusts rather than fighting against them.

"That's it, baby, let go." I peppered his neck in kisses. "My beautiful man, my perfect lover."

His entire body shuddered, and Morgan tightened around my cock.

"Come for me, Morgan." I stroked him. "Now, come for me now."

There was a moment of surprise on his face, but it quickly turned into surrender. He bowed off the ground with a shrill cry as the orgasm ripped through his body. Wet heat coated my hand.

My own need roared to life and the rush of euphoria knocked the air from my lungs. I buried a yell into the crook of his neck and lost myself to the spiral of release.

Morgan collapsed, chest heaving, body glistening in sweat. He held me, and we lay there while the sun slid behind the trees and the air cooled.

We shivered but stayed where we were.

Chapter Seven

I stood in line at the grocery store with a tub of Chocolate Extreme with Marshmallows ice cream, a bottle of wine, and a small box in my pocket.

A Friday night ice cream binge had become a ritual for Morgan and me. After we met with Abigail the second time and Morgan signed the stupid contract Mr. Day had negotiated with his team, we grabbed a half-gallon of ice cream, some cheap wine, and lay in the grass, sharing a spoon and glass until we could barely walk.

When the days got colder, we moved inside and lay in front of the wood stove. That went on for about a month, then I stopped going home except to finish random projects on the house. After the plumbing was finished, the hardwood floors stained, and everything that needed to happen to make it livable was done, I quit going altogether.

Morgan convinced me to rent the place out, and I moved in with him.

There wasn't a single morning I woke up with any desire for coastal waters or pristine sands. How could I when I had the most beautiful man in the world at my side each night and in my arms in the morning?

A month ago, I'd officially rearranged my finances and made Durstrand a permanent place in my life; leaving everything else I'd known, my shipping business, the FBI, even Rubio, behind.

This was my new life. Forever. With Morgan.

I stepped up to the cashier. Donna greeted me with the same smile she did everyone, but her eyes glittered with mischief.

The register beeped and the price of the wine flashed on the display. "So, is it true about you and Morgan?"

I pulled out my wallet. "What do you mean?"

"You know." She held out her hand and wiggled her fingers.

I was not surprised to find half the line behind me leaning forward to hear my reply. How the hell did they know about the ring I'd bought? I'd specifically driven a good two hours to the next city so the gossip mill wouldn't catch wind and spoil the surprise.

I'd waited until Morgan had gone to work that day to pick it up and I hadn't shown the damn thing to anyone.

"I have no idea what you're talking about." I handed her a twenty. The smile she wore withered, but the people behind me were already whispering. An old lady got out her cell phone, and I did my damnedest not to glare at her.

Must have failed 'cause she quickly closed it and gave me an apologetic shrug.

Damn it, I'd really hoped to do this right. Although by the time I got to the truck, I was wondering if maybe him finding out wasn't such a bad thing. It would give him the chance to save me from making an ass of myself while down on one knee.

I knew he loved me, and God I loved him, and while the ring was just a ring, there was a very good chance he'd see it as letting go of the last of his independence and forever binding himself to one person, for one life. You'd think I'd be the one who'd be scared of that idea. And I was scared, but only because I was afraid I wouldn't be good enough.

My entire life I'd never even toyed with the idea of getting married. In fact, I'd laughed at the few men I knew who had. Why? What for? So you could be miserable like all the hetero couples? Then to add insult to injury, only a handful of states recognized the union.

Although now the list was getting longer and cities who resisted were winding up in lawsuits. Jessie always seemed to crank up the volume when the topic came over the news. I don't know if he did it for my benefit or if he was really curious about the outcome.

Most of the patrons, at least the evening crowd, seemed indifferent. A few had choice words, but they were the kind of folks who probably voted against allowing the union between mixed race couples. Whatever they said was usually lost under the rest of the crowd cheering on the football game showing on the other screen.

Looking back, he might have been trying to give me a hint. If he was, it worked, because I found myself smiling every time the Supreme Court ruled in favor of equal rights and smiling same-sex couples held up their marriage certificates for the world to see.

Some of those people had been together fifty-plus years, a few used walkers and wheel chairs, and way too many looked like they were days from their own funeral, fighting death and old age, just to see the day they could have a piece of paper. Some stupid form to give you a tax write-off, said you shared your debt, and let someone else make choices for you in the event you couldn't.

No, it had never been an afterthought for me until I realized that's exactly what I wanted with Morgan.

If he said no, I'd understand why, but maybe he'd at least wear the ring. For me, a silly symbol that he loved me enough to be mine.

I'd just got to the truck when my cell phone rang. I didn't recognize the number. I figured the gossip mill had moved quicker than even I'd given it credit for.

I answered. "Hello?"

A male voice laughed and said, "Abracadabra."

"I'm sorry, buddy, but I think you have the wrong—" The line went dead. "—number."

I loaded the groceries in the passenger seat. All the way back to Morgan's, I kept touching the box in my pocket, and before long, the butterflies in my stomach were doing the macarena.

Porter's Creek was barely wide enough for two cars, let alone a truck as big as the old Chevy. So I had to ride the shoulder to get around the small compact beater sitting on the side of the road.

The headlights illuminated the dented door, slid up the side to the busted taillights. As the night swallowed the vehicle in my rearview mirror, the smile I'd been wearing fell south.

I turned into the driveway and took up my regular spot under the tree in front of the house.

Warm light spilled from the windows and the front porch. Music trickled out from the open front door. It was a scene I'd come home to many nights. Sometimes to find Morgan at work on a sculpture, other times naked in bed.

Usually I was out of the truck and taking the steps two at a time, but tonight something held me back. A shiver ran down my spine. My hands shook.

Nerves. It was just nerves.

Then a breeze caught the screen door. It swung a few inches before the bottom corner caught the decking leaving it tilted off the hinges.

My heart froze in my chest. I didn't even bother closing the truck door as I headed to the house. Gravel crunched under my heel. A paving stone in the walkway shifted when I stepped on it.

The first porch step squeaked. The second was silent. A smooth gash made a hole in the screen near the doorknob. A smear of dark red colored the white paint of the lower windowpane, where whoever had cut the screen, had also broken it out so he could reach through and unlock the door.

From there, I tracked the intermittent trail of blood through the house. Sometimes it was a shoe print, sometimes a bare foot, or the desperate slap of a hand looking for purchase.

With each step I took, the heavier my body became, until the very act of walking left me gasping for air.

I stopped at the pair of boots jutting out from behind the kitchen door.

Pots, pans, plates lay scattered around the kitchen. Broken bits of glass turned to dust under the soles of my shoes. Lying in the middle of the debris was a well-built young man slightly shorter than me, with dark hair, and dark eyes. His expression was a strange mix of anger and surprise.

Bloody pits punctuated his T-shirt. His belt was undone and his zipper down.

The world snapped back into place hard enough to send me stumbling. "Morgan?" My heart pounded so hard I almost missed the small high-pitched ticking sound coming from the back porch. I followed the noise to the shadows under the workbench.

Morgan sat with his knees pulled to his chest and hands pressed to the sides of his head. The gun was still in his right hand.

My knees gave out, and I crawled toward him. His lip was split, and there was a bruise on his cheek. He was naked except for the torn remains of his boxers, but there was so much blood smeared over him that I couldn't tell where it came from until he rocked forward and I saw the gash on his arm.

"Morgan." He didn't look at me. "Morgan…" My fingertips brushed his arm or maybe his shoulder, and he screamed. Not the normal kind of cry fed by fear, but a raw animalistic howl. Some sort of primal warning of eminent death.

I scrambled back.

The sound trickled away as he continued to rock and thump the stock of the gun against his temple.

I took out my cell phone. My hands shook so hard I could barely dial Aunt Jenny's number.

"Hello?"

"He's hurt." I choked back the sob.

"Grant?"

"Someone broke into the house. And he's hurt." I sucked in a watery breath. "Morgan won't let me touch him, Jenny. He won't…"

"Have you called the sheriff?"

I shook my head.

"Grant?" There was movement from the other end of the line. "Grant, have you called

Sheriff Parks?"

"No."

"Stay with Morgan. I'll call. I should be there in ten minutes."

I returned the phone to my pocket. "Shhh—it's okay. It's okay. It's just me. Just me, Morgan." I inched closer.

Back and forth, back and forth. Each tiny whimper echoed by the soft thump of the gun bumping the side of his head.

"Morgan... Morgan, sweetheart, look at me."

He didn't.

"Morgan, I need you to give me the gun."

Considering the damage to the dead man's chest, it was unlikely there were any bullets left in the clip, but it only took one to kill a man so I didn't want to take the chance.

"Morgan, please, baby. Give me the gun, okay? Please..." I reached for it, and he jerked. "Morgan, I'm just going to take the gun." I got a grip on the weapon.

He let go without a fight.

I pushed it off to the side. "Morgan?" He still didn't acknowledge me.

I crawled under the table. My knee brushed Morgan's thigh, and he slammed into the wall trying to crawl up it or through it, I couldn't tell which. But he fled so violently his fingertips split and his nails tore off.

"Morgan, stop, stop, you're hurting yourself."

He flailed, kicked, and snapped at the air.

"Baby, please, please..."

Finally, I did the only thing I could. I wrapped my arms around him and pinned him against my chest.

For a second, the way he looked at me was twice as horrifying as the terrible scream he made. I dragged him from under the table. He clawed, kicked, spit. My blood mixed with his, my tears soaked his hair.

Somehow I managed to keep my voice steady. "It's okay." He thrashed. "You're safe." He sank his teeth into my forearm. The jagged pain was nothing but background noise. "I love you, Morgan. I love you and everything is okay."

I don't know how long he struggled, but my muscles ached, my skin stung with scratches, bite marks on my arms. Then all at once, he fell limp. But it couldn't have been too long because Jenny hadn't gotten there yet.

I cradled Morgan and petted his hair. But he didn't move, he didn't make any sound, his gaze remained transfixed. Staring at nothing. Seeing nothing. Hearing nothing.

I carried him out to the front porch and that's where Aunt Jenny found us.

****

Aunt Jenny and I sat in the yellow-walled waiting room with its ancient TV. The picture was fuzzy and broken up by lines. I'm not sure if the volume was turned off or it didn't work. The cup of coffee in my hand had long ago gone cold. Or maybe it was never warm.

At some point Sheriff Parks showed up with a couple of deputies and gave us the name of the man who had attacked Morgan.

Dillon Barnes. He'd stolen a car just hours ago and come to Durstrand. How the hell he'd gotten out was on everyone's lips.

Deputy Harold closed his cell phone and joined our group. "The warden at Alamo won't be available till the morning, and the guy I talked to doesn't even have Dillon listed in his computer."

"Are you telling me he just broke out of prison and no one noticed?" Jenny cast an accusing eye around the room. Everyone squirmed. Hell, I would have squirmed. "Bullshit."

"He didn't break out," Sheriff Parks said. "If he'd broken out, there would be a BOLO out on him and they would have called Morgan to warn him."

"Well, if they let him out on parole, they were supposed to call and let Morgan know."

"He wasn't due to go before the board until next month," I said. "And if someone fucked up and got the dates wrong, they sure as hell should have called Morgan to warn him they'd let the bastard out."

"He wasn't let out," Harold said. "If he'd been paroled, he would still be in system, but there's nothing there. Like he'd never been in jail to begin with."

"Now how the hell does someone just magically disappear?" Jenny said.

Abracadabra.

The cup of coffee slipped out of my hand and left splatters on the gray tile.

"Grant?" Jenny gripped my arm.

"I'm sorry." I swallowed back the bile inching up my throat. "I'll get something to clean that up with." I stumbled in the direction of the men's room.

"You should have been a magician, Grant." I would have recognized Jeff's voice and whoever called hadn't been him. It had to be coincidence, just a stupid wrong number and some asshole looking to hurt someone. Two different events. Nowhere near related. I pulled a wad of paper towels from the dispenser. But Aunt Jenny was right, people didn't magically disappear from the prison system.

Everything spun, and I leaned against the sink.

Behind me, the door opened. Sheriff Parks's concerned gaze reflected in the mirror in front of me.

"You all right?"

I turned on the tap. "Yeah, just... I didn't eat any dinner... shouldn't have drank the coffee..."

He walked over. Could he see the fear and lies? "Is it true you and Morgan are getting married?"

I laughed. I couldn't help it.

"Even heard you already have a date set."

"Really? When?"

He leaned against the wall. "Oh, sometime in June."

"According to who?"

"Kelly Chapworth. She's head of the Red Hat Society."

"Don't know her." As if it mattered. I splashed more water on my face.

"But it's true?"

"I bought a ring."

"Did he say yes?"

I did meet his gaze then. "I didn't get the chance to ask."

His smile fell a little as sadness filled his eyes. "You will."

"Doesn't mean he'll say yes."

"Would you like me to start a gambling pool? Might make enough to pay for the wedding."

I pressed my thumb and finger against my eye. "I really don't want to talk about this right now." I made a sad attempt to cover up an escaped tear with another handful of water from the sink.

Sheriff Parks took off his hat and examined the inside as if it had a secret to tell. "I know I'm just a hick cop to you. But I'm also Morgan's friend, Jenny's friend, and I hope yours."

"I appreciate that." And I did.

"But I'm also good at my job. Pretty good at reading people. What I saw back there wasn't a man who accidentally dropped his coffee cup, it was a man who heard something that scared him."

"Well, finding out a person can walk out of prison undetected is pretty scary." I pulled out more paper towels until I had way too many. "Now if you excuse me, I have a mess to clean up."

Parks put a hand on my shoulder.

"Grant, if you know something, now's the time to say it."

"And what would I know?"

"You tell me."

I couldn't. He was a cop, and they were on the same team as the FBI.

Parks nodded as if he read my mind. "For the next five minutes, I'm not the sheriff, I'm not even a cop."

"Cops are cops even when they aren't in uniform."

"For the next five minutes, I'm not. Now I'm some good ol' boy and family friend. If you know something, or think you know something, I need you to tell me."

I crushed the paper towels in my fist. Did I trust him? And if I didn't, then what?

"While I was on my way home from the grocery store, I got a phone call. It was a man I didn't know, and he only said one thing."

"What?"

"Abracadabra. A certain FBI agent used to tell me I should have been a magician."

"I'm not sure I follow."

"Dillon disappeared, magically, as Aunt Jenny put it. And she's right, people don't vanish out of a high security prison without help."

"And you think the FBI might be involved?"

"Do you know anyone else who could access prison records and erase them?"

He put his hat back on. "Why would they do that?"

"The shipping business I ran didn't always attract nice people. But as long as they played by my rules, no guns, no drugs, no people, I helped them move things." He nodded for me to go on. "They seemed to think my client list would help them arrest some people. I disagreed, and I wouldn't cooperate and give them the information they wanted."

"But why would they let Dillon out?" He crossed his arms and gave me a doubtful look.

"Because his psychological profile almost guaranteed he would go after Morgan."

208

Sheriff Parks shook his head. "I don't know. That's a really far-fetched idea."

"Is it? You know of any other way Dillon could have walked out?"

"A computer error isn't impossible. I hate to think that, but it's happened."

"What about his records?"

"That I don't have an answer for."

"But it's awfully convenient, don't you think? And from what I've seen, the FBI pulling off something like this wouldn't be outside the realm of possibilities."

He smiled a little. "They'd still have to go through channels to get someone out of prison. Especially someone like Dillon. The circumstances would have to be extenuating. There would be documentation. It would take time. And the reason would have to be astronomical. Other than a bad drug habit, he didn't even have anything to offer the police when questioned. What reason could the FBI come up with to get the channels open to pull him out?"

"Like someone told me once, Homeland Security."

Sheriff Parks stood straighter. "That doesn't even make sense."

"Doesn't have to. They're two words that give the FBI a lot of power to go around a lot of things. And trust me, if they thought it would get them what they wanted, then they'd use it."

"I don't understand, Grant. If you ran your business like you claim, then why would they exert so many resources? Even the FBI can be held accountable. If it was found out they let a guy go because they knew he'd go after an innocent citizen, the agents involved would wind up in prison."

It was my turn to smile, and it wasn't a happy one. "Feds don't go to prison; they go to country clubs. With fences. But more than likely they'd just lose their jobs and probably get to keep their pension." The rules had always been different for people like them. I didn't expect Sheriff Parks to understand. He might have been a good man, but he was still a cop.

You know that old saying about how you shouldn't talk about the devil? My phone rang. The number was unknown. I answered it.

"You should have cooperated, Grant."

"Who is this?" I knew the voice. I'd heard it at least once before.

"There's a flight leaving for Chicago at eight a.m. Be on it." The hard edge to his voice clipped his words. It was practically a speech impediment. Special Agent Hines had talked to me the same way the day I sank my barge.

"Be on the plane. Next time, I won't set loose some punk kid."

"You son of a bitch..." The line went dead, and I strangled my phone.

"You know who it was." Parks got in front of me. "Tell me, Grant. Tell me, and I'll do whatever I can to stop this guy."

"You don't have that kind of power." Because, like he said, he was nothing but a hick cop, a good one maybe, but he followed the rules. Hines wasn't fucking Goliath to David he was Godzilla.

"And you do?"

I could. I had the money, the resources, and I was a criminal. Maybe it was time I played the part. No wonder people like Lorado left a body count. Seemed like blood was the only thing that got anyone's attention. Sure as hell got mine.

"Do me a favor. Keep a couple of your boys here at the hospital to keep an eye on Morgan."

"Are you going somewhere?"

"I have a business meeting I need to attend."

Parks searched my face. "Grant, what are you going to do?"

Something I should have done a long time ago. Something a good cop like Parks couldn't let happen because it was his job to serve and protect no matter who the asshole was. "I'm pretty sure my five minutes is up."

****

I'd just finished cleaning up the mess I'd made in the waiting room when a nurse came through the back door wearing blue scrubs. Her hair was pulled into a bun and almost the same shade of silver as her eyes.

A wrinkle in her smock hid her name tag, but Jenny said, "How's he doing, Anne?"

"He's resting." She offered me her hand. "I'm Anne Lindle. We've never met, but I've seen you around town."

I rarely forgot a face, but right then I doubted I could've recognized my own. We shook.

Anne glanced past us to the small group of cops gathered in the corner. Parks was on the phone, probably trying his damnedest to find some grain of evidence the FBI had let Dillon out. Going by the look on his face, he was failing.

"Can we see Morgan now?" I needed to hold him because there was a chance I might not get to again.

"Sure." Anne led us into the back where nurses and assistants roamed in scrubs and bits of equipment sat against the wall. We passed the beds separated by curtains down a hallway. She stopped at door 42.

Her gaze went to Aunt Jenny then me. "Before we go in, you need to realize we sedated him for the examination."

I'd almost forgotten.

Anne patted my arm. "Don't worry, everything came back clean. He's just bruised up and has a cut on his arm."

Jenny's exhale was almost a sob, and tension I didn't know existed bled out of me.

"But there are some concerns." Ann put her hand on the door.

"Like what?"

"Morgan's not responding to questions."

Jenny said, "But you sedated him."

"Not enough to make him incoherent."

"What are you trying to say?"

Anne let go of the door. "I'm not qualified to—"

Jenny gathered up both the other woman's hands and held them. "Honey, we went to school together. You sat behind Lori in Mr. Seigle's math class. You tutored me in English Lit. You were there when Lori brought Morgan home as a baby, and you were there when those plastic surgeons in Maysville put him back together." Jenny held the woman's gaze. "You know Morgan. Now I need you to tell me what you think. Not as a nurse, but as my friend. As Lori's friend and Morgan's."

A tear escaped down Anne's cheek, and she whisked away with a sweep of her thumb. "Morgan's suffered a trauma, but his situation is complicated because of the autism. I think he has a good chance of coming back, but it could be days or weeks or…"

Never.

The unspoken word hung in the air between us.

I had to swallow several times before I could get my voice to work. "Please open the door."

She hesitated again.

"Please."

"Just keep in mind a lot could change over the next twenty-four hours."

The shift from fluorescents to near darkness left me blind. Then slowly the soft light over the hospital bed revealed Morgan, lying on his side. There was an IV in the back of one hand. The other lay on his pillow near his face, flexing as if dreaming about the tics it liked to display.

His eyes weren't closed, but he didn't look at me when I walked up. Round bruises marked his throat and a bandage covered the cut on his arm. The fight he'd put up had left marks across the back of his knuckles.

"Hey." Morgan's empty gaze wandered upward. I touched his cheek, his shoulder, his arm. A high-pitched whimper ticked out of his throat, and he stared into the light.

All I could do was stand there. I understood then what Anne had been trying to say. "He'll get better right?"

Her eyes conveyed a million I'm sorrys. "There's no set rule when it comes to regression. Or autism in general. Morgan is very unique in his ability to adapt and manage himself. Most people with as severe a diagnosis aren't as lucky. They might be able to acquire basic skills, but they don't excel like he did."

"But he came back before."

"Yes, he did."

"Then it's possible." My vision blurred.

"The specialist will be able to give you a better idea."

Tears burned a path down my cheeks.

She put her hand on my arm. "But if anyone can do it, it's him."

It was just a grain of hope, but it was something. "Um." I wiped my eyes. "Would you two mind if…"

"You take all the time you need." Aunt Jenny tossed a thumb over her shoulder. "Anne and I will go get some coffee. I'll be in the cafeteria if you need me."

The door shut, and we were alone. Morgan arched his neck as if he was trying to follow something I couldn't see. I pulled a chair over. The bed rail didn't want to cooperate, and it wound up cockeyed, but low enough for me to sit and put my elbows on the edge of the mattress.

Morgan's wayward hand reached upward toward the light. I took it. There was only a second or two where he resisted, then his grip tightened and untightened over and over again.

"You probably already know this, but I bought you a ring. I should have given it to you weeks ago but…"

He blinked several times in a row and his gaze slid away.

I scooted closer. "I wasn't sure how you'd take it. You know, me asking—" My voice cracked, and I cleared my throat. "Morgan Kade, it would be the greatest honor in the world if you would marry me." He fell still for a moment, but any hope I had he might actually respond withered when he returned to watching that far-off place where the light held him prisoner and I had no ability to reach him.

I kissed his knuckles, his palm, I pressed his hand against my cheek. "I'm so sorry. I never meant for you to get hurt. I never thought—" Could I say that? Could I really say I never imagined he might get hurt, really hurt, or killed? What if Jeff hadn't lied? What if the people in business had decided to take me out? Why? Who knows? To make a statement? To make sure I never got back in business? I knew they didn't need a reason. But logic told me I wasn't worth the expense of getting the job done. After the long silence from the FBI, I'd assumed my secrets weren't worth the taxpayer's dollars either.

Now I knew differently. I had something that, for whatever reason, Hines had crossed the line between the good guys and the criminals. He'd become one of the monsters, and monsters didn't work on logic.

"I was selfish, and I don't deserve you. But I love you more than anything in this world." Could he even hear me?

I took the box out of my pocket. "I've got to make a trip, but I'm going to leave this here with Aunt Jenny. When I get back, if you'll let me, I'll put it on your finger."

And what if I made it back to Durstrand and Morgan was still like this? A sob burst out of my chest, and I buried the tears in the blanket on his bed.

I should have cooperated and given the FBI what they wanted, but I didn't and now Morgan was paying for it. Unfair wasn't even a big enough word. My conscience held me accountable, even if my gut told me it wouldn't have mattered what I'd done. Hines wanted something I had, and obviously he would do anything to get it. Hurt anyone. Even kill them.

And his reasons had to be personal because Sheriff Parks was right about one thing; Hines was taking a huge risk and stretching his reach to its breaking point.

After a while, I was empty of tears even though my heart continued to bleed.

Morgan whimpered, and I looked up. His wandering hand drifted from his temple to my face. He tapped a path down my cheek to my lip. For a moment, his touch lingered, then he withdrew again.

"I'll be back soon." I wiped my eyes and stood. "As soon as I can. As soon as this is over." I kissed him on the forehead. "And I don't care how long I have to wait for you, I'll do it."

I could only hope I wouldn't make a liar out of myself.

****

Jenny sat with Anne near the coffee machines. A younger woman sat with them. She didn't carry the air of a nurse, and she lacked the stiffness of an attending doctor. Her clothes, a cross between medical and business suggested she held some other position at the hospital.

When she saw me, she nodded a hello and excused herself, leaving behind a folder in the middle of the table. I grabbed a quick cup of coffee while Anne and Aunt Jenny exchanged good-byes.

As I walked over, Anne gave Aunt Jenny a sad smile, squeezed her hand, then nodded at me. "It was good to get to officially meet you, Grant. I just wish the circumstances had been different."

Who wouldn't? We shook, and she left. I sat across the small table from Aunt Jenny who stared at the folder, frowning.

"What's that?"

"Just some paperwork."

Just paperwork didn't normally make people look like they were about to cry. Definitely not people like Aunt Jenny. She held up her empty Styrofoam cup. "You mind?"

"Go ahead."

While she prepped herself a new cup of joe, I stared at the folder. I had no right prying into anyone's business but found my hand inching closer.

"Go ahead." Aunt Jenny returned. "You can look."

"What is it?" I pulled it over.

"It's an information packet on Walnut Cove."

It sounded like a vacation spot, but when I flipped aside the cover, I realized it was anything but. A shiny brochure showed the faces of disabled individuals, and several pieces of paper listed questions. Another sheet stated patient's rights. A few more made a contract for admittance.

I stared at Aunt Jenny, and for the first time, she dropped her gaze. "It's a just in case thing, Grant. I'm not signing anything."

"And why the hell would you need a 'just in case' thing."

"I think you know why."

"He'll be all right."

She nodded. "I pray you're right. But if he isn't, he's going to need round-the-clock care."

"Who says?"

The precision with which she lowered her cup to the table, off to the side, was done with a robotic movement screaming of untapped anger. "If Morgan has regressed—"

"You don't know that. Anne said herself, it would be a while."

Aunt Jenny turned her cup one way then the next. It reminded me so much of something Morgan might do. It never occurred to me his reasons for rearranging his plate might be to get his temper under control. But unlike Morgan, Aunt Jenny wore her intentions loud and clear in her expression.

"I know what Anne said. And I know his chances are good. But if, God forbid, he doesn't come back, he's going to need someone to take care of him."

"Then I'll do it."

"Grant."

"I love him. I want to marry him." I took the box out of my pocket and pushed it over to her. "I promised him as soon as I get back I'll put that on his finger."

"You're thirty-six years old, Grant. If Morgan doesn't come back, you will be spending the prime of your life caring for someone who is not the person you fell in love with."

"Bullshit."

Her mouth screwed up. "Grant, you have no idea how combative he can be. He could hurt you or himself."

"I've lived with Morgan for almost six months. I think I know him pretty well."

"You know the Morgan who isn't trapped inside his head. You don't know this Morgan. I do. I know what Lori went through. I know the hell it can be to work with someone as severely autistic as him."

"Hell?" How could she think of using that word to describe Morgan?

"Yes. Hell. Because most days it's a one-sided job, one that's lonely and stressful. You lose your friends, your family, your life. The person you care for is the center of your world."

"Because you love them."

"Yes. But also because the rest of the world isn't ready for them. I told you, Morgan lost friends, people who he thought he could count on. When he came back home after Dillon, the people who promised they would visit every day did, once or twice, and then never again.

"Seeing someone you love, so distant and lost that they fight you even to go to the toilet, it's an ugly reality even the people who loved him couldn't deal with." She scrubbed a hand over her face.

"You're talking about yourself, aren't you?" The guilt in her eyes was all the answer I needed.

"I was among the herd, yes. I thought Lori had lost her mind when she brought him home as a baby, and I was definitely convinced she lost it when she brought him home a full grown man, trapped back in the prison he'd been born to."

"But she helped Morgan excel, then she brought him back when he regressed," I said. "If she can love him enough to make it happen, why can't I?"

"Because love has nothing to do with it. If it did, every autistic child on this planet would excel like Morgan. The truth is, most don't. Every instance of autism is different, and Morgan is a very rare case among a whole lotta other cases."

"So you're just writing him off." I slapped the folder closed and shoved it at her. "You're just going to lock him up somewhere so you won't have to deal with him?"

"You listen here, Mr. Grant Kessler, don't think I didn't see how you looked at him when you walked in there. Don't think I didn't see the fear you felt. The revulsion."

The heat rising in my cheeks fell somewhere around my ankles. I sipped my coffee, it burned my tongue, but the nerve endings in my body appeared to have died. The sour trail it left to my stomach suggested my taste buds had done the same.

Aunt Jenny was right. More than right. And if I truly thought about it, I had no idea how to deal with a normal illness, let alone something as complex as Morgan.

"Lori made him better." It was all I had to defend myself with.

"Yeah."

"How?"

"I don't know. She was a very special person. Very unique. In some ways like Morgan because she understood him. I don't know how, but she could reach him when no one else could. She worked with him every day, Grant. Every waking hour revolved around Morgan's needs. Maybe it gave her an advantage when he regressed because the specialists begged her to put him in a home."

"But she didn't."

"No. Lori gave the definition of stubborn a whole new twist. She was my sister and I loved her, but I won't pretend to have ever truly understood her or be anything like her. I know I can't handle Morgan, and I'm the only family he has."

"What about me?"

"He loves you so much he would never forgive me if I asked you, let alone allowed you to."

I drained my coffee cup. Anger and frustration turned it into a crumpled wad in my fist. Even when there was nothing left to crush, I still squeezed. From across the table, the folder mocked me.

"Are they going to be able to give him therapy?"

"Some."

"Some?"

"Walnut Cove is mostly state funded. After Morgan's bank account runs out, he'll become a ward of the state and they'll cover his care."

"You think he'll get what he needs in a state-funded facility?" He wouldn't. Our government did a piss poor job of taking care of the veterans who sacrificed their body and mind for their country. I knew the kind of place Walnut Cove would be. ·

"It's a clean facility. I went there once with Lori. Toured the whole place. They specialize in young people like Morgan. They even take them out into the community at least once a week."

"But she didn't leave him there."

Aunt Jenny laughed a little. "Nope. She didn't leave him there. And when they called to make sure she hadn't changed her mind, she told them all the places she'd cram the phone if they dare contact her again."

"If she didn't want Morgan there, neither do I."

"Grant—"

"What if he had home care?"

"You're talking about a lot of money. Even what's in Morgan's account from that mess with the Days wouldn't cover the cost for a year."

"What if I paid for it?"

"Grant... I don't think you realize how much—"

I took her hand and squeezed it. "It would be nothing to me."

She searched my face. "He wouldn't want you to do that."

"Yeah, well, Morgan doesn't always get what he wants. And honestly, this isn't just about him." Maybe I was hoping for atonement?

"You said you were going to put a ring on his finger when you got back."

I sat back.

"Where are you going?"

I pushed aside the crumpled remains of the cup. "Chicago."

"Why?"

"To do what I should have done months ago. Cooperate."

"You're talking about the FBI guy who was following you around a few months back."

"In a roundabout way, yeah."

"I thought he dropped his case."

"I think he did, but his boss didn't."

"I don't understand."

The doors to the cafeteria opened and a small group of men and women came in. They chattered among themselves while they gathered up trays to enter the food line looking for all the world like high-schoolers getting ready to collect their lunch. Only it was the middle of the night, and they carried an air of fatigue only those who work relentlessly to save lives could wear.

"I think the FBI might have arranged for Dillon to disappear from prison."

"What? Why?"

"Because they would have had access to his psych evaluation. They would have seen his obsessive behavior concerning Morgan. They would have known he would go after him."

"That's illegal."

"Probably."

"How could they do something like that? Who would let them do something like that?"

"Not everyone obeys the law, even the FBI."

"Does Sheriff Parks know?"

"Yeah. I told him."

"And?"

"He's a sheriff of a small town; the FBI doesn't have to answer to him."

"Well, they have to answer to someone." She hit the table with her fist.

"It's supposed to work that way, but it doesn't." And never had in my experience.

Aunt Jenny stared at me. "I still don't get it. Why would they want to hurt Morgan?"

"I called Jeff on his scare tactics. I raised the odds with my own. And I think it backfired."

"They did this because of you?"

Someone laughed, and I jumped. My hands shook so I put them in my lap.

"Look at me, Grant." It would have been easier to face the business end of a gun. "You told me Morgan was safe with you."

"I thought he was." I did. I swear I did. My guilt and pain raked my muscles raw. I ached for tears, but there were no more. I'd left everything I had back in Morgan's room.

She clenched her jaw and shifted her gaze. I had no idea if she flexed her hands because she wanted to hit me or wished for that shotgun she'd once threatened me with.

After a long moment, she seemed to regain control. "So now they've got your attention, you're going to give them what they want?"

"Yes, ma'am."

"And you think that will make them stop?"

I opened my mouth to answer, then closed it.

"Yeah, in my experience, rattlesnakes aren't very trustworthy."

I snorted. "I think there is more to this than official FBI business. I have no idea what, but it's personal."

"And you don't know why?"

"No."

"What do they want?"

"My client list. The times and dates I shipped things. At least that's what they told me."

"What do you think they really want?"

Aunt Jenny's question held me in place. "I honestly have no idea."

She nodded as if she expected the answer. "You ever kill a man, Grant?"

"Yes, but only when I had to."

"Good." The coldness in her tone almost made me ask her the same thing. Then I decided I didn't want to know. "How long will you be gone?"

"I'm not sure. A few days. Less than a week, I hope."

"And what if you don't come back? What about Morgan then?"

"I will." I realized what she meant. Really meant. "But it... yeah. I'll make all the arrangements with my lawyer for Morgan's financial needs. Just promise me no matter what happens, you won't take him out of his home. You'll use the money to hire as many people as you need to take care of him and get him better."

Aunt Jenny pushed at the notebook with all its lies and fake pictures about happy residents. "Won't be necessary." She brought her gaze back up. "'Cause you're gonna be back here, then you'll put that ring on Morgan's finger, and get married."

Chapter Eight

I made all the necessary phone calls to Harriet while I waited to board my flight. Like a good friend, she didn't argue with me, but the tone of her voice conveyed her worry. I assured her everything would be fine, but she didn't believe me.

Thing is, neither did I.

Before we hung up, I made my first and only demand of her. "Make sure Morgan is taken care of." Such simple words and completely benign, but the tone of my voice would tell her exactly what I meant. If I wound up dead, he would always have what he needed, and if Hines survived and tried to come after him, FBI or not, he was a dead man.

Since I didn't use any kind of fake ID, I expected the FBI to know I'd returned to town, but I didn't expect them to be so eager to welcome me back.

Jeff stood propped against a post next to the luggage carousel. His dark glasses hid his eyes, but his smirk was blinding.

I collected my lone bag and tossed it over my shoulder.

Jeff fell in beside me. "Aren't you going to say hello?"

"Nope."

I walked through a gap in the crowd, and Jeff had to push his way around people to catch up. "So what brings you home? Business or pleasure?"

"This isn't my home." I stepped aside for a lady pushing a stroller. Jeff nodded at her and she smiled.

"Ah yes." Jeff followed me to the bathroom. "You've settled down, bought a house, maybe even a dog, and found someone to share it all with. Although I still think your choice for a partner is debatable. Of course there's still time to grow some ethics."

I stopped with my hand on the door. The fury burning in me must have shown in my expression because Jeff lost his cocky smile and took a step back. It could have been my imagination, but I think he even moved his hand closer to his gun.

I went inside. So did Jeff, but he stayed close to the door.

"So why are you back in Chicago?"

"Vacation." I put down my bag. "You know noise, wind, smog, just what the body needs to balance out all that wholesome sunlight and clean air I've been breathing for the past six months." It was tempting to piss on his shoes. If he'd been closer, I might have.

"Vacation? And you think the FBI is bad at making excuses." I finished and went to the sink. His reflection grew behind me. "I'll find out eventually, so you might as well tell me."

I dried my wet hands over the front of his shirt making dark blue stains on the pale cornflower fabric.

I grabbed up my bag and was almost out the door when Jeff said, "We know about you putting your client list up for sale. Out of curiosity how much are your so-called morals worth? A quarter million, half a million, more? We even started an office pool on who the lucky recipient would be."

I don't remember lunging for Jeff. Just one moment I was looking at him, the next I had him pinned against the wall. His sunglasses clattered to the floor. "Did you take bets on Morgan? So what's a man's life worth to you now days, Jeff, ten, twenty, thirty bucks?"

"What the fuck are you talking about?" Jeff twisted in my grip, and I slung him into the paper towel dispenser. A smear of crimson followed him back to the wall.

Jeff tried to say something, but I crushed his cheek against the wall. Spittle made white flecks on his bottom lip. I pressed harder, and tears formed in the corner of his eye.

"What was it you said to me, Homeland Security? Is that what you did to get him out, or did you just flash your FBI club badge and walk him to your car?"

"I—" His reply sputtered out with a shove to his back.

"You think that badge makes you invincible? It doesn't." I leaned closer. The evil in my tone crawled from the darkest parts of my soul. Parts I never knew existed or maybe hadn't until the threat of losing Morgan became real. "And it sure as fuck isn't big enough to protect the people you love."

Jeff rolled a look up at me. Fear, raw, unshielded, and real burned in his eyes. He swallowed several times. "I don't know what you're talking about."

Truth or lie? I studied his face. I inhaled the stench of terror forming beads of sweat on his skin. He trembled until his very bones rattled. I think for the first time Jeff realized the man I could have become.

I think for the first time, so did I.

I left him collapsed against the wall, gasping for air. The dark purple splotches in his cheeks turned red, then pink, and the color slowly returned to his complexion.

He touched his ear and crimson painted his fingertips. I said nothing while he used a few paper towels to stem the blood flow while checking the damage in the mirror.

Leaning forward, he opened his jacket and the butt of his gun showed clearly under his arm. At any time, he could have pulled that weapon on me and gotten away with killing me for attacking him.

He dabbed the paper towel under the faucet. "Now do you think you can tell me what the hell you're talking about?"

"You wouldn't believe me if I did."

"Try me."

I picked up my bag. "Just answer me this, did you know Hines was going to let him out?"

"Who?"

"Dillon Barnes?"

His eyebrows wrinkled. "Name's familiar but…" He shook his head. "Who is he?"

"A psychopath who went after Morgan."

"Is he okay?" Jeff turned. Either he was an Academy award-winning actor or his concern was real.

"Yeah, he'll live."

"Grant, we both know a man can live and not be all right. Is Morgan all right?"

"When I left the hospital, he was still sedated. I'll know more when I get back." If I got back. "Now if you excuse me, I need to go find a motel to check in to and wait for your boss to call."

"Hines? What does he have to do with this?"

I started toward the door and he cut me off. "Move."

"Not till you tell me what's going on."

"If you don't know, you don't want to."

"Who are you selling your client list to?"

I exhaled a bitter laugh. "You really want to know?"

"Yeah."

"Special Agent Hines."

He squinted at me. "What?"

"Yeah, and the price is Morgan's life." Or what was left of it. I pushed the thought out of my head. He would be fine. When I got back to Durstrand, he would be the same man I'd fallen in love with. He would laugh, he would pull his pranks, and most of all, he would build beautiful glass sculptures in an attempt to let the world hear the wisdom the light had to share.

I tried to push past Jeff but didn't have the strength and wound up propped against his shoulder one hand on the wall.

"Tell me what's going on."

"Why, so you can run and tattle to all your little cohorts?"

He cupped the side of my face and the warmth of his skin chased back the cold crawling through me. "No, because I'd heard about your client list going up for sale."

"And you wanted to put in a bid?"

"No. I wanted to find out what happened to make you willing to sell it. We both know you don't need the money." He swallowed, and his throat clicked. "I also thought maybe…"

"What?"

He stepped away again, picked up his sunglasses, and checked his reflection.

The bathroom door opened and a couple of other men came in. One went into the stall, the other the urinals.

Jeff indicated the exit with a tilt of his head. We walked out, shoulder to shoulder. Almost close enough to hold hands. When the crowds thinned a little, he said, "After our last conversation, I dropped the case on you. Hines wasn't happy. He insisted I stay in Durstrand. But it was my case by then and my call. He tried to go over my head, but the Deputy Director agreed with me. We'd wasted enough resources and had nothing to show for it."

"Still doesn't answer my question."

"Your case is fantasy fodder for a few new people. I was afraid if another agent started poking around, you might think I was involved and… I crossed the line with you, Grant. I've only seen you like that a few times and the last time was when you killed Caruso."

"I killed him to keep him from shooting you." As if he needed a reminder.

"I know. But you gave him a chance to stand down. He wouldn't, and you didn't even blink when you pulled the trigger. I saw the look on your face. I heard your voice. I heard that same tone when you called me before you were supposed to come to Maysville. You didn't even have to send a photo to prove your point, I was already convinced." We stepped outside and found a space of unoccupied wall in the sunlight. Outside, his paled complexion made the flush in his cheeks glow. "I want you to know I puked my guts up for the next hour."

And for some reason, I didn't feel a bit guilty. He was right, he did cross the line.

"Well, you can rest easy. I'm not here for you. I'm just here to see the sights."

He fished a pack of gum from his pocket, offered me a piece, and I declined. "Why do you think it was Hines who sent someone after Morgan?"

"Where should I direct my answer to make sure you get the best reception?"

"I'm alone and not wired."

"And I'm supposed to take your word?"

"If I wasn't, you'd be dead or at least in cuffs for the stunt you pulled in the bathroom."

He had a point.

"Because he called me, and basically told me he did. Then he promised to send someone more experienced next time."

Jeff blew out a breath. "I know the guy's a bastard but…"

"You can't believe he'd do something like that?"

"Putting a hit out on someone is illegal, no matter who you are."

"He didn't put a hit out on Morgan."

Jeff's eyebrows rose over the edge of his glasses.

"Dillon Barnes was serving time for almost beating Morgan to death several years ago. Hines arranged to let him out."

"How did he know—?"

"He'd go after Morgan?"

Jeff nodded.

"He was up for a parole hearing next month. Harriet had arranged for the doctor to speak to the board on Morgan's behalf. Since the guy pled out, the trial judge never heard the state shrink's eval. At the hearing, he was going to recommend Dillon be moved to a facility for the criminally insane. He felt Dillon needed treatment. The guy wasn't just short a few marbles, the bag was fucking empty. All Hines would have had to do was read Dillon's file. The odds were by far in favor of him going after Morgan than trying to disappear."

"Hines might have been Special Agent in charge of the investigation on you originally, but his reach only goes so far. He'd have to get approval to walk a prisoner out, and he'd have to have a damn good reason."

"Homeland Security? Isn't that what you said?"

"Still…" The busy city street reflected in his mirrored sunglasses. "To do something like that takes a certain level of clearance. Not to mention the prison guards who would be witnesses."

"I've have associates who've served time in prison and some who worked in them. Both sides will tell you, after a while, you get apathetic. The people in charge don't hear or see anything. You just go there, do your job, and try to get home in one piece. And the prisoners try not to get shanked or piss off a guard. It's the only way to stay sane. Believe it or not, Jeff, people don't get cured when they go to jail, they learn better ways to not get caught. And the people who work there? Some of them come out of the job a completely different person than they were when they went in. Maybe Hines paid someone off, or maybe he just told them he was going to rid the world of a piece of shit scumbag. Or maybe he didn't have to say anything at all and just flashed his ID. Who knows?"

"Would still be a huge risk for anyone to let a prisoner walk out without a court order. Even if the person taking them was FBI. If something happened to someone on the outside, even the prisoner, there would be questions."

"Not if there's not any evidence they'd been in their prison."

"How could there not be a record?"

"You tell me. Dillon's records were erased. It was like he'd never been there."

"How is that possible?"

"I figured the FBI had access to prison data with a few key strokes."

He crossed his arms and leaned against the wall. "Sure, we have access."

I shrugged. "So Hines slipped and hit the delete key?"

"I don't think it's that easy."

"Why not, you make people disappear all the time." A line of cabs formed at the curb. People got in, people got out. A tour bus cut around them, belching a cloud of burned diesel.

"I know he wasn't happy when they took him off as SAC and appointed me, and tried to run things from the backseat, but this is…" He shook his head. "He's risking his career, Grant. If anyone ever found out, he'd go to prison."

"I seem to remember another agent who was hot to trot for my list a few months ago. He was willing to hurt someone I cared about too."

Jeff dropped his gaze. "I might be an asshole, but I'm not a killer. I would have never done anything to put Morgan in real danger. I just needed your attention."

"Yeah, and you got it."

"I realized that." He scuffed his feet against the concrete. "What are you going to do?"

"Give him the list."

"And you think he'll let you walk away?"

"I don't know."

"If you're right, he's committed some serious crimes. And if he shows up with that list, the director is going to want to know how he got it. Scaring you never worked before. If they ask around, they'll find out about Morgan, then Dillon and the missing prison records. He'll get caught."

I nodded. "Has it occurred to you maybe he's not doing this for the job?"

"Then why else would he?"

"Something personal. My bet something illegal enough to risk losing his job."

Jeff rubbed his jaw.

"What?" I said.

"It's nothing."

"You're thinking about something, what is it?"

"Remember when I told you about Ruford and Zada closing up shop?"

"Yeah."

"That wasn't the complete truth."

"Have you ever given me the complete truth about anything?" Guilt, regret, and maybe even sorrow rippled through Jeff's expression. Before he could say anything, I said, "What was the truth?"

"Their bodies washed up in Grand Haven."

"Surprising, and not."

222

He nodded. "They were supposed to go into witness protection. Came forward while Lorado was doing his tour in Egypt. They were going to testify against him. Claimed he had law enforcement on the payroll."

"No wonder they wound up dead." I couldn't think of one person who had crossed Lorado and lived. Number one reason I never did business with the man. He stayed on his side of the docks; I stayed on mine. Also why I worked very hard to keep my clientele specialized. The last thing I wanted was someone who pissed him off, putting merchandise on my boat.

"Yeah, they were shot in the back, same gun, close range, and the decomp condition suggested they probably died about the same time. Hines was the agent in charge of picking them up."

"Isn't that dangerous? I mean, one agent for two very well-known killers."

"I thought so. Hines blew it off. He said they would only ride with him. Then he came back empty-handed and said they were a no-show."

"And that didn't throw up any red flags?"

"We're talking about Hines here. SAC at the time. He has twenty-plus years on the job and two Meritorious Achievement medals. So no, I didn't question him. And people like Ruford and Zada aren't exactly worth crying over." Jeff had a point.

"So now you've changed your mind? Why?"

"I didn't say that."

"But you're entertaining the idea." I jerked my chin.

"Maybe."

"Spit it out, Jeff."

"A couple of months ago, Hines's wife asked me if I knew if he was having an affair."

"What did you tell her?"

"No. Which was, as far as I knew, the truth. I asked her why she thought he was, and she said there was some money missing from their accounts and he was getting phone calls at odd hours of the night. She seemed pretty insistent, then last month for their anniversary they renewed their vows and he bought her a Mercedes."

I whistled. "Sounds like an affair apology to me and then a promise to keep it in his pants or else."

"I wondered that myself. Then something weird happened. Hines forgot his personal cell phone in his office one evening when he left. Damn thing kept going off every thirty seconds and I had work to do, so I thought I'd shut it off. Just as I picked it up, he came back into the building. Got pretty pissed. Wanted to know why was going through his stuff. I told him the thing was chirping like a wounded bird. He looked it over, I guess to see if I'd been snooping, then told me to stay out of his personal space and left."

"But you saw something."

"Yeah, a phone number. I only saw it for a second, but I swear it was the same damn number associated with Inman Enterprise." Which was Lorado's shipping company.

"And you just happened to know that how?"

"Because I used to stare at it every time a call came through to be recorded. But it was a long time ago, before I was assigned to your case. I thought maybe I was wrong, but now this."

"You think him and Lorado are doing business?"

"I don't know."

If Hines was keeping Lorado privy to information from the inside, it could give him a huge upper hand in moving his products. It could also explain why of all the big dealers, he never seemed to be bothered by the feds. Or at least not to the extent as his competition. And when he was tailed, the busts were always minor, and his lawyer always seemed to get the charges dropped.

It would also explain how a relatively unknown man had gotten so big so fast, taking over most of the shipping docks and the clientele.

If Hines and Lorado were working together, then things were even uglier than I thought. This was no longer just about Hines, but Lorado. Even Rubio feared the man.

"What are you going to do?" Jeff jerked his chin at me.

I shifted the bag to my other shoulder. "I should probably try to find a motel."

I turned, and he grabbed my arm. "Grant. If you're right, he's not going to let you walk away."

No, I was more likely to end up like Ruford or Zada. "I'll worry about that when the time comes."

"You need to worry about it now."

I pulled out of his grasp. "Look, I'm tired. I didn't get a lot of sleep, and I'm sure when Hines calls, he won't want to be kept waiting."

"Let me help you."

I laughed. I couldn't help it.

"Damn it, if he's gone bad, he needs to be brought down."

"Trying to earn one of those Meritorious Achievement medals?"

"This isn't a joke."

No, it wasn't. It was life or death. Hines or mine. Maybe even Morgan's. But I'd trusted Jeff one too many times and gotten burned. Sure, he'd been doing his job, trying to catch the bad guys, but still...

Jeff stepped closer. "I don't want to see you get killed."

"I gotta go." I headed to the line of cabs.

"There's a new café next to the old drug store that sells the ten-pound bag of gummy bears. I'm going to be there for dinner. Probably around six or so."

"Hope the food is good." I waved down a cabbie.

"If you'll join me, I'll buy."

"No promises." I opened the back door and tossed in my bag.

"I mean it, Grant, I want to help."

And whether I liked it or not, I needed all the help I could get.

****

I found a pay by the hour, day, or week motel. The kind where the vacancy sign was always lit and rattraps lined the hallways. I could have gotten better accommodations, but I needed a place where they only took cash and didn't ask for ID. Or if they did, you could show them a few Jeffersons and their copying machine would instantly break down and they'd transpose a few of the numbers on your driver's license in their logbook.

The man sitting at the front desk greeted me with a gapped smile. His toupee was lopsided. After he counted the wad of cash I'd given him for a week's stay, he fumbled around in a drawer until he came up with a key.

"Don't lose that, it's the only copy, and I'll have to charge you for a new lock."

The giant yellow tag attached to the ring stuck to my palm. It was probably gum, at least I hoped it was gum. As soon as I got inside the room, I washed my hands just in case.

Taking the plane meant leaving behind any weapons, but I knew where to go to score what I needed, although their storefronts wouldn't be open until past noon, a few not till dark.

Exhaustion left me lying on the ugly maroon comforter. At least it smelled clean. Either that or housekeeping had a stock in Febreze.

The nurse had said the anesthetic they gave Morgan would last a few hours. It was well past those few hours, yet I hadn't called the hospital to check on him. I wanted to. My joints ached to dial the number, but fear kept me from picking up the phone.

Besides, if there had been a big change, I was sure Aunt Jenny would call and she hadn't. I tried not to think of what that could mean, but of course it was impossible.

A strip of sunlight made a line across the bed beside me. I ran a finger through the beam, and the color in my skin was bleached away only to return when I moved outside the limits of the light.

I did it again and again for absolutely no reason, feeling nothing, hearing nothing, wishing I could understand what Morgan saw, heard, even felt when he danced his fingers in the fragments of light.

He'd told me there were hidden messages, or stories. I hadn't really given it much thought until then. In spite of what should have happened concerning Dillon, he'd gotten out, and Morgan had known he would.

Dear God, what if I had somehow convinced him to give me the gun the day I caught him shooting the bottles. It left me wondering what else Morgan knew or could know. What other secrets did the light sing to him?

My cell phone rang, and I jerked my hand from under the beam as if it had burned me. Another muffled ring had me rolling off the bed and stumbling to the door, which was all of three steps, where I'd dropped my duffle. I dug through it, found my phone.

A mix or relief and anger washed over me when the number came up unknown.

"I take it your flight was comfortable?" The noise in the background suggested Hines was either driving or somewhere there was enough traffic for the noise to carry.

"Out of curiosity, are you going to shoot me like you did Zada and Ruford or just slit my throat? Throat cutting is messy and personal, I figured you'd just shoot me."

Hines laughed. "I don't want to kill you, Grant."

"But you're not going to let me walk away. You can't. I'd be a witness."

"Is that what you think?"

"Yeah."

"Then why did you come?"

"You know why."

He laughed again, this time it was deeper, darker. "Yeah, I do."

"Just so you know, if you go back on your word, you will die."

"Really?" The background noise faded until it became a hollow echo. Underground garage? An alley? Was he close? "And how do you expect to kill me, if, like you say, I'm not going to let you walk away alive?"

"Same way I make things disappear. Like you said, Abracadabra."

His exhale rattled the speaker. "Unlike Special Agent Shaldon, I'm not afraid of you."

"Of course you aren't. I haven't given you a reason to be."

"Face it, Grant. You're soft. You've always been soft. Eugene was too, it's why he had a quarter of the fortune he could have had. You're just like him, you know. Pathetic and weak."

"Thanks for the compliment. Eugene had honor, respect, and the trust of a lot of people, I'm willing to bet you don't even have one out of the three, despite your FBI badges of honor. Tell me, Hines, does your wife know what you're doing?"

A car door opened then shut. The soft rumble of an engine filled the silence.

"You on your way home or to work? Do you plan on putting in your two week notice when you go criminal full-time, or are you just going to call in sick and disappear?"

"Shut up, Grant, I'm not in the mood to hear you talk about anything but your client list."

"Then get a pen and paper." I sat back down on the edge of the bed. A spring bit the back of my thigh and I had to move over.

"No. I'm not going to rush this. I don't want you to leave out a single detail. I want to look you in the eye when you give me those names so I know you're telling me the truth."

"Aww, are you asking me out on a date?"

"There's an old church near Randal's Pub. Be there in the morning, nine a.m. sharp. Don't be late, come unarmed, and alone."

"And who would I bring?"

"I know Shaldon met you at the airport. The Assistant Director might believe him when he says his job comes first, but I don't. If I find out you've said anything to him, I'll make sure you get a front row seat at his funeral."

I forced myself to keep breathing.

"Do we understand each other?"

"Yeah."

"Good. Nine a.m., sharp. Do not be late. If you are, even two deputies watching over your little retarded boyfriend won't stop me from getting to him." Hines hung up, and I was left trembling.

****

The café was some greasy spoon diner tucked beside an out-of-business cigar shop. The customers consisted of cabbies, truck drivers, and the occasional couple looking for a cheap meal.

Dressed in jeans, a polo, and a ball cap, I almost didn't recognize Jeff tucked in the corner where he had a view of the entire room. It was the kind of spot I would have chosen. Especially now, when I had no idea who was going to sneak up on me.

He caught sight of me, and his smile went crooked. The waitress taking his order nodded and walked away.

"I told her to bring you some tea. You'll have to sweeten it, though."

Chrome edged the checkered walls, and all the booths were red vinyl. "Classy joint."

"They're going for a 50s motif, I think."

"Hope the food's worth the migraine."

"Best hamburger you'll ever put your mouth on, and the onion rings prove there is a God."

The waitress came back with a glass of tea. "You boys ready to order?"

"Burger, double order of onion rings." Jeff handed her the menu.

"I'm not hungry, thanks."

"Bring him the same, I don't want him picking off my plate." She left, and I frowned at him.

"I said I wasn't hungry."

"When you smell mine, you will be."

I fished out sugar packets from the white box between the salt and pepper shaker. "Do you know whether or not you were followed?" I said it so casually I think it caught Jeff off guard because he stared at me for a moment before he realized I was serious.

"Why would I be followed?"

"Hines knew you met me at the airport."

"Of course he did, I didn't make a secret of it. Told the whole office I was going to find out whether or not I won the pot."

"What did you tell them when you got back?"

"That you gave me some lie about visiting relatives and told me to fuck off."

I laughed a little. "He doesn't trust you."

"Of course not. You and I were having sex. I compromised myself by letting my emotions get the best of me."

"Compromised..." One packet after the other, I emptied them into the glass until I had a pile of white topping the floating ice cubes. "Sounds so..."

"Impersonal?"

"Yeah." Especially coming from a guy who claimed to have loved me.

"The choice of verbiage is very important when chatting with the department shrink. Compromise shows I knowingly made an unwise decision but did it with the intentions of keeping an emotional distance."

I opened my straw and stirred my drink. "You see a department shrink?"

"Saw."

"PTSD?"

"No, I had to convince them I played the part I needed to play to get the information I was supposed to get."

"I could have told them that."

When I glanced up, his smile was brittle.

"Hines told me if he finds out I'm talking to you about this, he'd kill you."

The bells on the café door jingled, and a woman came in with a teenage boy. He walked with an exaggerated gait with one hand curled at his chest and the other hovering near his ribs. Occasionally he would reach out as if to pluck something invisible from the air around him no one could see.

The woman led him over to a less crowded area of the café. The boy jerked from her hold and spun away from the table. Without missing a beat, she caught him and turned him around. He sat but not before knocking the silverware onto the floor. The woman picked it up and put it aside.

Two waitresses cast a wary look in the teenager's direction. Both of them frowned. The blonde shook her head and the dark-haired woman went over to the table. Her forced smile threatened to crumple when the teenage barked out some random sound and slapped the table.

The woman who was with him didn't even seem to notice.

When the waitress left, the woman took out napkins from the dispenser and laid them on the table. The teenager kept his head turned to the side.

No matter how hard I tried to keep my eyes on my glass of tea, my gaze continued to roll up to the teenager as he rocked in his seat.

"Did you hear me?" Jeff said.

"Uh, no, sorry."

"I said I wouldn't be able to live with myself anyhow if anything happened to you and I didn't do something to try to stop it."

There was real longing in Jeff's eyes. I don't know if he meant to or not, but his foot brushed mine. As I pulled my leg back, our waitress arrived with our food.

"Here you go, two burgers, double rings. You two enjoy." She put down the plates and left.

Jeff prepped his burger. "How's Morgan doing?"

The question swallowed me in guilt. I picked at my onion rings. "He was doing okay when I left. Resting."

"You haven't checked on him?"

"I don't want him to worry."

The young boy in the back of the café yelled and knocked his drink in the floor. The woman with him tried to stop him from throwing hers down too but failed.

Other patrons turned in their seats. Some frowned. Some turned away quick enough to suggest they were disturbed by what they saw.

At first I thought the woman was oblivious to the strange looks, but then she flicked a quick look around the restaurant. More people came in. All of them stared for a moment before picking out a table as far away as possible.

The woman got the boy calmed down by handing him a paper napkin. He began picking it apart and piling the flakes on the table. She waved at their waitress, but the woman was more than hesitant to walk over.

The guy sitting beside us spoke to his female companion, "People like that have no business out in public."

My response was automatic. "Why don't you shut your fucking mouth and eat your pie?"

The guy turned in his seat. I held his gaze, and after a moment, he spit out a curse, threw his napkin down, and hauled his wife, girlfriend, whatever, over to the checkout line. I don't know what he said to the cashier, but her face turned red and she nodded.

"He's kind of got a point." Jeff held up a hand in defense. "Jesus, Grant, chill."

"I didn't say anything."

"You didn't have to, you already look like you're on the verge of roadrage."

Was I? The waitress left towels with the woman to clean up the mess and fled back to the counter where her companion stood by the display cabinet full of doughnuts.

I didn't know what was wrong with the boy, but the idea Lori had endured the same kind of treatment when she worked with Morgan turned the guilt inside me into a monster. Jeff was right. I was on the verge of some kind of roadrage. But not at him, or the ignorant pie-eating asshole, but myself.

Why? Because like everyone else in the fucking restaurant, I sat on my ass staring while she tried to maintain control of a situation that was way more than one person should ever have to handle. Had the boy been some cute three-year-old who spilled his milk, half the staff would have been over there, all smiles with a fresh glass and a mop. Instead they'd thrown her a handful of towels, then ran and hid.

And while no one else said anything, at least not within earshot, they wore the same expression my neighbor had. The same expression Jeff had. People who weren't normal shouldn't be inconveniencing those who were.

It left me wondering if I stared at the boy and woman the same way. The thought left my stomach rolling.

"I took precautions," Jeff said.

I pulled my attention back to the conversation at hand. Half of Jeff's burger was gone along with quite a few onion rings. He always could eat fast. I picked at the bun on my hamburger.

"What do you mean?"

"In case Hines did try to follow and listen in." He took what looked like an iPod out of his pocket and laid it on the table.

"What is it?"

"A sure fire migraine for any kind of listening devices. Works up to a half mile radius."

I picked it up. "So what do you do? Fill their headphones full of Barry Manilow?"

"Not funny."

"I've never found your taste in music funny. Disturbing, yes, funny…"

Jeff took the device from my hand, fingers brushing mine, leaving behind warmth under my skin. A smile pulled at his lips like he knew exactly what the light bit of contact had done to me. I ate an onion ring.

"Good?"

I chewed. I swallowed. Then picked up another. "Not bad."

"They're incredible. Admit it."

The batter was light, crunchy, with just enough grease to keep it from being dry and some sort of salty spice that set off the natural flavor of the onions, turning it almost sweet. He was right they were incredible.

"Like I said, they're okay."

Jeff shook his head at me. "Has Hines contacted you yet?"

Hines. The reason why we were there. Or I was there. I had no idea why Jeff was still in Chicago, he should have gotten to go home if they officially closed my case.

"Yeah."

"What did he say?"

"Gave me a place and time."

Jeff stared.

I ate a few more onion rings.

"Well?" Jeff said.

"Why aren't you back in DC?"

A wrinkle formed between his eyes. "Where did that come from?"

"You said you closed my case, so why are you still here?" I waited for the telltale glint of a lie, instead he blushed. "Can I wait until after we eat before I embarrass myself?"

A clatter of breaking glass and shouting cut off my reply. The boy was out of the booth waving his arms and the food they'd ordered lay in a mess on the floor. The woman tried to corral him back into his seat, but he twisted and turned, knocking her aside.

One of the waitress said something about calling the police and the woman yelled out a no. "He's fine, he's just…" He swung his arm and caught her in the temple and she tumbled into the booth.

I didn't even realize I was walking over until Jeff said my name. Didn't matter I had no intentions of stopping. One of the waitresses had the phone in her ear. I pointed at her. "She asked you not to call the police."

"But he's…"

The kid screamed at the top of his lungs and pulled his hair with both hands. "Brian," the woman pushed herself to her feet. She grabbed napkins and held them out to him. He didn't acknowledge her. "Brian, it's okay. Everything is okay." While she spoke to him, she watched me with frightened eyes. Did she think I was going to hurt him?

People stared, half of them stood, a few pushed their kids out the door. Yeah, she probably did.

I don't know what made me do it, maybe it was because of all the times it had helped Morgan. It could have easily been the wrong move, but the waitress hadn't put down the phone and the last thing we needed was a bunch of cops in there trying to wrestle the kid into submission.

I put both my hands on the side of Brian's head. "Hey." My voice trembled, but I cleared my throat. "Hey, Brian. Look at me."

His beet red face squished into a mask of what could only be described as pain. He pulled against my hold, not to get away, but side to side.

I rocked with him, letting the swing of our bodies threaten to take us over. The yelling stopped, and he let go of his hair and put his hands over mine. After a long moment, he opened his eyes. He hummed and the vibration rode up through my palms. I hummed with him, trying to hit the same pitch, failing, but coming close enough that his crumpled features fell slack.

"I'm so sorry," the woman said. It was barely a whisper, and she stared at me with an awed expression. "Do you have an autistic son?"

"No."

"Brian." The woman tugged at one of his hands, and he let go. She put some napkins in his palm, and his focus shifted to the white sheets of paper. I disappeared and so did the world as he turned the sheets into tiny paper snowflakes one pluck at a time. She sat him back down at the booth. "He was doing so good. I thought he would be okay going out today. It's his birthday and…"

She was too young to be a parent. If I had to guess maybe only a few years older than Brian.

"Is he your brother?"

She nodded. "Mom and Dad don't get to see him as much as they used to." In my head, *don't get to*, translated to *don't want to*.

"He doesn't live with you?"

She dropped her gaze to the mess on the floor and started to clean it up. I stopped her. To some of the staff hiding behind the counter, I said, "Can you get a busboy out here, a mop, and bring them a fresh plate?"

"No, no, I don't want to bother anyone. We should go."

The busboy got as close as two tables down. I took the bin from him and his towels. Together, the woman and I cleaned up the mess while Brian sprinkled tattered napkins all over the table.

"How did you know what to do?" she said as she scraped up the last of the french fries and tossed them in with the broken plates.

"I have a friend who's autistic. He gets overloaded sometimes, and that's what worked for him. I didn't know if it would or not. But I thought I'd try."

"I've never done it that way before. Usually, if I can just get his attention and give him a napkin, he's happy." She opened her purse. "What's your name?"

"Grant."

"I'm Suzanne, or just Sue." She took out two twenties and laid them on the table.

"What are you doing?"

"Paying for our food." And obviously leaving a tip these people didn't deserve.

"You haven't finished eating."

"We can eat lunch at the home…"

…the rest of the world isn't ready for them.

"No, you'll eat here."

Her face flushed. "We've already caused enough problems. We should go." Tears shimmered in her eyes.

I put a hand on her shoulder. "Sit." She did. "What normally causes him to overload?" She fumbled with the two twenties on the table. Brian reached for one and she slipped another napkin in his hand instead.

"Noises sometimes, and smells. I think maybe it was the waitress's perfume. I can't take him to the mall because he can't stand the smell of the perfume. But to be honest, I don't know."

"He can't tell you?"

"Brian can't talk. Sometimes he makes sounds for certain things but never words. Mom always hoped he would at least learn to talk. His therapist said it's different for everyone. I just…" Sue slumped in her seat and watched her brother make a mess.

"Stay right here."

I went over to the counter where the waitresses were huddled. "Is there anyone not wearing perfume?"

The black woman glanced at her friends.

"You?"

She gave me a slow shake of her head.

"Do you mind waiting on them?"

"Is he going to do that again?"

I glanced back at the table. Brian's sister made a sad attempt to mop up the mess on the table. "He didn't do it on purpose. He was just…" What did I tell her? Because I didn't really understand myself. I took out five twenty-dollar bills from my wallet. "Wait on them. If there's a problem, I'll take responsibility."

231

"You gonna replace the plates he breaks?" The cook walked over. He was taller than me and a good fifty pounds heavier, but he watched Brian with the same kind of fear the waitresses did.

I took out a few more bills and laid them on the counter with the rest. "Buy a whole new set."

The black woman took the money I'd given her and put it in her apron. "I'll get a mop to get the rest of that up." Then she stopped. "That won't make him mad, will it?"

I knew mad wasn't the right word, but explaining it was useless. "I'll check." I went back over to the table. Brian made lines on the table with the pieces of napkins he'd torn up. "Will he be okay with them coming over and washing down the floor?"

"He should be." She gave me an uneasy smile.

I relayed the message, but just in case, I told the waitress to make sure there was no cleaner on the mop, then waited close by until she'd finished.

Whispers and murmurs from the people in the restaurant turned into low chatter and the waitresses went back to work. I returned to my table. Jeff glanced back at Brian and his sister.

"Don't stare." I sat. "She's embarrassed enough."

"She probably should've taken him home."

Jeff was wrong, I knew he was wrong, yet part of me agreed with him. The scared ignorant part that had once judged Morgan for what I saw, not for who he was. I'd hoped it had died, but in that moment, I was forced to realize it hadn't.

And it scared me because I was forced to realize just how unprepared I was to face the reality of what I might find when I went home. My cell phone lay next to my coffee cup. A paper weight for the confession of my cowardice. I put it in my pocket.

Our waitress came to our table and refilled our glasses. Her perfume wasn't cheap, or unpleasant, but it was definitely strong. "Do either of you need anything else, coffee? Dessert?" She smiled, but it didn't hide her nervousness.

"He wasn't trying to hurt you," I said. She blinked at me a couple of times, then glanced over her shoulder. "He got overwhelmed."

"Because of my perfume?" she said, like she was calling bullshit. Then she dropped her gaze. "Sorry, I'm just not used to people like him."

"Maybe you should consider doing some volunteer work at one of the long-term care facilities around here?"

"Honey, I barely have enough time to sleep. I work two jobs, have three kids to feed."

"And lucky for you, they're perfect and you don't have to worry about something as simple as a smell making them panic."

She gave me a sour look. "I'll get you your check."

After she left, Jeff said, "So now what? You're a patron saint to the mentally handicapped?"

"Don't be an asshole. I was just beginning to enjoy your company."

"Does Morgan do that?"

I wanted to tell him no. "Not exactly."

"But you knew how to calm him down."

"I guessed. Brian could have as easily punched me out."

"Brian?"

232

"Ever met a *person* who didn't have a name?"

"That wasn't…" He sighed and pushed his plate back some. "Doesn't it bother you at all?"

"What?" I took a bite of my hamburger. It was barely warm, but still good.

"What? Seriously? You have to ask me what I'm talking about?"

"Apparently so."

"Your relationship with Morgan."

I glared at Jeff over the bun, took a bite, chewed. Extra slow. He waited with his arms crossed and attitude painted all over his face.

I wiped my mouth with a napkin, more to give myself time to think about what I wanted to say and how to say it than anything else. "First of all, there's nothing wrong with Morgan."

"Grant, I've seen him, he acts a lot like that guy who just threw the temper tantrum."

"There's nothing cognitively wrong with Morgan."

"Then why does he act the way he does?"

"It's hard to explain, truth be told I don't know if I even understand it myself. But I know without a doubt, under the tics, he's as normal as you and I, and perfectly capable of making life choices." I started to pick up my burger, then put it down again. "And so what if he wasn't? What if he was mentally handicapped? There are a boatload of people out there who wouldn't get out of the double digits of an IQ test and they do just fine in life."

"That's different."

"How?"

"Because they don't act…"

"What? Crazy?" I flicked thoughts at Jeff, and he found something more interesting across the room to look at. "Newsflash, crazy people have rights too. Mental illness isn't a crime, and they go on to live productive lives. Hell, I'd bet more than half of the students at MIT would qualify as Asperger's."

"So?"

"Asperger's is a mild form of autism."

An argument played through his eyes. "Still not the same."

"Why? 'Cause you say so?"

"Because those people act normal."

I laughed. "Holy shit, Jeff, you're kidding me, right? I know a guy Vince who works in a multi-million dollar company's IT department, forty-something, and refuses to throw anything out. He organizes old outdated motherboards by shape, then the color of the little capacitors. Has an entire room full of them. Housekeeping went through it one day when he was out, and he had a meltdown. The boss made them go dig it all out of the garbage."

"Was he a client or just a personal friend?" Jeff said it with a smile, but it might as well have been a verbal insult.

"He rented a space in one of my buildings. He didn't like people so he didn't want to live in an apartment. He had no TV, no furniture, earned a six-figure income, did nothing but build computers and tinker with robots. I just thought he had a few screws loose like the rest of the world. I had no idea who he was, or worked for, until I got ready to sell the place. He asked if he could buy it. I thought he was joking. He asked me how much, and I tossed out a number. Ten minutes later, I had a plastic bin full of hundred dollar bills in my hands."

"He gave you cash?"

"Didn't believe in banks, because he knew how easy they could be hacked."

"You sold him the building?"

"Only after I made him promise to get a whole lot of new locks, a floor safe, and not let anyone know he had large amounts of money lying around."

Jeff moved his silverware from one side of his plate to the other. "Is there a point to this story?"

"Yeah. Morgan might be autistic, but he excels in ways that super genius Vince didn't. Even with only Asperger's, the concept of how dangerous having money out in the open could be was beyond him.

"Morgan may be autistic, but he is a normal man with a mental condition, not a mental condition who is a man."

****

We finished our meal and paid our bill. Where the setting sun could find a space between the buildings, it cast fragments of red and gold on parked cars. In the shadows, it was already twilight, and even though it was spring, the air held a chill. Air that stank of diesel fuel and rot.

In Durstrand, the only smell there to choke you out was the chicken manure trucks hauling waste from the laying houses to spread on pasture and corn fields. I never in a million years thought I'd miss that smell.

There was something—or someone—I missed more. I took out my phone.

"Hey." A clatter of bells followed Jeff out of the restaurant. He grinned as he walked up. I put my phone away. "You need a ride?" He took out his keys.

"Probably not a smart idea for us to be seen together."

"We can make it look official, and I can drive you over to the office and we can play twenty questions."

A shiver ran down my spine. It was more than the chill.

"Look, I'll call the Assistant Director, let him know I'm meeting with you in an attempt to find out who's interested in your list."

"Why, so you can arrest me?"

Jeff rolled his eyes at me. "No, in hopes you'll reconsider cooperating, you know for the good of the people and all that."

I snorted. "And he's going to fall for that line of bullshit."

"Yes. Because it'll be true. We'll talk, you'll claim ignorance, I'll get mad, and we both storm out."

"And what purpose does that serve?"

"I'll take the long way around, and we can discuss what to do about Hines."

He pulled out his keys. "Why on earth would you waste your money on a car?" Especially here, where the traffic was hell, walking was faster, and parking could top the price of a mortgage. "Because I hate taking the subway."

"Your apartment is a block from the office."

"Was." Jeff jabbed a thumb over his shoulder. "I leased a place at the new complex they built."

"That's almost twenty miles out."

"I know."

"Why?"

He stared at the keys in his hand. "I'm resigning after this year."

"No, you're not." The look he gave me said he was serious. "Why would you resign?"

"Because, there was this guy I fell in love with and I knew as long as I worked for the FBI he'd never give me another chance." Jeff stepped off the curb and walked over to a mint green Prius.

I made a face. "I take that back. You didn't buy a car."

"Come on, it's gas efficient."

"You actually fit in that thing?"

"Lot roomier than it looks."

"Why the hell did you get green?"

"I got a very good deal."

"So they paid you to take it off the lot?"

He laughed and so did I. Then I caught myself. "What made you think I would come back to Chicago?"

He shrugged. "I leased the place before you left, it just wasn't move-in ready yet."

"So you thought after all this was over, the FBI had what they wanted from me, you and I'd just live happily ever after." It sounded like the plot for a bad comedy skit.

"Yeah, something like that."

"When I left here, I had no intentions of ever coming back."

"I know. That's why I didn't re-sign my lease."

"That means ever coming back to you too."

I never imagined you could see a man's heart break, and maybe Jeff's didn't, maybe it was just the shadows of the coming night.

He clicked the key fob and the car beeped. If you could call it that. Not sure if the sound was even low enough on the decibel scale to qualify for an actual beep. More like a mouse fart.

"Let me give you a ride back to where ever you're staying."

"What? Not gonna invite me over?" For a second his smile fractured, then he pulled out his sunglasses and put them on.

I got in the car.

"Now about Hines." He turned the key. I wasn't sure if it had even started until the dash lights came on and we pulled into traffic.

"What about him?"

"Let me put a wire on you. Get him on tape and have him arrested."

"If he's working for Lorado, that would be like poking a hornet's nest."

Someone honked behind us, but the light was already red at the intersection. "What if he's not working for Lorado? I mean. Was, but isn't now."

I tried to sit back, and my knee hit the dash.

"You can adjust that. Lever's under the front."

I reached down and wound up smacking my forehead when he started moving again. "Never mind, it's not that far. Take a right two lights down." I pointed. "Why would you think he was working for Lorado but isn't now?"

Jeff thrummed his fingers on the steering wheel. "What was it you told me a thousand times over? There's nothing on your client list Lorado would want."

"Hines wants it."

"Exactly."

"I still don't follow."

"Lorado has no interest in your contacts because they don't deal in the stuff he moves. You said yourself, he makes in a day in drugs what you do a month in stolen coin collections."

I smirked. Then I thought about what Jeff said. He was right. "Then if they're working together, why do you think Hines wants it?"

"I don't know, but I think that unknown makes this situation ten times as scary." He pulled up to the motel's curb and leaned forward, eyeing the place over the rim of his sunglasses. "You sure it's safe to stay here?"

"Probably not, but I'll be all right." I started to get out, and Jeff stopped me.

"Tell me where you're meeting him tomorrow, and I'll help you."

"How?"

"Keep him from killing you for starters. Then get enough evidence to put him in prison."

Whether I liked it or not, Jeff was right. There were too many variables for this to be as simple as handing over my list. Whether Hines was in bed with Lorado or working out something on his own, I had no idea, but it was very unlikely he'd show up alone. And I had a very good chance of winding up dead.

"Nine o'clock at the old church near 76th."

"Did he give you any specific instructions?"

"Come alone and unarmed."

"Predictable."

"He'll kill you if he sees you."

"He won't see me."

"What do you mean?"

Jeff opened the dash and took out a quarter-sized disk. "Wear a shirt with a collar or a jacket and stick this under it."

"What is it?"

"The latest and greatest recording technology."

"You just keep these lying around your car?"

"Boy Scout code, always be prepared."

"Figures."

He flipped it over and showed me how to turn it on by snapping the fitting down over the pin. "Make sure it doesn't show, or he'll know what it is on sight." He put it in my hand. "I'm going to go by that church tonight when it's dark, and find a place to set up."

"Set up what?"

"I want to have a clear shot if I need it." My confusion must have shown in my face. "I'm sure in all your digging you saw where I was in the Marines."

I had, but he'd gotten honorably discharged after only a few years and there were no details. "Yeah."

"They wanted me to be a sniper after I graduated top of my class in Marine Scout Sniper School."

I raised an eyebrow. "Why were you discharged?"

Jeff took off his sunglasses and fiddled with the earpieces. "The CIA wanted me more."

"But you work with the FBI as a field agent."

"Yup."

"If you have that kind of skill, why the hell are you wasting it out here?"

"Because I didn't like the idea of the sole purpose of my job being to kill someone."

"You would have had other duties."

"Yeah, I would have. But the only skill they would have cared about was being able to get a kill shot. That wasn't me."

I looked at Jeff. Really looked at him. Maybe for the first time since all the bullshit blew up between us. And for the first time, in a long time, I saw the man I'd fallen in love with. I'd been wrong to think he was the FBI playing the common man, he was the common man playing the FBI.

"Why did you get into this job the first place?"

He shrugged and put his glasses back on. "Pays the bills."

"Bullshit."

He laughed. "Maybe. Doesn't matter anyhow. Just know I'll be there, okay?"

"Are you really going to be able to shoot Hines if he pulls a gun on me?"

"Absolutely."

His tone left no doubt in my mind he meant it.

****

The Church of the Seven Patron Saints was long overdue for demolition. Why anyone would put a pub in the area, I had no idea other than the rent had to be cheap.

On the right of the church, a crumbling ice factory. On the left, a building of unknown history. It resembled a sanitarium to tell the truth. One of those from the forties when an institution was more of a house of horrors than a place of healing.

No wonder they put the church there. Those people needed all the prayers they could get.

Stone towers topped with metal roofs reached into the cloudless sky. The crosses on the peaks beacons of warning.

Broken windows were sightless eyes and fragments of stained glass lay spilled on the streets from where the neighborhood kids, or some bored drunk, had tossed pieces of brick through them. There was enough left in the arches to create jagged rainbow edges in the folded stonework. Faceted corners made the edge of the building and trash clogged the tiers at the base.

A cardboard sheet, empty cans, and a hypodermic needle marked a sleeping spot. The lack of bird droppings suggested the occupant had recently vacated.

I checked around the corner of the building. The rear of an SUV and sedan jutted out from beyond a pile of crates. There was no sign of Jeff on the building tops.

With the broken windows, a scope, and a good eye, there would be more than enough opportunity for a clear shot from any angle.

Just in case, I'd made a phone call and picked up a G19 and a GLOCK from a kid on a bike. The ankle holster and boots came from the pawnshop about a block from our exchange. It was the first time I'd bought a gun illegally, but I'd never needed one so fast. Considering what I was walking into, I figured I could make an exception.

Hines told me to come unarmed, but he also knew I wasn't the type to follow orders. I expected him to find the GLOCK hidden in my coat. The pocket would be too obvious, the lining between the layers of material a little less.

I figured it would be enough feed his ego and get him to lower his guard, thinking he'd completely disarmed me.

The one in the ankle holster was less likely to be detected. First off, an ankle holster was the absolute worst place to hide a gun if you needed to get to it fast. Second, the boots would make getting to it even more difficult, so of course no one in their right mind would stick a gun there.

I'd also worn jeans, another obstacle, but again for appearance because I'd split the edge making it possible to yank it to my knee if I wanted. Tucking the hem into the boots concealed the tear.

I practiced getting to it a few times in my motel room only to come to the conclusion it was definitely going to be a last-ditch effort for me to defend myself.

Hopefully it wouldn't come to that. If it did, Jeff had better be good as he claimed.

The final touch to my wardrobe, the microphone hidden in the coat. I tried several spots, the collar, the chest, but I wanted to make sure wherever I stuck it, the sound would be clear. I settled on the arm of the jacket. It was black, three of the buttons running down the cuff were black and about the same size. I tore one off, stuck it in place, and as long as Hines didn't inspect the details of my clothing I was pretty sure it would go unnoticed.

I wouldn't have noticed it. But then I didn't make a point in keeping up with the latest and greatest FBI surveillance equipment. For all I knew, the condoms Jeff and I used had hidden cameras in them.

A hard squeak echoed from the hinges and stray sheets of newspaper stuck to my shoes. Hines stood, arms crossed, with two other men who wore smug smiles.

"Welcome to the party, Grant. Glad you could join us," Hines said.

"I'd say likewise but I hate to lie." I stopped halfway down the aisle flanked by rotting pews and forgotten Bibles.

Hines waved me closer. "C'mon over, join the party." One of his men picked up a metal folding chair leaning against a table. It was too clean to have belonged there. Bringing seating arrangements was not a good sign.

"I'm fine right here."

"Do as he says, Grant." I don't know what shocked me more, the sound of Jeff's voice or the fact I'd walked right by him where he stood in the niche beside the main entrance. "I told you I'd be close."

I'd never wanted to punch a grin off a man's face as I did in that moment.

"Unzip your jacket."

I hesitated.

"Don't make me do it for you."

The teeth on the zipper ticked.

"Now open it."

I did.

He ran his hand along my ribs. "Turn around."

I did.

He slid his fingers into the waist of my jeans deep enough to fondle my ass crack. His

238

breath was hot against the shell of my ear. "I told you a long time ago, one way or the other, I was gonna fuck you." The outside of my jacket was next. He groped the weighted edge. Jeff tore the opening in the seam until the gun practically leapt into his hand. "I thought it was understood you were to come unarmed."

"I thought we agreed you weren't a back stabbing son-of-a-bitch, so I guess we're even."

He continued down, squeezing my groin, running his hands down the leg of my jeans. He found the tear and pulled the leg out of the edge of my boot.

"You really should do something about your wardrobe."

Any second he was going to find the ankle holster and I'd be up shit creek with a concrete block around my neck. Hell, I already was up shit creek with a concrete block.

He ran a look over my boots. "Jesus, Grant, you can't even buy decent footwear. What are people going to say when they see you in those at your funeral? Or are Mountain Man mud stompers the redneck standard for Durstrand?" As he stood, he wiped his hands on his pants as if just touching the boots had left dirt behind.

Maybe they had. I didn't really check their cleanliness status when I put them on. Beyond making sure there were no spiders in the toes.

Jeff tucked the gun into his jacket pocket.

"Should I hand over the listening device you gave me or is it even real?"

"Oh it's real. Like your choice of location." He indicated the cuff of my jacket. "But there's no one to hear and if there was…"

He took out the small iPod shaped gadget, flipped it, and stuck it back in his pocket. "Now." Jeff shoved my shoulder. "Let's get this done, shall we?"

Warm rays crossing the aisle caressed me in blue, red, and yellow as I was led to Hines and the men waiting for us at the front of the church. Jeff stopped me at the chair and pushed me into the seat. The metal squeaked.

"You realize if you'd just cooperated, it would have never come to this." Hines took out a pocket knife. "But that's okay. You're here now and that's all that matters." He flicked open a thin blade. Definitely not the first choice for killing someone.

Quickly.

"And since I have neither the time nor the patience, you're going to answer my question." Hines knelt and held up the blade so I could see it.

"That's why I'm here." Sort of. I glared at Jeff. He met my gaze, but his expression remained blank.

Hines snapped his fingers at me. "Down here, Grant." I obeyed. "Now, I'm only going to ask you once, if you hesitate, if you give me any reason to doubt what you tell me, I'm going to start cutting pieces of you off, after Richey back there shoots you in the knees."

I squinted at Richey. He'd been the driver of the Bronco and there at Toolies when they'd harassed Morgan. I almost hadn't recognized him with a freshly broken nose.

"You're gonna need a pen and paper," I said. "Lot of names, dates, and places. Unless of course trained snipers have photographic memory."

Jeff's eye twitched. Hines looked back at him? "Trained sniper? Is that the line of shit he told you? Jeff couldn't hit the broad side of a barn." Hines had already looked back at me when Jeff slid his gaze over to the man. There was something in the way he stared at the back of Hines head that sent a chill down my spine.

"Got that pen and paper yet?"

Hines tapped the blade of his knife on my knee. "I only have one question for you to answer."

"What?"

"Tell me how you moved your loads."

"How I... what?"

"I want to know how you moved your merchandise, Grant, and how Jeff never saw you do it. One day you'd have an Aston Martin; we'd pop the crate and you'd have a shipment of kit cars. And the paintings, the gold coins, anything and everything. How did you switch the containers with no one seeing you or move the stuff in and out with no one seeing you?"

"Why the hell do you care about how I moved my merchandise?"

"Don't worry about my reasons, just worry about telling me." Hines put the tip of the blade against my thigh.

The doors to the church banged open and a dozen men with assault rifles walked in. Lorado stormed in surrounded by a protective ring of bullet fodder. His crisp gray suit a silver lining to the darker black and browns worn by his gunmen.

Seconds became minutes, minutes became hours. The rush of men turned into a series of swinging limbs, rustling fabric, hands moving out guns with fingers on the trigger. Angry voices bellowed, ricocheting off the church walls until they rolled like thunder.

A bullet whistled by my head. Hines fell back. The pulpit splintered, the guy standing near Jeff drew his gun. At the same time, I dove to the floor and crawled in the direction of the pews.

Lorado held out his arms. "What the hell is this, Hines? You think I wouldn't notice? You think I don't keep count of every bullet, every ounce, every time someone moves things in my operation?" He followed Hines as he scurried across the room. "I told you what would happen if you fucked with me. We had a good thing, and you had to go and screw it up. Where's my merchandise? Or are you gonna tell me some sob story about how it was accidentally loaded onto one of Grant's shitty barges or someone else's?"

Gone the menace in Hines's voice. Now he was just the scared kid trying to hide behind an overturned table, fumbling for his gun. Blood soaked his shirtsleeve and ran down his fingers in crimson strips. He couldn't seem to get his weapon out of the holster.

Lorado fired off another series of shots. Craters formed in the stone walls above Hines's head.

He finally got his gun in his hand, switched from the right to the left. Everyone had a weak side. For his sake, I hope he wasn't too weak, but his shot was so off target Lorado didn't even blink.

More bullets plugged the walls. Dust and paint chips became snow. One of the other FBI boys rolled under the stage and disappeared. A second later, the curtain fluttered, pushed by flying lead. A blond guy carrying a Sig in each hand went down. Another was tossed off to the side between the pews. His ragged breathing was snuffed out by more bullets.

"You know," Lorado said. "The first time, I let it slide. I saw the empty containers left behind with your surveillance setup. You cost me valuable merchandise. But I let it slip 'cause I knew there was no way you were stupid enough to try again."

Men moved closer. I yanked up my pants leg and palmed the G19. The weight difference was awkward compared to my.45. Movement to my left caught my attention. Jeff slid down one of

240

the other line of pews and behind a stack of old boxes.

I was so intent on tracking him, I almost missed the guy with the automatic. He swung around the corner, and I nailed him in the throat. A fan of crimson painted the Bibles stacked on the edge of the pew. He dropped his gun in favor of trying to stem the blood flow.

I crawled in Jeff's direction. He had turned his wrist, watch held close to his lips. His gaze flicked from Lorado to the front of the church. Was he going to try to make a run for it?

Lorado's voice filled the church. "All you had to do was play by the rules, Hines. I would have made you a very wealthy man. Fuck, I was making you a very wealthy man."

Hines caught my gaze. Anger warred with fear. Fear warred with guilt. I was right. He'd been playing with the bad guys and tried to beat them at their own game. I could have told them there were no winners in the criminal world. Some just lived longer than others.

I used to think you could get out and increase your chances, but I'd been wrong.

The dark-skinned FBI agent popped up from between a row of pews. Muzzle flashes chased him as he backed up in the direction of a side door. Lorado hit the ground when the man flanking him took a bullet to his chest. Two others made chase.

They both went down, but I had no idea where the shots came from. The guy under the stage? Hines?

Jeff moved down the aisle. Disjointed shapes of color paved the rotting carpet. The effect was so close to the light fragments cast by Morgan's kinetic sculptures, for a moment I was there in his backyard. Fresh grass and the dew of early morning mixed with the ghost of last night's cookout. When the sun broke over the trees, we'd sit in silence while he adjusted strings of metal around smooth droplets of glass.

There was a very good chance I'd never have another simple moment with him, one filled with love and his strange magic. The anger inside me broke loose. I might die, but I'll be damned if I let Jeff walk away from this.

I rolled over a mound of trash, glass broke, things shifted under me, a sharp jab to my ribs made me grit my teeth. Using my elbow as a prop, I was able to steady my hand even in the seconds of chaos where my heart slammed into my ribs. Jeff didn't see me until he rotated on his hip to take out another couple of men as they cut between the pews in his direction.

I couldn't name the expression on his face. Not fear, not guilt. He was too calm for a man about to die.

The light blinds.

Jeff had searched me.

The light blinds.

He hadn't fired a single shot in my direction.

The light blinds.

And now staring down the muzzle of my gun, knowing I could kill him with a squeeze of the trigger, he watched me.

...and sometimes the trust you think is broken is just a little dented up.

Trust. What I saw was trust. I pulled back behind the seat. If I was wrong, I'd hate myself tomorrow. If I lived till then.

More voices invaded the building, this time with military precision. Heavy boots thumped the floor, and the click of weapons being readied. Then the words I couldn't understand at first fell into place.

241

"FBI, drop your weapons."

Lorado made a half turn, and Hines shot him in the back. The rest of the men tried to scatter, but side doors opened and more men dressed in swat gear and vests marked with Jeff's frat house logo spilled in.

I dropped my gun, spread my arms out, and rolled onto my stomach. Maybe no one would shoot me in the back if I looked harmless enough.

Black shapes descended, and my arms were twisted between my shoulders. Searching hands groped my legs, ankles, lingered at the holster hidden inside my boot. Whoever it was, yanked it off my foot. My pants leg was lifted then let go.

I turned my head and my face was abruptly shoved into the carpet. "Don't move."

"Special Agent Hines, don't fire." Hines stood from behind the overturned table. He took a couple of steps, and I lost sight of him between the gap in the pews to my left. I couldn't understand what he said, but it started off crisp, only to be cut short by demands for him to drop his gun. His face hit the floor, and we stared at each other from the space under the seats.

Someone called for an ambulance. The death rattle of a dying man made it through the hum of voices. Someone else cried out, and one of the other men with Hines identified himself only to be answered with a command to drop his weapon and get down on the ground.

"He's fine, let him up." The sound of Jeff's voice caught me off guard. Unlike Hines and the other, he wasn't on the ground in cuffs.

The weight pinning me to the floor vanished. My arms protested as they slid to my side. I was careful to keep them out. Last thing I needed was for someone to think I was reaching for a weapon.

"You okay?" Jeff knelt.

I watched the agents as they checked bodies and handcuffed survivors. There weren't many.

Outside the steady flow of light dimmed behind a cloud and the broken swatches of color faded.

"I guess I owe you an explanation. And a thank-you for not shooting me."

I got to my knees. The rush of adrenaline receded, leaving my lips numb and my fingertips cold.

"Grant? You okay?"

I rubbed my face, then nodded. "Yeah, yeah."

Jeff stood and offered me a hand up. I declined in favor of using the arm of one of the pews. As soon as I put weight on my right leg, a bolt of pain shot up through my ribs, then a wave of nausea knocked the air from my lungs. Everything flickered and a warm rush soaked my thigh.

"Shit." Jeff hooked an arm under mine just in time to soften my landing back on the floor. "Where's the EMT? Danny, get the first aid kit."

A well of blackish-red blood soaking my side spread wider. "Red." I held up my fingers. "Like the bottles Morgan bought."

Jeff's expression pinched. Someone brought towels. "Let me see." Jeff tore open my shirt. A twisted piece of metal jutted out from below my ribs. He cursed, and I stared. All the glass on the floor, and it had been a piece of metal torn loose from a window, a wall, or just randomly laying around.

Jeff packed the towels around the metal shard.

"Hang on, an ambulance will be here in a few."

There was so much blood, and it was really dark. "How long have you been playing double agent?" My attempt at a laugh ended in a grunt of pain.

"Be still."

"Well?"

"You gonna tell me what was in those empty containers on the barge you sank?"

"Told you, didn't—" I coughed and copper coated my tongue.

"We'll argue later. We just need to get you to the hospital."

There was so much blood and it was so damn dark. "If I don't make it, I need you to do me a favor."

"Shut up, Grant, you'll be fine. You took a bullet to the chest. This is just a splinter in comparison."

But the bullet had been a through and through, and whatever the piece of steel had pierced was not as forgiving as muscle, tendon, and bone. "I promised Morgan I'd put a ring on his finger."

Jeff stuttered in his rush to pack the wound.

"I was going to ask him to marry me."

EMTs came through the door. A gurney was lowered.

"I think it might have hit his spleen," Jeff said.

Someone stuck me with a needle; a fluid bag hovered overhead. I grabbed Jeff's arm. "I promised I'd be back to put it on his finger. If I'm not..."

Jeff leaned in. The tears on his cheeks landed on the cushion beside my head. "If you want to put a ring on your boyfriend's hand, then you'd better survive, because I'm not doing it for you."

I think I called him an asshole before I blacked out.

Chapter Nine

The shard of metal missed my small intestines by millimeters and nicked my spleen. An almost sixteen inch long razor sharp sliver of tin should have perforated everything. But somehow it avoided all my major organs by curling up between the space behind my ribs.

I was in the hospital six days, but only because of the risk for infection. I'd always healed up pretty well in my life, but this time, even I was surprised.

Don't get me wrong. It hurt like a bitch. Every time I breathed. Moved the wrong way. Laughed.

Took a piss.

I think it wasn't as noticeable because of the pain in my heart.

I still hadn't called to check on Morgan, and with every passing day, it became easier and easier to rationalize why I shouldn't.

What if I put him in danger again?

What if he couldn't forgive me for almost getting him killed?

There were more excuses, but it's all they were. Excuses. My lame attempts to cover up the truth.

Could I spend the rest of my life looking at Morgan lost in his head? And worse, was I willing to?

"I heard they were going to let you go home."

I hadn't seen Jeff except behind a cloud of pain meds. The two days I'd been sober, he'd been MIA. Now here he was, leaning against my doorframe.

"Yeah. Food sucks and I haven't had a decent beer in over a week." I struggled to pull the shirt over my head.

"I see the clothes I left fit." Jeff walked over.

"Jeans are a little big, but yeah, they fit." The stitches pulled, and I grunted.

"Need help?"

He didn't give me time to answer. He untangled the shirt where it bunched up in the back. The warmth of his touch followed the hem down my ribs. He lingered until I slid off the corner of the bed.

"You never did answer me." I said.

Jeff made a face. "About what?"

"How long have you been playing both sides of the fence?"

He smiled and dropped his gaze. "I suspected something was up for a while. But I knew for sure when you sank the barge."

"Freak accident. Not my fault."

His mouth cocked to the side. "Well, that freak accident outed Hines. He lied about where the barge went down so they couldn't recover the equipment. And I'm not talking a few feet off, but miles."

"Why?"

"I asked the same question, so I did some scuba diving."

"You've got to be kidding me."

"I told you, I take my job seriously."

"You dove, in that water, in the fucking winter." That went beyond dedicated and into the realm of crazy.

"Not that seriously. I rented a submersible from a treasure hunter store."

"I'd think the FBI would have stuff like that on hand."

"Oh, they do. But I didn't want Hines to know I'd gone back to look."

"What did you find?"

"The barge, the FBI surveillance unit, and what looked like lots and lots of drugs. Or what was left of them. There was another container on that barge too, open and empty. But I'm guessing you wouldn't have a clue as to what was on it since it wasn't your container."

I gave Jeff my best poker face. "Mix up in the paperwork. Happens sometimes, wind up with the wrong container on your boat. All I can tell you is Lorado was pissed as hell when he received my Aston Martin. Can't imagine anyone not appreciating an Aton Martin, can you?"

In a way, Hines saved my ass. Otherwise Lorado might have thought I'd tried to steal from him. I wondered at the time why he didn't ask more questions, but figured he didn't want to stir the proverbial hornet's nest.

"Well, whatever it was must have been related to Houdini."

I arched an eyebrow. "Why do you say that?"

"Well, it was unlocked and was empty. So either it disintegrated or swam away."

"Current probably carried it off."

"And the unlocking part?"

"Maybe they forgot to padlock it?"

"No, I found the padlock, it had been cut."

One of the few things you never go without on a barge, bolt cutters. Just in case, you know, you wind up with something you need to get out of a container really fast and shove into the water.

"Some people have all the luck." I gave a dramatic sigh. "Just think what would have happened to Hines if the FBI had found that surveillance setup filled with drugs."

"Forget them. Lorado. That load was five years' worth of skimming. He had a buyer and was riding your barge to meet with them because Lorado knew he was SAP on the case. So if he ran into Lorado or any of his customers, it wouldn't have looked out of place."

"What about the other two men on the boat with him?"

"Richey and Mark were already in on it. So I went to Hines and said I wanted a cut."

"A little risky. He could have put you in a container on one of those shoddy barges."

"I'm sure it crossed his mind. But my undercover work on you gave him an excuse to hang around some of the hot spots. It almost fell apart after the boat *accidentally on purpose* sank, because he had some very angry customers who wanted their money back."

"The missing money from his bank accounts."

"Yeah. It was only a partial apology. He had to work fast after that. Take more than he had been, more often. Keeping me around gave him an excuse to stay in the field. But he got greedy. And Lorado took notice. Him showing up at the church was not a part of the plan. I'm sorry about that."

"If you'd told me what you were trying to do in the beginning, I wouldn't have been so reluctant to help."

"Would you have believed me?"

Would I? "I don't know. Maybe."

"I wouldn't. And honestly, I wanted to keep you as far away as possible from the melee when it finally went down. You'd taken a bullet for me once. I didn't want to risk it again."

I rubbed my scar.

"Thanks to Lorado showing up at the wrong time, you still wound up in the line of fire."

"Not part of the script huh?"

"Wasn't supposed to be. But I guess he could have found out at any time. Just sucked it had to be right then." Jeff shrugged. "Anyhow, you moved to that dirt bowl, and I let Hines talk me into following and trying to threaten the info out of you. Then you know the rest."

"Town is called Durstrand. It's actually a nice place. Real pretty in the fall."

"Yeah, but you always talked about the beaches."

I had. The smell of the ocean, the feel of the sand, the sight of the tide washing in and out. I'd only gone once as a kid, but it stuck with me. As an adult, I'd swore that's where I'd retire.

"Things change."

"I was thinking." He handed me my shoes.

"Don't you need to file some paperwork for permission to do that?"

He laughed, but it died pretty quick. Not in a sad way, but as if he was saving his breath for something more important. "Why don't you stay with me for a couple of weeks? At least until you're healed up enough to dress yourself."

"I'm good." My attempt to reach my feet ended in a cold sweat.

"You can't even put on your shoes."

I dropped the sneakers on the floor and crammed my foot into them. The tongues bunched up, and the heel collapsed. I didn't give a fuck. "See, shoes are on."

"Grant." And he said my name in a private way, belonging in quiet moments wrapped in someone's arms. "Don't do this to yourself." I looked up, and he dropped his gaze.

"Do what?"

"I think you know."

"Obviously not."

"Maybe you should call before you go back. Or is there a specific reason why you haven't?"

"I was a little busy. Getting shot at can really make for a rough day." But the look on Jeff's face said he already knew.

"You called."

"I didn't have to." Jeff stuck his hands in his pockets, then took them out. They wound up on his hips for a split second like he didn't know what to do with them. "You said some things when you were out of it."

"Like what?"

"You said you didn't know if you'd be able to handle seeing Morgan again."

My cheeks burned.

"You said something had happened and 'he'd gone away.' You kept asking him not to step off the cliff. I tried to get you to tell me what you meant and finally you said regression. I didn't even know what it meant until I looked it up."

"Morgan regressed once, a long time ago. He was fine, though."

"But it's happened again because he was attacked." Jeff made it a statement.

"When I left, the nurse wasn't sure. He was sedated, and it hadn't worn off yet. Plus he was in shock. He shot a man." A man he'd lived in fear of for years. The creature of his nightmares. How many times had Morgan cried out in his sleep and I held him until the worst of it went away? Thinking about it then made me realize he never really woke up from those dreams, he just slipped somewhere else until they were over, then went back to sleep.

"It has to be bad, Grant."

"Did someone call?" I looked around for my cell phone. It was in the bag on the rollaway with my wallet. Dead of course.

"No, no one called, but you said you made Aunt Jenny promise not to put him in a home."

"The hospital gave her a pamphlet. It was a 'just in case' thing."

"I should have called after I checked in the motel."

"You were scared."

My guilt forced me to have to sit on the edge of the bed. "Yeah."

"What are you going to do if you go back and he hasn't come out of this"—Jeff waved a hand—"whatever?"

"He came back once before, the nurse was pretty sure we were just seeing a reaction to the sedative they gave him." It didn't even sound convincing to me.

"I asked one of the psychiatrists here about regression in autism patients, and he said his experience hasn't been positive. He also said it can happen anytime, not just with trauma."

I wadded up the plastic bag with my belongings. "Yeah, well, he doesn't know Morgan."

"What if you go back and he stays regressed? What if he'll never be normal?"

Normal. But then Morgan never was normal. Remarkable maybe. But never normal.

"Then I'll get specialists, therapists, anyone…" Surely to God someone could help him. If only Lori had been alive but she wasn't and I doubted even the experts knew her secret.

If Morgan was anything like I feared, I'd become his caregiver for the rest of my life. Loving him, but not mentally, physically, or emotionally able, to deal with the trials to come.

"No one would blame you if you didn't go back." Jeff cupped my cheek.

I shook my head. "I promised him I'd come home." My eyes burned. "I promised him I would put a ring on his finger. I promised to marry him if he would let me." No tears fell, but the world wavered. "I can't break my promise."

Jeff grabbed me by the shoulder and stopped me from falling off the bed. "Breathe, Grant." He picked up the call button. "I need a nurse in here."

I shook my head.

"Yes, you do."

I shoved his hand away, and even though everything exploded in multicolored spots, I forced myself to my feet. A nurse ran in, took one look at me, and ordered me back in the bed.

"I'm going home."

"Grant…"

"Goddamn it, I'm going home." Screaming took the last of my strength. I collapsed on the floor. Another nurse was called in, and with Jeff's help, I wound up lying in the hospital bed with

247

the rails pulled up.

I threw my arm over my eyes. One of the nurses took my vitals, the other put an O2 monitor on my finger.

"His blood pressure's a little high," said one nurse. "I'll let the doctor know."

They left, and I yelled at the closed door. "I'm going home no matter what the fuck he says." I tried to sit up. Jeff wrestled the railing out of the way, and I wound up sagging in his arms crying on his shoulder.

He petted me. "I just don't want you to go back and find nothing there."

Nothing. As if Morgan had died and there was an empty space. Only, in some ways, he had. In some ways, it was even worse. If he was lost in his head, what lay in wait for me was something I knew I wasn't prepared for.

If I'd thought for a second love would have brought Morgan back, I would have been running out the door. But Aunt Jenny was right. If love could fix something like autism, then parents would never have to face it.

"I have to go back." I barely recognized my voice.

"Not this minute, you don't. Take a few days. A few weeks. Rest. Think about this."

Only I didn't want to think about it, because when I did, the excuses grew.

"I've got a spare room in my new place. You can stay there until you decide."

"No."

"Grant, please."

"No. I can't."

He made me look at him. "Why?"

"Because I love him."

****

I had the cab driver drop me off at the end of Morgan's driveway. I hoped the walk would give me time to get all my thoughts in order, but it was like trying to pick up a thousand toothpicks with my toes. Correction: Fifteen hundred toothpicks, there had been a five after the one.

Aunt Jenny's car was parked out front. A white van with some sort of medical logo sat beside it. Home supplies, oxygen, lift chairs, and physical therapy transport was written across the back in blue letters, and on the side, windows in white. The front door opened and a black man walked out with Aunt Jenny. He wore jeans and a crisp yellow shirt. They laughed, hugged, and he waved. It wasn't until he pulled out of the driveway that Aunt Jenny saw me.

Her mouth fell open, and she came running down the steps, and I wound up crushed in her arms. I must have made some sort of sound 'cause she pushed me back and looked me over.

"I'm okay." I pressed a hand to my side. "Just a little banged up."

Tears pooled in her eyes. "We thought you weren't gonna come back."

"I promised I would. I'm sorry I didn't call to let you know. But to tell the truth, I thought I wasn't coming back either. I was scared, Jenny. I didn't know, I still don't..."

She shushed me. "You were in the hospital... needed some time to heal. Totally understandable."

"How'd you know I was in the hospital?"

"Sheriff Parks called the locals there. They couldn't tell him much; FBI wasn't sharing info.

But that man, Hines, he was on the news. They arrested him. Said there was a shoot-out. Is that what happened to you?"

"Nothing that exciting. It's a puncture wound. I rolled over on a piece of metal while hiding under a pew."

"Still gotta hurt. How long were you in the hospital?"

"Got out this morning."

She looked over my shoulder. "Where's your truck?"

"I left against doctor's orders, and he wouldn't clear me to drive so I took a taxi from the airport. I figured I could go back and get the truck in a couple days. Might have to bum a ride."

She grinned. "God, Grant. I'm so happy to see you." She started toward the house.

I stopped her. I needed to ask her. I needed to know before I went in there. But if she told me what I feared, I wasn't sure I'd be able to walk up those steps. I couldn't even say for sure I wouldn't turn around and walk back to the end of the driveway and call the cabbie back.

I think Aunt Jenny knew, because she took me by the elbow and turned me toward the house. I let her lead me like some lost soul through the front door.

"He's doing really well. Anne thinks it's because we brought him right home. Goes to PT twice a week, well, three times now since he messed up his ankle."

I stopped. "How did he hurt his ankle?"

She propped her hands on her hips. "I suspect he tripped over that damn puppy he picked up. Stupid creature is always underfoot."

"You don't know?"

The living room had been cleaned up, and there was a new coat of paint on the walls. The couch had been replaced. I couldn't remember how badly it was damaged, but the dining room table was there. One chair was missing.

In the kitchen, all the pots and pans were back in their place. More new paint. Even part of the doorframe leading to the back porch had been redone. No blood stains, no sign of any of the terrible things that had happened.

I knew without asking, Morgan had done the work. It screamed the care and love he'd put into the house. A person, who only accepted perfection, who took care of the smallest detail to the best of his ability.

My heart fluttered in my chest.

"He still hasn't talked."

I turned.

Jenny squeezed my arm. "The specialist thinks it's just a matter of time. He said to think of Morgan's progress as a slow reboot. He was quiet for a while after Lori died, then started talking again like nothing happen. So don't worry too much."

"So, he's okay."

"He's doing everything else on his own but…"

"What?"

"Part of him is still missing." The hope growing inside me shriveled. "Personally, I think it's because he's been waiting for that part to come home." Jenny took an object out of the pocket of her overalls. I almost didn't recognize the ring box. It seemed so small in the palm of my hand. I nodded and slipped it into my jeans pocket.

I didn't see the puppy until it ran through the back door, tongue hanging out the side, tail wagging a million miles an hour. Jenny scooped it up before it could latch onto the ankle of my jeans.

"When he starts talking, first thing I'm gonna ask him is why the hell he got a dog?"

I laughed, and she glanced at me. "Now, c'mon. He's out back working on something." With the puppy tucked under her arm, she led me to the back porch.

"What?"

"I have no clue. Not his normal thing. You know, glass. This is wood. And it's big. Gave me a list to give to Berry, and they delivered the first load two days after he got out of the hospital."

We walked down the back steps and into the yard. Morgan rocked long slow movements, following the planer in his hands, as he stroked a length of wood set between two sawhorses. Curling flakes covered the ground. Other pieces were set off to the side. The curve in them was deeper like rib bones.

Sweat glistened on his tanned skin, and his jeans hung low enough to reveal he'd dressed in his preferred way. Every muscle in his shoulders and arms contracted with the push of the instrument in his hand.

"He does this all day long, nonstop. Still haven't a clue as to what he's supposed to be building."

"A boat," I said.

"Yeah," Jenny snorted. "Well, if I didn't come and check on him, he'd starve to death. Starts at sunrise, doesn't quit till he can't see." She shook her head. "Why the hell is he building a boat?"

I scratched the puppy behind the ears. "Because a dog isn't a hobby." She gave me a look, and I added. "Long story, I'll tell you later."

"Well, maybe you can get him to eat more regularly. Damn jeans are about to fall off. Then he'll be mooning the neighbors."

She was right, and it made me smile. Jenny laughed. "Not everyone wants to see his ass, Grant."

Over and over again, Morgan shaped the wood. Sometimes stopping to test the angle with a caress of his hand. His gaze was in that far off place where the sunlight spilled its secrets. Nothing existed for him except the tool he held, and the focus of his attention. My fear returned, but I stomped it down.

"Hey, boy," Aunt Jenny said. "Look what the cat dragged in." He continued to work. "Morgan." Aunt Jenny made one of those ear-piercing whistles and he looked up. His shoulder jerked and his hand tossed thoughts. Then he stood straighter and the veil of blond curls hiding his eyes parted.

The man I loved met my gaze.

Morgan stumbled on his way around the bench, hopping on one leg in my direction.

"Crutches, Morgan," Jenny said as she tried to control the wiggling ball of fur in her arms. "Doctor keeps telling you to use the damn crutches."

He didn't make it halfway before I had him in my arms. His good leg wrapped around my waist the one in the cast hung by my knee.

His mouth met mine, his tongue pushed in. Either he'd eaten something sweet recently or I'd forgotten just how good he tasted.

Behind me, the screen door shut, and it was just him and me standing in the sunshine, dappled in colored pieces of light.

"God, I missed you." I petted his face, and he peppered my cheeks in kisses. "I'm sorry I didn't call. I should have. I was scared. I thought... I thought..." I shook my head. "Forgive me."

He kissed me again, and I lowered him to the ground. His thigh rode over the lump in my pocket. His left eyebrow went up, and he snapped his fingers.

"I promised you I'd be back to do this." I got down on one knee. My side protested. Morgan gave me a worried look. "It's nothing. Nothing important. Not right now." I took the box out of my pocket. My hands shook so hard I couldn't get a grip on the top. Morgan held my wrists. "It's okay if you don't want to. I know it's asking a lot. But I wanted..." He took the ring out of the box and turned it over and over in his fingers. The sun caught the edge, searing it in lines of white.

I put the box on the ground and held his hand. Then I took the ring. I didn't put it on his finger until he met my gaze again. "Morgan Kade, will you marry me?"

No beach in the world could have compared to his smile. He kissed me again, this time long, slow, exploring my mouth while he mapped my face with his fingertips. When we broke apart, he held me and then one word caressed my cheek. "Yes."

Chapter Ten

Surrounded by grass so green it looked painted, half of Durstrand, and about a thousand cud chewing bovine, Morgan and I exchanged rings and vows. The rumor mill saved us the need for sending out invitations to anyone local. Although I did mail out one, but wasn't surprised to hear nothing back.

Not that it mattered, with the number of people who chattered about going, one less person wouldn't be noticed. As the numbers grew, Toolies was out of the question, so was Morgan's house, Aunt Jenny's, and the rec center.

Then we thought we had it beat when Reverend sent a personal invitation to use the church.

The only problem with the rumor mill is details like dates, and times and even names get mixed up.

Reverend Harvey apparently planned on solving that issue by announcing to everyone the right day and time at Sunday morning service. Morgan and I went, mostly to show our appreciation. That was how Reverend Harvey found out I was not in fact marrying Candace Jones on June the eighth, and he turned the Sunday morning service into a lecture about the sanctity of marriage.

He was about three sentences in when Berry stood up in the middle of it all and asked him if he needed a bottle and a nap. No one laughed, but the good Reverend turned ten shades of red and the service took a quick left turn.

Morgan and I left him to his preaching, followed by at least half the church and reconvened at Toolies. There Mr. Newman informed we were to utilize his drive-in theater. The cows insisted.

The cows. How can you say no to cows? Especially when they're being sacrificed in your honor.

Somewhere between our second hamburger and the wedding cake, I'd spilled punch on my white jacket. Morgan's was black. Thank God he'd gotten the white pants and mine were black, or I would have looked like I'd taken a shot to the leg.

"It doesn't show that bad." Morgan dabbed at the stain some more. It was useless.

"Put some baking soda on it, dear." Mrs. White leaned on her cane and examined the blotch. "Cold water and baking soda."

"Vinegar." That from her friend. Dorothy, I think. She always wore her hair in a big blue beehive. I made the mistake of commenting on the color once, apparently Dorothy is a bit color blind.

Mrs. White huffed at her friend. "Nonsense, that'll just make him smell like a pickle. Baking soda, at the most, some peroxide."

Robert from Jenny's garage stopped. His cheeks bulged, and green icing coated his lips. He had a plate in his hand with at least three more untouched pieces of cake. "They got stuff at the dollar store that will take it out." Bits of crumbs sprayed the air landing on his shirt.

"I'm sure it'll be fine," I said.

Dorothy glared at both of them, and what started as advice turned into an all-out argument. Morgan pulled me away. We walked through clouds of smoke billowing from the open grill. Hotdogs, steaks, hamburgers. If my ribs didn't already feel like they were going to split, I would have eaten something else. As it was, I was close to having to undo the top button of my pants or risk it popping off and shooting someone's eye out.

Now wouldn't that be a wedding day story to tell. We'd be front-page news.

Again.

Apparently the issuing of a marriage license to a same-sex couple won out the announcement of the county fair, a supposed Big Foot sighting, and the breaking and entering of Big John Porta Johns.

Nothing was stolen. Morgan suggested maybe someone just had to go really bad.

I continued to wipe at the stain, and Morgan undid the carnation on the opposite lapel and used it to cover up the pink blotch. "See, all better."

And a lot less work than baking soda, and it wouldn't leave me smelling like a pickle.

We held hands and made our way through groups of screaming kids, balloons, and streamers of white broken loose from the fence where the cows stood chewing cud and watching us. Someone had rented an inflatable bouncy ball house. I have no idea why, but it added color and kept most of the kids out of the way and gave something for the teenagers to laugh about.

I didn't know half the people who showed up at our wedding, and I was willing to bet three-fourths didn't even live in town—they were there for the food, the cake, the laughter, the all-out weirdness of it all.

I didn't mind. Tonight I'd have Morgan all to myself and we could exchange the private vows we'd written to each other. And kiss. Really kiss. Without worrying about it winding up on YouTube.

"I was thinking." Morgan tossed thoughts, then plucked a balloon from the fence and bopped me on the head with it.

"What were you thinking?"

"We should try out the boat."

The sailboat. Thirty feet long and built by Morgan's hands. Okay, I helped. Some. When he let me. After telling me all the ways I was doing it wrong. With the inside finished out, it was now as cozy as any cabin. And was great for nights we wanted to stay out late and watch the stars, then only have to move a few yards to get to the bed.

Currently Morgan's work of art sat in the backyard on a cradle to keep it off the ground. When the sun hit the portholes just right, the colored glass threw beautiful kaleidoscope patterns all over the ground. The boat belonged in a millionaire's toy collection, not the backyard of two simple men, where it was the favorite sunning spot for one lazy yellow lab.

"I don't think it would do much in Tom Greer's pond." I doubted Tom's pond was even deep enough for it to float.

Morgan laughed, then he tilted his head. Fragments of light sparkled off the silver garland someone had edged the table where the wedding cake sat surrounded by other cakes. "What about the ocean?" He let go of the balloon in favor of chasing the sunlight glitter reflecting on my jacket. After a long moment, he stopped and raised his chin. "It would work in the ocean. That's where most people put sailboats."

"Yeah." My heart hadn't beat so hard since the first time he spoke or when I realized he'd somehow snuck back into his old self without me even realizing it. As if nothing happened and the world had gone right again. "Ocean's a long way off from here."

"I know."

"You sure you want to try to go so far from home?"

"I built the boat, just like the house. So in a way, it's home." His shoulder jerked and his grip tightened. "I want to try, even if we don't get very far, I'd still like to try."

"Why?"

"Because it would make you happy."

"I'm happy now."

"Okay, happier."

I started to argue, and he held up a finger. "Okay, fine. I would love for us to try a trip to the ocean, but if it's too much, we'll turn around and come home. Deal?"

To see Morgan on the beach, drenched in sunlight, skin golden brown, hair bleached white, it was nothing more than a fantasy I was pretty sure, but then, he did build a boat with no experience, no instructions, just intuition.

In much the same way he'd changed my life.

I leaned into him. "Just make sure you lather yourself head to toe in sunblock."

"Why?"

"'Cause I don't want your important parts to get burned."

"I plan on wearing swim trunks."

"Not if I have anything to say about it."

He grinned at me, and I kissed him again. A few ladies carrying casseroles passed by with forlorn looks on their faces.

"Don't people usually bring food to funerals?"

Morgan snickered. "It is a funeral, for their fantasy fodder."

I laughed and so did he. We started over to where Jessie and Aunt Jenny were making friends with the beer kegs when a trail of dust popped up on the distant road. Newman had insisted all the cars park at the far edge of the pasture. This one however, ignored the orange cones, continuing toward the crowd.

People turned and conversation hushed. The car stopped just beyond the rows of seating and the stage where Morgan and I had exchanged rings. Covered in a rich blue rug, you never would have known the platform had been built out of old pallets collected from the hardware store.

Orange dust settled on the sedan, taking away the gleam of a fresh wax job. The driver's side door opened, and Jeff got out. He stood there surveying the crowd, picking at his suit, before sliding on his sunglasses.

Jenny, Jessie, and Berry walked over, plates in one hand, beer in the other, looking to do battle.

"Tell me that son-of-a-bitch ain't gonna cause no problems," Aunt Jenny said.

Mr. Newman joined us with a set of keys. "Here." He held them out to me.

I took them, reluctantly. "Uh, what are those for?"

"Chipper shredder, all gassed up, haven't fed the hogs yet." I almost laughed, I mean, there was no way he could be serious, then Berry said, "Have to bury the car."

Then there was Jessie's reply. "I got the perfect spot."

Morgan raised his eyebrows. I gave Mr. Newman back his keys. "I don't think we'll need those today."

"Well, he better have one helluva good reason to be crashing your wedding," Jenny said.

"I sent him an invitation." All eyes turned on me. I shrugged. "I didn't think he'd come." Obviously I was wrong.

Jenny pointed a finger at me. "You and me, boy, we gonna have a talk after all this, just you, me, and Maybelle." She walked away, everyone followed, but they didn't go too far.

Morgan nudged me. "Don't worry, when the beer wears off she won't be so..."

"Scary?" Even with my back to Jenny, her glare all but burned holes through my skull.

"Yeah. And who's Maybelle?"

"Her twelve gauge."

I hoped to God she didn't have it in the trunk of her car.

Jeff made it through the crowd. "Wow, this is..." He surveyed the mix of overalls and Sunday dress, the inflatable bouncy house, the tables, and tables of food, the cows, who had no problem staring back, and the lines of open smokers where hotdogs, hamburgers, and steaks disappeared as fast as they turned brown. "An interesting setup. Definitely a different kind of wedding."

"Folks got a little excited about the idea of Durstrand issuing its first gay marriage license."

"I would have thought the protestors would outweigh the partygoers."

"Well, we did have two."

"Three," Morgan corrected.

"The Reverend Harvey, Chad Grizzle, and his dog."

Jeff looked around.

I said, "They gave up as soon as the steaks hit the grill." I pointed to Reverend Harvey standing by the fence talking with a group of older women, then Chad sitting under a tree by himself with his dog, who still had his cardboard sign tied around his ribs but had chewed half of it off.

"Still a lot of people. I didn't think this many people lived in Durstrand."

"I'm pretty sure only half are locals. But apparently when Mr. Newman fires up the grill, people come from all around." I picked up a cup of punch off the table, sniffed it to make sure it was virgin, then offered it to Jeff, he declined with a raise of his hand. "Promise, no alcohol."

"I'm good, thanks, though."

I drank it.

"So. How is everything?"

I couldn't see his eyes, but I had a feeling he wasn't referring to life in general. My suspicions were confirmed when Morgan said, "You know, if you're worried about whether or not I'm okay, all you have to do is ask."

Jeff dropped his chin, still smiling, although it was different. Relieved but at the same time sad. "Something tells me you're still gonna be more than a handful." But he said it in a good way. One that left you grinning 'cause you knew you'd gone and done right.

"Of course I am. But I'm worth it."

"Humble, isn't he," Jeff said.

I shrugged. "No need to be humble when it's the truth." I drained the glass and dropped the empty into the garbage bag taped to the edge of the table.

Jeff shook his head while giving the place another look around. "You really went and did it."

I held up my hand, flashing my ring finger. "Yeah."

He nodded again, this time more to himself.

I slapped him on the arm. "C'mon, fresh load of burgers are about to come off the grill."

Jeff tossed a thumb over his shoulder. "I can't stay, I'm transporting someone to Marco Island."

"Florida?"

"Yeah?"

"Why would you drive from Chicago to Florida?"

He laughed at the face I made. "I like to drive." Then Jeff shrugged. "Besides, I had somewhere I wanted to stop along the way."

I cleared my throat. "So what's in Florida?"

"I told you I didn't renew my lease. I just stuck around to see what Hines would get, then took a job in Miami." Jeff stared at the movie screen, then took another quick look around. "Is this a drive-in theater?"

"Yup."

"I know Durstrand is fifty years behind, but this is a little rural even for them."

"Wasn't built for the townspeople," Morgan said. "It's for the cows."

"The cows?"

"They like to watch movies, makes them taste better."

Jeff started to say something, but I shook my head. "I'll explain later, when you have more time to talk."

Morgan tossed thoughts in the direction of Jeff's sedan. He tilted his head enough to flash his distant gaze. The sun glinting off the windshield did a better job of hiding the interior than the tinted windows.

"What happened to him?"

Jeff glanced back. "Who?"

"The man in the backseat?"

"Nothing that I know of."

"Then why do you have him in your car?" In my experience, people didn't wind up in an FBI agent's car for no reason.

"He showed up at the office. Asked to speak with an agent."

"You?"

"No, no. I was cleaning out my desk."

"And?" I said.

"Nothing to tell. I overheard him asking how much a bus ticket would be to Florida, and since I was headed that way I offered him a ride."

"On a whim, you just offered him a ride."

"Sure, a twenty-something hour drive can get pretty lonely."

"But you like to drive, remember?"

"Doesn't mean I don't appreciate company." Jeff shrugged. "Might as well have gone alone, so far he has been much for conversation."

"You don't plan on driving all the way through?" If he'd come from Chicago, he'd been on the road for eleven hours already and had to be exhausted.

256

"I'll get a hotel in the next town over. Since he didn't have to buy a bus ticket, he should be able to cover his room."

Morgan took a few steps closer, tilting his head one way then the next. "You should listen to him."

"Like I said, he hasn't spoken except to ask to stop to take a leak."

Morgan lifted his chin. His gaze lingered around Jeff's shoulder, but I think it was close enough to eye contact to get his attention because he took off his sunglasses.

"He didn't tell the agent what he knows because he got scared," Morgan said. "You need to hear what he knows." He walked back over to me and pecked me on the cheek. "I'm going to see if there's any peach bread left; Mrs. Hatchet has already stuffed two loaves into her purse." With his lips against my ear, he added. "Jeff should try harder to get him to talk. He needs to let the guy know he can be trusted. They'll be really good for each other."

With that, Morgan wandered over to where Mrs. Hatchet was trying her best to fit another piece of napkin wrapped peach bread in her already bulging purse.

"Out of curiosity," Jeff said. "How did Morgan even know there was anyone in the backseat?"

"Saw him?"

Jeff gave me a bored look. "Can you see anyone back there?"

Between the tinted glass, the glare, who could? "No. But then I can't see a lot of things Morgan can."

"He hear things too?"

"Only light."

Jeff made a face. His gaze went from Morgan, to me, to Morgan. Then he put his shades back on and his eyes were hidden. "Thanks for the invitation. In spite of... well, you look happy."

"That's because I am."

"And I'm really happy for you."

"I know." But he was hurting too.

Jeff stuffed his hands in his pockets and took a few steps back. "I better get going."

"I find it hard to believe you drove all this way just to leave."

He pulled a pale gray envelope from his jacket pocket. "You sent me the invitation."

"Yeah, but you didn't stay."

He gave the festivities another looking over, as if maybe he might have missed something, or imagined it. The smile wore was sad. "No reason to." Jeff opened the driver's door.

"Hey," I walked over. "About what Morgan said. You should take his advice." Jeff chuckled and I put my hand on his arm. "Seriously, Jeff." I lowered my voice. "If Morgan thinks whoever it is in the backseat of your car has a secret they need to get off their shoulders, then they do."

"I know some people put stock in psychics..."

"Morgan isn't psychic, he just sees things most people don't or sees things in a way we don't or can't. He told me the guy needs someone to trust. He also said you two would be good for each other."

Jeff rolled his eyes and pulled out of my grip. "I'm going. I'll call you when I get settle to let you know how the beaches are." He wouldn't. I had a feeling Jeff had no plans to ever speak to me again. Not because he was angry, because he was afraid of bleeding to death.

It was a fear I understood and one I was glad I hadn't let stop me from coming back to Durstrand.

He got in, but before he could shut the door, I caught a glimpse of his passenger. Dark olive skin, darker hair, eyes as turquois as the ocean water.

There was a scar on his upper lip, another under his chin.

And I'm sure if he'd taken off his shirt, there would have been more. Some burn marks, some cuts.

Rubio had been more worried about the sharks than the bullets when we dragged his son into the water. Bleeding and barely alive, he'd practically been a calling card for a feeding frenzy. He'd been the last of his surviving children we'd been able to track down. I never expected to find him alive in that Cuban hell hole, neither did Rubio. But we had. Only the last time I saw the boy, he'd been nothing but a breathing corpse.

Now there was life in his eyes and the spark of fight. I didn't know whether to be relieved he hadn't lost his soul to whatever happened to him, or terrified of why he'd left home.

Jeff backed out, turned around, and then headed back up the road.

My cell phone rang.

"Is he safe?" The sound of surf and seagulls was loud enough to suggest Rubio stood directly on the beach.

"How long has he been gone?"

"Four days."

"You should have called me sooner."

"I knew where he was going."

"And you let him?"

"Yes."

"He went to the FBI." And if he did start talking, it could come back on Rubio.

"I know."

"Why?"

"Lorado is dead." There was no elation in Rubio's words. Just the tone of a man stating the fact. A task needing to be completed, and now it was, all was well. If only it were so easy.

"If he said anything, they didn't believe him."

"I told him they wouldn't, but he insisted on going."

"Why?"

"Because he left friends behind, had friends die."

"How did you know where he was?"

"I recognized the name of the agent they logged as taking him back to Florida." I didn't even want to know how he had access to the FBI database. Some things were best left unknown.

"Are you going to pick him up?"

"I have a boat waiting for him if he will get on it. I just needed to make sure he was safe with Agent Shaldon."

"Yeah, he's safe."

"Good. That is all I needed to hear."

"What if he tries to go back there?" To that place of misery, torture, and death. Where deranged men seemed to think twelve-year-old boys had valuable secrets that needed to be extracted.

"He is a grown man now, Grant. I cannot stop him from hunting the hunters."

"Will you call me if you need help?"

A child laughed in the background. Water crashed against the sand. A rush of wind cut across the cell phone. More than ever, I hoped Morgan would one day get to see the water.

"No."

How did I reply?

"You are happy, Grant. You are safe. Your battle is over. Live your life, be happy, love deeply. Good-bye, my friend." He hung up.

I was still staring at my phone when Morgan walked over. His gaze met mine, and I stuffed my phone in my pocket. Nothing else mattered when I looked at him. Nothing at all.

"Who was that?"

"Rubio."

"Is he okay?"

"Yeah."

"What about you?" Morgan wrapped his arms around my neck and we began rocking to the sound of nonexistent music. Or at least music I couldn't hear, but then I didn't need to. I had him.

"I'm perfect."

"Feeling a little humble today, huh?" He kissed one corner of my mouth and then the other.

"No need to be humble when it's the truth."

The End

CPSIA information can be obtained
at www.ICGtesting.com
Printed in the USA
FSHW04n0804240418
47377FS

9 781511 581110